Praise fo

"Dawn Kurtagich really is the queen of darkness . . ."

—Josh Winning, author of *Heads Will Roll*

"Scary stuff!"

—R. L. Stine, author of the Goosebumps and Fear Street series

"Kurtagich is one of my favorite writers."

—Evelyn Skye, *New York Times* bestselling author of *The Hundred Loves of Juliet*

"Dawn Kurtagich has an amazing mind. Creepy, but amazing."

—Christopher Pike, bestselling author of the Thirst series

"Kurtagich's horror imagery is satisfying and affecting."

—*School Library Journal*

"Kurtagich's writing is evocative and fearless."

—Cat Winters, author of *In the Shadow of Blackbirds* and *The Raven's Tale*

Praise for *The Madness*

"Sharp and relentless, *The Madness* has a bite that won't let go."

—Kiersten White, *New York Times* bestselling and Bram Stoker Award–nominated author of *And I Darken*

"Fiercely feminist and fantastically eerie, *The Madness* is Welsh Gothic at its most intoxicating. Dawn Kurtagich really is the queen of darkness, drawing beautifully on Bram Stoker's *Dracula* to deliver a story that's smart, fresh, and frightening in equal measure. This book wraps itself around you like a wraith and refuses to let go."

—Josh Winning, author of *Burn the Negative*

"If you thought Mina Harker deserved more credit, more power, and more agency, this *Dracula* remix is for you. *The Madness* zeroes in on the original's undercurrent of sexual violence and puts its targets—young women—in the starring roles, arming them not only with wooden stakes and arcane lore but also with love and solidarity. Kurtagich's vampires, like Stoker's, are vicious, calculating predators, but this time the prey bites back."

—Amelinda Bérubé, author of *Here There Are Monsters*

"In *The Madness*, Dawn Kurtagich has created a stunning *Dracula* retelling—creepy, insidious, and visceral. This book will haunt me for a long time—in the very best way."

—Amy McCulloch, author of *Breathless*

"Exquisitely dark, disturbing, and clever as hell! Kurtagich's hypnotic retelling electrifies and relentlessly propels the reader forward with one cliff-hanger after another. If you think you've heard this story before, think again. *The Madness* is a tour de force of feminist horror."

—Paulette Kennedy, bestselling author of *The Witch of Tin Mountain*

"*The Madness* is genuinely chilling and endlessly compelling. Welsh folklore, small towns, and secrets—this story is Gothic horror at its finest."

—Emily Lloyd-Jones, author of *The Bone Houses*

"I devoured *The Madness*. A modern interpretation of *Dracula* cast with familiar characters, the story is deferential, referential, and yet wholly its own terrifying achievement. Kurtagich's writing is lively and gorgeous. This original spin on a familiar tale is guaranteed to keep you turning the pages until the sun comes up."

—Joshua Moehling, author of *And There He Kept Her* and *Where the Dead Sleep*

"Kurtagich has taken *the* classic horror novel and dragged it into the twenty-first century in this fabulous, feminist, and fierce retelling. Mina Harker was one of the most passive women in literature, representing Victorian virtue until she is attacked, and then is considered soiled because of it. The Mina of *The Madness* is intelligent, flawed, and fiercely relatable. She takes matters into her own hands, and forms a band of badass women, reimagining Stoker's boys club in a manner that will leave you pumping your fist in the air with triumph."

—Ann Dávila Cardinal, award-winning author of *The Storyteller's Death*

"A retelling with teeth, *The Madness* is exquisitely timely and elegantly told, reimagining vampires into our current world with rich imagination."

—Hannah Whitten, *New York Times* bestselling author of *For the Wolf*

"An atmospheric and immersive read! This feminist take on *Dracula*, focusing on victim experiences and with spot-on commentary about the parallels between men and monsters, is as fast-paced as it is carefully wrought. With bone-chilling imagery and deep characterizations, this is a fantastic reimagining of the classic *Dracula* tale."

—Wendy Heard, author of *You Can Trust Me* and *Hunting Annabelle*

"*The Madness* is a mesmerizing indictment of female exploitation sculpted from the decaying bones of a classic. An intricate and empathetic reimagining that haunted me in more ways than one. My new favourite thriller!"

—Isabel Agajanian, author of *Modern Divination*

"Dawn Kurtagich's official debut novel! My reading experience of *The Madness* consisted of the investigation of mysterious psychic trauma . . . strong female protagonists, and a labyrinthine, Welsh castle, all of which are drenched in the pervasive echoes of Bram Stoker's *Dracula*. I especially enjoyed the mixed-media storytelling including bits of letters, texts, and message board discussions—so interactive and immersive! *The Madness* checks a lot of boxes for thrill seekers and horror hounds!"

—Sadie Hartmann (@mother.horror)

"A propulsively dark Welsh Gothic reimaging of *Dracula*, which centers on the compelling and lushly drawn women of the tale. Dawn Kurtagich masterfully weaves local folklore with a malevolent conspiracy of powerful men to deliver a novel that is viscerally creepy and unforgettable."

—Danielle Paige, *New York Times* bestselling author of the Dorothy Must Die series and *Wish of the Wicked*

"A chilling Welsh Gothic that sinks its teeth into you. Darkly haunting and fiercely clever, this is Mina Murray like you've never seen her before!"

—Mia Kuzniar, bestselling author of *Upon a Frosted Star*

"*The Madness* is everything a great horror novel should be and more—a creeping tale that gets its claws into you and doesn't let go. It's a story about pain, trauma, and ultimately hope, and needless to say, it belongs at the top of your TBR pile."

—Gwendolyn Kiste, three-time Bram Stoker Award–winning author of *The Rust Maidens* and *Reluctant Immortals*

"Edge-of-your-seat storytelling plus assured writing make this chilling take on the *Dracula* story a compulsive read. Five stars from me!"

—Juliet Marillier, author of the *Sevenwaters* and *Blackthorn & Grim* series

"*The Turn of the Key* meets *Underworld* in this gloriously chilling, feminist take on *Dracula*. Set against a brooding Welsh backdrop with lush imagery hiding its darkly beating heart, *The Madness* will stay with you long past the final page. Truly stunning!"

—Kat Ellis, author of *Harrow Lake*

"Writing an original story about vampires is a monumental task, but Dawn Kurtagich has done it. With spare prose and a feminist twist, meet the newest vampire classic. Part thriller, part horror, and 100 percent compelling."

—Samantha Downing, international bestselling author

"Darkly evocative and thought-provoking, Kurtagich is one of my favorite writers."

—Evelyn Skye, *New York Times* bestselling author of *The Hundred Loves of Juliet*

Praise for *Teeth in the Mist*

"Dawn Kurtagich breathes life into Faustian lore."

—Hypable

"Kurtagich delivers a creepy, atmospheric tale of subjugation, female self-empowerment, and redemption."

—*Publishers Weekly*

"Kurtagich's writing is evocative and fearless. *Teeth in the Mist* abounds with atmosphere, mystery, and horror and gleefully plays with the Faust legend in ways both modern and classically Gothic."

—Cat Winters, author of *In the Shadow of Blackbirds* and *The Raven's Tale*

"Delightfully disturbing . . . an eerie, atmospheric, satanic spooky story."

—*Kirkus Reviews*

"In *Teeth in the Mist,* Dawn Kurtagich weaves genres, time periods, and sets of characters with deft fingers. Connecting all is the mysterious Mill House. Readers will be fascinated, perplexed, often freaked out, and always wanting to turn the next page."

—Juliet Marillier, author of the Blackthorn & Grim series

Praise for *And the Trees Crept In* (*The Creeper Man)*

"Will haunt readers with its raw emotions, palpable pain, and consistent character voices . . . Frightening and compelling, this gothic will easily sweep fans up into its creeping sense of hysteria."

—*Kirkus Reviews*

"*And the Trees Crept In* is a hauntingly immersive tale of insanity, terror, and what happens when you're not even safe in your own home."

—Hypable

"Kurtagich's horror imagery is satisfying and affecting—her descriptions of the day-to-day decay the girls face are as rich and scary as the monstrous man who scuttles around on all fours and the teeming mud pits that are waiting in the woods. A great next read for teens who enjoy being scared."

—*School Library Journal* (starred review)

"Kurtagich evokes an all-pervading atmosphere of horror with dark imagery and language evoking rot, decay, and death . . . This unique novel is for teens who enjoy being immersed in a dark, complex horror story."

—*Voya* (starred review)

"Kurtagich has created an incredibly assured, claustrophobic horror with a fractured and troubled teen narrator that will have you gripped to the very last page."

—Book Trust

"Horror fans will be caught by the gripping cover image, and there's plenty to scare them here, even during the second reading that the surprise ending might encourage them to undertake."

—*The Bulletin of the Center for Children's Books*

"Dark, twisted, and terrifying, *And the Trees Crept In* will keep your stomach in knots from page one. A must-read for horror fans everywhere!"

—Susan Dennard, *New York Times* bestselling author of *Truthwitch* and *Windwitch*

"*And the Trees Crept In* should come with a warning label: Best read in the light of day, with lots of smiling people around, and candy canes and unicorns and cute babies. A beautifully written, gorgeous nightmare of a novel."

—David Arnold, bestselling author of *Mosquitoland* and *Kids of Appetite*

"An enthralling, unsettling fairy tale that will have you turning pages long into the night."

—Michelle Zink, author of *This Wicked Game* and *Lies I Told*

"A fight for survival, an encroaching forest, a cursed manor, and dark secrets . . . Kurtagich's terrifying take wrapped my heart up and squeezed until I was as cold as the dead things haunting its pages."

—Alexandra Sirowy, author of *The Creeping* and *The Telling*

Praise for *The Dead House*

"A haunting new thriller . . ."

—*EW*.com

"Kaitlyn/Carly Johnson is troubled. Suffering from dissociative identity disorder, Carly is awake during the day and Kaitlyn owns the night. The personalities leave each other notes to help smooth the transition; they lead separate lives. When the parents die suspiciously, Kaitlyn/Carly is moved to a psychiatric hospital and then a school for troubled teens. When a doctor integrates the personalities, Kaitlyn emerges; she believes that other forces are possessing her and trapping Carly. Then other teens go missing or are killed. This book will pique readers' interest on multiple levels. Told through diaries, police interviews, psychiatrist's notes, emails, video transcripts, and newspaper articles, this unique format puts the reader in the position of investigator. Finally, there is the horror component, which will keep many readers anxiously waiting to see what comes next."

—Library School Connection

"A horror tale made creepier by the integration of diary entries, grainy pictures, interview transcripts, newspaper clippings, doodles, stills from video recordings, and other media, Carly/Kaitlyn's story is told as 'found footage' pieced together by followers of 'the Johnson incident,' which remains an unsolved mystery. Kurtagich maintains the creepy and dark tone through to the end, where readers are not given a neat a tidy ending—ghosts still haunt, pieces of the story remain missing, and life goes on despite the terrible tragedy at the prestigious Elmbridge High School."

—*Voya* (October 2015 print issue)

"Kurtagich's debut is a taut, psychological suspense novel centered around disturbed teenagers Carly and Kaitlyn Johnson and the horrifying series of events that culminated in a deadly fire at a residential high school. The timeline is recreated through a series of police files, diary entries, transcribed video footage, and newspaper stories, revealing that Carly/Kaitlyn share the same body, with Carly occupying the daytime hours and Kaitlyn the night. The two communicate via a series of notes, and, although Carly's therapist believes she suffers from dissociative identity disorder, it's not clear which girl is the primary persona and which is the alter ego. When the Carly personality disappears from Kaitlyn's consciousness, she embarks on a grisly quest to find her in the 'dead house' that is her mind. Not for the faint of heart, this is a gory and grimly compelling story, made more so by the novel's visual elements. Readers will be left wondering if the supernatural elements are real or all part of a troubled girl's damaged mind."

—*Booklist*

"This creepy boarding school novel meshes real-world issues with a paranormal mystery in a fun but scary debut . . . Fans of horror novels will appreciate the creepy photographs scattered throughout, and the multiple perspectives are smoothly integrates . . . a worthy addition to high school horror collections."

—*School Library Journal*

"I do love an unreliable narrator (or two), and this endlessly twisty psychological horror manipulated from the off. A Buzz Book of the Bologna Children's Book Fair in 2014, this is Orion imprint Indigo's biggest debut title of the year."

—*The Bookseller*

"Insightful characterization and a detailed exploration of the importance of the emergent identity to the teenage self."

—*Publisher's Weekly*

"What an evil and original story. You can't stop reading Kaitlyn's diary. But is she real? It's a mystery inside a mystery—and the shocks keep coming. Scary stuff!"

—R. L. Stine, bestselling author of the Goosebumps and Fear Street series

"All I could think when I finished *The Dead House* was that the author, Dawn Kurtagich, has an amazing mind. Creepy, but amazing. I loved it."

—Christopher Pike, bestselling author of the Thirst series

"Full of twists, buried secrets, and enough disturbing corpses to please the most discerning horror lover, *The Dead House* is a thoroughly engrossing read. Diary entries, psychiatrist records, and transcripts from the investigation keep the pages turning late into the night. This is a harrowing tale, cleverly told."

—Kendare Blake, author of *Anna Dressed in Blood*

"Kurtagich weaves a terrifying and mind-bending tale reminiscent of H. P. Lovecraft. This is one of the best horror debuts I've read in a long time!"

—J. R. Johansson, author of *Cut Me Free* and The Night Walkers series

"*The Dead House* is a seamless blend of the supernatural and the psychological. Creepy, compelling, and compulsively readable."

—Victoria Schwab, author of *The Archived* and *Vicious*

"Spine-chilling, gruesome, and mysterious; an exciting debut . . . difficult to put down, and even harder to forget."

—@TheBookbag

The Thorns

OTHER TITLES BY DAWN KURTAGICH

Teeth in the Mist
And the Trees Crept In (The Creeper Man)
Blood on the Wind
The Madness

The Dead House

The Dead House
Naida

The Thorns

Dawn Kurtagich

THOMAS & MERCER

This is a work of fiction. Names, characters, organizations, places, events, and incidents are either products of the author's imagination or are used fictitiously. Otherwise, any resemblance to actual persons, living or dead, is purely coincidental.

Published by Thomas & Mercer, Seattle

www.apub.com

ISBN-13: 9781662526978 (paperback)
ISBN-13: 9781662526961 (digital)

Cover design by Zoe Norvell
Cover photography © Tamara Obukhova/@toucheconomy

Printed in the United States of America

For Twin. You're a chop. 😉

TRIGGER WARNING

Dear Reader,

When I was eight years old, my mother (at the insistence of my stepfather) drove me to a boarding school in the middle of the desert and left me behind. What happened at this school inspired the novel you are about to read. Leaving me there was a last resort on her part, a desperate way of coping with huge and turbulent events in her life. There is a lot more to that story, but it isn't mine to tell.

Books are my safe space, and they should remain yours too. My hope is that you're able to open these pages and live in Bethany's world for a time, and then leave, secure and whole. But you should know these pages, this sand ocean, is littered with paper thorns. Please be aware that this novel deals with darker themes, specifically bullying, sexual violence toward a minor, gaslighting, self-harm, chronic pain, minor alcohol and drug abuse, reference to animal harm, and mental health crises. The sexual violence is not gratuitous or graphic, but it *is* present and necessary for the story. If you feel unable to go safely into these choppy glass waters, I would prefer you don't, leaving them for when you feel your boat is secure enough for sailing.

This book is the culmination not only of almost twenty years of toil but of certain periods of time in my childhood. The specifics of my life are mine to tell or not, but many of the elements in the novel have their origins in real experience. I have decided to leave it at that.

This novel is also a psychological thriller, straddling the line of horror. Horror, like books, is my safe space. A magical land where we can direct our fear and unease, purging them from us, and then safely finding our way out again.

I hope you will find a path through the thorns.

Yours,

Dawn Kurtagich

January 2023

1

The Devil

NOW

I have been trying to kill Sally Pierson for seven months. I've tried thirty different incarnations of murder.

Hanging.

Flaying.

Skinning.

Acid attack.

Drowning.

Car crash.

Plane crash.

Decompression sickness.

Jungle accident.

Motorboating disaster.

Natural catastrophe (earthquake, volcano, tidal wave, hurricane, tornado, tsunami . . .).

Starvation.

Cliff dive.

Stabbing.

Shooting.

Cancer.

Poisoning (arsenic, strychnine, cyanide . . .).

Spider bite (black widow being the favorite).

Bee attack.

Hornet attack.

Burning.

Snakebite.

Impaling (I was watching a rerun of *Buffy*).

Beheading (*Highlander*).

Other forms of decapitation.

Spontaneous combustion.

Death by piranha.

Concussion.

Anaphylaxis.

Old age.

I have thought a *lot* about murder. And yet, Sally survives. None of these do her justice. Sally has been with me for seven books, the main character of my Sally Chronicles: a 1950s heroine-housewife, assassin, spy, psychopath, and perfect pot roast preparer. She irons her husband's shirts, packs her kids' lunches, and has an exquisite spinning back kick. She's deadly. Almost good enough to catch a bullet in her pissing-perfect pearly whites.

She's too perfect to die.

"Shit."

I lean back in my office chair and gulp down the last of my cold black coffee. Sally has outwitted my attempts to decompose her at a molecular level, and I am seething resentment.

I hate my creation.

Touché, Dr. Frankenstein. Touché.

I lean in close to my laptop and lower my voice. "Listen, you bloody buggering bitch, I'm going to kill you one way or another, and you're going to bloody well stay dead. And when you're gone, I'm never going to type the name *Sally* again. Ever."

Unless she kills me first.

I peer down the corridor to see if Bruce is up yet, but I can still hear his snores. He sleeps with an ease I can't fathom, and in the early hours of the morning, those blue-tinged whisper hours, I envy him. He's left a Post-it next to a little bowl with my medicine in it. *Yum-yum*, it says.

It's a good day, and I don't need my wheelchair. I grab one of my crutches from where they rest at the edge of my desk and hobble to the front door. London in the morning is something entirely different, and I've gotten into the habit of sipping my coffee on the front stoop, watching the commuters pass by the fence.

I've been out a few times already, each time hobbling back inside with another idea about my Sally problem, only to be defeated and end up on the stoop once more. Half a cup of cold black coffee sits on the bottom step, a depressing sludge, and as I step down to reach for it, something sharp presses into my foot.

It is sitting in the middle of the front step.

A devil's thorn.

A singular thorn.

My entire body goes cold. *There's a devil's thorn on my front step.*

I back away, searching the street; my heart is flooding my body with adrenaline. I've spent so much time writing about it that I've almost forgotten I have the capacity to feel it. Terror.

I stagger back into the house, dropping my crutch, and shut the door, throwing the lock closed.

This can't be real.

My computer dings at me from across the room, the distinctive sound of an incoming email. On autopilot, I make my way to my desk, ignoring the searing pain in my shins, and collapse into my chair.

I click over to Gmail

and freeze.

My God.

It's you.

In my inbox.

I take a breath, close my eyes, count to ten, and then look again.

It's still sitting there, in bold type and unread, screaming for my attention. But then, you always did have my attention.

My hand shakes as I glide my finger across the touch pad and click:

> To: Sloane@BethanySloaneAuthor.com
> From: StaceyPreston@gmail.com
>
> Subject: Long time no speak
>
> Well, well, Bethany Sloane. God, it's been a lifetime. Stumbled across one of your books in my local and nearly had a heart attack.
> A bestselling author—are you kidding me? I never would have predicted that one! I'm delighted for you.
> I read you're in London now! You'll never guess, but I am too. Small world, huh?
> If you fancy a coffee and a catch up, do email back.
> From an old (and getting older!) friend,
>
> Stacey

You're here.

On the other end of the internet. Somewhere out there in this city. And maybe as close as my front step, if that devil has anything to say.

Stacey fucking Preston.

The flash of a blade, glinting in the sun. *Prove you love me.*

Oh. Holy. God.

2

Humiliated Ball

THEN

A devil's thorn is sticking out of my foot.

Caught from the low-lying yellow-flower weeds that litter the school grounds, it's the size of a five-cent piece. The orange light of the evening sets it aflame, ocher hues bleeding into scarlet, waging war on the tiny barbs. It smirks at me. I smirk back, even though I know the thorn, not me, is the victorious party. I know this because my feet are tough.

A tough foot means no blood.

I *want* there to be blood, thick blood that gushes from my heel to stain my uniform and splatter across the cracked soil. That would give me a reason to go to Matron Monday and have a bandage put on. It would look good to have a bandage. Everyone would be impressed.

Even Stacey.

I fantasize over the thought for a few minutes, rolling Stacey's name over my tongue. I wonder if I could walk across broken glass and whether I should try. It would have to be when Stacey was *sure* to see, without it being planned. It couldn't appear staged. Then it wouldn't count. Unless it was a dare.

I can't sit down because I know what will happen. When I first got here, I did what everyone does their first time: I sat. Landed in a pile of devil's thorns and had to have the sharp teeth plucked from my sore buttocks one by one by Matron Monday. No one ever forgets after that. It's like a branding. No one forgets the hand that scorches her.

The only way to avoid getting devil's thorns in your feet—the only way the *new* ones know about—is to stay inside. I was one of them once: new. I stayed inside too. But no one ever does that for long. I was lucky, because Stacey chose me, so I learned quickly. She took me under her wing and showed me the way to survive, and we became the Thorns: me, Stacey, and Bernadette. The three of us could survive together.

Settlers, an hour north of Pretoria, can be warmer than Mum's oven on summer days, and when we have free time that is ours and not the matron's, we run free in the bush. We run over the thirsty orange South African ground—cracked because of hell below it—through the tall scratchy yellow grass with the devil's thorns. We are lions seeking out our prey, or maybe we are magical elephants with blue trunks that can split into two, or maybe we are lost sisters on a desperate trek through the wild to find our forgotten family.

Maybe we can fly.

We refuse to remain cooped up in the musty dormitories, where the air is as thick as vomit. We'd rather face the thorns, the dry and dusty air, and the glare of the cruel sun, like warriors facing certain death. Stacey tells me it is about faith and about flying.

Stacey is leader, and she waits for me. It's her right to lead because she's fourteen and Bernie and I are thirteen. She knows more than us; she's been through and learned everything first, in her extra year of being alive. She lives in the future.

She says she's not in Atlas, the "Big House," because she has to watch over us, and when we graduate into the Big House, she'll go too.

"It's my duty," she says.

But she's been inside Atlas, and I am in awe. I don't ever tell her this, but she can read it in my face. If I stare at her for a bit too long, she will smile and blink, then turn away, as she always does. She contemplates my adoration. I follow her and watch her intently. I memorize her. Stacey makes sure the Thorns know what to do and when. She knows all the rules; she keeps us safe.

The day I arrived, five years ago, I wore blue sandals. My bed wasn't next to hers; it was the one next to the one next to hers. She had a cotton bedspread the color of weeping rubies. I wished my own block-blue bedspread didn't look so different. I mumbled to my mother that I wanted a new one. She laughed, patted my head, said "Don't worry, darling" in an accent I'm beginning to forget, and then she left to go back to England with her new Afrikaans husband. They could have taken me with them. They could have put me in a boarding school in England, even, but Stoffel insisted I stay here, where he could be sure I'd be raised "right." And what Stoffel wants, Stoffel gets.

Stacey called me over with a twist of her head, glanced at my blue sandals, and showed me the bottoms of her feet. Her dry heels, badly cracked and filled with dirt, demanded my attention. The skin was white around the edges, broken, dry, and filthy. I was overcome with a reverence.

I didn't wear shoes after that.

I know that is why the devil's thorn doesn't cause me to bleed—my feet are becoming strong. I am becoming a Thorn. But it does make me angry to see there are no cracks in the thickening heel. Aggressively, I pull out the devil and look at it; it is a baby lying helpless in the palm of my hand, the thorns tiny, only partially developed. I am angry that I felt it at all. I snap off the sharp edges until it is a humiliated ball in my hand and then throw it away with a sadistic pleasure.

I have done everything right today.

3

Dirty Diner

NOW

I shouldn't be doing this.

The streets are burning with the heat of another restless summer, the people languid and sticky. I'm standing outside a shitty '50s-imitation diner, once haute couture back in the late noughties, after absinthe and Vogue cigarettes. Jesus. That was a long time ago.

The bell rings halfheartedly on its rusting hinges to announce my arrival—*Thank you, herald.* It has given up the ghost but hasn't been allowed to die in peace. Zombie door. Undead door. Let-me-fucking-die-already door.

I motion to the guy behind the counter; his skin is cement gray. I take a seat at the back by the window, hidden in shadow.

You're late.

I rummage through my bag and pull out a ciggy, popping the menthol capsule and lighting it with shaking hands. It burns down in my hand, a prop and nothing more.

"Those things'll kill you."

You're here. You're standing in front of me. Your hair is as wild as ever, lioness, eyes muddy and full of secrets, even now. And suddenly I smell the sand of the desert. I feel thorns between my toes, glass under my eyelids.

"Jesus."

"Not quite," you say, sitting down across from me and leaning on your elbows.

Your fingernails are short, clean, and unpolished, and I stub out my smoke and hide my red manicure beneath the table.

"This is a huge mistake." I hesitate. "Right?"

You shrug, then turn around and gesture to Cement Face. He hurries over with a percolator pot and pours you a coffee, like we're in some cheesy American sitcom, then shuffles back to his post. I don't even warrant a cup of coffee. Even here, eighteen years later, you're the boss.

Touch a line, break your spine!

You drag a finger over the edge of the cup before taking a sip, eyelashes caressing your cheeks.

I lick my lips and glance away. Glance back.

You watch me with those eyes. Those eyes that clawed secrets from the darkest places. Those eyes that saw things I couldn't see. These eyes. Here. Older. The same.

I take out another ciggy and light it, contemplate taking a drag. Will it shock you? I don't; I just let it sit and burn.

"I dream of the Tractor Tire," you say, still looking with those eyes.

I flinch, remembering our spot, those towering rubber walls. "Fuck."

"Yeah."

You take the cigarette from my fingers, and it's yours now. You always knew when I was faking.

"Fuck," I say again.

And you laugh.

4

Tractor Tire

THEN

Stacey sits on the Tractor Tire, her left leg dangling into the hole, her right leg propped up, one slim arm wrapped around it. Short brown curls fly about her head, a halo both awesome and wild. Bernie perches beside her, legs together, skin lobster red under the harsh midday sun. She wriggles her nose like she wants to pick it, but sitting next to Stacey, she wouldn't dare. My stomach lurches to see her with Stacey, alone. What secrets have they shared? What precious moments have I missed? One thorn, two . . . my mind ticks over like an engine, trying to work out how I can steal the moments back. I am nervous; Bernie smirks at me because she knows it. I am late.

"Where have you been?" Stacey asks, her voice even, eyes still. She doesn't look up, and I know it's a bad sign. She runs a tall piece of grass up and down the inside of her thigh, so softly it's torturous to witness.

I am sweating.

"I got a devil in my foot," I say. I know this excuse is not good enough. Bernie knows it too. She smiles and looks away, because she is not the one in trouble today.

Above me, the gulls screech in mockery.

"And what did you do with it?" Stacey looks at me then, her mucky-brown eyes searching my own. I feel confident, but my hands are sweating, and there is a pressure in my bladder.

I look at Bernie with defiance and reply. "I took off all the pointy bits and threw it away."

Bernie looks at Stacey uncertainly, with her hands pressed together, her fingers turning yellow. I try not to laugh as I imagine her as a Simpson, with yellow skin all over. Her dirty-blond hair, which is always greasy with sweat, would look better with yellow skin than it does now, clashing horribly with her red face.

Stacey considers me for a moment. She is elemental to me, like a goddess—body as still as the earth, eyes like fire, lips moist as water, hair flying untamed in the breeze.

I try not to swallow, but fear is closing in on my throat. My neck itches, and so does my toe, but as a test for myself—to prove how serious I am about pleasing Stacey—I don't move.

Stacey blinks, and her lashes are so long and thick they ripple the air. Then she smiles. "That was very good," she says, putting the piece of grass between her glistening lips. "Well done. Now nobody can be bothered by it again, and it won't have any babies. *You* wouldn't have thought of that, Bernadette," she says, turning to Bernie, who blushes even more red and looks down.

Already, tears form in her bubble-gum-blue eyes. I want to whoop! I want to run circles around Bernie and laugh: *ha ha ha-ha-ha, ha ha ha-ha-ha!* Instead, I just smile openly (because I am now allowed to).

Bernie is the Thorn Stacey is angry with, and I think that maybe it is because Stacey has had to spend so much time alone with her while I was gone. I take pleasure in thinking Stacey is glad to see me, basking in the thought that she may have missed me.

Stacey sits in silence, examining her right foot, covered in brown dirt. She's like a cat, seemingly elegant and sleek, but wild and nocturnal. Bernie and I remain still, our eyes scrutinizing her. We wait for a sign. Every muscle in my eyes is fixed on her, because I don't want to miss anything. If I miss something and Bernie catches it, then it might become important later. I count to ten, and she still doesn't move. I count to twenty. She looks up at me. She smiles and looks down again. I count to forty. Her eyebrows twitch, and I almost gasp.

What is she *thinking*?

"There was once a boy who died here," she says slowly, framing each word with care. She raises her gaze to look at us, waiting for a reaction.

"Died?" whispers Bernie, her eyeballs large spheres of mostly white. She's like a child.

Stacey rolls her eyes and purses her lips. "Isn't that what I just said, Bernadette?"

Bernie blushes.

"What happened to him?" I venture meekly; I can't help my fanatical curiosity from peppering through. Death, like detention, is a topic that demands full attention. My mouth is pregnant with questions; my tongue is heavy. But then I realize it's not words pressing against my palate: it's saliva. I lean forward and spit out the gooey mess my mouth collected, and the words go with it.

Stacey stretches her leg, toes flexing wide, and examines her foot. "He used to go to school here. A long, long time ago. He had no friends and no family, only a guardian who left him here year after year. He came out at night, to this same old tire, and he sat all alone, in silence, communing with his dead family."

Bernie gasps and covers her mouth. I smile and stare at Stacey, enraptured.

"He would call, 'Sarah . . . Sarah . . . hear your brother! Come and sit beside me. Keep me warm.' Well, a blue-gray shape would appear out of the center of the tire, rising up like water falling backwards, and floating there would be his little sister. Her body was all ashen and torn, and blood gushed out of her mouth when she tried to speak. Her eyes would stare at him, right into his very soul. He knew that she had risen out of hell."

Bernie shrieks and blocks her ears.

"Stupid ninny," Stacey says at the same time I think it. She half smiles, and my stomach leaps.

I grin. "Why was her body torn?"

"His whole family died in a car crash. He was the only survivor." Stacey looks at Bernie with a frown. "Bernadette, open your ears! If you don't listen, how will you know how to keep yourself alive?"

Bernie stops her sobbing and looks at Stacey. A line of sticky clear snot runs into her mouth.

"Well," says Stacey, leaning back, "one day, after he had been here for four years, he decided that he wanted to join his family. He was tired of living in a world of silence and loneliness. He called out to his sister, 'Sarah . . . Sarah . . . hear your brother. Come and claim me. My life is yours.' He sat silent, calmly waiting for her to take him away, as the watery figure rose out of the Tractor Tire. But as her face materialized before him, he had a terrible shock and realized his mistake.

"It wasn't his sister's face at all. Her eyes were bloodred, shimmering with death; she had a wicked smile on her face, and blood oozed out from between her glass teeth, all congealed and dead. He knew that he was looking at Glass Man! 'You have called me,' she said, 'and now I claim you, Henry Dertz, as my own.' Glass Man raised his arms and slithered forward, and Henry was engulfed, drowning in midair.

"The school reported him missing, and no one saw him ever again. Since then, every few years, children go missing at this very spot. Glass Man comes to claim them for his own. You don't see him at first, but you hear him whisper into your ear—'I am Glass Man. I claim you as my own'—before you drown in your own blood, or he leads you away down, down, down into hell, right through the ground on this very spot."

Bernie pulls her legs up out of the Tractor Tire and grips them with her arms. She isn't brave enough to run away without Stacey, but she wants to. I wish she would. I wish Glass Man would eat her. She isn't a proper Thorn.

"Now," says Stacey, standing up on the tire so she is ten feet tall. She raises herself up onto her tiptoes and then lifts her left leg off the tire. She is balancing on one dainty foot, like a ballerina. "Who's brave enough to stand in the center until I say?"

Bernie stares at Stacey with wide eyes. "Stand?" she asks. "In the *center*?"

Stacey smiles, still on her tiptoes, perfectly balanced. "In the center."

This is it. This is my chance.

"I will," I say simply, though I am scared enough to wee in my knickers—panties, I mean. For once, I am grateful Stacey can't hear my thoughts. If she heard me say England words again, she would call Glass Man for *me*.

Stacey smiles and then motions me forward with her index finger. I climb up the Tractor Tire, which is actually five of them stacked on their sides, towering over us. I use the ridges in the rubber as a ladder. On the top, I feel slightly dizzy looking down, but I manage not to sway.

"You can climb out after you've counted to sixty."

"Okay."

"Ten times."

I hesitate for less than a second, but she sees it and her eyes narrow, so I nod as confidently as I can and climb into the center. I look up at Bernadette and Stacey, and I hope that none of Bernie's snot will fall on me. The middle of the tire is very shadowy. Above me, Stacey nods. She whispers something to Bernadette, who then begins to climb down the outside. She looks at me for five seconds, and I think I see a tiny smile, but I am not sure. Bernie hops off the tire.

I feel a jolt of wonderful shock when I think maybe Stacey is going to stay with me by herself. That would be wonderful. But she regards me, eyes like quicksand, and then she steps backward off the tire—her irises never leaving my face—and she is gone.

My stomach lurches into my throat, and my heart hammers. I hear them scuttle away through the scratchy grass.

"Stacey?" I call. My voice is small, lost in the shadowy space.

She left. She left with Bernie. Stacey and Bernie. Together. I'm proving myself to her . . . and she left.

The sun is setting, casting long, leering shadows all over. I want to climb out of the hole, but I know I can't. I try not to look around me at the inside of the tire, filled with cobwebs and secret shadows. I try not to think *Glassy, glassy, cut my arsey; glassy, glassy, cut my arsey; glassy, glassy . . .*

I clench my fists and my jaw, and I try not to be angry. Stacey is making sure I do it right. Maybe when I'm done, she'll smile and laugh and tell Bernie to go away forever.

My Stacey, I think. *I can do this.*

I gaze at the orange sky, I smell the cinnamon air, and I begin to count in a resolute whisper.

"One, two, three, four, five . . ."

I lift my skirt and pull aside my panties. The hot yellow stream hits the ground loudly. It feels like a sacrifice of appeasement.

Please don't get me.

I continue to count.

5

Peanut Butter and Bovril Sandwiches

NOW

It's strange, the things we remember. Like the upside-down peanut butter, bread, and milk concoction at breakfast. Slathering the sickly sweet peanut butter and golden-syrup mixture, which they passed out in small tin jugs, on top of white bread, putting it upside down in plastic bowls, and covering the glutinous mess with full-fat milk. We thought we were such geniuses.

"How about the peanut-butter-syrup-glob mix and Bovril?" I offer. "Remember that?"

"Best invention ever," you say at the precise moment I say it, and we giggle like girls.

"Can't imagine the British tongue craving peanut butter and beef-extract spread, though," I comment.

"Likely not."

And then there are the things we can't remember. What subjects we took at school. What the teachers looked like. Their names.

"Matron Monday," I blurt, and you frown.

"I don't remember that one."

"She was fat. Huge. She had this long white hair growing from her chin."

"Was she old?" you ask.

Funny. I can't remember that. Maybe. I don't know.

"She wore white."

"A uniform . . . yeah. I think I remember something about a uniform."

And there is more. Endless, blazing weekends. Torture in the sun. Brown hair turning gold at the ends. Mosquitoes and lizards.

Prove you love me.

I shake my head, swallowing down sudden bile. Things are different now. I've grown and evolved since I was a girl, and I bet you have too. The idea that we can have a normal friendship is alluring, despite the niggling question of why you've suddenly reappeared in my life.

On and on we chat, finding our way through the fog of time.

Coffees numbers three and four have been consumed. My body is buzzing with the caffeine.

You tap the edge of your cup: *ping, ping, ping*. "Remember Joe?"

"Joe?"

You laugh, spilling some of coffee number five on the table. You wipe at it with your fingers, drawing patterns of art only you can see. "You don't remember *Joe*? The janitor, remember?"

I shake my head.

"God, we used to sneak out at night and go see him. He was nice. His son was the groundsman."

My skin prickles uncomfortably, and I smell . . . "Cocoa."

"Exactly. He'd give us hot cocoa."

"He kept reptiles or something, didn't he?"

"He's dead now, I suppose."

"I guess." I grin. "We must have been terrors!"

You laugh, and I want to hear that sound forever, for always. "Yes, we were."

A beat of silence.

"What else?" I press. "What else do you remember?"

I want it all. Your memories of us, your impressions. Everything you experienced, every color, scent, and feeling.

You shrug and sip your drink, grinning in a sly way that seems familiar. Are you playing games with me? Are you still the same creature you were back then?

"Who else went to school with us?" I press. "We could have fun and try to look them up on Facebook. See how they look now. God, what if they have kids?"

"I . . ." You hesitate, and you don't like not having answers, because you shrug off the idea and stand up. "Who cares? It's all gone and done, isn't it? Best to live in the here and now."

And just like that, this conversation is over.

Something stirs in my bones. A memory.

Stacey knows all the rules.

And you're still making rules, aren't you? Well, that's fine. I don't plan to follow.

"What are you doing here?" I finally ask it, and I don't know why I should be so nervous to hear the answer. Don't know why I feel so afraid.

"You were on my mind." You say it without looking at me, and I want you to look at me.

Look at me.

I want to point out that you never talk about the past. It's one of the rules, isn't it? Or is that wrong? I can't remember. Such a long time ago. I could make a joke out of me being on *your* mind, turn it into a funny quip, a powerless lure. I'm not at risk of falling under your wing, not now.

Still. Beads of sweat are breaking out on my brow.

I don't feel very well, and all of a sudden, I regret coming out to meet you. My curiosity has been satisfied. You are here, you are Adult, you are alive and thriving. That's all I needed to know. I can close the door now, before it gets worse. Before you get worse. I can go home and finish my book and sleep now.

And I'd very much like that.

"I've got to go to . . . I have a thing." It sounds ridiculous coming from my mouth, and I wish I had Denise's flair for half truths. I wonder if my publicist had training for that specifically, or whether she's just a natural.

"We should go out one evening. Have a laugh, get smashed."

I almost agree—it seems I still have the habit—but catch myself at the last minute.

"I'm . . . I'm really busy. It was nice seeing you again."

Something is cracking in my bones, and I need to be at home now. I need to be gone.

And then you're turning away, and I have no idea if my mouth is hanging open, but it hardly matters. Because you are the one striding from the diner, and I am the one left behind, gawking.

6

The Invisible House

THEN

The House is a long distance from the school, and the way to it is a secret, one that Stacey shared with Bernie and me on a Saturday afternoon exactly three weeks after I met her. Even though it was barely past noon, the day had been a long one, dragging on with endless futility. The sun sieved surprising winter heat directly to us, and we felt our ears begin to sunburn. I relished the thought of peeling them later, like it was summer again. We followed her all the way there, one Thorn after the other, Bernie behind me, me behind Stacey.

She took us almost the entire way to the schoolhouse, but at the crossroads she turned, not right—the direction that would lead us to the school—but left down the lengthy road through empty grounds. The road eventually leads to the outer gate and to the quiet road outside the school.

"We're going outside," Bernie whispered in my ear. "She'll leave you there for the vultures."

"Shut up, Bernie," I said. "Don't be stupid."

Stacey stopped then and turned to face us, her face blank and expressionless. Her dark eyes were fixed on Bernie; Stacey's skin, always so pale, made them seem black and forbidding. "Have you got anything to say?"

My stomach flipped in pleasure, but I kept it silent and hidden, as I always tried to do.

Bernie blushed. "Are we going outside?"

Stacey's eyes narrowed. "What do *you* think?"

"I—I . . . I don't know."

"Keep it that way. Follow on and be quiet. Bushmen might ambush us with the racket you two are making."

She led us along the dirt track until I could see the caretaker's hut in the distance, a white spot on the orange earth. Then, abruptly, she turned off the road and headed in the direction of the colossal corn tower. It loomed in the distance like a specter, dark, empty, abandoned. I knew the stories; I knew it was haunted. Everybody knew.

"Are we—" Bernie began, but then fell silent; Stacey's earlier rebuke surely still burned in her ears.

The surrounding area was unnervingly exposed; in the open fields we were easy targets for searching eyes. I looked around, worried that we may have been seen and followed, but nothing moved in the swaying yellow of the fields.

"We're almost there," said Stacey.

The fields grew wilder as we neared the fence of diamond wire. Stacey bent down and pulled up the edge of it. Surprisingly, it gave way, twisting skyward to reveal a hole at the bottom, small enough for the three of us to slither through on our bellies.

"Go."

I didn't hesitate.

On the other side of the fence, the corn tower looked eerily close. Yet I could see that it was not in this field, as I had suspected, but in the one after, or possibly farther away still. It didn't matter. I still felt its presence, a cold wraith that peered down at me. I resisted the urge to lift my face to look directly at it.

Stacey led us through the second field to a small square building of dark-brown brick. She didn't seem concerned that anyone could be there, so I followed, unperturbed. A small whimper escaped Bernie's mouth, and she followed us closely, walking on my heels.

"This used to be the very edge of the school years ago," Stacey said. I didn't ask her how she knew this: She knew it because she'd been here forever. The school was Stacey. "The fence was pushed forward a ways because they had no money. A man used to own the corn tower and lots of the farms around the area. But one day, he just disappeared. He went into the corn tower one night because some kids had painted it and smashed the windows, but he didn't come out. The tower was shut down, corn still inside, and it's been left ever since."

I risked looking up at the tower then. The windows at the very top—the only windows—peered down like eyes. Inside, a huge bed of dry corn was left to rot.

"These are the old toilets," Stacey said, tugging on the rusty padlock hanging from the door. "Boys round the back, girls here. That was before the separation. Round the back is our new house."

We followed her around the small toilet block to where a large umbrella tree stood. The branches covered the corrugated tin roof of the bathroom and extended outward to provide a large area of shade, which looked glorious even from a distance. But I wasn't allowed to say I was hot unless Stacey was hot.

The L-shaped building and tree together provided complete seclusion from anyone who might spy. Scattered about on the ground were clam-like seeds, some closed, some open, spilling papery sheets on the ground.

"Clip-claps," Stacey said, following my gaze. "If you rub them on concrete, they get hot enough to burn you."

I scooped up a handful of the dark-brown sand. It was softer than any I had felt before, like cooking flour. I put it to my nose and sniffed, imagining it might taste like cocoa.

Stacey didn't say much to us after that. She sat on the ground in the center of the tree's shadow and stared at the brick wall with blazing eyes and a frown on her face.

That was a long time ago. Since then, we've come to the House on the nonschool days we aren't with our parents. Bernie's come every second weekend, and she cries when they leave. Stacey's mother is dead. I think it happened before Stacey came to live here, so it must have been a long time ago. Stacey doesn't talk about her mother, and I'm not allowed to talk about mine. She never says it out loud, but I *know* it. Once, a long time ago, Stacey said, "I don't recount the past. It belongs where it is." I know what she wants, so I don't talk about Mummy. I don't mind. There isn't a lot to say anyway. Stacey's father hardly comes at all, but when he does, Stacey goes quiet.

Stacey is setting out the rooms. She uses the big stick we hide in the hollow of the tree to outline the walls of the Invisible House. We follow her, using our hands to scrape away the excess dirt and clip-claps. We collect the big hard seeds and use them to make benches, beds, the lines that are doors—anything we think of. A terrace, perhaps, looking out on a valley, or a swimming pool, or a waterfall.

Bernie happily sweeps the floor with the little broom we made out of twigs and twine. She is such a little housewife.

Such a little housewife. Mum used to say that in a snickering sort of way about her pretty friends—friends with rich old husbands and too much time. Now *I* think it. I think it about *her*, with her new crinkly husband who has no proper teeth and a wallet that is always full for her.

Bernie finishes sweeping and uses her hands to throw out the excess dirt. I have an impulse to step on her neat little partitions, but I know it'll make Stacey angry. It will make her hate me.

"Who will be the evil stepmother?" I ask, hoping it's not me.

"I'll do it," Stacey says.

She's been doing it more and more. She is so good. She always chooses the most boring role.

I beam inside.

I don't mind having to pretend that Bernie is my sister, because *I* always get the beating, and she is always the weak one. Last week I was locked in the cellar for two months without a lick of food or water. I almost died.

Today we serve food. I load the tray with apples, sausages, mash, pap, wors, grapes, and toffee. Stacey smiles as I point each item out to her. I sprinkle fine sand over the top and say, "Monkey-gland sauce." She begins to eat, and my invisible tray grows lighter. I kneel on the hard ground, and my knees begin to ache.

Stupid Bernie. I fume, trying to hold still while I think of how Bernie swept up all the soft sand. I am convinced she did it on purpose.

Stacey eats, and I watch her mouth move. She doesn't sit at my meal table, so this is the first time I have seen her chew. I am mesmerized . . . it looks like she is the first person to *ever* chew. Like she invented the chew.

We go on like this for a while. The weekends were tedious before the House. Now, they go too quickly. Before I am ready to see the sun set behind the corn tower, Stacey puts down her invisible whip and stands up, heading for the fence.

"Supper."

It takes me a little while to get my mind back to the here and now—I am still sitting in the cellar with a bleeding back and torn blouse.

Bernie gets up right away. She never has any trouble finding the invisible door, like me.

◆ ◆ ◆

It's movie night tonight. Matron hands out plastic cups of hot chocolate. It's watery and not very sweet, but I drink it like manna from the gods. Precious ambrosia. I can never hold myself back long enough for the cocoa to last through to the end of the film. I get halfway, and then I forget, or I get desperate, and gulp down the last few sips. Then I stick my fingers into the cup and scoop out the sugar and chocolate powder that is locked inside the gooey bits that have touched the water.

Stacey's hot chocolate lasts right until the end credits, as usual, and she never touches her goo. I asked her if I could have it only once, and the look she gave me turned my insides watery. But, in secret, I'm always desperate for her goo.

After the movie, we prepare for bed in silence. Sal and Chena have gone home for the weekend, so Stacey and I are alone. The whole dorm feels empty and dark. Somehow abandoned, like we are, inside it. Stacey removes her gown and hangs it inside her cupboard, gathers her toothbrush and toothpaste, and walks out of the room, down the corridor to the bathroom.

Later, in bed, before Matron walks through the corridors turning lights off, Stacey whispers, "Don't go to sleep."

7

Mirror, Mirror

NOW

Denise arranged everything. I found the text message on my phone.

> Be ready. Thursday the 9th. 4pm.

And on precisely that date and time, an Uber beeped from the street. Denise could plan a war on her iPhone and still get a good night's sleep.

Bruce hovers behind me in the living room as I get my crutches. "How are you feeling?"

"All right."

"Did you take your meds?"

I nod. "Yum yum."

He kisses my earlobe, and I giggle. "See you later."

I'm not the only author Denise is responsible for, but I know I take up the bulk of her time. It takes consistent effort on my publisher's part to keep me presentable. And that is Denise's job. I wonder what her memos look like. *Dress and paint Bethany. Deliver Bethany to award ceremony. Make sure Bethany doesn't arrive in her onesie and unicorn slippers.*

Even now, here at this hairdresser (it has some clever name, like *The Snip* or *Sheers*), Denise has thought of everything. Every mirror in the whole place has been covered because of my preference of not seeing myself. There are no other patrons because I hate crowds. There is exactly one man doing my hair, because I don't much like men outside of Bruce, and one lady in the back waiting to "put on my face" (she hovers, popping her head around a curtain now and then to see if I'm ready). I don't like to be looked at for very long, nor for too many eyes to be on me at one time. I wonder how much they had to fork out for me this time.

Maybe all of this is because it's the penultimate Sally book, and they need the buzz. It was long listed, then short listed, and now it might win a literary award, though God knows why. If it wins, they expect the last in the Sally series to explode. They'll want more, but there's only so much I can bleed onto paper.

Hell, maybe it's because they feel sorry for me.

But the longer I sit in the chair, waiting for Mr. Designer to fix my hair into something other than a short bleached mess, the more I think I'd rather be able to see what he's doing.

I'd rather be able to see what *you're* doing.

"*Et voilà*!" he cries, spritzing my hair with something to make it set like clay. He's a cliché of himself.

I'm passed along to the young lady in the back. She's wearing what can only be described as an artist's pallet around her neck, except it displays a plethora of creams, eye shadows, and lipsticks instead of bright acrylics and oils.

"Fresh canvas," she murmurs in a sexual voice, the hint of a smile in her cheek, and there it is, confirmed. I am unworked art, ready to be discovered. I wonder who she'll turn me into. Could she turn me into you? Could she give me that enigmatic gaze, sharp and unfocused at the same time? Could she make my lips seem to curve just so . . . narrow my nose and raise my eyebrows into sharp arches?

Were you wearing makeup at the diner? Or are you, like me, the fresh-canvas type of face? I can't remember, and it bothers me. Lip gloss or bare? Mascara or not? You were perfect, and I wish I had your photograph, and I hate that I've changed myself so much in the years since we were children. But that's what growing up is, I remind myself. Safety from the feral creatures we used to be, a veneer of civility. I feel the walls of the Invisible House all around me, keeping me safe.

Twins, they used to call us. Wild, curling brown hair that bunched around our faces, skinny legs, and sandy feet. And I can't remember why I did this to myself. I can't remember *when* I did this to myself. There is a vague memory of cutting off my hair, seeing the locks of brown fall into the sink. Bruce telling me to stop. I remember that. But when did I go platinum blond? And when did I chemically straighten my hair?

"Relax your jaw," the lady with the palette says. "You're gritting your teeth."

I unclench and release my breath. "Sorry."

"Not used to this kind of pampering, are you?"

"No."

"Such a shame," she says, and the sponge she uses on my face is cold and wet, and I want to tell her to stop. Stop. Stop it. Please stop. "You're pretty. Now I will make you beautiful."

Your feet were beautiful, hard skin cracked with lines of permanent dirt, a Thorn for the thorns.

"Would you like to see?" she asks, sometime later. "I haven't chosen a lipstick color. I thought you may like to have a say for yourself, depending on the dress you wear."

"Sure."

It is my most casual reply. I should win an Oscar. This little girl has no idea what she's asking me.

Did we play lying games out in the sun on top of the broken ground? I have an eerie sense of memory—this lie feels so familiar. The nostalgia deeply unnerving. I could cry. It's like the hint of a scent passed beneath my nose too quickly to capture.

The girl reveals my reflection like a stab.

Quick and sharp, she pulls the black silk covers down without counting down, without giving me a chance to prepare. I see Mr. Designer hurry over, but it is too late and he knows it. He wants to cover the mirror and undo the damage, the damage that my publicist warned him might be done, but he is curious. Like all humans watching a car crash—his morbidity takes over.

And there it is. My reflection. At first everything is where it should be. Eyes. Eyebrows. Nose, mouth. Slim face. White-blond hair pin curled and sprayed stiff. Only so much you can do with it this short. The girl has done a good job with what she was given. I am now suitable for the award ceremony. Suitable for publishing at night, which is a whole other beast than its daylight counterpart of sweat, greasy hair, and coffee-stained lips. I look human.

The cracks are there, though. They always are. Tiny fissures, like fractures in glass, and then one big *crack*.

It begins at my jawbone, a parting of the skin even through the foundation, concealer, and powder. But not like skin at all. Sharp, sudden, revealing not bone but a blackness beneath. It is with horrified fascination that I watch it spread, across my cheek and over my nose with a *crunch*, to the pink corner of my eye, where it stabs like a shard of broken mirror.

The glass is in my throat now, and I can't swallow. The shards rise and rise until they are behind my eyes, and I am blinking the blood from my retinas.

The world goes red.

And then black.

And the pain is intolerable.

I rub my cheek, and the cracks close up. They were never there.

They'll come back, of course, these things I imagine, but I like the disguise. And though my hands are clean, my nails perfectly manicured, I still feel the blood on them. A writer's imagination.

"Lovely," I murmur, and then I turn to the girl who made me human for the evening. "Red lipstick should be fine."

"Beautiful," the girl says, and she is the antithesis of you, and I want to make her stop, make her change, crack and morph into something less appealing. Her youth and joyfulness aggravate me. She may only be five or so years younger than me, but I've been old for a very, very long time.

She applies the lipstick, and I am a vixen.

A long languorous creature yawns somewhere in my left thigh, a body haunting, and I smile.

They help me to the door, and when it closes behind me, I hear Mr. Designer and Miss Makeup break into whispers.

I have become a story in their narrative.

As you are in mine.

8

Stacey's Girl

THEN

Stacey stands over my bed like a tokoloshe, teeth bared and eyes blazing. A scream builds in my throat, but she claps her hand over my mouth, smothering it.

"I *told* you not to sleep!" Tiny white balls of spittle have gathered in the corners of her mouth.

Tears fill my eyes. "Mm-mmommee," I apologize against her hand, muffled.

She removes it and wipes it on her nightgown, then steps back and folds her arms, her lips curling. Her eyes flicker over my face and my body, and I shrink downward into the bed, terrified of the disgust in her eyes. What is she thinking? How can I make up for my mistake?

"I'm sorry," I say again.

"Hurry up."

She already has her school shoes on, so I hurry for my own, feeling the phantom hand on my lips where hers was a moment before. I resist the urge to touch it, knowing that if I do, it will vanish.

At night, wearing shoes is sometimes allowed, though I don't know why. Sometimes it is and sometimes it isn't. Stacey knows the rules. I think she must read the signs in the sky, smell them in the air—know in the cells of her flesh when things are safe and when they're not.

I eye Stacey's lace-ups, which were once her brother's, as I do up the stupid ninny buckles on my own. Stacey hurriedly stuffs our beds with our pillows and then heads out the door into the corridor. She doesn't even hesitate.

The clock that sits on the wall above the outer door throws ticking noises across the corridor. They echo back. It's the sound of ghosts; I shudder at the thought, so I stay close to Stacey.

If we get caught, we'll be in detention forever; breaking the rules is a big mistake. Being out after lights-out is the biggest one. Once I had to write a thousand lines because I forgot to push my chair in. Another time Matron Monday forced me to clean the toilets for a month after I broke a bowl at breakfast. Detention varies from teacher to teacher, but the matrons dole out the worst. Bernie had to stand with her back against the wall once, squatting like she was sitting on a chair, for a whole hour. She was a wreck. I pointed and laughed some. I can't remember what Stacey did, which means it wasn't much, which means it isn't important.

It doesn't matter. All that matters is Stacey. She wouldn't do anything wrong. She knows everything, so I follow on.

It's too dark to see anything because the moon is hiding. It's also unusually cold, which makes me think the ghosts are *definitely* out. Will they be watching us, like I'm watching them? Will they notice the trespass of the living?

Please don't get me, Glass Man.

I glance out toward the grounds and force myself not to scream at the abyss that meets me. I imagine all sorts of things waiting to pounce, critters crawling over my feet, up my shoes, and under my pajamas. I shudder. It's creepy being out . . . exposed. Except, no—it's not. Stacey is out. I am out. We are both fine. *Fine, fine, fine.*

"Calm the fuck down, will you?"

I gasp in a huge mouthful of air, surprised that Stacey's sworn at me, and I nod.

I want to ask where we're going. Is it safe? Why are we doing this? When will we come back? I'm sleepy. I need the toilet. This doesn't feel safe. I bite down on my tongue and follow her, mute.

We run along the black road, which cuts the grounds in two, until the school is just a speck in the blackness.

"Are we going to the House?" I ask. Maybe we are going to the Tractor Tire, and she is going to make me summon Glass Man.

She doesn't answer. She stares past me, her face twisting in what appears to be alarm, as though she sees some hideous creature behind me. With my mind full of Glass Man, I feel pins and needles in my chest, and I think I might faint.

Somehow I think I can *feel* the thing that must be behind me.

"What?" I breathe. "What is it?"

Her eyes widen and her lips part slightly.

I spin around, sure someone or something is behind me, but the night is as black and empty as ever, which is worse. Her footsteps rush away, and my stomach drops out from under me. I can picture her scolding me, even as her back vanishes into the blackness. *Not quick enough,* she might say, eyes glinting opaque in the gloom. *Not by a bloody long shot.*

It is so dark tonight that Stacey is hard to see. I give chase quickly, terrified to lose her to the night. Terrified to be alone. I find her fast enough, and then I make sure to stay close. She skirts the roads, keeping low as a salamander, until we can see the caretaker's hut. She walks up to the front door, breezy in her confidence, and knocks.

I hide behind her, peeking out from the space her shadow would occupy in the sunlight. At night her shadow is invisible, but it's still there, and I feel it. What is she doing? What will she say? What is her goal? My heart pulses in my chest and my neck; the veins push, like little hands, against my skin in predictable rhythms—*What now? What now? What now?* I can almost hear it. What is she doing? What are we doing?

The door opens torturously, slowly, and only by a crack. Joe, the caretaker-cum-janitor, regards us with amusement. His wrinkly old face is kind, and his bushy eyebrows remind me of Father Christmas, so it's hard to stay afraid. Somehow I manage it anyway.

"Little Stacey Preston," he says in a warm gravelly voice, rich as gravy on pork chops.

"Hello, Joe."

I stare at her and, if it's possible, the wonder I feel as a constant when she's near magnifies until it encompasses both of us like a big impenetrable bubble. I've never heard this voice before. It's an octave higher, wider as she smiles, whole and round like a carefree and spontaneous laugh. It's . . . pleasant, natural, young, innocent. It's all the things Stacey is not. It's all the things that our parents want us to be, the things that are safe. The things that stop awkward questions. It's not the voice of terrible stories about boys with demonic sisters, nor the voice of rules and order, nor power and control. It is not a glass voice.

"And you've brought a guest?"

"This is Bethany." She gestures to me but doesn't look. I'm like the product she is advertising, so I try to shine. "She's my best friend."

My smile turns into a ghoulish chasm as the shock of Stacey's words sink in. *She's my best friend.* I can see it all already—our whole future is written in those words. We'll spend our lives together, finish school and go to university. We'll meet boys who are brothers and have identical weddings. Our children will be born on the same day, and they will fall in love and have their own children, merging our genes forever, leaving us immortal and combined. I laugh awkwardly at the enormity of the thought, but Stacey's jaw clenches, and I know I have gone too far.

"Well," Joe says, looking down at me with small blue eyes that have some white on them, like pieces of fat, "aren't you two the pair of twins?"

Happiness—perfect, serene happiness—never felt this complete. Fluttering in my chest signals to me that I ought to be breathing. But if I move, then this all might shatter, vanish, dissipate. I don't even want to blink in case what has happened is merely something stuck in my eye, itching to be blinked away. If I can hold on to this moment and keep it within me, I could float away. My body betrays me, and I gasp in a tiny breath. The feeling remains, weighty, significant, humbling. I nearly drop to my knees in awe of it.

This is Bethany. She's my best friend. Well, aren't you two the pair of twins?

"Well," he says, and the moment becomes ordinary once again. "Come on inside, then."

Stacey walks in with deliberate steps, chin raised. She knows exactly where she's going, and I tail her closely, looking around with wide eyes. She's been here before; it is abundantly clear. But . . . when? I don't remember ever being out of her company. I mean, why would I? I step where she steps and try not to get anything wrong.

"So, what's new?" Joe asks as he limps across his small living room. A brilliantly white snake is curled on the sofa. Stacey bends down to stroke its head, and I stare in wonder. Stacey isn't afraid of snakes . . . of course she isn't. Maybe this snake is friendly.

I glance at Joe, and he smiles, eyes crinkling. "That's Molly. She's friendly."

I go over and give Molly a stroke, dazzled by her cool glassy skin. She lifts her head and looks at me, tongue dashing out.

The walls are cracked, and there is no paint on them. But Joe has a TV, and I stare at it in wonder. It's even better than the one we have on film nights. I bet he even gets *actual* TV channels, something I haven't had since last summer. It feels like forever ago.

Stacey shrugs and goes to sit on his sofa, next to the snake. "Nothing much. How is Molly doing?"

She pets her absentmindedly.

"Ag, she's good," he says. He chuckles and shakes his head. "Ol' Moll likes you quite a bit, hey?"

Stacey grins and plants a kiss on Molly's head. I seethe.

"Still can't sleep?"

She shrugs. "Not really. You want me to go and try, instead of visiting?"

"I suppose I should enjoy your company as much as I can." He chuckles. "When Sakkie gets home, there won't be room for such delightful company."

Stacey's face darkens, but Joe is looking at me now, so he doesn't see.

"Sakkie is coming soon?" she asks. He can't hear the iron in her voice, but I can. I shudder.

"Sure is, *liefie*. Few weeks, maybe. Be good to have my boy home again. But there won't be room for you chickens here, I'm afraid. You be sure to remember that, okay?"

Stacey looks away, and her face is marble. She has stopped caressing Molly, who shivers in her desperation to be petted.

Joe doesn't skip a beat. He just stares at me. "Well, Bethany." I can't help but shy away a little, because he looks less like a Father Christmas in this light and more like a father demon, with his wild white hair. "Would you and Stacey like some warm cocoa?"

My spirits pick up immediately. Maybe he isn't so bad after all. "Yes, please."

He laughs. "I had a hunch." Glancing at the snake, he adds, "And do you want an egg, Molly?"

He smiles again kindly and limps out of the room and into what must be the kitchen. I go to sit beside Stacey. I want to ask all sorts of questions. Why are we here? When has she been here before? Why did she come? Was she alone? Or was she with Bernie?

I dry retch.

"Don't look so wimpy," Stacey says. She doesn't even whisper. She just strokes and strokes and strokes the snake.

I wish I were Molly.

I blush. "Sorry."

"If you're going to be my twin, you have to be braver than this."

I'm sure that I must be sitting, smiling, breathing, blinking—but I feel none of that. Can you die of such contentment? I feel like I am made of nothing more than light. I have come so far.

If you're going to be my twin, you have to be braver than this . . .

Stacey said the same thing to me once, five years ago.

It was cold that morning, a wintry August day, late into the school year, and I stood in a small room with the stranger who was my mother. I kept glancing at her blond hair and her big chest, confused. She faced a big counter that I was too small to see over, but I heard her sign her name on some sort of paper. Then, with a kiss and a wink, she was gone.

A fat woman who smelled of rotting wool and mothballs told me to follow her, so I did. I remember my shoes squeaked on the linoleum floor, announcing my presence in a grating scream. The wing was empty, so Matron let me unpack alone. I didn't know how to fold my clothes, so I just moved them from my bag as carefully as I could and put them in the drawers I knew would be mine.

When Matron didn't come back, I snuck outside. There was a group of girls playing a game I had never seen before, involving long strips of elastic band, laughing and jumping and singing. One of them spotted me, tapped another girl on the shoulder, and nodded in my direction.

A ripple of laughter followed as they took in my woolen hat, complete with bobble; my red mittens; and my plastic sandals.

"Cold much?" one of the girls called, and then all of them exploded laughing. I was humiliated, confused—I didn't understand what was going on. What was so funny?

That's when I saw Stacey. She reclined on her elbows under the cold midday sun, observing me. I bit my lips and began to take a few steps backward. I needed my mother. I needed her to take me home right now.

She sat up and dusted off her hands. Then, with a glare at the other girls, she walked up to me.

"Nice hat," she said, and I felt like her comment was genuine. The other girls stopped laughing, stumped mute in the face of her contradiction.

I knew then what she was doing. She created a door for me to step through, into their world—into *her* world. She gave me an opening and offered me a way to bypass the tests those inferior girls might otherwise have put me through.

"Thank you."

She smiled and put an arm around my shoulders. Then, so none of the other girls could see, she whispered, "If you're going to stay here, you'll have to be braver than that."

I sniffed, wiped my snot on my mittens, and nodded.

"Good."

I blink back to the present. I stare at Stacey, delight caressing my face. Her twin? If I want to be her *twin*? Really? I've finally made it here, to this moment. I try not to look too happy, because I know Stacey will be angry with me, but inside I'm doing backflips.

"Okay," I say as blandly as I can. She knows this word is enough of a promise. It conveys more than the four letters it's made of.

She knows I am hers.

9

Games

The morning bell sounds, and I yell; the sky is bright blue outside, and I'm petrified because I don't know if I'm back in the dorm room or if I fell asleep on Joe's sofa. My first thought—*Where is Stacey?*—pounds on the inside of my skull. It won't relent. I turn to look at her bed. There she is, getting up already.

I jump out of bed, my heart racing. I can't remember what's real. I can't remember if we really did go to Joe's house last night. I can't remember if we drank cocoa and watched TV and nibbled on pieces of sugarcane.

I glance at Stacey, but she is icy and distant. She strips off her bedding efficiently and quickly, leaving the pile of material on the floor at the foot of her bed, then grabs her toothbrush and toothpaste and runs to the bathroom, like every other morning. And like every other morning, I strip my own bed and follow, just a little too late. Always a little too late.

Back in the bedroom, I walk over to Stacey, where she stands making her bed. "Did we—"

Matron Monday cuts me off with a whip of her tongue. "Sloane! Look at this bedding. Get to work!"

I rush over to my bed and make it as fast as I can. Stacey is already standing beside hers, waiting for inspection.

Matron circles my bed. "Get rid of those wrinkles if you value your free time."

I get rid of them. I also send up a silent prayer of thanks that it is Saturday, which means our underwear and socks won't have to be inspected, and we can wear whatever we like.

"Move it, Sloane. We don't have all day. Good work, Preston."

I can't wait to talk to Stacey. I'm burning to ask her about our adventure. But Matron seems determined to keep me from speaking. I bite the inside of my cheek and wait until it is clear.

"Breakfast," Matron says.

I file out after Stacey, still biting my cheek. She stares straight ahead as she walks, and I know that now is not the time to ask. We walk in silence to the food hall, and I grudgingly make my way to my assigned seat. Chatting will wait a bit longer. The Big Girl who sits at the head of the table ignores me as usual. She is bored and apathetic, leaning her cheek on her hand and sighing a lot. I sit down and wait, but I can't keep my legs from bouncing in my chair.

I've been looking forward to breakfast since last night. I hope it's delicious. My mouth waters when I think of Bovril and syrup-peanut-butter mix, or peanut butter bread put upside down in a bowl and covered with milk.

Not today.

We have porridge again. Plain *mealie* pap.

I eat the spoonful put into my bowl, trying not to vomit it up again. There is no sugar today, which must be some kind of punishment or else is "character building." I fantasize about gnawing on a stick of sugarcane and wonder if I can get Joe to ask the sugarcane ladies for some more.

A tide of effervescing laughter threatens to bubble out of my mouth.

Well, aren't you two the pair of twins.

After breakfast, Stacey doesn't wait for me, and I'm sick with worry. I rush through the corridors, imagining her alone with Bernie, and I'm nearly hyperventilating by the time I reach the dorm. Stacey is lying on her bed, her face toward the door.

Her eyes are round and shining. "Were you leaving without me?"

She mistakes my stunned silence for affirmation and turns away. I rush to her bedside and kneel. Explanations usually annoy her, but in this case, I think she needs one. Am I learning to sense her tone better, now that I am older? I'd like to think so.

"I was coming to look for you," I say. "I didn't see you in the hall. I looked everywhere."

She turns back to me, and her eyes look like someone else's. "You won't leave, will you?"

I blink. "No. Why would I leave?"

She nods, and her eyes droop. I wait for a long time for her to do something, to tell me to do something, but she is immovable, and the silence drags on.

"Are you sick?" I ask.

"No."

"Do you need to sleep?"

"No."

"Can I help?"

"No."

I sit and watch her patiently. I wait for a sign. What will happen if Stacey isn't Stacey anymore? *Stop it.* I'm horrified by indecision. What do I do? What would Stacey do? She'd wait. Yes, she would wait it out.

So I do.

It's not long before Bernie comes into the dorm. She has heavy footfalls, and her presence annoys me. Also, she's wearing a stupid pink color that matches her cheeks but clashes with her hair. She sniffs, and because Stacey can't see, she picks her nose and eats whatever it is she finds. Even though I hate to admit it, she has a restorative effect on Stacey, who stands up right away.

"Come on," she demands, leading us out of the room.

I scowl at Bernie before I follow. She looks confused and even upset but says nothing.

The Tractor Tire is different today. Stacey is too quiet, which changes everything. The sky is gray and moody, at her request, I think. We take our cues from her. The wind is blowing in irregular gusts, which catches us off guard and whips up our dresses. I can smell the dirty scent of the dry day, and I feel quite depressed. There is nothing to look forward to, and Stacey's silence has me on edge. I can also smell the loamy scent coming off Bernie, and something that smells like cat spray or sage. I decide she must have peed herself.

I fiddle with a baby devil's thorn between my fingers. The spiky bits are very small but very sharp; like a kitten's claws. I feel sorry for it, not wanting to break them off. It feels sort of . . . mean. I glance up at Stacey, but she isn't looking at me, so I slip it into my pocket unharmed. I'll make it my pet and hope Stacey never finds it.

"Bernie, go away," Stacey says at last.

My eyes widen, and a grin spreads across my face. I replay the sentence in my mind. *Bernie, go away. Go away. Go away, Bernie.*

I choke back my laughter and the niggling feeling that I would hate to be where Bernie is. I force the sympathy away and out of myself. This moment is for me.

Bernie's eyes turn very white and big, and her jaw slackens until I can see her shiny tongue. It twitches a little, as though she might try to say something to change Stacey's command. Like me, she will do anything she can think of to reverse a decision that puts her out of favor. She wants to try to deflect Stacey's disdain onto me. Her eye spasms, so I smirk at her, and when I'm sure Stacey isn't looking, I stick out my tongue. Her face crumples, lips stretching back over her teeth in an ugly grimace. Big tears well in her eyes. It's like the best TV show I've ever seen.

"Now," Stacey says.

Bernie gets to her feet slowly and walks away, being very careful now that she doesn't have Stacey's footsteps to follow through the paper-thorn patches. She looks lost, uncertain. When she reaches the safe track, she begins to run, her bum wiggling.

I suppress the urge to whoop in triumph.

I get up, climb the tire, and sit next to Stacey. Her face looks brighter.

"Last night was fun," I say.

"Ssh! You never, *ever* speak about the night during the day."

I nod. "Okay."

Of course. I'm so stupid. I should have known that.

"Have you ever played Glassy, Glassy?" she asks.

Jolted, my skin feels like it has been dipped in ice water. Why would I play *that*? "Of course not."

Stacey looks out into the dry yellow fields of wild grass behind the fence in the distance. "I did once. When I was six."

I can hardly believe her. She must be testing me. The idea of that . . . *game* is more terrifying than breaking the rules at night. It's more terrifying than Stacey.

She licks her lips. "Glassy, glassy, cut my ars—"

"*Stop!* Don't say it!"

Stacey's mouth is still open from almost finishing, but she slowly closes it and smiles.

"Got you," she says.

I laugh, but I don't think she was joking. In my head I hear it. *Arsey. Arsey. Arsey, arsey, arsey. Glassy, glassy, cut my*—stop!

I control my breathing by counting to ten. I watch my toes, and every time I go up a number, I go up a toe. When I reach ten, I think I am okay.

"We're twins," Stacey says at last. "Maybe we were separated at birth."

"But you weren't adopted."

"But maybe *you* were. Maybe both of us were and we don't know it."

I contemplate. It's true that I don't look like my mother much, but I used to. This new possibility is enticing. I want it to be real.

"Yes," I whisper. "Yes! We *must* be twins." It seems logical. I force it to be.

"Prove it."

"How?"

She takes a razor blade from her pocket and hands it to me.

I shudder. "What do you want me to do?"

"Cut your arm. Prove you love me."

I finger the blade, and before I have time enough to think, I swipe it across my arm. I don't feel the cut at first and think I must have done it wrong. Then spots of blood pepper my skin in a line, and it stings.

Stacey's eyes bore into my bleeding flesh with adoration, and she raises my arm to her lips. She kisses the wound tenderly.

"Poor twin," she coos with bloodred lips.

I love you, I think. But I never say it.

Now that this discovery has been made, I feel a little bold, and I take Stacey's hand in my own. My stomach jumps into my mouth when I feel her smooth hand inside mine. I feel like a dirty, snotty, sweaty girl holding the hand of a goddess.

Stacey lets me stroke her hand, and nothing more is said. After I've bled onto my summer dress for a little while, she gathers some dry grass and presses it to my wound. "Like in the olden days," she says. Then she takes my hand and walks me back to the dorm.

I have to wait until the sun has set to ask Stacey about what is happening tonight. I stare out of the window until the sun has fully gone, each and every ray disappeared over the dry horizon, and then I turn to her where she sits on her bed, staring at the wardrobe.

"What will we do tonight?"

Stacey looks at me with a blank expression. "Don't go to sleep," she says.

10

Mountains in Memory

NOW

I circle the room; I circle people.

This is something you would never understand. The lilting music. The low hum of conversation. Like bees. Everyone glitters just a little.

You never glittered. I don't recall a single nail polish, hairband, lipstick, or sticker. Nothing shiny. Nothing lacquered. Just the proud, sandy scent of the relentless summer, the cinnamon dryness of the earth. That sandpaper-in-your-throat kind of desperate breathing that made it hard to swallow.

The women are strapped in and perfumed up. The men haughty, discussing the short list. Who among them will take home bragging rights? It's a boys' club. Worthless—unless they win. They all secretly think they will.

"That's right," they'll chortle, "I'm a Brentwood and Baron Award–winning author." It's their accreditation. And if they lose: "It's a pile of politics, nothing to brag about. I've set my sights on the Pulitzer."

Strange, though, Stacey . . . no matter how hard I try, I can't remember a single book between us. I can't remember a single classroom, or a single subject, or a single teacher. I don't recall our learning. All I have are fuzzy recollections of dusty roads, the white chapel, and the Tractor Tire. Ethereal memories with no substance, except your magnanimous presence in it all. You are larger than a mountain in my mind. You are a solid part of the things that make up me. So why can't I remember more of these things?

Don't go to sleep.

"Bethany, darling!" Denise, wrapped in an elegant black toga-style dress, slides through the crowd toward me. She has a young man in tow. Twenties, plain, a sparkle in his eye.

"Hi, Denise."

"You look absolutely fabulous. I told you that place was amazing! And you seem to have survived it well enough." She laughs and gives me a kiss on each cheek. "Where's that husband of yours gone to?"

"He's getting drinks," I say and glance at her companion.

"Oh, darling. Let me introduce Ralph Mullens. We've just acquired him for a speedy thriller. We're absolutely delighted. It was a nine-house auction—very exciting! But we got you in the end, didn't we, Ralph?"

The young man, Ralph, grows beet red, but looks thrilled.

"Ralph," Denise continues, "this is Bethany Sloane."

"Miss Sloane, I can't tell you how much I enjoy your novels."

I raise my brows. "Really?"

"I grew up reading Sally's adventures under my duvet covers."

I smile. I feel *old.*

Age is a good thing, I remind myself. Distance is a good thing.

"Ralph is our twenty-year-old shiny new star," Denise says, answering my unspoken question. Women are attuned to age.

"I'm so excited for the new book," Ralph says. "When's the publication date? I couldn't find one online."

I am going to vomit.

"Don't tell me you started the party without me?"

You are glorious.

A marvel in black velvet so deep it sucks in the light. Somehow the darkness you radiate makes you look more radiant than everyone else. I forgot that I ended up inviting you to come. I never thought you actually would. You—mucky, wild, untamed you—here, in this roped-in, phony imitation of manners.

You really have changed, I realize, and breathe easier.

Denise takes Ralph's arm and slips hers through. "We don't give Bethany deadlines. She's far too important for that. A true artist's artist. But you, young buck, will have plenty."

Ralph looks absolutely overwhelmed and impressed, and I give Denise one of my thank-you-you-are-my-savior looks.

Ralph tries again. "Miss Sloane, I wanted to ask you—"

"It's missus, actually," Bruce says, arriving with two tall glasses. To the untrained eye, it might look like his and mine are the same, but I know his is champagne and mine is sparkling apple juice.

Ralph blushes furiously again. "Oh—oh, I'm so sorry, I—"

Bruce slaps the poor kid on the arm. "I'm messing with you."

Not for the first time, I wonder if it was a mistake keeping and publishing under my maiden name. Maybe, subconsciously, I did it so you'd always be able to find me.

"They're going to be announcing the winner in a few minutes," Denise says, winking at me. "Better get to our seats."

I turn to introduce you, but you've gone to the back of the room with the nontabled guests. You sit down with the rest of the audience and raise your chin, eyes sparkling with amusement.

Bruce helps me to sit at our assigned table, frowning when I wince. "You okay?" he mouths.

I placate him with my hands and whisper, "Just tired."

The speeches go on for a long time, and I feel myself fading out of the room. The laughs and murmurs of encouragement around me transform into gentle waves lapping at some distant shore.

When they call my name, I don't hear it. I don't even realize what's happening when everyone turns to me, their faces alight, clapping. It's only when Bruce stands, bowing to me, and then makes his way to the stage on my behalf that I come to. I won. I won the Brentwood and

Baron Literary Award for a series of books I can no longer write. For a series of books I have come to hate.

"Bethany Sloane," the announcer says again, as though to wake me from my shock.

But all I hear in my head is your voice, telling me stories.

Don't go to sleep, Bethany Sloane.

You sit beside me in Bruce's now-empty chair as the applause grows louder and take a sip from my drink. You pull a face.

"Jesus. Is that apple juice?"

I nod, keeping my eyes on Bruce as he mounts the stage and shakes the hand of the announcer.

"My medicine," I say simply, trying to hear what Bruce is saying into the mic.

Thank you. I'm delighted to accept this award on behalf of my beautiful wife, Bethany, who . . .

You scoff. "No alcohol for poor medicated Bethany."

I glance at you.

. . . an immeasurable talent, and very much beloved . . .

You raise your brows. "And he takes your award too?"

You're trying to get to me. But it won't work.

"I can't get up on the stage. And I don't like people looking at me."

"They're *all* looking at you."

And you're right. Everyone is turning to look at me, no doubt wondering why I'm not up there.

. . . and I know she would say the same . . .

You scoff again and pass back my drink, then get to your feet and leave the venue entirely. I wish I could follow. Instead, I sip my invalid juice and smile.

11

The Trap

THEN

To keep myself from falling asleep, and thereby defying Stacey, I pinch the insides of my thighs until my eyes stream. By the time Stacey gets up from her bed, I can feel the bruises, and there are dozens of little half-moon punctures in the soft skin. Stacey doesn't notice I have been waiting for her; she walks to her closet, grabs her sweater, and makes for the door. She doesn't look at me.

"Hey." Has she forgotten me?

She turns around, but I can't see if she looks at me, and for some reason this really bothers me. There is too much space between us, and I need to sense the contact of her eyes focused on mine. I want to feel her gaze touching me, like a physical caress.

She turns back to the door. "Hurry."

I scramble for my closet and my own school sweater, but Stacey doesn't wait for me, and I have to walk down the hall alone. Without her I feel like I'm drifting through a haunted place again, like a graveyard. In every shadow I feel the presence of the other, the thing that isn't me, the thing that isn't real. Everything screams at me silently; every shadow looms up around me. It feels too cold, and I'm not wearing enough. The protection that Stacey's proximity affords leaves me cold when it's withdrawn. If I go back for a jersey, I will have lost Stacey—not just tonight, but forever. She won't forgive me. She'll think I'm weak and that I can't keep up. I square my jaw and rush on.

Outside, I make to sprint in the direction of Joe's hut, but a sound arrests my progress.

"*Pst!*" Stacey is waiting in the shadows on the other side of the doorway. "This way."

We run in the opposite direction into the dead night. Not even a breeze exists this evening; the world is as still as my anticipation. We scurry along the brief area of the school that is tarmac, over the giant center circle—which reminds me of roundabouts back home, except bigger—and over to the boys' side. I have never been to where the boys live. I expect it to be dirty, but it looks just like our side, minus purple crocuses.

Stacey leads me to where the older boys live, which is farther in. Their building doesn't have the same basic shape as ours: it's newer. There are lights still on in the dorm, behind green curtains. The dark shadows of bodies move behind some of them, shadows in boxes made of brick. I want to giggle, being this close to their personal space.

We tiptoe around to where the showers are. Some of the boys are in there; we can hear the ruckus from outside—bawdy laughter, yelling, and slapping noises as they run in and out. Now I really want to giggle, but Stacey's severity turns my insides out.

A window to our left, near the level of our knees, looks down into the boys' shower room. Stacey inches up to it and peeks inside. The boys' heads are lower than the level of our feet, and for some reason this is the most amusing thing to me. They're showering underground. They're *naked*, showering underground. I'm so close to laughing that I stick my fingers into my nostrils, hoping to suffocate the chortle that threatens to burst out of me.

I cover my mouth and try not to make that horrible hissy-laugh-through-my-teeth sound. It would be horrendous to giggle now and give her away. I watch her face carefully, wanting to see even a minute change. Nothing happens. She watches them with little interest, her nostrils flaring. Maybe they have swimming trunks on. Maybe there's a concealing wall.

"Why do they shower so late?" I ask.

"I think they're the swimming team," she says. "Late practice, when the pool's free."

I wait for what feels like a long time before Stacey finally notices me standing alone, waiting. I'm aching to take a peek too.

"Look," she mouths, nodding toward the window.

I kneel and peek through the glass. The boys—young men—ignite my cheeks in a furious blush. I have never seen a naked boy before . . . it has never occurred to me to look. I blush and look away. I'm an invader. I've never had this role before. It feels like it doesn't quite fit.

"Don't be a ninny."

I look again, this time more carefully. I'm captivated; I'm warm all over. I don't understand the way I feel. I want to escape. I wonder what it would be like to kiss one of them. They all look the same . . . but also they look different. Some have hairy arms and armpits, some have hairy chests, some look like there can't possibly be any hair on them except for their heads. Some have muscles, some are skinny. But they all have a distinctly male aura, like a scent I can pick up, even out here. Every single one.

It feels like an age before Stacey says she is bored and we go back to the dorm, and I have no way to know what has been set in motion by her wandering eyes and mechanistic mind. I have no way to know that we can't go back from what we've seen.

"You were perving on them," she says to me once I'm in my bed.

I send up a silent thank-you prayer that Chena and Sal are away; to have them snickering at Stacey's rebuke would be bad. To have witnesses hear that Stacey thinks I'm a perv would be enough for me to kill myself.

"What?"

She tricked me. She let me look, and I didn't know it was bad. "Don't talk," she tells me, and she climbs into her bed, facing away.

I'm so tired and shaken that I don't remember climbing into bed. There's only the sensation of blinking and it suddenly being light.

I feel like I've had an out-of-body experience.

Is Stacey still mad at me?

I glance over at her bed, but she's missing.

The fever has Stacey, and she's quarantined in sick bay until further notice. I would hate to be in her position, but I hate being in mine even more. Without Stacey I am lost . . . I don't know what to do or when. I don't know the rules. I am bored. Bernie has gone off with the girls from her dorm, and they don't like me, and I don't like them, and when I try to follow, they laugh. So I wander the school grounds alone after chapel, killing time.

Bernie is different without Stacey. I don't like it. She's not as pathetic. She kind of looks . . . calm, as though she suddenly has a little bit of confidence. Almost. It bugs me. Without Stacey's backing, I can't make her feel fat or unworthy, and I want to because she laughed at me with her stupid friends, and I have no one.

Bernie isn't a real Thorn.

Whatever. I don't care, anyway. Only Stacey is important, so Bernie can go down the Tractor Tire hole for all I care.

Except . . .

Except.

Except I don't like this at all. I don't want to be alone.

Sometimes I try to hide in the empty dorm. I don't want anyone to see that without Stacey, I am nothing, have nothing. Without Stacey, I don't exist. I cry for a while, and when I hear someone come closer along the corridor, I escape outside again, and I cry some more. It's a pinching in my chest, a fleeting thought, but it's there—I miss my mother. How long has it been since I've yearned for her comfort? How badly I seem to need it now. The tickle of her hair across my face, the softness of her lips as she kisses my brow, the way she brushed my hair behind my ear. My need disgusts me, and I swallow it down like the bile it is.

I wander all the way to Joe's door before I comprehend what I have done.

I knock and wait for him to open it.

"*Ja*?"

It isn't Joe but rather a Joe-like man with sandy-colored hair and gray eyes. He has little bristles on his face that look like tiny shards of glass. I take an involuntary step backward.

"I . . . I-is Joe here?"

The man, who I know must be Joe's son, Sakkie, steps back and regards me. "No."

"Oh." I finger the corner of my dress. "Okay."

"I'm the new groundskeeper." His mouth twitches up. "You can wait for him if you want. Inside."

I glance behind me, but I am met with the sight of the hot, empty school grounds and more long hours of hiding.

"Okay." I step over the threshold.

He closes the door behind me, and most of the light disappears.

NOW

You're there in my mind when I take off my makeup. The black-cat-eyed, ruby-lipped vixen is coming apart one swipe of a micellar-water-moistened cotton pad at a time, revealing me, and all my cracks, beneath. A clown, sinister and grinning as the lipstick smears. And you are with me.

Mindfulness.

We're supposed to practice it, right?

The cotton pads build up in a disgusting colorful pile. My cracks are back. It's not like I'm insane. I know the cracks aren't really there. It's my overactive imagination. I've always had that problem—and yes, it is a problem. Even for a writer. You remember, don't you, Stacey? You were just the same, back then. The stories we would invent. The places we would inhabit. Neither of us were very good at reality.

The cracks are wrinkles or pores, but in my mind, they fissure and splinter, wider and longer than they ought to be, so when I look at myself in the mirror, I see an ancient porcelain doll, the paint all chipped and eroded.

It's a pretty nasty picture. Somewhat sinister.

Touch a line . . .

That's why I avoid mirrors. Because, after a while, even the mirror begins to crack.

Glassy, glassy . . .

Bruce appears behind me, kisses my neck. When did he come in?

"You were wonderful tonight," he murmurs, breath warm and champagne flavored.

I didn't do anything at all, and I can still hear you scoffing.

"That dress was . . . rather lovely."

I am smiling before I feel it. "Oh, really?"

"Utterly"—he kisses my collarbone—"mesmerizing."

He puts my pills on my vanity, along with a glass of water.

"Thanks." I don't touch the offering.

"What do you say"—he slides one of my bra straps off my shoulder—"to putting it back on"—the other bra strap is down now—"and coming to bed—take your pills, my love—so I can rip it off you again?"

Take your pills, my love.

He sneaks it in there in a whisper. Does he even realize? Would I have remembered had he not brought them to me? Likely not. He's keeping me safe. Keeping me healthy. But I feel like a child. *You* make me feel like a child.

I stand and grab Bruce's face, planting a kiss on his lips. His arms slip around my waist, and he presses me to him, his muscles flexing. We kiss like we haven't in years—deeply. Wildly.

We have sex. Or, sex has us.

While Bruce is inside me, I try to remember all the things I can about you. The day we first met (I can't exactly remember the details), the first thing you said to me (blank), why we were friends (why?). By the time I come back to myself, Bruce is done and lying beside me, frowning, and there is a cold, sticky wetness between my legs, thinning as it oozes out of me onto the sheets. Did I take my morning pill? Another thing I don't remember.

He touches my cheek. "Where were you?"

"Hmm?"

"Is everything okay?"

"Yeah. Just . . . distracted. The final Sally book is looming, and I'm stuck."

"Want to talk about it?"

I shake my head.

He caresses my arm. "You're an award-winning author now. You've got this."

I should be focusing on Sally Pierson, instead of you.

Sally Pierson.

Stacey Preston.

My God. Have I been writing you all along?

12

Done, Undone

THEN

Joe's house looks different during the day. It's as though the magical veneer that exists in the half light of the evening has been stripped away to reveal the cracked core beneath the facade. It is dim, sparsely furnished, run down. I go to the sofa without thinking and sit.

"Do you have cocoa?" I feel bolder with this younger man here. I have a hunch he won't refuse me.

He smiles. "Yes. I'll make some."

I follow him into the kitchen. "Are you Sakkie?"

"That's me."

"How old are you?"

"Twenty-eight."

The number means little to me in actual terms. I hold out my hand, thinking it is the proper thing to do. "I'm Bethany Sloane."

He takes my hand with an amused raise of his eyebrows. "And how old are *you*, Beth?"

I feel an impulse to lie, but since I think he must already know my age, I tell the truth. "Thirteen and two-thirds."

He laughs—a pleasant sound—and begins to putter about the kitchen, getting mugs, cocoa, milk. Filling the kettle and putting it on the stove. "How much sugar?"

"A lot."

He puts down the spoon he has been using to ladle in the white granules and instead tips the sugar pot into the cup. Some of the sweet sand scatters all over the counter, but Sakkie doesn't seem to mind.

I chuckle. I have decided I like Sakkie. I'm going to make him into a second friend if I can. We finish making the cocoa, and then I follow him back into the lounge where he sits on the old sofa. I mimic him, trying to look like I know what I'm doing, but I don't know if I should cross my legs or not, if I should fold my hands in my lap or sit on them.

Sakkie breaks the silence with ease. "So you're a friend of my dad's?"

"Yes." I pick at the loose thread on the corner of the cushion. "We sneak out to see him at night sometimes."

"We?"

Her face floods my mind like a tidal wave. "Stacey and me." I sip the cocoa. "She's my twin."

He raises his eyebrows, and I get the feeling he thinks something is funny but that I wouldn't understand. His eyes seem to ridicule me all the while they burn.

"So you, like, break the law to come and visit an old man?"

"Yes. Joe's our friend."

He chuckles. "Perverted." He puts down his cocoa and faces me on the sofa. "You're a pretty one," he comments, rubbing his chin. It makes a scratchy sound that's so appealing I want to try it.

I flush and bite the insides of my cheeks. Stacey told me four months and three days ago that supermodels do this to make their jawbones look bigger, which reminds boys of their lips. I haven't yet discovered the significance of lips, or why boys need reminding of them.

"Too bad you're so young."

"I'm not young," I insist, sucked-in cheeks forgotten. Will he ask me to leave? "I'm *not.*"

He raises his eyebrows like he doesn't believe me. He reaches for a box on the table beside him and pulls out a cigarette, turns to me, hesitates, and then offers me one. I take it confidently, without showing that I don't know how to hold it.

He lights his, then passes it to me and takes mine. I put it between my lips and inhale. My lungs immediately contract and protest, pain searing my chest. I'm mortified by the coughing, spluttering, suffocating noises I make. My face burns because I know I look really stupid. The cloud of smoke I have choked on conceals my chagrin for a split second, obscuring my features.

Sakkie pats me on the back. "Easy."

I hand back the cigarette and bite back frustrated tears. Stacey would have done it right, when I always do it wrong. She would have been disappointed in me.

He puts it in the ashtray and then regards me again. His eyes twinkle, and he spits out a stray piece of tobacco onto the floor. "Have you ever kissed a boy?"

I pull a face. *Eugh.* "No."

He sighs. "That's what I thought." He reaches for his cigarette and takes another long drag. "So young. I first kissed a girl when I was *ten*. That's three and two-thirds years younger than you are now."

Has Stacey kissed a boy? Of course she has. No wonder she wasn't bothered by the naked boys in the shower room; she's probably seen it all before. Being so behind deforms me, makes me less. Can she sense this about me, this lack of mouth-to-mouth experience? Is it something vital, like a rite of passage I am late to pass through? Is something wrong with me?

Sakkie leans forward, and I let him kiss me on the lips. It is brief and sort of nice; his lips are dry and cracked, full of texture and life. I am pleased with myself, but Sakkie frowns and leans back, looking away from me. He reaches for another cigarette, lights it, and takes a drag.

"You kiss like a child," he says through the smoke. I chew on my cheeks again to keep my embarrassment from showing too obviously.

I think I might hate myself. If Stacey were here, Sakkie would never have thought that. If Stacey were here, she would have enchanted him.

If you're going to be my twin, you have to be braver than this . . .

Stacey's voice in my head. Powerful.

I lean forward for another kiss with the mind to press harder, but he puts down his cigarette and wraps his arm around my waist, pulling me closer; his other hand he puts in my hair at the back of my head and holds it firm. I try to pull away, startled by the sudden closeness of his glass-hair-rimmed lips, but he forces me nearer, lowering his mouth onto mine, kissing firmly. It pricks like sharp needles. Then he parts my lips with his tongue.

Brave. I'm brave. Can you see, Stacey?

In the moment it takes for me to gasp in a breath, I'm crying. My tongue is now waxy and tingling; I'm shivering but I'm not cold. My teeth chatter, and tears stain my dress.

He glances at the door and then claps a hand over my mouth. "Ssh!"

It's cold. Suddenly, it's too cold. I want to stop this now.

Braver than this. Braver than this . . .

He releases me again when I've stopped struggling, so that our faces are only centimeters apart and I am looking at him cross-eyed.

Sakkie stinks like a boy. Only deeper. Dangerous.

He takes a second drag of his cigarette and then puts it down again, blowing the smoke onto my chest. I sit on my hands to keep them still, but I'm still shivering.

He unwinds his warm hand from around my back and lets it fall on my chest, on my barely-there breast. It surprises me, this contact, but mostly because Sakkie seems hesitant. He is rapt with attention now, less languid, less unimpressed with me. I poke out my chest a little to show him it's sort of okay, and I see his eyes glint curiously. How funny that I can make a man's eyes stand at attention!

You're so brave.

I'm your twin. I can be like you.

"You're going to be quite a beauty," he whispers, and I let myself believe him. If Stacey were here, he would prefer her. But she isn't. I like to think that today, *I* am Stacey. My weakly waving hair is really the wild, untamed frizz of Stacey's mane. My eyes aren't the watery blue of a fading summer sky but Stacey's hard, brown, foundational eyes, the color of the earth and soil beneath my feet. For years I stepped where she stepped, did what she said, believed what she told me; I flowed on her rocky surface like changeable water. Rightly. But today *I* am the one setting the footprints in the sand. Today what I say matters. I'm not the silent shadow resident; I am the shadow maker.

I know how to do it. I've studied Stacey for five long years.

And this is my reward.

I giggle when Sakkie moves his hands back and forth, then slips his hand under my dress and squeezes me.

I laugh. "It tickles. Stop!" I begin to cry again.

He laughs at me, taps my cheek, and kisses me again, and then his lips trail down my neck, over my collarbone, and disappear into my top. I am shivering; I don't know how to act. I don't know what to do.

Maybe I should stop it now. Maybe that's enough for today. Maybe I should go and find Bernie and ask if she's seen Stacey. I should talk to Stacey. I could tell her all about Sakkie and his glass-shard face and grappling hands. We could laugh.

Braver than this.

He stops and glances at the door, and maybe I should leave, but then he stands, walks over to it, and turns the latch. I am locked in, but I don't think I mind. It's warm in here, and Sakkie wants to be friends with me and he's kissing me and touching me and . . . Bernie isn't here, and I am Stacey, and I can do anything.

I take a breath. I can do anything.

Sakkie's eyes scatter all over me.

My body has been changing, causing a kind of embarrassed curiosity in me, but with Sakkie looking, I feel almost powerful. I really am almost Stacey, aren't I? I want to put my hand on my hip and raise my eyebrows, but instead I hug my arms around myself.

An image drifts lazily across my memory. Stacey lies on her bed, watching me. Except for her blinking eyes, she never moves. So I don't move either.

Stacey waits. She always waits.

So I wait.

Sakkie steps closer to me and circles me like a vulture, lightly brushing his fingers across my shoulders, my back, and my neck, drawing closer with each rotation. Around and around like a merry-go-round. My teeth chatter because I'm afraid of something to come, but I have no idea what it is. The look in Sakkie's eye is wild and frightening and . . . What will happen now?

Then suddenly he is behind me, pressed against me, warm and solid. I look up into his heavy-lidded eyes.

"You're special, Beth," he murmurs. "So special."

I glow under his praise, melting into his words, but I think I better leave now. "Sakkie . . ."

"Beautiful Beth," he murmurs, covering my mouth with his broad hand.

I should leave.

You can't leave. You're Stacey today, stupid. Don't be afraid; don't be chicken. If you leave, you are Bernie; if you stay, you are worthy.

I'm like a world map, and Sakkie is plotting his course. I am like the dragon fruit that he can scoop, clean, and ingest. He touches me, and I wonder if I'm supposed to feel anything more than the knot of fear inside of me.

He pushes me onto the sofa, collapsing on top of me, grunting and breathing and kissing.

"Beautiful Beth," he murmurs.

I—wait. What's happening? I thought it was over. I thought that was all. The touching and the kissing—that was all, right?

At first, I can't tell what he is trying to do, but then something in my brain clicks. I want to scream because I sense that I'm not ready for this thing; I want to stop.

For a few seconds I'm torn from this moment and into another, one that exists in my memory. Stacey is pounding at the unrelenting earth with a sharp rock. Her arms, powerful and quick, create an explosion of fine orange dust as she pounds, pounds, pounds. Over and over, she hits the ground; the hole she is creating gets bigger and bigger, deeper, and deeper. There is fire in her eyes; she is determined and unrelenting. She doesn't stop until the soil becomes looser, moist, more red. She's approaching hell's ceiling, and I want to beg her to stop, but how can I? I'm just as curious as she is. So I watch her dig; I watch the earth submit to her violation, and I say nothing. The water doesn't resist, does it? No. The water flows *into* the hole and sees how deep it goes.

I am no longer the Bethany I was before, and in my mind, seared to my eyelids, is the image of Stacey staring at the hole she has made, gripping the sharp rock between exhausted fingers. Am I the same Bethany that watched her do it? Or am I closer to Stacey now, holding a rock of my own? Maybe I'm the earth that has been churned and excavated, standing exposed with a gaping hole filled with red?

I close my eyes.

No. I'm more than that.

Suddenly I'm his Beautiful Beth.

I'm still clutching him when he makes a move to get up.

"Don't go!" I gasp. "Don't leave! Don't go!"

He squeezes my hand reassuringly and smiles in a way that transforms his face. It is a tender expression and the first sign of softness this stranger has given me.

"I'll be right back, Beautiful Beth."

I grin at him, but my lips quiver, and suddenly I think I'm going to be sick on the floor, and then he won't be happy at all. I curl in on myself, a tiny, tiny ball, and wait for the sickness to pass, but I have a feeling it won't. I have a feeling it's inside me now, forever.

Stupid ninny.

As I occupy the smallest space possible, I contemplate the sensations I feel now: a heat slowly fading, throbbing pain, something bigger. Am I more than I was before? Less? Is this something Stacey would be proud of? Something has changed, and I didn't expect it to. I wasn't ready to be this yet.

My hands start to shake, and my stomach contracts. I clench my jaw and try to figure out what's wrong with me. I scratch my head, I block my ears, I hold my breath, but no matter what I do, the tidal wave inside me is closing me up, making me hurt, getting closer. I want to wash my hands. Suddenly they feel so dirty I can't stand it. I have to wash my hands.

Sakkie comes back.

"You're pretty special, Beth."

It sounds like goodbye.

"When will I see you again?" I ask, and it comes out sounding more like a demand. This can't be it, surely. I still don't know anything at all.

He is surprised. "I don't know." His smile lengthens. "Can you get away tonight?"

Stacey will still be in sick bay, so I know I am free to make this decision. "Yes."

"Do you know where the sugarcane grows?"

I pull a face. "There?"

"Don't like that place?"

"Well . . . the washerwomen live there. It's not private at all."

"You're right." He frowns. "I know: at midnight, go to the road that leads out of the school. I'll meet you there and take you somewhere special."

I rub my arms, pleased to have something beyond my contracting stomach and tight palms to focus on. "Okay."

He takes my chin in his hand; it's a little too firm. "You'll really come then?"

"Yes."

He leans over me and wraps me in his arms. I inhale the scent of car oil and soil, smells that will become memories later. They mingle with the sharp pain deep inside, and I wonder if I need to pee. Is that the pain I feel?

He releases me slowly and just stares at me. "You're beautiful, Beth."

I blush, and then the lock turns, the door opens, and Joe walks in with Molly, humming an indistinct tune under his breath. When he sees me, he stops, blinks. Molly is wrapped around his neck, judging us silently.

"Bethany?"

"Hello, Joe. I came to visit you, but you were out."

He glances at Sakkie, and an expression I can't understand crosses his face. His eyes widen as though he's alarmed, but his mouth contradicts them by shivering slightly before pulling back to expose his teeth. He might be angry if not for those eyes; he might be scared if not for that mouth.

Joe looks at me and smiles, slowly, like it's an effort. "Is that so? Have you been here long?"

I shake my head. "No, I just got here. Stacey's sick, so I wanted to let you know we won't be coming to see you tonight."

Joe looks relieved, and so does Sakkie. "Aw, well, that's a shame. Never you mind. Just tell her to get better now."

I smile and head for the door, patting Molly on the head as I pass. "I will. See you later, Joe." I turn to his son. "It was nice meeting you, Sakkie."

"I hope you come again soon."

I laugh and almost cry by accident, then hurry out the door. How different the school grounds look now, on the other side of those few moments.

13

Little Stone

NOW

The cursor blinks at me expectantly. Blink. Blink. Blink.

What[BLINK]are[BLINK]you[BLINK]going[BLINK]to[BLINK] write[BLINK]Bethany?

And because I have a stupid brain, the beat of the cursor draws me in, and I start counting the blinks.

One.

Two.

Three.

Four.

My fingers spring into action with the rhythm.

Fuck.

You.

Piece of.

Shit.

These are the five best words I've written in months.

I click over to my browser and sign in to my email. Nothing from Denise (thank God), a plethora of congratulations emails, promises of coffee or lunch or whatever "soon" from people half-remembered. Nothing from you. And then—

> From: Forna Loucam
> To: Bethany Sloane
> Re: PAGES?
>
> Hi Bethany,
> Yes, I'm chasing. Any more pages to share? I'm salivating to know what you're doing for the final SALLY novel! Ten pages? Five?
>
> Tick-tock,
> Forna

Forna has been my editor from the beginning. She took a chance on a young nobody writer with a housewife-turned-assassin novel and changed my life. I suppose Sally changed her life too. She was a junior editor at an independent publishing house when she pulled me from the slush, and now she's editor in chief. Neither of us expected it to hit any list, so when it hit them all, Pointer Publishing got a massive jump into the limelight, Forna and me along with it. It's been nothing but Sally novels since.

I'm drowning in Sally. I need her to die so she can never come back. I promised Forna a final book no one would ever forget.

That was ten months ago.

And I have five useless words to show for it.

Another email pings into my inbox.

> To: Dr. Sumani Morgan Client List
> From: Ruth Pienaar
>
> Subject: Sorrowful News

Dear Bethany Sloane:

As you are a former client of Dr. Sumani Morgan, I am writing to inform you of the sad news of his passing last Tuesday afternoon. Dr. Morgan was a pillar of hope and inspiration in the local community, and more recently had been helping clients as far as Johannesburg, Cape Town, and Durban. His family are mourning in private but have agreed to let us, the staff here at Pretoria Mental Health Hospital, hold a wake in his memory. You can find details of the event in the attachment to this email. We are certain that Dr. Morgan changed your life as he did for so many others, and we hope that you can attend to celebrate his extraordinary life and honor his legacy.

Yours Sincerely,
Ruth Pienaar
Executive Secretary to Dr. S. Morgan and Mr. E. Pistorius
Pretoria Hospital, Pretoria

I squeeze my eyes shut, trying to ignore the sudden infestation of army ants in my chest. I try to take a breath, but it won't come.

This is hell's ceiling. Are you scared?

I slam my laptop shut and hurry for the front door, almost falling without my crutches, my skin vibrating right off my bones. I fling it open, hanging onto the frame, gulping air. After a while, I fumble in my pocket with shaking hands and pull free my pack of cigarettes.

I light up, take a real drag, step out onto the stoop, and pain shoots up the arch of my foot.

"Ow, fuck! Bastard!"

A devil's thorn sits innocently on the step. I pick it up, staring at the strange black-gray coloring, as though it's been burned. I fiddle with it for a while before putting it into the pocket of my robe. A deep sense of unquiet is growing on my skin. How could you possibly know where I live? I remind myself to be rational.

I continue to smoke, watching London pedestrians pass me by.

Bruce finds me there sometime later. He takes the cigarette from my fingers and stubs it out in his coffee.

"You're smoking again?"

I shrug, not looking at him, your words ringing inside me. *And he takes your award too?*

What would you know about marriage? We have a life that works for us, me and Bruce, and that is something I don't have to explain or prove. I shut my eyes, annoyed that I've let you get to me again.

"I think we should go away somewhere," Bruce says. "Get some air."

"I'm on deadline."

"They'll wait for you."

I feel my hackles rise. "I can't do that."

"Well," he says, wrapping his coffee-free arm around me. "You can write from anywhere."

"I feel like I'm close to a breakthrough. I don't want to lose that."

"Okay." He kisses my ear and goes back inside.

When I close the door and retreat back into my office, the sun is setting and I have no more written. Forna's email screams at me from my cold laptop. But your silence screams louder.

14

Meeting Place

THEN

Waiting for midnight to come is sort of like living through a panic attack brought on by indecision. Something tells me not to go; something forces me to. I lie in bed, twitching, as though giant malarial mosquitoes are biting me with their poisonous proboscises. I nibble my lip and breathe too fast and feel like my body is too . . . alive. Too real. I've changed from what I was into something unfamiliar.

I'm sore.

I wish Stacey were here. I want to tell her everything that happened so she can help me break it down and explain it. How should I have acted? Did I do the right thing? Does she know about this too? Has she seen the world on the other side of that thin veil of pain?

Stop it, I tell myself. *Stacey wouldn't ask all these stupid questions. She'd just know.*

I jiggle about like I've had a sugar OD, but mostly that's because I'm trying to convince myself I'm not scared of the shadow that has watched me from the corner of the dorm for the last hour. It appeared out of nowhere, subtly, and then refused to budge. Sometimes, when you dream, you think shadows are there, and when you turn to look, they've faded into an innocuous shape.

Not here.

The shadow just lingers, malformed and out of place. Too big for the darkness of the room. Too big to be *just* a shadow. It watches me, though I see no eyes. I sense its regard.

It's not real, I tell myself, and then it shifts, and I jiggle faster. *It's* not *real. It's my imagination.*

Think of Sakkie. Think of what happened on Joe's old sofa. Think about what you are now.

A giggle escapes me. I'm still sort of excited and happy when I think about it. I wish Stacey were here so that she can see how well I'm doing. What I've discovered. I can just see her face smile down at me. Maybe she will stroke my cheek. Maybe she will tell me that she knows, too, that she has discovered this . . . thing.

I can't wait to see Sakkie again: *my* Sakkie. I fancy that I know everything about him—his smell, his history, his body; how he tastes. That's all I can think of in relation to one person, and it's enough.

My Sakkie, my Sakkie, my Sakkie.

The shadow laughs at me, a tinkle of glass, and I tell it to shut up, sure that I must be dreaming or going crazy. But the laughter stills with my rebuke, and I choke back my hysterical chortle.

I watch the clock on my bedside table tick away the minutes, and I count every one. I glance at Stacey's collection of pencil shavings. That's what my insides feel like. My mind is full of what has happened and what has been done. Parts of Sakkie's body, so new and fresh, flash before my eyes. I bury my head in my pillow and sob, and my fingertips squeeze the pillow until they feel cut up and broken.

When I close my eyes, the shadow steps closer. I throw my head up and stare at the corner of the room, daring it to come nearer, terrified it will. But nothing is there. No shadow; only the dim white paint in a pool of moonlight.

For a few moments, I almost feel like I would rather not exist.

Should I go? Should I stay? I debate with myself, and I fade away a lot, into illusions and fantasy. In my own world, Stacey and I would look the same. I would tell her about Sakkie; she would give me her secrets in exchange. We would call my mother—the original one—*Mummy*, and we would call her father *Dad*. What I've done would be okay. She would understand and explain the feelings inside that I can't describe. She would catalog them, and together we would file them away until there was nothing left but clarity. Clear as perfectly polished glass.

Eventually, I decide I *must* go. I have to. The choice is out of my hands. It's in the hands of destiny.

I have a lover, I sigh, *just like Emma Bovary.*

I'm out of bed and in my school dress and shoes before the minute hand is at a quarter to midnight. I tiptoe out of the dorm—past the snoring Chena and tooth-grinding Sal, both of whom are back from visiting their parents—into the night. It's warm, dusty, and dry, but for the first time, I don't care. I skip along the ground, heading for the main road, without a care or a thought for anything of a practical nature.

I'm in a world of fantasy now. I've escaped reality. I'm a fleeing princess in a long, trailing gown, going to meet my Rodolphe. I'm not real: I am imagination. I am moonlight.

Sakkie is waiting for me with his hands in his pockets. He stares out into the distance with a frown on his face and shifts from foot to foot nervously, glancing east and west, north and south.

"Sakkie," I call.

His face lights up, and I give in to the urge to run to him like in a movie I'm sure I've seen but can't quite remember. He picks me up as I reach him, and I wrap my legs around him like I would my mother. How I would have preferred Mummy to marry Sakkie instead of Mr. Oldie-Pants! Sakkie would have been much cooler as a dad.

"You came," he says and kisses me over and over. His hands are in my hair, pulling a bit too hard.

I giggle because his little glass hairs prickle, and then I nod.

"You okay?"

My teeth chatter, even though it is warm. "Mm-hmm."

He chuckles. "Let's go," he says.

I resist. "Wait . . . Where are we going?"

He kisses the tip of my nose, a gesture that tells me I'm adored. "It's a surprise."

He puts me down and takes my hand. His legs are long, and he pulls me along so firmly that I'm nearly running. I laugh at first, but then a hand closes around my lungs and I'm out of breath. Around us everything is dark and quiet, but the moon is growing fuller every night, brimming with possibilities. What's that called again? Waxing.

I swallow the rising fear in my throat and tell myself I'm safe.

How can you be safe if Stacey's not here? She knows all the rules.

I don't immediately notice, but Sakkie is taking me in the same direction as the House, and I wonder if that is our destination.

I bite my lip, flashes of the day coming to me in unbearable snippets that make my body pulse like blood flowing under an artery. My whole body is a beating heart, full of pressure. I'm afraid of pain, and I hope that he will be gentler with me.

"Are you taking me to the House?"

As soon as it is out of my lips, I wish the words back. I sound *so* stupid, like a little kid. The darkness of the evening hides my blush from his sight.

He frowns. "What house?"

"Oh . . . I, um, I thought there was a house around here."

"Nope. Not for years."

We keep walking, his hand around my wrist, me jogging to keep up. Underneath the musky scent of dry earth, the moist, dewy fragrance of the early morning is getting stronger. It's the smell of almost-rain, almost-moisture—almost-coolness.

It only takes me a moment to cotton on to the only other location he could possibly mean to take me to.

"Not . . . the corn tower?" I whisper, pulling back my arm, which he releases.

His smile is hideously beautiful. "It's perfect."

"No!" I clutch both hands over my mouth.

"Why not?"

"It's haunted."

He laughs fiercely, throwing back his head and clutching his free hand over his flat stomach. "Haunted? Beth, you can't be serious?"

I look away. "Well, it is."

"Well, I can protect you."

I shuffle from foot to foot, undecided. "Promise you won't run out and leave me there?"

I wish Stacey were here with me.

He sniggers, but then sighs and says, "Of course not. Grow up, will you?"

Because I want to be a grown-up, I agree, but I plead inwardly for Henry Dertz and any other lost soul to leave us in peace.

Please don't watch, I add silently, sure that in limbo they can hear me.

Grow up, Bethany Sloane, a nickering voice says. *Grow up!*

It takes a long time to get to the tower, and the temperature is dropping. Because I am wearing my summer school dress and my school shoes without socks, my skin is full of hideous goose bumps, like chicken skin, by the time we reach the staircase that runs up the outside of the tower all the way to the only door it contains. The doorway looms above us like the eye of a Cyclops; I can hardly believe we're going to be willingly eaten by it.

"Sakkie," I murmur, shaking. "I—"

"Don't be scared," he urges me. "I'm going to protect you from everything. You're *mine.*"

He says it with such confidence. I am his. He is mine. I'm saturated with a sort of divinity of feeling, warmth that blocks out the nighttime air, even though I keep shivering. Warmth that penetrates to the core of me, which I think must mean I love him.

We climb the rickety staircase, and Sakkie pushes open the door; the resounding echo from inside is the sound of a haunted place. I almost scream, and my body lurches inward, retracting into a smaller form. I feel the tightness in my belly. The echoes are the whispers of an invisible place with many doors and halls and locks, places to disappear into forever, like a ghost ship lost on a silently turbulent glass sea.

I hide behind Sakkie.

Inside it is dark, but I can make out the edges of an iron platform and balcony, which runs around the circumference of the tube like a betrothal ring. It smells a little like thistle bush. The center . . . down below is as dark as my worst nightmare. Full of dried-up, old, rotten corn. I wonder if the corn looks full and heavy to the dead who watch it. I wonder if the ghosts wonder why we don't eat it.

Sakkie doesn't bother to close the door—we are hidden from all eyes already—and the moon casts a hazy silver light over our bodies.

I'm scared and desperate. "Can we just talk for a bit?"

He laughs; it's harsh. *"Talk?"*

"Please, Sakkie," I ask again, when his hands begin their eager roaming once more, pulling at my flesh, stretching the skin, his mouth all over my face and neck, urgently seeking.

"What do you want to talk about, beautiful?" he says in a husky voice, pulling at my dress.

My cheeks are on fire. "I . . . I don't know . . . just, Sakkie," I protest, feeling afraid and a little humiliated. "Just please."

I don't want him to touch me, but I also want nothing more than for him to touch me again.

He steps away from me with a smirk, and the cold air between us terrifies me.

"Please come back," I beg, squeezing my legs together.

He folds his arms and doesn't budge, his eyes cold and hard as flint.

"Please, Sakkie."

"Are you begging me?" he asks in a low voice.

"Yes!"

"Beg me."

"Please, Sakkie, please!"

"Good," he murmurs almost inaudibly, stepping closer. "I like it when you beg me. Beg again."

"Sakkie . . ."

He steps away, toward the door, and the blackness intensifies as though to claim me.

"Please! Please, please, Sakkie!"

"Good girl."

Wrong. This is

wrong.

Stupid ninny.

Sakkie kneels beside me and gathers me into his arms. "Beth Sloane," he murmurs. "My beautiful girl."

I give him a quivering smile as I start to cry.

15

Fuck

NOW

Fuck this novel. Fuck Sally and her fucking death. Fuck this career.

Fuck everything.

I can't write. All I have in my head is you. What are you doing? What are you eating? Why haven't you emailed? A terrible cloud is hanging over me, coming closer like some awful gathering storm. Like a horrible foreshadowing.

Touch a line . . .

Dread wells in my stomach every time I think of you, out there somewhere, a growing sense of doom. It makes no sense.

You could be up to anything.

And the devil's thorn on my stoop shows you could be closer than I think.

A scent catches in my nose—foreign perfume. Not mine. I frown, tracing it through the air to my own jumper. It smells of spices: cloves and cinnamon, maybe. Not my signature Chanel.

A horrible thought rises like a miasma: Bruce is cheating on me. But no. There are no signs of that, and I know it to be impossible.

What, then? I was wearing this when we met up, wasn't I? Did we hug? Is this *you* I'm smelling on me? Fire and brimstone. Thorns and glass.

. . . break your spine.

The image of you is enough to break me out in a cold sweat. But we're not girls anymore. We're not the Thorns anymore.

The past is the past, where it belongs.

I stare at my blank Word page, the blinking curser.

The past is the past, and I am fine.

Fuck.

16

ALONE

THEN

The sun is rising as I return to the dorm, dripping and exhausted, shivering and empty minded. I am the cocoon husk left behind once a butterfly has taken wing. I am broken.

I hurry along the corridor, hoping to beat the morning bell. I breathe easier when I am inside my room, proof positive that good things do happen once in a while. I unbuckle my shoes and place them in the wardrobe, then remove my dress and hang it up. Every movement feels like the first; I am very aware of my aching muscles. There is now a blood stain on my school skirt, but laundry isn't for another three days, so I will have to wear it. It's a badge of where I've been. I am desperate to curl up into a ball under the duvet and lose myself in sleep for a little while—to absorb some of the hardness that is surrounding me and make it soft again.

"Where were you?"

My heart jolts into my mouth when I hear her voice. Stacey has returned from sick bay and is sitting up in bed, watching me; her eyes are empty—awaiting explanation. She can penetrate so deep that I blink more than I should.

"Where *were* you?" she asks again, because I am frozen.

My pupils dilate, like a girl flying high. "I . . . I . . ." I shiver. I'm shaking. My whole body exhales the one truth before me. Stacey is back. Stacey is here. I'm safe. "Stacey," I breathe, full of so many different things that I can't pick one away from another.

I'm overcome with the urge to reveal my secret to her, to tell her about the metamorphosis that has begun—to tell her how divinity couldn't feel as powerful as her return. I let go of the weighty sigh that boils in my chest, and it washes outward, into the room. I want to touch her face and cry on her shoulder. I stare at her with fat tears rolling down my face, and I'm happy.

Stacey, Stacey, Stacey.

"Where?" she asks again, but her voice is smaller than before.

I hiccup and laugh and cry. *I'm different now, can you see it?* "I . . . nowhere. I couldn't sleep. Oh, Stacey!" I rush forward to kneel at her feet. "I'm so glad you're back!" *Can you see?*

Stacey's face is stone. "Liar. You can *always* sleep. Did you go to Joe's house again?"

I shake my head. I'm glad I don't have to lie to Stacey about this. "No."

"Where, then?"

I wipe my nose, an excuse to look away. "I couldn't sleep. I told you. I promise."

Tell her where you were, says a voice inside my head. *Tell her and see.*

Stacey doesn't comment. In the silence, I feel the gap between us like a tangible thing. The air isn't like a barrier, not really; it's more like the potential to become one. I want to say something, to fill up that gap and break the possibility lying there, but then she speaks, and it's too late. The moment has passed.

"I see."

"When did you get out of sick bay?"

She looks away, and I feel nervous affection. "I left tonight. I felt better, and I missed my bed."

I get up and sit next to her on her mattress, something I have never done before. "I'm so glad you're well again. Now we can go and see Joe together." And Sakkie.

Stacey nods just as the bell rings. I don't notice that both Sal and Chena are awake and have been listening to us. They act as though they don't care and strip their beds as usual. They will never know the electric show going on inside me at this very moment. They will spend their lives trying to capture this fleeting but powerful feeling.

In the bustle of the morning activities, it seems my nighttime adventure has been forgotten. Stacey is my point of focus. Every movement is studied; every gesture and facial expression is cataloged. And while I watch, a dawning realization slowly sinks in.

I can never tell Stacey about Sakkie, not ever. She will never tolerate another person having my affections, which makes me love her more.

In the bathroom, she doesn't speak to me, as usual, but I feel a sense of power that I've never had before. Back in the bedroom, I give her a secret hug and tell her I am glad she has come back, that nothing was the same when she was gone.

She doesn't look at me. She just makes her bed with perfect, nimble fingers.

"We'll be going to the House together this afternoon," she tells me.

She looks at me then and smiles faintly. She has such pretty eyes. There is a tiny gap between her front teeth that I wish I had. I consider shoving paper or plastic in there to create one, like the tooth version of the lip plate. It needs further meditation.

"Okay," I say.

And she adds: "Alone."

Happiness can't be more complete than this.

Alone.

17

Masticatory Archetype

NOW

We are at dinner, and I keep pinching my arm under the table because I can't believe this is real. You and me eating dinner together. Even at school we didn't eat together. We weren't assigned to the same dining table, which means I don't think I've ever seen you eat, and suddenly that is all I can think of. I wonder if you're a camel chewer. Jaw working in circles, round and round, caressing your food rather than mashing it. Or maybe you're an up-and-down-hammer kind of chewer. Maybe you pause to consider your food—the flavors, the texture . . .

What kind of chewer am I? What will you think of the way I eat? Will it seem weird to you? Will I offend you? Disgust you?

I'm so glad you emailed. Or did I email? I can't remember. The nights without sleep blur everything together, but that hardly matters now. You're here. You're here with me.

I reach for the water on the table and pour myself a glass to have something to do, because all I can think of is *swallow, swallow, swallow, swallow,* and I wish you would teach me to swallow the way you do, and I need to stop.

This feeling is familiar, like a haunting. Was I always this obsessive?

"You been here before?" I ask, tearing my eyes away from you and looking around. It's a local place. Not a chain restaurant like the ones Bruce likes to eat at. This place looks old, like it's been in the same family for generations, serving perpetual soup. Like the food will be amazing despite the fact the walls haven't had a new lick of paint since the '60s. And for the first time since I can remember, I'm not concerned about the hygiene rating.

"I come here a lot," you say, and grin like you're keeping a secret, the queen of sealed lips.

Are you playing games? Why am I following along?

"Where do you live?" I blurt.

I need to know more about you. Now. Right now. What do you eat? What do you drink? What music do you listen to? What's your local grocery store? What do you do for a living? Are you a hippie artist or an HR manager? City serpent, corporate slave, or self-employed? My old obsession is rising, warm and familiar. Tell me everything about you, Stacey. Tell it all.

I ignore the tiny voice inside that tells me I need to know these things to keep myself safe.

From what?

You grin. "How long have you been wanting to ask me that?"

I laugh, a breathy release of tension. "A while."

It was a bad morning. Bruce didn't want me to come out.

You pour water from the carafe on the table into the small glass but don't take a sip. "Why wait so long?"

"It felt like prying." It's the only answer I can give. I can't tell you the truth—that I haven't asked you because I know that you'll enjoy making me writhe while you sit and look at me and don't answer. But maybe that's wrong. Maybe you've grown out of those games.

All of a sudden, a memory. A scorching day, but humid. Brutal. We are lying on our beds, breathing in soup. I am watching you. Waiting to see what we will do. You are my sole focus because focusing on anything else would mean I give in to the terrible discomfort of the day. I will not cry. *I will not cry.*

Your eyes, brown and textured, amused, and something else. The way you watch me watching you. And how you turn away so I can't see. So I can't read you. The torture of the day comes back, but I focus on the back of your head. I have to focus on you. If I don't, I will break.

"I live in Highgate for now. I move a lot. I get bored easily." You consider me, then say, "I've had a burning question too."

I blink away the memory of your brown eyes to focus on the real brown eyes in front of me. The waiter brings us our drinks, and I wait for him to leave before responding.

"Oh?"

"Your husband."

I gulp some vodka tonic and laugh. "That's . . . vague."

You lean back. "Well?"

"We've been together a long time," I manage.

"Don't tell me you've been shackled by marriage to one man for more than five years?"

"Try twelve."

You don't react right away, but your eyes narrow. "What about your wild oats? Unless you guys are the cool kind of married?"

"The cool kind?"

You're not the type to roll your eyes, but you narrow them again, and I can feel your exasperation.

There was always a language you spoke that I was desperate to learn.

"Open," you clarify.

Hot humiliation prickles my cheeks.

"Oh." I stir my drink with my straw. "No."

Your grin is wicked, and I squirm. "You've missed out."

This is a new game, one I'm unfamiliar with.

"Bruce is my best friend. And I don't really . . . you know . . . care for it that much."

"What, sex?"

I clear my throat and we *are not* talking about this, holy fuck. "Er, yeah."

You grin in that way of yours. Half pity, half mischief. "You really *have* missed out. Poor little Beth."

My beautiful Beth.

A shard of glass in my stomach, and I feel that impending sense of doom again. I down the rest of my drink because I hate this. My life must seem so ordinary to you. So plain. Boring.

"Do you remember the heat?" I ask. "At school?"

"Not really, no."

"It's burned into my memory." I give a mirthless chuckle. "Literally. I used to think I'd die of it. At night, I used to slide my hands under my pillow on the cool side just for some relief. And breathing—swallowing—it was all just . . ." I let the sentence die. It hardly matters if you don't remember.

"Like sandpaper," you murmur.

"Exactly. Breathing felt like sandpaper in my throat."

"Yes, the air was so dusty."

I grin. "I can't believe they sent kids there. Like a gulag or something."

Your eyes are flinty. "Maybe we deserved it."

The silence hangs between us, heavy. Brittle.

"I can't imagine being with one person forever," you say at last. "Not least a man. And you really plan to just . . . do that? With someone who takes credit for your work and makes you drink baby juice?"

My heart is hammering in my throat, but I will not engage.

I pick up the menu. "What do you think the soup of the day is?"

You watch me for a few moments before picking up your own menu. "It's usually red pepper."

I close my eyes for a moment, grateful to have the menu to hide behind.

You've let me escape, and a flood of relief washes over me. But when I lower my menu, there you are, on the other side, perceptive as ever.

"Oh, Bethie," you murmur. "You forgot how to be free."

18

Star Crossed

THEN

Stacey is the evil stepmother again; I am the daughter. I have been chained to the rusty pipe in the cellar for six weeks without food and without light. I am going mad from it. Stacey watches me starve with cold eyes; she circles me, chin protruding, eyes searching. She whips me over and over, and my back arches with every invisible flog she delivers.

I can smell the invisible blood.

"Secrets are evil," Stacey says, her nose wrinkling and her lips pulling back over her teeth in a feline snarl.

I shiver with the ferocity of her stare and whimper, "Yes, Mother."

"Keeping them is like having a disease—a disease that will send you to hell!"

She lashes out with the invisible iron rod, and I flinch away. I imagine the red welts that will come up from such a beating, and I am delighted. She may have to dress the wounds like she did the other week. If she does, she'll make a magic serum out of spit and sand and spread it on my skin with her bare hands.

Stacey isn't happy when I let my excitement show, and she slaps me. This slap is no invisible hand but her cold, hard palm—digits that are my mistress. I am thrown backward, heat and pain flooding my cheek.

"Where were you?" she yells, her face two inches from mine. *"Where?"*

I am startled to realize that we are no longer playing, and that there are tears on Stacey's cheek. I stare at them in wonder. They represent something not quite definable, but I'm sure if I figure out what that something is, I'll have grasped some hidden truth about her.

I jump up, invisible chains forgotten, and I stare at her, disbelieving. I choke on my surprise, it is so real in my throat.

"You forgot about me," she murmurs, her shoulders heaving.

I shake my head, more to dislodge the shock than to disagree. "Never—we're twins!"

"You've found someone else to take my place. Maybe Bernie. You've abandoned me."

This magnificent and alarming change merely from being gone with Sakkie? This adoring display of real emotion aimed at me, simply over the risk of losing me? I am humbled, powerful. The hot, dry grounds look even emptier than normal. They are too still; not even a breeze flutters the long grasses or stirs the cracked earth.

What if she decides I really have abandoned her? I know her. She'll counterattack before I can explain, unless I do it now, quickly.

I grab her shoulders and shake her. "Stop it!"

"Walking alone at night, without me," she says with a scowl. This alarms me. Stacey has all the answers. Stacey shouldn't need *me*. "Go away then," she snaps, turning her head. "You're not my twin."

Everything gets dark, everything gets still. It takes me a full three seconds to hear what she said.

"Stacey . . ."

"Go."

"Stop it!" I cry. Is she cutting me loose? Is she pushing me away? My throat closes, and I want to cling onto her like a drowning victim. I want to beg her not to abandon me, not to leave me like Mummy did. I reach out and try to grab her shirt, but she moves away.

If she doesn't want me, what will I do? If she thinks I don't want her, it's even worse. She is shelter I can't afford to lose, and because of this, I know I can never tell her about Sakkie. I can never tell her what has been done—of how I have changed and of the secret I have learned. If I do, it will only be confirmation that I've moved on without her. It will only prove I've abandoned her. I can see that for her to learn the truth would be for us to shatter. Stacey and Bethany, the singular, would cease to exist. The horror of being without her pushes everything else out of my head, and the open grounds suddenly seem like a vast ocean I will drown in if she chooses to walk away.

I was so sure Stacey would be able to tell . . . to smell, see, hear something. I was so sure that the signs would be there to read on my face and on my body, like a map. That she would *know* and understand. That she would be able to tell me what to do now.

Stacey has all the instructions, but not in this.

She won't tolerate competition for me. And I won't tolerate competition for her. Stacey is important, and nothing else is. The idea that she might one day find out anyway, on her own, terrifies me even more. If she learns about it later and realizes I didn't tell her . . .

In my terror I hug her to me, tightly. "I'm your twin, I'm your twin!" I say it over and over until she is saying it too. It becomes our own private mantra. It becomes a secret language blended into one long word containing all the fervor we feel, commingling like the spit and mud she laid on my skin.

IamyourtwinIamyourtwinIamyourtwin.

If Stacey finds out, the matrons will find out, Mummy will find out. My terrible ugliness would be exposed for them to examine. They would know something about me I want to keep hidden away. Thinking of them with this knowledge about me, having them see how I have been opened up and what Sakkie has done to me, is enough to make me realize I need to lock it away, bury it inside.

I shut the door on these phantom sensations—these memories—and I bolt it closed.

With Stacey back, I am once again her girl. I don't know when I will see Sakkie again.

Maybe never.

Every evening, I have nightmares—terrible dreams of getting lost in long dark corridors that twist and turn and have no exit, of bleeding razors and of Stacey's taunting voice. Sometimes the voice is Sakkie's. A cold shadow always lingers at my shoulder, and occasionally I think I see a face. Maybe, like Esther Greenwood, I am going crazy. Maybe I'm trapped in a distorted bell jar, looking at my reflection in the warped glass, seeing shadows that are really only me. In the morning, the nightmares are like Sakkie's kisses. I can't see them, but I know they're there.

It's a film night tonight, and I look forward to the concealing darkness. It's a time for me to think things through without being seen, without having to hide the look on my face. The weekend, long and empty, is going to take some mental preparation to survive. Last weekend Stacey was too observant. I was too careless with my face.

The film is *Superman*. I let the colors flash past my eyes but never really see them. They are never more than indistinct shapes and sounds that make no sense. It is over too quickly, and my cocoa cup is still full when the lights go up.

Stacey frowns when she sees it. "Are you sick?"

"Oh." I wonder if I should lie about it so that I can escape to the sick bay. "No," I eventually concede.

We walk to the dorm in silence. Chena and Sal aren't with their parents this weekend, so there isn't much talking. Stacey convinced Sal to switch beds with me, so now I lie right beside Stacey. It is an honor I never expected. For three nights in a row, I have fallen asleep to the sight of Stacey's back, rising and falling beneath the duvet covers, nothing but empty space between us.

As we near the dorm, Stacey leans closer to me. "Don't go to sleep."

This means we are going out. I sigh inwardly, though I don't mind the distraction. If we go to the boys' shower room, I would like to take a better look. I want to compare them to my Sakkie.

We prepare for bed, and soon the lights go out. I lie in bed for a while, trying to clear my head of all the thoughts running around freely inside it. Stacey is facing away from me, so for a while I just watch her breathe. If I could reach across the gap and touch her, maybe I could absorb some of her energy, her confidence—the answers she seems to have to everything. Maybe some kind of understanding could be reached. A way she could let me have Sakkie.

There is a moment when I am terrified of her being asleep. I am terrified of Chena and Sal being asleep. It means I'm alone because their minds are far away.

But I don't feel alone.

A trickle of a familiar sensation runs down my spine. Is someone watching me? I lift my head from the pillow and stare out of the shadow-rimmed doorway and into the empty, black hall. I could have sworn someone was spying on me from there only a moment before. I felt observed. I frown and then lean back again.

As soon as my head is on the pillow, I feel it again. Someone is staring at me from the shadowy corridor, standing in the doorway not ten feet away. I lift my head as quickly as I can, hoping to see whatever it is, but the corridor is as cold and empty as before. I'm uneasy and panicky. I desperately want to crawl into Stacey's bed, but something keeps me from putting my legs down on the ground, as though the thing watching me might be under my bed, ready to grab at my ankles from below.

I shudder and glance at Stacey. She lies as though asleep. My heart beats hard enough that I can hear it in my ear canals, and I swallow air down a throat as dry as the Sahara.

I shut my eyes and count. I have entered a sort of rhythmical state of semiconsciousness when Stacey stirs. The presence is gone. I check my bedside clock. It is eleven o'clock; we have been in bed for almost two hours already.

Beside me, Chena snores slowly. Sal grinds her teeth, and the sound is a bit like the nibbling noises of a chipmunk, only squeakier. I follow Stacey on padded feet, through the halls, in my pajamas. It is another cool night outside.

"Where are we going?" I ask when we are far enough away from the west wing that my voice won't carry inside.

"To see Joe."

My insides go cold, and I stop walking.

Stacey turns to me. "You said you loved his cocoa, and you didn't get any tonight."

Her eyes dare me to protest.

"Oh."

"Come on then."

I follow, numb. What can I do? What will I do? Maybe Sakkie won't be there. Maybe he will be asleep. What can I do? What will I *do*?

Stacey knocks on Joe's door, and I hear slow footsteps on the other side. I grind my hands together, squishing the fingers into one. What will I do if I see him? What if he says something that Stacey notices?

"Hello, Joe," Stacey says.

Joe smiles a little reservedly. "Little Stacey," he chimes. "Back to the land of the healthy, I see."

She laughs once. "Yes."

Joe glances past Stacey to me, where I'm trying to be invisible; his smile drops a little, and I blush. "Bethany, hello."

I wipe the sweat off my upper lip. "Hi."

"We only want to visit for a little while," Stacey says when Joe still hasn't invited us in. I sort of hope he won't . . . like he's too tired or something.

He blinks. "And some cocoa, too, *ja*?"

Stacey grins. "That would be *lekker*, thank you."

He steps back, chuckling and shaking his head. I walk in past Stacey, my heart pounding and my fingers sore from all the squishing. I survey the room; it's empty. I breathe a sigh of disappointed relief, and my shoulders relax a little. The pounding in my head slows down.

Joe offers us a seat and then goes to make the cocoa. I sit down beside Stacey, and she takes my hand, and the touch sends a tingle up my spine. I imagine Bernie watching this, her cheeks red and indignant.

Joe returns to the lounge without the cocoa, and I imagine the water is still boiling. I can see the kitchen in my mind, as it was on the first day I met Sakkie, and I blush furiously. On this very sofa, where Stacey now sits . . . I feel slightly dizzy; my stomach roils.

Stacey eyes me but doesn't say anything. I wipe my lip again.

"You girls need to be careful coming out late at night."

Stacey laughs. "We always do it."

"Still," Joe insists, and his voice is harder. "Young girls should be careful."

His eyes glide to my face and away, and I bite my lip. Does he know? How could he know?

I'm so agitated that when Sakkie comes out of the kitchen, beautiful in blue, holding a tray of cocoa, my vision shakes, my heart races, the room spins, and I feel weightless. I am lost to the ether in the hammock of sleep.

Then the floor hits me in the face, and I think I see someone in the corner of the room, bathed in shadow like a penumbral gown.

"Get out of here," someone growls.

"Bethany," another voice calls. It is Stacey. "Twin?"

I groan. "What happened?"

"Easy now," Joe's voice murmurs. "Sit up nice and slow."

I open my eyes as Joe is helping me to sit up. "Did I faint?"

Stacey nods.

"Oh. I forgot to breathe."

Joe frowns deeply. "Has this happened before?"

"My mother used to get it," I admit. "I'm sorry."

I look around. Sakkie is nowhere to be seen. The shadow is gone, too, and the room looks bright and open.

"Where's Sakkie?" I ask before I can stop myself.

Joe's glance hardens. "He's gone to bed now."

Stacey's eyes narrow. "You know Sakkie? How?"

"I came to visit Joe when you were sick," I explain, hurriedly adding, "just to explain that you were ill and so we wouldn't be around to visit. But Joe was out. Sakkie was here."

"Oh."

"I didn't stay long," I add, trying to be convincing, but my face blazes.

Joe clears his throat and gets to his feet. "Well, I think that's enough excitement for one night. Drink your cocoa and then get off to bed."

Stacey's eyes widen in rare surprise. "But—"

"Quick now," he insists. "You need sleep at this age. You're very young." He says the last three words more to himself. "You're very young."

Joe hands me a cup of warm cocoa, and I frown into it. I want to go up and see Sakkie, but I can tell it is forbidden. Stacey forbids me, and Joe forbids Sakkie. I feel like Juliet, the star-crossed lover. When will I see my Romeo again?

Despite my decision to cut Sakkie out, seeing him is suddenly all I can think of.

19

Change

Touch a line, you break your spine; touch a crack, you break your back.

The police have been to the school with sheets of paper for everyone to fill in. There has been a drought alert issued, and the water has been cut off except for twice a day—morning toothbrushing and evening baths. Stacey has been allowed to take baths by herself because she got her period and is now A Woman. I heard Matron Monday say so. I have to bathe with Chena, which is better than with Sal. We are allowed very little water. We have to use our clenched fists, pressed at the bottom of the tub, as a measure. Once the water reaches the line of our wrists, we've got the volume we're permitted. There is no hot water; the evaporation is a waste.

Stacey doesn't like to talk about her period, even though I want to know more about it. When will it happen to me? When will I be A Woman? Will I feel as different as I did after Sakkie taught me about pain?

It's almost the weekend again; two weeks have passed since I fainted. Tomorrow night Stacey will go to one of the lodges to be with her father and siblings. They have come to visit for the second time this year. After they come, I won't see Stacey until Monday morning, and when I do, she will be weird.

We walk along the road toward the chapel. I try to pay attention; I don't want to step on a line and break my spine. I don't want to step on a crack. The chaplain has ordered a Thursday sermon to pray about the drought. Last Sunday he slapped my hand because I crossed myself with the wrong hand. I've decided to hate him.

I peek at Stacey. She stares ahead, focused, so I try to pay attention.

After the sermon, we are released. We don't have to go to afternoon classes either. We suddenly have hours free. Because it is so hot, we are allowed to walk around in our bikinis after visiting Matron for sunscreen. My bikini is pink and yellow and blue. Stacey wears a skirt over hers because she is scared about her pad showing. I try to look for a sign of it when I think she isn't looking, but I can't see it. I thought it must be like a baby's nappy, but the tiny skirt she is wearing makes that impossible. Maybe it's like a plug.

The thought makes me flush, and I think of Sakkie. I haven't seen him once since that day. Not once. I am scared he has left the school. I am scared Joe sent him away. I resolve to spy on Joe's house tomorrow night, once Stacey has gone to be with her family. I'll see Sakkie too. I will see my Romeo again. With Stacey going away, I am allowed to think of him like a real boyfriend, and not competition for Stacey. My plan is foolproof, and I feel very confident, but Stacey shatters my schemes.

"I'm going to ask my father if you can stay with us this weekend," she tells me.

"Huh?"

She nods, smiling. "You're my twin, aren't you?"

I nod but don't say anything. I am horrified my goal has been taken out of my hands. I'm torn in two directions—drawn to two ends of a spectrum by strong magnetic forces, leaving me trapped somewhere between them. The division within me, forced by Sakkie and by Stacey, is one that is sweet poison. Though I want to say something, to make some decision, I know the weight of such a choice is too big for my hands, even if that choice is about my own life. I'm smothered by the weight of a concept I don't understand, a decision I'm incapable of making. I feel like I am going crazy. The fever in my body keeps growing and growing, and Stacey has plucked away my secret treasure. I bite the insides of my cheek and taste blood.

Should I want to be away from Stacey? Shouldn't I relish the chance to be with her and her family, like the twin I am?

Stacey calls her father from the booth using her shiny phone card, and an argument ensues. Stacey is livid by the time she exits, her face pale, her lips red, her eyes dark. It is the look of fury.

"He says no" is all she says to me. The same weird darkness is creeping into her expression.

I shrug. "Oh, well. I'll miss you. Maybe I can come for lunch on Sunday."

Stacey raises her eyebrows, a sign that she has brightened slightly at the idea. "Yes."

I don't talk to her again since she is too angry. I am learning to read her. I watch her like I watch a film, for two long hours. We have been playing "England, Ireland, Scotland, Wales" with Gogo and Uri. Stacey and Uri are the only ones still in. Gogo and I stand across from each other, five feet apart; we have the long elastic band around our hips, around mine and across to hers. Stacey swivels, her long slim legs rotating perfectly.

I fiddle with a lock of my hair, which is still dark, but the ends are turning a golden color. Stacey says it's the sun doing it—my hair absorbs the golden sun. I am secretly excited and horrified about the idea of turning into a blonde. If I do, I will look more like my mother (shudder), but I will also look more pure (glee).

I feel the phantom sensation of Sakkie's hands, and I flush. Next to that sensation is another one, deeper inside me. It's like the phantom sensation, but vastly more . . . real. It feels not like a touch, but like the absence of touch. It's located inside me, somewhere I can't reach, somewhere dark and lonely and hostile. It's like there is something missing from deep in there, but I can't discover what was there before. It's something near my soul, or part of my soul.

I try to shake it off, to revert to my original state, but the hole lingers.

We start the game over, and I am back in. It is my turn. I stand with a leg on either side of the elastic threads and begin my turn, jumping from one side to the other.

"England, Ireland, Scotland, Wales, inside, outside, inside, on!" I jump the final move, pinning both sides of the elastic under my feet. I look up, smiling with my victory. As I do, I see him in the distance, watching me with burning eyes.

My Sakkie.

My eyes meet his—hot, feverish, wild. His lips are drawn into one tight line; his hands turn white where they squeeze the secateurs. My heart thuds furiously, and my palms grow sweaty. What if Stacey notices something? What if she hears my heart thrum furiously in my chest. She can smell terror, can't she?

I feel naked in my bikini top, and unconsciously lift my hand to cover my chest. His proximity to me, with my friends here too . . . it feels obscene. I flush. My whole body flushes. The bottom of the pulsing river of my heartbeat sweeps me away.

I look away hurriedly, hoping that because I'm ignoring him, he will leave me alone and get on with other things. The last thing I want is for him to come over and talk to me. Stacey would know if he did that. I can't help one last glance through my hair, and I see Joe frowning deeply behind Sakkie. I don't like to see Joe upset. He is a nice old man. It is almost as bad as seeing Sakkie upset. That, I can't stand.

Joe turns away with slumped shoulders and directs a wheelbarrow toward the dumping area.

"That groundskeeper is so weird," Gogo says, but I tell her to shut up and she does.

"Bethany," Stacey calls. She and Bernie are several feet away in the paper-thorn patch. I tear my eyes away from Sakkie and hurry to catch up. My back skin burns under the sun and Sakkie's gaze. I hope I will be able to peel it off later.

Bernie looks shocked that I would make Stacey wait. Stacey eyes me but makes no comment, a silence I am, for once, thankful for. I'm not sure I could answer any questions at the moment without telling her the utter truth, and then she would leave me, and the bricks would keep falling until there was no empty space left between us.

He hasn't left the school, is all I can think. He hasn't left. He's still here.

It has come to my attention that the change he has made in me is a big distraction. Stacey stared at me for two whole uninterrupted minutes earlier today before I realized it. I know that while I am Sakkie's girl, I can't possibly be Stacey's girl too.

I am going to break up with him, even if I never find the little missing piece he took from me.

I dry retch at the thought.

I wish there was a way for me to contact him, to get to a meeting place, but there is none. It is up to me to be quiet, to seek him out at home and risk Joe seeing me. I feel like a secret agent. I feel like the assassin Nikita. I have an invisible gun strapped to my back, and I wear an invisible catsuit. No one knows I'm really in disguise.

We play for the rest of the day, and then Stacey takes Bernie and me to the Invisible House, where we are tortured for another hour. The sun is setting, the swaying fields bathed in orange all over, and it is dinnertime, so we make our way back. Bernie grins from ear to ear. She has returned to Stacey's good graces. She thinks things are finally back to normal after a long punishment. She has no idea this change of state is permanent, and nothing is the same as before.

We eat, which feels like a chore. The hard plastic chair underneath my thighs feels too hard, the steel fork in my hand too cold. I'm burning where I sit, distracted, until the bell finally rings five minutes later and I push away my plate, untouched. I feel like I am one of those people who sit at a desk from nine until five and watch the clock, *tick-tock*, *tick-tock*, slowly, slowly, slowly; killing time, waiting for life to speed up.

Tick. Tock. Tick. Tock.

Stacey leaves on Friday after school is out. Now all I have to do is wait for night to fall; then I can slink out like a vampire bat.

20

Like a Cat

NOW

Denise leans forward. "Give us more," she says, her voice struggling to restrain pressure. She is good at author management, but patience can only last so long when publishing schedules revolve around one author. And I'm the reason thirty other titles are hovering in limbo. "Something. Even a chapter. We're salivating over at the office."

She laughs and leans away, slapping the table like Bruce does when he's particularly jovial. Nice cover. She's dripping irritation. Like Bruce was this morning when I told him about this impromptu meeting.

Don't stay out too long. What time will you be back?

He'd offered to come with me, but then his phone rang, insistently shrill, and the moment passed.

Your voice rings out in my memory: *Don't go to sleep.*

"It's coming along," I tell Denise. It's what I always say. *Coming along. It's going well. Can't rush creativity.*

There was another devil's thorn on my stoop this morning. Are you messing with me? Reminding me you're here? Reminding me that you know exactly where to find me?

"It's been almost months, darling," Denise says, easing herself in. She tries to be gentle with me, and usually it works. But I can see the seams beginning to open on her kind, understanding face.

I fiddle with the tablecloth, watching my chipped red nail polish and wondering why I use the stuff. You don't. Your nails are perfect. Always were. No need for the veneer.

What do you do for a living? I forgot to get an answer from you at dinner. Got distracted. Got panicked. I can't imagine you as a writer. You sitting at a desk and typing away at the keys? No. Then again, I can't imagine you sleeping in a bed, making coffee, using the toilet, taking a shower . . . nothing so mundane. Maybe you don't work at all. Maybe you speculate. Maybe you own properties and have a passive income that more than meets your needs.

I move a lot. I get bored easily.

Speculation, then. That's most likely it. I'll have to ask you. And where have you lived? That's another pressing question. London, yes. Highgate, didn't you say? Dubai? Italy? Scandinavia? Greece? I can imagine you in Egypt, conversing with the Sphinx.

"Bethany?" Denise breaks in to my thoughts, and I realize I've been sitting with my mouth hanging open. "Are you . . . okay?" She touches my forearm in that way people do when they're worried you've had a death in the family, or that your mental facilities aren't quite up to par. Non compos mentis.

I snap my jaw together. Swallow.

Like sandpaper. "I'm fine. It's going well. Really. Forna doesn't need to worry. I just needed time to think it all through."

"So, can we have the opening chapter?"

"Sure."

I wish my mouth wouldn't open sometimes.

Denise smiles, and her shoulders drop. She exhales through a laugh. "Excellent. God, we were getting worried. I'll let Forna know she'll have the first chapter in the morning."

Fuck.

I nod, force a smile. "I think she'll like it."

Denise throws up her hands like a comic book character made 3D. "Darling, you have no idea—*no idea*—how happy everyone will be at the office. A new Sally chapter, after so long! Listen, though, I must dash. Stay as long as you like—they have the company card details here. Write if you wish," she says suggestively. "You have made me the happiest woman in London."

I should feel wanted. I should feel great.

I want to vomit.

Denise's smile drops as she turns to leave. "Author care" achieved.

She turns back and calls, "Just . . . remember how to be free!" She winks and grins, then leaves, weaving between tables, quick as a dolphin.

Poor Bethie. You've forgotten how to be free.

I lean back in my chair with sudden emptiness. What the hell am I doing? With my life, with my time, with . . . everything?

Maybe you're here to burn it all down.

My phone buzzes. A message from Denise.

Give us the end, Bethany. Make it legendary.

I open a new text and compose it without analyzing.

I'm going to kill myself with this book. I hate my main character, Sally. She's going to be the end of me.

You reply right away.

Kill the bitch. Move on.

I laugh so loudly that the maître d' looks my way, eyebrow raised. I grab my coat and head for the door, my fingers itching in their gloves. Screw the drink.

Kill the bitch. Move on. Simple.

Too goddamned right.

Back at home, I pull out my laptop and begin to write. I channel you. Your nonchalance. Your freedom. Who cares how Sally dies? So long as she does. I can murder as well as the next person.

The words come like a torrent, and I'm reminded of the early days of my writing journey, before the agents, before the book deals and the lists and the awards and the press. Back when I wrote at night with a small windup lamp, cramped into a plastic chair at the laundromat, scribbling with pencil and paper, furiously churning out my secret lives into the woman I had dreamed up. Sally. Powerful, clever, intelligent, and whole. Sally Pierson. Heiress. Housewife. Thief. Assassin. Overall badass in disguise.

Sally Pierson. Stacey Preston.

Now I'm her assassin, and I'm taking her down. Boring is criminal. Vagrancy is art.

I write,

and write,

and write.

The light changes.

I write.

The light fades. Bruce brings me tea and medicine.

I write.

The tea gets cold; the house gets dark.

I write.

And all I can think while I'm doing it is: *Goodbye, Sally. Hello, Stacey.*

I remind myself this is about the book, and nothing more. You're inspiring me to work, but that's all. There is no greater meaning here, and I am not being roped into your world. They are just words on a screen.

Eventually, I close my laptop, my fingers aching from the speed with which they hit the keys, and sip the dregs of cold tea.

Ding-dong, I think, grinning from ear to ear. *The bitch is dead.*

I attach the chapter to an email to Forna, copying Denise, and press Send.

A thrill runs through me, and I lean back in my chair, my hands roaming up and down my body. I feel the smoothness of my stomach, the pertness of my breasts. I let my hands explore my skin like they haven't in years, tingling all over.

I caress myself, feel the dips and curves of my flesh. The moisture and the tension. Heat rises in me like an old friend, and I touch myself, move with myself, closing my eyes.

The orgasm is intense and sustained, and my toes curl up like cats. I gasp for breath, laugh, and laugh, and laugh. I cry.

Then I reach for my phone and hesitate. This is a bad idea . . . I should disengage. But you're so tempting, and it *has* been many years, and you deserve to be given a chance to show your evolution. I send you a message.

You mentioned having some fun? I'm game.

I'm finally game.

My God. Where have I been?

21

Night Prowl

THEN

The moment has come, but I'm afraid. I'm afraid not of being unsuccessful but of actually achieving my goal . . . of actually *seeing* Sakkie. If I do, will Stacey know? Will she sense it? And me? What will I do when that fire overcomes me? How will I survive it? And if I *don't* go? Would I survive that?

But I have a purpose. A higher purpose to what I'm going to do.

I slide my legs out of bed, flesh on cotton, and then I walk to the cupboard, flesh on laminate. I don't put on my shoes; I want to risk nothing. No sound, no exposure. My feet are tough, I tell myself, even in the dark. No devils will get me. No Glass Man tonight. I'll be safe.

I convince myself the devils and I are in league tonight. They will make a righteous path for me to follow, and when I go wrong, they will draw blood and pain to tell me, warn me. They are little shards of glass—of mirror—showing me the way. That's what being in league with the devil means. He'll hurt you to love you.

I don't bother to climb into my school dress either. My pajamas are safer. Less material, soft cotton, more silence. Less to get snagged, intangible like water. Glass made liquid. There's water in my lungs, too, but I can't cough, can't breathe.

Around me I feel the eyes of someone watching again, but I'm full of liquid glass, and nothing can stop me.

"Go away," I mutter with a flick of my hand, not wholly sure if what I sense is my imagination or the ghosts that are out in the moonlight.

On the way to Joe's house I catch five devils, four in one foot, one in the other. Either we aren't in league, or they are just testing me. I don't bother plucking the thorns off. I slip them all into the pocket of my nightdress like I'm a collector of pain, humming "Who's Afraid of the Big Bad Wolf" in my mind. One thorn anointed, bloody where it pierced the arch of my foot.

I almost turn around, sensing the thorns want me to; I actually take a step backward. Cowards do things like that; cowards hide and run and never, ever act. Not even when something like Stacey is at risk.

Outside Joe's house I'm not sure what to do. I stand in the shadows and stare at the glowing orange windows, willing Sakkie to peek through. I stare at the peeling paint on the window frames, and I stare at the grimy glass panes; I yell at him with my mind, telling him to open one and see me.

Pull back the curtain, I chant. *Pull back the curtain. I'm here; I'm here.* The thorns chant with me. *Pull back the curtain. I'm here; I'm here.*

He doesn't. How will I reach him? How will I know which room is his? I panic when I realize I'm locked out. I'm on the outside in the open night, alone and invisible, with the ghosts. On the other side of the wall, my Sakkie is going to sleep, not knowing that I'm here, waiting for him. Each second he doesn't see me is a second closer I come to Stacey's return, and although I want this more than anything, I'm dreading it. I need to do this one last thing first; otherwise, it will all have been for nothing. Otherwise, this will always be between us. I have to cut Sakkie out. I have to cut out the rotten bits inside.

I gasp in shallow breaths, clenching my jaw to keep the tide of panic away. But it rises fast.

The water in my chest evaporates, leaving behind horrible worms. They wriggle in my lungs, and I can't even cough to get them to stop. I clench my jaw, clench my fists, unclench my jaw, flex my fingers.

Eventually, I walk around to the back of the house and sit pressed up against the wall, knees tucked in. What am I doing? I know I should go back. I know I should give up or try harder. Stacey would. But I can do neither. All I have the capacity for is to sit in a little ball and to *not think*. If I don't think, I can't crack up. If I don't crack up, then that would be good.

That would be good.

So I do nothing.

I am not made of glass.

Glass Man can't get me.

It is a long time later that the downstairs window goes dark. Then I see Sakkie briefly through the narrow window near me, climbing the stairs. The grime on the glass looks like Stacey's eyes, peering out at me, judging my inactivity as well as my intentions. I peer in to see which way he goes. He turns left. The one in the middle is the bathroom, which has special wavy glass, so the next one must be Sakkie's room.

I get to my feet, joints stiff and cold, searching for something to throw at the glass. Stacey's dusty eyes continue to laugh at me. I reach into my shallow pocket and withdraw the devil's thorns. I think they must have something to do with this fantastic turn of events. Maybe they are grateful I didn't pluck them and steal their pride. I throw three devils at his window and miss. I throw the fourth, and it barely makes a sound. Useless. Four useless weapons. Four useless tools.

Glassy, glassy, cut my—

I swallow Stacey's voice, which rings in my head.

You're doing something wrong if the thorns have abandoned you.

I hunt around for stones small enough to throw until I have a little pile of six. I hit the glass on the third try, but nothing stirs from within. I try again and again, and finally, on the fifth try, he appears behind the curtain, squinting into the night.

I wave frantically. *Please see me. Please!*

His eyes stop their roaming and fix on my face. His expression flickers, his eyes sharp; then he is gone, and I run to a safe distance to wait. He comes out the back door and searches for me. Eventually he spots my pale-blue pajamas in the distance and runs toward me.

Impatience to touch him sears my stomach from the inside; the fire is so strong. It boils downward. My heart sends jet streams of adrenaline coursing through my body, always beating the same *obsession, obsession, obsession*. The same *hurt me, hurt me, hurt me*. Love me, please, just love me. Somebody.

My lungs greedily breathe in the dusty air, desperate for some hint of Sakkie's scent, but there is nothing but the dead sand, the cracked earth, and the dry horizons.

Stacey's eyes linger in the dirty window, as though she is staring into a magic mirror, searching for me, finding me, and I feel suddenly reluctant.

I let out one cry that is mostly howl, and then the obsession and his form in front of me, so real, so proximal, send me shooting into his arms.

"Why haven't you come to see me?" he asks. His eyes are wide, surrounded by thin, fragile wrinkles in the skin, and I'm afraid of the frantic emotion barely withheld by the thin membrane. He has gunk in the corners of his eyes, and I wonder if what Stacey says is true. Is it left behind by the sandman when he brings us our dreams?

"I was afraid," I whisper.

"Afraid of me?" Sakkie says, drawing me back to the dark now.

"Afraid to tell you . . . that it . . . can't carry on."

"Why?"

I don't have any more words, so I use Stacey's again. "It can't carry on."

His hands ball into fists around my hair; his teeth are out. *"Why?"*

"'Cause," I mumble.

"That's a child's answer. Tell me *why*."

"Because . . . I *am* a child. I'm thirteen, Sakkie. You're twenty-eight. They won't let it happen, will they?" Though I'm not exactly sure who "they" are, Sakkie seems to know "they" have power over us.

He looks like he is about to protest; his hand slackens in my hair.

"You won't tell. I can make you not tell."

"They will find out, eventually."

He swears in Afrikaans. Then his eyes soften. "So what? We love each other, right? What can they do? We can keep it secret. Secret until you're old enough."

Love. Is that what this is?

A secret love affair sounds like a fairy tale, but I know the reality of the rosy image he's trying to plant in my mind. The reality is the choice I must make between Sakkie and Stacey. The real fairy tales are like the ones Stacey tells, the ones with broken sisters, with hell and Glass Man down tractor tires and haunted corn towers and invisible houses. Those are the real fairy tales. *This* is.

This is the inevitable choice that would eventually catch up to me. And, if I left it until the choice reached me instead of me reaching the choice, it would be impossible to make.

Or worse: It would be made for me. By Stacey.

I shake my head. "No."

"Bethany," he hisses and pulls at my hair. "Why come here if you were just going to end it? Your passions won't let you stop." He pulls my hair again. "You're like me, a creature of obsession. You're a wild, untamed bird; you can't be caged—there's no escape."

Each time he pulls my hair, I cry out and the tears spill over. But I won't change my mind. If I give up Sakkie, then I can keep Stacey. If I keep Sakkie . . . I can't even think of it. I put my hand into my pocket and feel the sharp prick of a baby devil's thorn I've forgotten. I squeeze it between my forefinger and thumb, and the pain clears my head. The dust eyes in the window are smiling.

I square my jaw. "You're wrong. I'm not going to see you again after tonight."

He raises his other hand in a warning. He turns it into a fist. "Don't say that. Don't!"

The ghosts come closer, and they are comforting in their interest. Why have they come now? I can feel my arms shivering, a sure sign they are intrigued. The moon is out, I think. They travel along moonbeams.

"I'm warning you," he says.

I squeeze the thorn harder.

"I don't care," I tell him, raising my face, daring him to strike.

"You're going to stay with me."

Squeeze.

"No. I'm going to pretend you never existed."

And then there are tears on his face, running into the glass hairs. "Why, Beth? *Whywhywhyareyoudoingthistome?*" His pleas are indistinct, rolling into one another, one long whine. I have never seen a man cry before. It's guttural, snarling, more like a growl than a cry. He bares his teeth and his gums glisten; his brows draw together until they nearly touch.

His fists clutch the roots of my hair.

You can't do it, says the voice in my head. And because she said it, I do it.

Squeeze.

"I didn't even know about you a few weeks ago," I tell him, "And now things are going all wrong! I'm acting like . . . like a stupid wild animal or something; I'm keeping secrets . . . all I can think about is you all the time and—" I break off. I can't tell him how Stacey has been watching me, noticing something has changed. What good would it do to tell him I am breaking up with him because I love Stacey more?

I take a breath. "I'm sorry . . . all I want is for you to hurt me all the time, and I hate myself, and it's confusing. I'm sorry."

"I love you, Beth," he whispers, moving his hand from my hair to my cheek. He caresses. "I love you."

The caress hurts more than the pain.

"I . . . I'm sorry."

"You won't leave me," he says, seeing the regret in my eyes. "You won't, will you, Beth?" The corners of his mouth pick up at the edges, almost a smile.

No, you won't.

Squeeze.

"It's over, Sakkie." When I say this, I know it's true. He loves me. So what? I love Stacey. It's enough. It's enough. It has to be. Besides, if he loves me, he'll wait here until I'm eighteen. He'll wait for it not to matter anymore, for my age to not be a problem anymore. For Stacey to not be a problem. It will give me time to tell her, when we are both grown up. He just can't see it. When I've gone, he'll see that, and he'll wait until we can do it right. My questions can wait a little while longer.

I feel older all of a sudden, as though I have some secret knowledge that gives me the power of age.

Sakkie's cheeks puff with each furious breath as the anger swells inside him.

"*No!*" he hisses at last, pulling my hair violently. "You're mine, goddamn it. It's not your choice! Don't I get a *fucking* say? Don't I have something to do with it, you little tease?"

He slaps me.

I scream as a surge of shock and pain pumps through me when some of the strands in his left hand come loose from my scalp. They almost twang like the snapped strings of a violin strung too tightly.

"Stop it," I cry. He pulls harder, yanking my head down, and then he tugs at my clothes again, and I lose my grip on the thorn. He chants my name over and over, his hands too strong; his will too strong.

"Stay with me," he says, breathless, and his voice is brittle.

I tell him I can't.

He hurts me.

A surge inside: Excitement. Not mine. Hers. Beastly Beth. Wrong Beth. Other Beth.

"No, Sakkie! Not now, okay? When I'm grown. When I'm older . . . stop, okay? Please stop."

He slaps my face again. Spits on me. "Ugly girl," he says. "You're disgusting. Stay with me. I'm the only one that wants you."

I'm crying hard, being ripped in two. I'm little more than a husk of a girl.

Stacey wants me, I tell myself.

He bruises my breasts, my thighs; he rips me open with his body. I try to stop him, try to resist, but he is so strong. So powerful.

"Stay, Beth," he whispers when he is finished hurting me. "Please. I need you."

"Sakkie?"

I freeze.

Joe yells for his son from the entrance to their house. Light spills from the doorway, washing away all the ghosts I felt before. I don't know if Joe can see me behind the tree, but I stay still and keep my breathing shallow.

Sakkie frowns down at me, his eyes screaming *You are mine.* I shake my head, and then he is walking back to the house, back rigid, fists clenched.

Joe yells at him, but I don't know what is said. I am too busy feeling empty, weak, alone; slowly wiping away the blood in patches all over my body. The bruises begin to pulse.

The door closes with a thud; the sound of finality, bringing with it the blackness of the night. The light is contained within those four walls. Nothing is left over for me.

I walk as far as I can on shaking legs connected to shivering knees and hips. I fall often. Each time I collapse, I force myself torturously to my feet, gasping for breath. But I always fall again. The moon is curtained behind clouds that have no silver lining.

By the time I reach the west-wing dorms, I am crawling, and my knees are bloody. If the devils were my allies before, they aren't now. I am sure that most of the damage to my skin since I left the tree has been due to them.

Matron Monday is on duty tonight. When she sees me, she gasps. It sounds like an inside-out scream. She raises her hands to her mouth and shakes her head.

"*Sloane*? What is it, Sloane?"

"I—just—need—a drink," I breathe between the painful contractions in my heart and body. "Water."

"Lie down, child! Lie down!"

I manage to climb into the bed, but then I begin to sob; the sounds I make are strange, whining, low and then high, uneven, breathy. I sob Sakkie's name, but it sounds more like garbled words. I sound like I've cracked up. I curl into the tightest ball I can. I want to be small. Smaller than a grain of glassy sand.

Matron Monday comes back into the room with a tall glass of water and a small white pill. I drink the water and take the pill, and within twenty minutes I feel calmer. Matron Monday removes my dusty pajamas, which have been ripped near the armpit area and along the elasticized waistband, putting them in a wicker basket. She then goes into the bathroom section of sick bay to fetch a basin of water and a rough white cloth.

I watch it all with detached vision, like I'm standing at the end of a fuzzy corridor or at the bottom of a brackish well.

She begins to wash away the dust and grime on my body, frowning at the blood that comes away with it, harsh crimson against a pale orange. She avoids my legs. All I can think about is what comes next. What happens now? Is this it? Will Stacey be sure now that I am hers alone? Will I have to tell her, or will she sense it? Will all those bricks that have fallen into the invisible wall between us just . . . fade away?

I'm nearly fourteen, I tell myself. The rest of my life is a long time to live without him, with this feeling rising up inside me. I hope he waits for me. If he loves me, he'll wait for me. He'll try to keep me. He'll try to win me back. Eighteen. That's all I need. I can die if I win him. Eighteen years of life is enough.

I'm the only one that wants you.

I love you.

I watch the basin grow darker and darker, and I imagine my body becoming cleaner and cleaner. With every wipe the matron delivers, my body shudders and contracts in on itself. My throat and stomach are clenching like I'll be sick. Will it feel like purging? Will this water wash away this horrible feeling I have? The one that makes me want to claw away my skin, the feeling that is the voice inside me, taunting me and laughing at me?

So stupid, the voice says. *So wonderful.*

What is the name for this feeling? What is it called? It's like guilt, only worse—darker, more violent. Will I get cleaner if the water gets darker? Is that how it works?

Once, before Mum left me here—I think I was six or seven—she took me to Florida Lake. We bought hot dogs and walked along the bank together. Just the two of us. It wasn't a sunny day; it was cold and gray, so we were alone. My hand was swallowed up in hers, warm and safe against the drizzle we waded through. It was like walking on a cloud. I felt like a whole person then, completely unaware of my body or my mind. I just *was*, and that was enough.

Even if I had a lake as big as that one, lost in my memories, it wouldn't be enough to wash me clean. Can it ever be washed away?

What about the disembodied hollow space inside me? The one that exists in the center of the chaos, silently echoing long and loud, ringing in my ears so that I want to shriek to block out that horrible silence. What about the rising absence of feeling in me? This abyss that is slowly growing bigger, devouring feelings, good, bad, all of it, until I am a husk left behind. Can you wash away a vacuum?

There is a cave-in; the folds of my mind close in around themselves, and I begin to drift. My eyes shut before I pass out. Matron Monday bustles around me, her heels clicking on the hard floor. I lose consciousness for a second, and when I wake, the day is in full bloom, and I am in unfamiliar white pajamas.

22

Parting the Sea

NOW

Bruce is wound tighter than a guitar string. He paces up and down in his office, muttering into his phone, closing the door when I wheel past. He wears his Bluetooth headset to bed twice, falling into a fitful sleep and then jerking awake when calls come in at stupid hours.

He smiles stiffly when I wrap my arms around him under the covers and is already gone when I wake.

"What's going on?" I ask on Wednesday morning when I find him bent over the kitchen island, head in hands, a teapot and empty cup before him.

He starts and stands straight, shaking his head.

"Don't say 'nothing,'" I warn. "I'm not blind."

He looks at me, then laughs, his shoulders releasing stress. "I didn't want you to worry."

"I worry when you keep me locked out."

And I wonder if you are making me see things, notice things I might otherwise have ignored. I have begun to pay close attention again, watching for signs of disruption.

He nods. "I'm sorry. Things are tense. Magauri is trying to buy out the company by tempting the shareholders to sell their stock. If it works, I'll likely be let go."

A vision of you plucking spiky bits from a devil's thorn, laughing as you toss it aside.

I am enraged on Bruce's behalf. "How can they do that? You started the company."

I won't let you become a humiliated ball.

"I own less than fifty percent. It's a mess. A power move. I don't think Trace and Myers will go for it, but I can't be sure. Being over here . . . it feels like I can't tell what they're thinking."

I sit down on one of the stools, resting my crutches against the island. "Maybe you should ask them to come here for a while."

Bruce shakes his head. "I did, but it's impossible right now." He hesitates, opens his mouth to say more, than pours me a cup of tea from the pot sitting between us. "Have you taken your meds?"

I nod distractedly. "Tell me."

He sighs. "I think we're going to have to go over there."

I laugh. "To South Africa?"

My stomach jolts, and I taste cooking-flour sand, see your face looming over mine, deep in shadow, spittle in the corners of your mouth.

I told you not to go to sleep!

I break out in a cold sweat; wipe my palms on my jeans. "Bruce, I can't . . ." I desperately search for a reason. Any reason. "I'm in the middle of the last Sally book. I'm finally making progress."

"You can write there, surely?"

My skin prickles with faux fever, and my ears whine with tension. "If I change the environment, it could stop flowing. You know that."

He's been well versed in my writer rituals and paranoia for more than a decade. He should know better.

"You go," I say finally. "You go and sort this out. I'll stay."

"No." He snaps it, the answer out of his mouth before he's even considered it fully. "I'm not leaving you."

"For God's sake, I'm not a child."

I feel your hands on invisible wires, puppeteering me.

He looks devastated. "Of course you're not—"

"I don't need you to baby me, Bruce. I'll be fine. I have to get this book done, and you're a distraction."

He rubs at his eyes. "I don't know. It feels wrong, leaving you here alone."

"I won't be alone. I've got Denise checking on me every two seconds."

And you. I've got you. I shouldn't want you. I should know better . . . but I do.

I force a smile and lean over to take his hand. "Go. Talk to the guys. See what's happening over there. I'll save my career, and you save yours."

He closes his eyes and presses my knuckles to his lips.

"Okay."

I feel a thrill of excitement at the idea of being left alone.

Finally.

23

Dress-Up

THEN

"Can you tell me why you were out of doors so long after lights-out?"

"I sleepwalk." The lie slides out on its own, preservation personified.

I am in stalemate with myself unless I let the lie take over.

"Oh." Matron looks surprised. I am worried this is going to take the whole day. "And the . . . ah, wounds?"

"I must have fallen."

My voice sounds all wrong, like a robot. Flat, insipid, depthless.

"Some of the cuts had a peculiar shape," she says, wringing her hands. She sighs a few times and then plunges on haltingly. "Bite marks, almost."

"I must have been dreaming," I say. I try to look perplexed. "I don't know."

"Well." Matron looks like she wants to change the subject, to wash her hands of this line of conversation. "Well, yes. Yes, I suppose so. Well, then . . ."

"Can I go?"

"Yes, yes. If you feel fine, then by all means."

I get up, and she hands over my dusty pajamas. As soon as they are out of her hands, she looks happier. She gives me a winning smile and tells me to "Have fun, now," and then she goes back to pottering around her medicine cupboard.

I find out a few days later that Sakkie has left the school. Joe says he got a job in the city and he won't come back. I am paralyzed for a day after I hear this news. I can't even collapse under the shock of it. Stacey sits with me every moment she isn't in school. I don't tell her anything, and she doesn't ask. The school calls it a cold and tucks me up in bed and forgets about me. Out of sight, out of mind. If only it worked that way for Sakkie too.

He has left me no note, nothing.

Why would he? The voice in my head says. *He got what he wanted, silly billy.*

In a week I'm on my feet again, and within a few days I begin to feel things are returning in some measure to the state they were in before. Sakkie is on my mind less and less—only at night, really, when the shadows of the past raise up into those other shadows, which watch me from the corner of the room. When I lie in my bed, I can feel something with me, something watching me, but I am always alone.

During the day I continue to vie with Bernie for Stacey's affections; at night I bite down on my lip until it bleeds, think of Sakkie, and feel waves of sorrow build around me. Then I sob until the black hole descends.

A week later I turn fourteen. My mother comes to visit me with her husband in tow. He gives me a wet kiss on each cheek, his saliva drying on my skin. My mother gives me a makeup kit, which pleases me, to her complete astonishment. It is full of blue, green, and yellow eye shadows as well as red, pink, and brown lipsticks. I take to the red, applying too much and getting it on my teeth.

I imagine that if Sakkie ever comes back, he will see a beautiful woman with ravishing lips and a full bosom. I imagine how the red lipstick will look smeared across his face, on his torso, on his body. To see *him* in bloodred for a change. I blush, want to cry, and try to think of something else. But I'm caught in a perpetual cycle, a torturous loop in my mind, and it churns round and round with no thought for my sanity. Emptiness, Sakkie, memories, Sakkie.

Round and round like a merry-go-round.

"Well," my mother says, surprised. "You're becoming a woman now."

I smile at this. "I know."

Shaking her head and raising her thin eyebrows, she seems delighted and perplexed in equal amounts. "Well," she says again, "the red suits you very well, darling."

I smile again. "Thank you, Mummy."

"Oops, better teach you how to avoid getting it on your teeth." She laughs, a *hawhawhawhaw* sound, and pulls out a white handkerchief.

I lick my teeth clean before she can get to them, and she laughs again. "Don't want anyone to say you've been drinking blood now, do we?"

"No."

"Like a little vampire." She finds herself very amusing. "Take your index finger," she says, holding up her manicured digit, "and slide it through your lips." She inserts her finger deep into her mouth and then pulls it forward. I can see the circle of red left behind near the ring position. "See? Easy as that."

I copy her. "Easy as that." I stare at my finger, at the little red circle. It's a wedding ring made of blood, and I don't wipe it away.

She beams. "Oh, Stoffel, dear, doesn't she look delightful?"

Stoffel nods without looking and then goes back to reading his newspaper. I think his neck is even longer now than it was when I saw him last. I am amazed to realize I haven't seen my mother in seven months. She looks the same. Still a Barbie that smells of baby powder and vanilla. I'm even more amazed that I don't care.

Stacey has filled the place inside me where my mother used to be. Pain shoots through my heart. I need her. I need Stacey. Right now. If I could inhabit her body for a day, I'm sure I'd have enough of her essence to last my whole life. I just need a little bit of her, just a little.

You're addicted, the voice says.

"No," I say.

Mum frowns. "What's wrong, sweetie?"

"Nothing."

"I've also brought you something else," my mother says with a knowing smile. "Come into the bedroom, darling."

I follow her into the back part of the cabin. Waiting for me on the bed are at least twelve bras with matching underwear. Some are simple cotton in various colors. Others seem bigger, with firmer material.

Do you think Stacey wears a bra?

"I . . ."

My heart beats so fast at the sight of these womanly items that I feel quite faint with excitement.

"Are these all for me?" I ask in a half whisper.

My mother beams. "Yes, darling! We're going to see which ones fit you. Where would you like to start?"

I eye the lavender one that is silky and bulkier than the others, but I am too embarrassed to pick it first. Instead, I point to a white cotton one with no distinct shape and try to ignore the voice that sneers *chicken* in my head. The bra looks rather like a minitop with an elasticized waist.

"All right, darling," my mother says, her smile a little hesitant around the edges. She sighs with a look at the other, more elaborate bras, and then she hands me the plain one with another little sigh. I feel like a giant Barbie doll playing dress-up.

I try it on in front of my mother. It doesn't occur to me to hide my body. But as soon as my top is off, she gasps.

"Darling! What are those bruises?"

I glance down. My small breasts, torso, and back are riddled with purple and blue bruises; some are turning splotchy and yellow. I'd forgotten.

"I was sleepwalking," I mumble. "I fell down a lot, but I don't remember."

She raises a shaking hand to her lips. "Oh . . . Do they hurt?"

I shrug. "No," I say, even though it is a lie.

They hurt beautifully. With this I can agree.

"Well, let's get you into some bras."

Most of the bras are too big, including, to my dismay, the silk one with padding. I'm afraid my mother will take it away. Two bras fit perfectly: both white cotton, both without the wire underneath. I am annoyed that I have such little breasts. I try to think what Stacey's breasts look like, but I can't remember them. Have I ever seen little bulges under her top? Or is she perfectly flat as the day she was born?

No one is that pure.

"Well, I'll take the others home until you grow a little bigger."

"Can I . . ." My voice trails off, and I eye the lavender bra and matching panties.

My mother smiles shrewdly. "Why don't you keep this one, darling? It's pretty, and it wasn't *too* big for you."

I shrug. "Okay, whatever."

She packs up the rest of the bras, chuckling and shaking her head, and I go to the bathroom. When I come out, I am wearing the new bra and my chest looks bigger.

"Ah, isn't that just darling?" I hear my mother murmur to Stoffel when she spots what I have done. "So adorable."

I let her think me cute, but inside I feel like a vixen. If only Sakkie would come back. If only he could see my new gifts that make me look womanly. Will Stacey think that too? Will she notice?

Lesbo.

I swallow the tide of emptiness inside me when I think of Sakkie and Stacey not being near, and I go and have lunch with my mother.

24

Old Blood

On the last day of her stay, my mother asks me to walk with her. She wants to talk to me about "womanly things," so I agree to go out of curiosity. It feels like my life has been spiraling away from me for a while, so I want the chance to be alone with her, to see if it changes anything.

I hardly expect Stoffel to take an interest in women's affairs, and he doesn't surprise me. Since they arrived, he has neither addressed a single word to me nor looked at me, if it could be helped. This arrangement suits both of us just fine. This way he isn't burdened with another man's blood, and I don't have to keep swallowing my upchuck whenever I look at his crinkly face or long turkey neck.

"Now, darling," my mother says, "have you . . . well, what I mean is, are you . . . Did you get your"—she gives a little giggle—"period yet?"

"No."

"Oh. Well, then we'll need to talk about it. Do you know how it works?"

"My friend got hers the other week." A bit late for her to play "Mummy" again.

My mother nods. "I expect she's told you all about it, then?"

I nod. Stacey has never talked about it, but I don't much feel like hearing the details. Blood is blood, and no concern of mine.

"Now, when your period comes, you'll need to be prepared, so I packed some sanitary towels for you."

"They're called pads here," I say.

"Oh. Yes, well, pads then. I brought enough for five days in case you start while I'm away. If you need any more, just telephone me and I'll send some up."

"I think Matron has them," I mutter, "so you won't need to worry."

Everyone is all interested in blood. I'm interested in Stacey's; my mother is interested in mine. But the only kind of blood I'm interested in is the blood I can never get back.

Her eyes drop, and she forces a smile. "All right, then, darling."

Even though I don't want to discuss this, *especially* with my mother, I have a burning question. We circle the cabin twice before I have the nerve to spit it out.

"When will I start? Will it start soon, now that I'm fourteen, like Stacey?"

"Stacey is your friend?"

"Yes." *She's my twin.*

"Well, it's different for everyone. I was much younger than you are now. But the one thing you must remember is that when it comes, you'll be more interested in boys. But you have to be careful."

I act surprised. "Oh."

She nods and puts her hands together. "Yes. Boys will want to be special friends with you, but you should avoid them."

"Avoid boys? That's stupid."

"No, it's not, dear. Boys only want one thing from girls like you. *Beautiful* girls like you," she adds, beaming at me in a nauseating way, teeth and gums exposed under straining lips. I don't want to be her little darling anymore.

I also don't want to ask what the "one thing" is because I already know, but if I don't, my mother will tell me anyway.

I settle on saying "Really." In her ears it will sound like a request for more information, but I will have the peace of mind that comes with knowing that I never asked.

"Yes. Boys will want to see more of your body . . . to do things that only married ladies and men do when they love each other very, very much and want to have a family together."

She thinks I'm five.

She is prattling like she does when she gets nervous. She cocks her head from one side to the other as she talks, as though she is writing what she is saying in the little notebook in her brain.

"Okay" is all I say.

I've never before seen my forthcoming period and the things Sakkie did to me as linked. Love and blood—one big enigma.

"Remember to say no if a boy wants to kiss you," my mother adds for emphasis.

"The boys live in the other block," I say with a shrug.

"Good. That's good."

Her mood eases a little after "the conversation" has been neatly dealt with. Now she can fold it up and put it in a drawer and never have to think about it again. Job done. Tick.

I become a little tearful when my mother and Stoffel prepare to load the car. The sight of my mother's retreating form, going to the car and back again, reminds me of when I first got here, and I was so little that her leaving felt like her death. I would shake as the hours to their disembarkation approached, and when the final hour arrived, I thought I would die if they didn't let me go away with them too.

For a moment, the world feels something like it did back then, when I needed my mother, when I was a small eight-year-old. I feel the rising surge of panic, like a tidal wave chasing me, and I try to stay ahead of it. I am close to begging them to take me with them. This is intensified by the fact that Sakkie, too, has left, and that Mummy and Stoffel are flying back to England from Joburg, where Sakkie has also gone. I don't want to be the one left behind like a once-loved-and-now-forgotten piece of luggage, like the gum wrapper thrown out the window once the sweet contained inside it has been ripped free.

"Mummy," I whimper, the old habits returning, "please take me with you. Please, *please* . . ."

She sighs. "Now, darling, don't be ridiculous. It's the middle of the school year."

I become hysterical in the instant it takes her to utter the word no. Like I did when I was eight. It doesn't make any sense. It's pure instinct now; the tidal wave has reached me. "I don't care! Please take me!"

Save me.

"Stop it, Bethany," she snaps in a clipped voice that sounds more English and natural. "It's preposterous to think of you coming with us. You need to stop doing this."

She's embarrassed, even though no one can see us. It's all about maintaining appearances now. About social etiquette. Wasn't that why she sent me here to begin with?

"Why?" I whine. "*Why?* I'm your daughter. Don't you love me?"

My mother has heard all this before. To her, it sounds no different from my usual sobbing pleas at the end of her semiannual visits. To me, it is worlds apart, and only partly out of habit. If she doesn't take me with her, what will happen? Where will my body take me?

"Darling," she says, drawing me to her bosom with a heavy sigh, "Mummy is married now. You need to learn to live without me running around after you all the time."

My sadness is replaced with red-hot fury in less than a second. Running around after me all the time? When exactly does she think she does that? She's abandoned me to the care of a matron in this desert school and only comes to see me every few months. If she had been here, I might have been better equipped to deal with Sakkie. I might have survived his absence. I might have been whole.

It might never have happened at all.

I boil in my rage and indignation, because *she* left *me* six long years ago to fend for myself in the bush, and look what happened.

"Running after me all the time?" My voice is tight, like it's a crucible waiting to explode.

"You need to grow up just a little bit," she says gently, placing a freshly manicured hand on my shoulder. Leaving me here to rot is "running around after me all the time"?

"Go. To. Hell." I say it very quietly.

She stumbles back a few steps, looking startled. "What did you say?"

"Go to hell."

"Darling—"

"Go *away*!"

"Bethany *Sloane*."

"Go *fuck* your new husband!" I yell, and spittle flies from my mouth and lands on her cheek, white. "I *never* want to see you again!"

I spin around and I run, ignoring my mother's furious demands for my return. Everyone has abandoned me . . . Sakkie, Matron, my birth father, my mother. The only constant now is Stacey.

Thank God for Stacey.

Stacey, who knows nothing of the disgusting things I have done.

"Bethany!"

My mother's last scream is from the woman I remember as my mother and not from the Barbie. It is the deep voice of the brunette, the entrepreneur, the slim and regular-breasted woman. It almost makes me turn, but then I remember that woman no longer exists. The Barbie killed her.

When I tear into the bathroom and lock myself in one of the stalls, I feel mugginess in my underwear. I pull them down. The white cotton is full of mucky burgundy *stuff*, and red runs down the inside of my thigh, sticky, wet. A disconcerting feeling of something once good, now leaving. I'm agitated and alone.

I ball up my hand, bite down on it, and scream.

25

Bats

My mother calls for the next two weeks. Every day. She also writes me letters. I ignore her. I'm too angry to respond, but I am also too embarrassed. Stacey knows I am angry with my mother. This has been a solidifying thing between us.

I don't tell my mother that her little darling is now A Woman, as she understands it. I don't tell her that her little darling has been a woman in another way for a while now.

During recess I sit beside Stacey, trying to think of what I want to ask her. I have a burning desire to talk about my mother—to get some kind of understanding about why I feel the way I do and why she does the things she does—but I know I'm not supposed to talk about her.

"What did you used to do with your mother?" I finally ask, and then I hold my breath.

Stacey shrugs, tapping her thumb to her fingertips one at a time. *Tap, tap, tap.* "We don't talk about the past," she says evenly. "The past is behind us for a reason."

I don't try to ask her about things like this again.

Nighttime trips are now impossible. Since the incident with my "sleepwalking," the matrons have bolted and padlocked the front doors after lights-out. This new confinement has me crawling in my skin, something I would have been (silently) thankful for in the days before Sakkie, when Stacey insisted we go night walking, and all I wanted to do was keep hold of the sleep I so rarely attained in the heat of the desert night. There has been an ongoing investigation into the events of that night, and I am scheduled to meet with a doctor in a month.

Stacey is more attentive to me than usual, and I begin to feel wrapped up in her affections. She is my security blanket . . . she keeps the warmth in and the world out. She is my barrier, my cage in the shark-infested sea. We walk, hand in hand, toward the green that sits in front of the chapel, waiting for the time when the sun will dip below the horizon and the bats will come out, flying above us by the dozens.

I stare at the sky, waiting for the telltale black flapping streaks. Chena, Sal, Gogo, Uri, and Bernie have come to join us.

"There!" Gogo yells, pointing above her head; her finger traces erratic patterns as she tries to follow the bats' course. Gogo has the quickest eyes; she always spots them first. But I can hear them. I hear the strange pulsing *squeak* of their sonar long before the others.

"I see them!" Uri confirms, and so do I. Their dipping bodies and webbed wings feel magical, like dark fairies.

I remove my flip-flops and get ready. We try to hit the bats in the air; it's a lot of fun. If we don't get them, they might dip low and entangle themselves in our hair. I was there when Lucia had a bat fly into hers. She screamed like she had seen the devil, running all over, scratching at her head. The bat got so tangled that it scratched her scalp until it was a bloody mess. The bat suffocated and had to be cut out, nothing more than a breathless corpse. Matron Rosi drove her into Pretoria to get her hair cut after that, because it was all wonky on the left side, and when she came back, she looked like a pretty boy.

I'm too mesmerized by their flighty dips and bends to throw my shoe. The sound they make when they fly too close, a clipped sound—*clkclkclk!*—reminds me of the corn tower. I don't mean to remember . . . I forbid myself to think of that night, but the sound throws me back and I can't help it. I remember that smell, the icy metal wall at my back, Sakkie's proximity. The endless pumping.

Memories injure as much as the source, only they're worse because they linger longer.

"I'm not feeling well," I mutter in Stacey's ear. I don't know if I will be allowed to leave, but I hope I can.

Stacey takes my hand and leads me away from the green, walking with a purpose. Bernie looks after us but doesn't follow. There is a particular iciness in the air tonight, and I wonder if it might rain. If it does, we'll be able to take regular baths again. I would like that. I would like to feel clean.

Stacey takes me all the way to the dorm and tucks me into bed. I look at her blankly as she sits beside me on the mattress. In the corner of the room sits the shadow that wasn't there before. It's as if the corner, where no light makes it from the dusk, is suddenly closer to my bed. I don't say anything; I just listen to my glass heart beat furiously in my chest and look up to Stacey where she sits, staring down at me.

When the bell rings for dinner, she tells me not to move. I almost ask her not to go, but nothing comes out except a feeble squeak. The shadow in the corner looks like a person. It has the shape of someone. It's been there, unmoving, for a while now. I want to blink and for it to be gone, but when I blink it only seems all the darker and more menacing. I think I must be doing that trick where you make pictures out of the clouds and then, no matter how hard you try, all you see is the picture until the vapor shifts. But the shadow never shifts.

Ten minutes later and Stacey has returned with two plates of pap and wors, with monkey-gland sauce. I don't know how she managed to bring the food to the dorm, but because she is Stacey, I know that what is impossible for me is not for her.

I don't eat a lot, and neither does she. I watch her chew with fascination. It is not the same as the invisible meals we have now shared countless times. I notice she chews on the left side of her mouth more than the right. I do the same. When I am done eating, she takes the trays back to the food hall and returns.

"We're not going out tonight," she says to me, stroking my head like my mother never does.

I already know this, but I nod as if it is news. "Okay."

"Sleep," she says, and I close my eyes as commanded.

26

Short Circuits

NOW

I have never been in a club. Thirty-two years old and I have never even been in a real bar. The music swells like a living beast, the building's own Cthulhu; the lights dance and buzz like fireflies. I can barely hear myself think, let alone talk. But . . . I like it. My God, I *love* it!

You dance through the hoards like you've done this a thousand times, a serpent, and I lose you.

I lose you.

Stacey.

Stacey?

Stacey!

Are you playing games?

And then you're back. Two glasses. Wine? You're laughing, saying something I can't hear. You hold out one glass, and I take it, sipping without smelling. I never developed a palate. I can't taste or smell the hazelnut undertones or the hints of caramel. It's rather vulgar, actually.

You find a table at the back, a circular booth, and help me to slide in. You take my crutches from me and lean them on the side. It takes a few tries—they like to slip and slide.

Useless.

Then you're in after me, and we have to sit close to hear each other, and anyway, there isn't much space. My stomach jolts with something like excitement or apprehension. You sip your wine and grin out at the people, watching them move and glide over each other, and I burn with wanting to know what you're thinking.

I wonder how often you come to places like this. To *this* place.

"Glass Man has come!" you yell, and I freeze, my skin going numb.

"What?"

"I love this song," you shout into my ear.

I watch you, wondering if this is a test, but you're swaying with the beat, and I shake my head. I have to stop thinking you're playing tricks. This isn't the desert, and we are different people.

It hadn't occurred to me to listen to the music. It's something I don't know, but the melody is a little sad. Strange how it evokes that emotion, yet the beat hits hard and fast.

Conflict.

Contrast.

Like you. Like me. Like us.

The Thorns, I remind myself.

You finish your wine, and I've still only had one sip.

"Drink up," you say, teeth flashing. "You'll get left behind!"

I sip again, grimace. *Touch a line, break your spine!*

You laugh, but I don't hear it. "Not a wine girl, then?"

"I . . . I don't think so."

You look at me for a moment too long, and I can tell you have just realized—or confirmed—something about me. I try to shove down the feeling of needing to prove myself to you, not allowing myself to be pulled back into those behaviors.

"Wait here," you say—or mouth—and then ease out from the table, weaving through the crowds again.

Several people call out to you or stop you on the way. You laugh and chat to them one at a time, or with several of them; your grin is so wide I could hide inside it. This is a you I haven't met, and I'm . . . jealous. Protective.

You're supposed to be mine.

You are a natural, and I feel so . . . ungainly. So useless. So out of my depth. When you're out of sight, the anxiety returns, and I wipe my palms on my jeans, hoping no one will try to come and sit down. That no one will try to get me to move. I don't want to move. It's safe here. My legs were sore before; now they aren't.

I keep an eye on my crutches, convinced someone might make off with them. I watch my bag on the seat next to me and then wrap the straps around my wrist once, twice, three times. I check for the exit, but I can't . . . I can't see it—people are everywhere. Strangers. Men. So many men.

My heart begins to thump in my throat. What if there's a fire or an earthquake or—what if you never come back? What if something happens to you and I never realize it because I've just been sitting here, waiting?

What if one of the men who was smiling at you was actually . . . what if one of them takes you—

My head races through every threat so fast I can barely keep up.

Smoke inhalation—

Death by crushing—

Injury by stampede—

Fire—

Earthquake—

Flood—

Kidnapping—

Drugging—

Asphyxiation—

~~Rape~~—

NoNoNoNo—not that, not that—

Where are the doors Where are the doors wherearethedoorswherearethedoors Where are *you* Whereareyouwhereareyou—Stacey? Stacey? StaceyStaceyStaceyStaceyStacey—

I sink lower into the booth—everything is beginning to get louder, harder, faster, brighter—please stop, make it stop—

Brain short-circuits

StaceyStaceyStaceyStACeyStaceystAceYStac-
eysTaCeyStaceyStaceyStaceyStACeyStaceyStaceyS-
taceyStACeyStaceystAceYStaceysTaCeyStaceyStac-
eyStaceyStACeyStaceyStaceyStaceyStACeyStacey-
stAceYStaceysTaCeyStaceyStaceyStaceyStACeySta-
ceyStaceyStaceyStACeyStaceystAceYStaceysTaCey-
StaceyStaceyStaceyStACeyStaceyStaceyStaceyStA-
CeyStaceystAceYStaceysTaCeyStaceyStaceyStacey-
StACeySTACEYstaceystyaceystaceyStaceyStACeyStacey-
stAceYStaceysTaCeyStaceyStaceyStaceyStACeySTACEYstaceysty-
aceystaceyStaceyStACeyStaceystAceYStaceysTaCeyStaceyStac-
eyStaceyStACeySTACEYstaceystyaceystaceyStaceyStACeyStacey-
stAceYStaceysTaCeyStaceyStaceyStaceyStACeySTACEYstaceysty-
aceystaceyStaceyStACeyStaceystAceYStaceysTaCeyStaceyStaceyStaceyStAC-
eySTACEYstaceystyaceystaceyStaceyStACeyStaceystAceYStaceysTaCeyStaceyS-
taceyStaceyStACeySTACEYstaceystyaceystaceyStaceyStACeyStaceystAceYStac-
eysTaCeyStaceyStaceyStaceyStACeySTACEYstaceystyaceystacey

"Here!"

I yell. It is absorbed by the music.

I stare at you, because you are here, and you are not dead and what the fuck is wrong with me. Fuck. *Fuck.*

You are holding a blue drink in your hand. Neon blue.

You slide into the booth quickly. "What happened? Did something happen? Did someone say something?"

My mouth flaps.

You uncurl my fingers, which are in a tight ball. You put them around the cold glass.

"Deep breath," you say into my ear, lips so close I feel their touch. Lip balm. Strawberry.

Step in my steps, through the paper thorns.

"Deep. Breath," you say again, and I close my eyes and force myself to inhale.

All there is is you. You tell me to breathe in, to breathe out. To hold my breath. You are so close to me—you are a protective wall.

"Now sip this." You lift the glass until my fingers take its weight, and I sip. Some dribbles over my lips and I am fucking useless and why am I like this and why do you have to see me like this?

I look at you, and you are the only thing in focus. A beacon in this black ocean. "It's sweet," I manage.

"Thought you might like an alcopop better. That's more for beginners. What do you think?"

I drink the whole thing down. "Better. Nice."

I take a few calming breaths and stare at you, watching your calm face, your calm smile—wishing, more than anything, I could be like you.

"I thought you'd gone," I mumble. You frown and put your ear to my mouth, and I repeat myself.

You take my hand and squeeze, your eyes burning. "I'm not done with you, Bethany Sloane."

And for some reason this is the best and worst thing you could have said to me, and my eyes well up. I squeeze your hand back and give you a quivering smile.

You study me for a moment and then seem to make a decision. Two fingers in your mouth and you whistle, loud and high, and motion over one of the guys who was talking to you. He grins and bends low to hear whatever you're saying, then winks and heads off.

"What did you do?" I ask, but the panic is less because at least you didn't leave me again.

Mr. Man returns with six alcopops. Two blues, three yellows, and one red. They look like liquid jewels under the pulsing lights. He puts them on the table, then leans over to say something more. I grit my teeth. Why did you call this bum over? I don't want his shitty alcopops.

But to my surprise, you say something caustic, and he leans away from you, frowning.

He says a word; it is lost in the tumult, but I know what it is anyway.

Bitch.

You smile, heavy lidded, like *Who gives a fuck* or *Yeah, I am, dipshit.*

You always were good at throwing people away.

He stalks off back to his mates, who are laughing, bent double and sweaty faced. He shoves past them and vanishes.

He's gone. He's really gone. And *you* sent him away.

We are alone.

"I'm going to take care of you," you tell me.

I don't know what time it is when we stumble into my apartment, but it doesn't matter. I'm buzzing and laughing, and you're right behind me. We collapse onto my sofa, and you help me put my feet up on the leg rest.

"I can't feel my face," I say, and you laugh.

"Jesus, you are a party virgin, aren't you?" You get up, but I don't want you to leave. "Where's your bathroom?"

I point. "Down the hall. Hurry up. I have to go too."

I wonder how long you'll stay. I wish I had something to drink so we could continue this night, but I know you'll probably have work or something in the morning. Wait. What day is it? Thursday? Friday?

By the time you get back my bladder is screaming, so I hobble to the bathroom as quickly as I can.

"Need your sticks?" you ask.

I wave a hand and lie. "Nah. Strong as an ox."

I stare at myself in the bathroom mirror for a long time. I am flustered, but intact. There are no cracks in my skin. My skin is . . . skin. Living, human, woman, flesh. Not a lick of glass in sight.

I brush my teeth and wash my face. The cold water clears my mind. When I go back to the living room, I'm half-terrified you'll have left without a word and half-terrified you'll still be here.

I don't know what to say to you. I have questions, but you never did like questions, and I wonder if that has changed?

You're here. On the sofa.

Looking at my phone.

You look up at me when I enter. "Bruce."

"Oh." I didn't expect that, and I'm not really sure why it bothers me. "Did he call?"

You hold up my phone so I can see the screen. Six missed calls. Eight new text messages.

"Bugger." I take the phone and sit down.

You look at me silently, and I can't bear it. I put the phone down in my lap.

"You should check the messages."

I nod. "I guess."

"Do it, then."

I open my phone and begin to read.

Hey, I just got done.

Can I call?

Bethany? Are you okay?

You must be sleeping.

Bethany?

Meds?

Bethany, getting worried.

Call me.

Jesus, Bethany.

Pick up.

What's going on?

I swallow. "I should . . . I should call him."

You are still looking at me, muddy eyes and ruddy face.

I rub my arm. "What?"

"Why does he treat you like you're a child?"

"I . . ."

"I mean, Jesus. How many messages did he send?"

I want to plug up my ears. You don't understand the dynamics of a marriage.

"He's just . . . he worries."

You raise an eyebrow. "My dad worries."

I laugh nervously. "He's away in Pretoria. On business. He just wants to make sure I'm okay."

You lean back into the sofa and curl your legs under you like a cat. "O-*kay*."

I shrug. "He loves me."

"We were out for *two hours*, Bethany."

"He's used to me being home, I guess."

You watch me, resting your cheek on your fist. You were always good at appraising me. I remember the feeling with sudden nostalgia, and my cheeks burn like they always did.

After a long, uncomfortable moment, you say, "What about these?" You're holding my bottle of pills in your hand, between slender thumb and forefinger. "I saw one of the messages come through. He checks whether you take your meds?"

"I get anxious."

"Pills for anxiety?"

"Yeah. He likes to make sure I take them. He doesn't want me to forget while he's away in case I have a panic attack. I used to get them pretty badly."

You look dubious, and I know I shouldn't let you get to me like this. "How long have you been on them?"

"Years. I can't remember when I started, exactly. Ten years?" *More.* "But they help."

You lean forward. "Bethany—"

My phone rings.

"It's Bruce. I have to get it." I turn away from you and press Answer. "Hey."

"Oh, God, you're okay," he says, breath leaving in a rush. "Bethany, where have you been?"

"I was asleep."

I hate lying, but I'm not ready to tell Bruce about Stacey. I'm not ready to share you yet. And . . . I'm not ready to share *him* either. I wonder who I'm protecting.

"You scared me."

"I'm sorry. I'm here now."

"Did you take your meds?"

"Not yet, but I will. I have them here." I turn back to you, and you're staring at me. "Listen, I'm still pretty tired and I haven't eaten. Chat tomorrow?"

"Okay. But don't forget your meds."

The heat rises to my face, and I turn away and mutter, "I won't."

"You'll take them?"

I feel your eyes boring into my back. "Yes."

"Okay. I love you."

"Love you too."

"Chat tomorrow. Bye."

I hang up and take a breath. My life consists of:

Me. Bruce. Denise. Forna.

And none of them in the same room. Ever. Except at the award ceremony, a one-off.

So speaking to Bruce while you are sitting on the sofa was weird, to say the least. I suddenly realize how isolated I've become, but I can't pinpoint the moment it happened.

I don't even speak to my mother anymore. I don't know when that happened either.

"He sounds . . ." You don't finish your sentence.

"Yeah," I say, turning back to you with a smile. "He's amazing."

You sigh, short and sharp, and then stand up.

"Listen, Bee, I don't know what you have between your husband and your job, but . . . I have to tell you, being on anxiety pills or whatever this is for over a decade is hard core. Have you ever tried to wean off them and see how you cope without them?"

"No, I . . ."

"Because I know about anxiety pills, and I've never heard of these."

"Well, you're not a doctor, are you?"

You might be, for all I know. I feel a surge of anxiety that I challenged you, quickly quelled. We are adults, for fuck's sake.

"No, I'm not. But, I mean . . . How do you feel in yourself, generally?"

"Can we talk about something else?"

You come over and take my hands. God, you're so gentle. So soft and warm and familiar.

I swallow. "I'm tired. My legs . . . I get tired. Sore. I sleep a lot."

You nod, and you never take your eyes away from mine. This feels like a confessional, and before I know it, I am telling you everything.

"I don't have friends. I write, sleep, eat. I don't know. Nothing else, really."

"How many hours a day do you write?"

"An hour. Two, maybe."

"Okay, add in three hours for your meals. Another eight or nine for sleep . . . that's fourteen hours. What do you do for the other ten hours in the day?"

"I . . . I'm not sure. Time just flies—you know how it is."

"Bethany." You squeeze my hands. "These pills . . . these are tranquilizers or something. They keep people calm. Make them sleepy. Make them . . . easy to control."

I pull away. "What are you saying?"

You love playing games. This is just another game. Another endless, looping, fucking game. I tell myself not to get roped in, but I can't stop listening, can't stop hanging on your words, your lips, your everything.

"I'm saying your husband sounds like a bit of a dickhead control freak."

"Don't!"

I turn away from you. I can't hear this. I won't.

I love my husband. I love him, and he loves me, and we're together. We will be together forever. Him and me versus the world. The way it's always been.

"Bethany, don't hide from this. I just want you to *think*. When was the last time you went out? When was the last time you had energy? The last time you felt happy, even? *Think!*"

"I can't." I shake my head. Grab my hair. "I can't."

"You have to."

You're behind me, and then your arms come around me. I shouldn't have had those alcopops . . . Was this the plan the whole time?

"Be strong. Just think and answer me. When was the last time you were happy?"

And I burst into tears. "I don't . . . I'm so confused."

"Ssh," you breathe. "I'm here. I'm not going anywhere. It's okay. It's okay."

We sink to the floor, and you hold me and I cry. You don't let go, not even for a moment, and when I fall asleep, I can still feel your arms around me.

You are gone when I wake, and unease churns in my stomach.

You know where I live now, I remind myself. Maybe you did before, if those devil's thorns on the stoop are anything to go by . . . but now you *really* do. No denying it. No avoiding it. No alcohol to lower those inhibitions. You know exactly where to find me.

An email from Forna beeps at me from my phone.

> The chapter you sent was corrupted. Can you re-send?

I resend the chapter and sit at my desk, pinching the skin of my fingers.

Your accusations ring in my ears. *Your husband sounds like a bit of a dickhead control freak.*

Am I being controlled?

Are you right?

. . . Why didn't you stay?

27

Detention

THEN

In maths class, I fiddle with a devil's thorn and ignore Gert Van Dyck. He calls me pube fringe in the hallways and kicks the legs of my chair over and over, but I am lost in memories, drowning in my seat.

I wonder what ugly, ginger, freckly Gert would look like naked. I wonder if his hands would hurt.

Beside me, Gert kicks my shin and laughs under his breath, which smells like onions and banana. I'll either vomit or slap him. I slip my hand under the table and punch, once. *There.* He gives a little squeal and falls off his chair, and I'm trying so hard not to laugh that I have to hold my breath to force the hysterics back down my throat. He is in too much pain to speak when asked what's wrong, and Matron is sent for.

He'll think twice before he kicks me again. Before he kicks another girl, too, I hope.

"Miss Sloane, care to venture a guess?"

My eyes snap open. I didn't realize that I had closed them. "Huh?"

I'm suddenly very dry and everything is very real and very sharp. I want to make things softer again, to tune up the blur on my vision.

Mr. Mollier's face darkens; his square jaw seems to harden. I can't help but notice how his eyes seem to scowl, and how he looks better when he's angry. "If you paid attention in my class, you might know what it is I asked you."

I blush. "Sorry, sir."

His eyes look me up and down. "Detention, Miss Sloane. Today after school you will come to my office for one hour."

I slump in my seat and mumble my agreement to be present, and then the lesson continues. If I had my way, Mr. Mollier would beg me to kiss him, beg me to let him do the things Sakkie did to me. He'd be powerless. I resolve to perform an experiment after school in detention with him. I resolve to attempt a seduction. A challenge like this quells the turmoil in my belly, and for a while I think I'm excited.

The bell rings, resonating in my fragile head like a choir of shattering glass, and I shut my book, having written not a single line. Lunch is chickpeas and spinach, green and puke beige. I eat some of it and then sit, waiting for the bell to explode in my head once more.

I sit through history class, science, and swimming before the final bell rings.

"Come on," Stacey says when I approach her. Her arms hang limply at her sides, and her eyelids are heavy, curtained with eyelashes like centipede legs. When she blinks, I expect to feel it ripple the air. She reminds me of one of John Carpenter's children of the damned. She looks as though her eyes could coerce anything out of anyone, light up like a laser and burn through the minds of men.

"I can't. Mr. Mollier gave me detention."

"Mr. Mollier hates you."

I am embarrassed by the idea of him hating me, but it only makes my challenge more interesting. If he hates me and I seduce him, the victory will be even sweeter. I can imagine his head hanging on the wall of my mind—my own little trophy. If I do it, I'll feel better. I know it. My ranking with Stacey will increase, too, even if she doesn't realize. And maybe, just maybe, he will force Sakkie out of me.

"Take this," Stacey says, holding out her detention pencils. She has glued four pencils together to make line writing go faster. She's a clever inventor. She makes things out of other things—she turns them into something better. I wonder if that's what she did with me. Took what I was and made me better.

"You think he'll just give me lines?" I ask, and I think I might surprise her and bring back the pencil shavings for her jar.

Stacey raises an eyebrow, unconvinced. "Sure."

"Thanks. He said I only had to stay for one hour."

"Come to the Tractor Tire when you've finished."

I nod, and then she leaves. I slip the line pencils into my schoolbag, and they sit quietly under the folds of my notebooks. I head for Mr. Mollier's office. Outside, I hitch up my skirt so that it is very short, and I check that I don't have any bruises on my knees or any grazes that will put him off. There is a scratch on my thigh, so I smooth it over with spit.

"Come," he calls when I knock. "Ah, Miss Sloane. Sit down."

I take a seat and cross my legs. Mr. Mollier hasn't looked at me yet, so I innocently unbutton the top three buttons of my school shirt and pull it open so that part of my new lavender silk bra can be seen. My heart thumps in my chest. Can I do this?

Inside something stirs, insatiable, dangerous, and I let it rise.

"I want you to write me an essay," he says, fishing in his desk drawers for some paper. "An essay on why mathematics is important for a girl to know."

I raise my eyebrows. "A girl?" I ask.

Mr. Mollier nods. "I want to know why mathematics is important for *you* to know."

I put down my pen immediately. "I can't write that essay."

"Why not?"

"Because I don't believe mathematics is important for me to know."

Mr. Mollier looks at me for the first time, leans against his desk, and crosses his arms. The challenge has begun. "And what is your rationale for that conclusion?"

"I think it's a waste of time. I don't intend to pursue a career that will involve maths in any way."

"I see. And what career is it that you have in mind? Because I can tell you, Bethany, that *all* career options need mathematics in some way."

"Mine doesn't."

"And how do you know what you'll want to become? You're only thirteen."

"Fourteen," I correct.

"Fourteen, then. You don't know what you'll grow to like or who you'll become."

"I know what I'm good at."

Mr. Mollier smiles despite himself. "So you've it all figured out, yes?"

I nod. "I think so."

Mr. Mollier looks at me for a long time, but he is looking at my face, not my chest, so I can tell I'm losing the challenge already. My heart misses a beat, and I swallow.

"What is this maths-less career path?" is his response.

"I'm going to be a high-class hooker."

I have struck Mr. Mollier dumb; his tongue is a tangle in his mouth.

He briefly makes as if to reply, realizes what I have said, and then snaps his mouth shut. He opens and closes it a few more times, his nostrils flare, and I patiently wait for him to respond. He's like a little fish out of water. He's like a new pet.

"If this is all a joke to you, Miss Sloane," he rebukes, "then I am *not* amused."

I frown. "I'm not joking."

What else am I good for? I have a special talent, don't I? Sakkie told me that once . . . or did I dream that?

"Bethany, I don't want you to *ever* utter those words in my presence again."

I ignore him, feeling bold. I *want* to put these ideas into his balding head. "And I don't think that I need mathematics for that, do I?"

Mr. Mollier sighs explosively and seems to become resigned. He rubs his eyes as if he is very tired. Then he brightens. "Don't you? Well, if you want to be a *high*-class"—sigh—"hooker, then you'll most certainly need mathematics."

"Why?"

"You'll need to know how to make a profit. You don't want to be poor. So you'll have to make daily calculations about the number of"—sigh—"*clients* that you need in order to maintain a profitable lifestyle. So, Miss Sloane, I'm afraid that"—long sigh—"hooking is one of *the* most mathematically involved professions in the world. Therefore, *completely* unsuitable as a career path."

I am surprised to realize that I have a newfound respect for Mr. Mollier. It has sprung up out of nowhere like a mirage in the desert.

I laugh, and I am startled that Mr. Mollier does too. "That's okay. I was only joking."

He chuckles again, shaking his head, and then he sighs once more. "Bethany . . . it isn't a good idea to talk like that, not at your age, and . . . not ever."

"Why?"

"People don't think that those kinds of jokes are funny. And the older you get, talking like that and joking like that, the more people will think badly of you and make all kinds of assumptions."

"Let them," I mutter. "I don't care."

"I know you feel invincible," he says, leaning forward. "Youth does that to you. But you're not. People's opinions of you will affect you in ways you can't yet comprehend."

"I don't care what people think," I repeat.

"Bethany, no one likes to be labeled a cheap girl."

"Maybe I *am* a cheap girl," I whisper, suddenly thinking that maybe I am, in actual fact, valueless. Maybe Sakkie used me and left me because I am worth nothing to him anymore. I feel what he did to me in my body, and my mouth fills with bile. I cough, trying to suppress stubborn tears that have decided to make an appearance.

Mr. Mollier sits in the chair next to me, and it creaks a little under his weight. "Now, come on. No child is cheap." He smiles. "It's impossible. God would never allow it."

"I'm not a child," I mutter.

"All teens think that," he says, amused. "God wouldn't allow any child—or young teen—to be cheap, okay?"

I swallow, my throat contracting, overcome with that same unnamed emotion I felt for days following the last night with Sakkie. I clap my hands over my mouth, afraid of looking ugly, afraid of crying. My challenge is going all wrong. I'm ruining it all by myself.

"I . . ." Talking is hard.

Mr. Mollier puts a patient hand on my shoulder. This is all wrong.

"I d-don't think God th-thinks about m-me at all," I splutter at length. What's wrong with me? Why am I talking to Mr. Mollier? I hate him; I *hate* him!

I am trying to convince myself.

"Of course he does. He thinks about all children. Children are the heart and soul of heaven."

I hold my breath until I stop crying, suffocating to prevent the option of tears.

Eventually I say, "I'm not."

"Now, Bethany," Mr. Mollier gently reprimands, "stop it."

"Don't you think I'm beautiful?"

"Bethany, stop it," he says.

I need something to replace the hole that Sakkie left in me, the deep aching chasm. Mr. Mollier walks to the other side of the room, rubbing his face. "Shit," he mutters.

I'm quiet for a long time, but inside me it's very loud. My mind is screaming, and it sounds like a crowd. What's wrong with me? Why doesn't he want me? Am I repulsive?

I risk a glance at Mr. Mollier. He rubs his stubbled face and stares out of the window.

"Don't you like me?" I hate how small my voice is.

He sighs, his head dropping. "I'm your teacher. I know it's normal at your age to have . . . crushes. But they should be for boys your own age, not silly old men like me."

The pain in my soul is unbearable.

"But I—"

"I think you've learned your lesson. I'm going to consider this detention fulfilled, okay?"

"I'm sorry," I whisper, unsure how to act now that I've crossed this line. "I'll . . . I'll pay more attention in class, sir."

His jaw clenches as he looks down at me, and he shakes his head, as though suddenly seeing what I really am. The tears well up again. I bite my lip and then walk out of the class without looking back. I can hear him slamming his desk drawers—the sounds echo after me down the hall, chasing me even when I sprint to get free of them.

I am a black hole. There is nothing but darkness inside me now. I doubt I am a child of God. I want to be, but I don't think God will have me. I walk in a sort of daze toward Joe's house, everything gone from my mind.

I knock on Joe's door, hoping he is in. I need something from him, but I don't know what. I knock on his door again. Joe opens, and a look of astonishment crosses his wrinkly Father Christmas features.

"Bethany?" he asks, peering closer.

I nod. "Hello, Joe."

"Are you all right?" he breathes, leaning closer. "You look like a wraith, *liefie*."

"Where's Sakkie?" I ask.

His face darkens. "He's gone away," he says in a clipped, closed voice. "You know that."

I hiccup a little sob. "Where did he go?" I ask again in a small voice.

Joe frowns, his shaggy eyebrows covering his eyes a little. "Come inside, child."

"Please Joe, just . . . just . . . can I have his address?"

"I don't think so, Bethany. He's not a . . . *suitable* friend."

"If I write him a letter, will you post it to him?"

He sighs deeply and rubs his weary face. He leans on his left leg and then shuffles to his right. He puts his hand on the doorframe and leans his head back, eyes closed.

I am desperate, forlorn. "*Please*, Joe," I whisper.

He looks at me again, closer this time. Maybe he sees how much I need this, or maybe he just knows that it's right. "All right. I'll pass along a letter if you want."

"Thank you," I gasp, giving him a spontaneous hug amid laughs and tears. "Thank you, Joe."

Writing the letter has been difficult. I have it all in my head, ready to be transcribed, but finding a chance to be alone to actually *do* that is almost impossible. Finally, I relent and write it during three English lessons and a maths lesson. Because I am a good English student, Mrs. Kilpatrick surely takes my secret scribbling to be note-making. During maths, Mr. Mollier lets me do whatever I want. He doesn't look at me. When I am finished, the letter is simple, but it contains all the love and hope I have.

I have twelve more minutes of maths before the school day will end, and because he said I'm not worthless, I use the time to pay attention to him. He is clean shaven, his shirt looks crisp, he is wearing a new tie . . . but he has dark rings under his eyes. Could I have done that? Am I infecting everyone with the black inside me now?

I wonder if I am like Henry Dertz, waiting to be summoned by someone who wants me, waiting to rise out of hell to consume them to feel whole, if only for a moment until they roll off me.

Where is Bethany Sloane?

The bell rings, and Mr. Mollier hurriedly leaves the class. I pay no attention, pack up my pencils in my Hello Kitty pencil case, zip up my bag, and head for Joe's.

"Finished it?" he asks when I approach him where he is working in the garden.

I nod. "Do you have an envelope?"

"Sure, *skattie*."

Joe produces a brown envelope of more than double the size needed for the letter, and then licks it and seals it with my letter safely tucked away inside.

"I'll send it tomorrow."

"Thank you, Joe. If he sends a reply . . ."

He sighs, and his shoulders slump. "Then I suppose I'll put it in your pigeonhole. But no more after that. I can't be responsible for it. Also . . . I wouldn't expect much. He's a busy man now, with his new job."

"Okay."

"Go and play," he mutters. "Enjoy your youth."

I calculate that a letter to Joburg should only take one or two days to deliver. So, if Joe posts it today, then I might get a reply as early as next week. I buzz with anticipation. If he writes the address on it, then I can keep corresponding until I am old enough to go to him and we can get married.

I spend the rest of the afternoon following Stacey as she collects clip-clap seeds in her skirt. I am not really with her today; I am drafting the second, third, fourth letters to Sakkie in my mind, writing them in the air, in an invisible secret language.

When Stacey looks at me, she sees I am obediently helping her collect. But in reality I'm soaring through the clouds, miles above the earth, singing songs of praise and hope, drunkenly bouncing around in the space my imagination has provided.

28

The Sleepover

NOW

"Marco . . . ?"

"Polo."

"Marco?"

"Polo."

"Maaaaarco . . ."

This is the best sleepover I've ever had. I feel like a kid again. You are a breath of life in this empty apartment, but I don't tell you that. No sentiment, just fun. No thinking, just sensation. We don't get dressed. We don't shower. We don't keep mealtimes. We eat whatever we want and watch movies during the day. This is how it should have been when we were kids; we're making up for lost time.

We are awake all night. Sometimes we drink and sometimes we don't, but we choose whatever we want, whenever we want. At 3:00 p.m., when I wake up, I find popcorn in my hair from our food fight last night, and I can't help laughing. I pull it free and pop it into my mouth.

I've never woken up laughing before.

Yet here I am, giggling like a girl, ecstatic over the fact that I know you'll be on the sofa when I get up. Knowing that, like every afternoon for the last week, you'll have breakfast waiting for me. What might it be today? So far, you've provided bacon sandwiches, chip butties, pancakes, peanut butter, and pizza.

I close my eyes and inhale the scent of you. It's everywhere. In the pillows, the duvet, the air.

I am in heaven.

I can't find words profound enough to describe how I feel about you taking time off work to stay with me.

You're in the kitchen, and we dance around each other, you frying banana and peanut butter sandwiches ("We are Elvis, baby"), while I grab a glass and reach for the orange juice.

"We'll have to go out soon, you know," I say. I don't like the idea, but there isn't much food left.

You spoon out peanut butter from the jar and pop it into your mouth, shrugging. *Who cares?*

We devour the sandwiches on the kitchen floor, under the table, because why not? You have to help me to my feet, and I spend the rest of the day in my ancient wheelchair, which is depressing, but then you make it a game, and we run up and down the hallway, speeding up until you release me and I go flying into a pile of pillows that you've stacked on the floor.

Where have you been all these years, you beautiful, cherished friend?

Late that night, we bring the pillows into the lounge and build a fort with blankets and the chairs from the kitchen. We hide inside and listen to the storm outside, talking in whispers over our torches while you rub cream on my legs.

"Did we ever do this when we were kids?" I whisper.

"I don't know."

"Did we eat peanut butter and banana fried sandwiches?"

"I don't know."

"What *do* you remember?"

"The heat. Now that you've reminded me."

"Yeah."

"It was so hot we couldn't sleep. I remember that now."

I close my eyes. "Shouldn't we . . . remember more? I've been thinking about what I do remember, and it's like I have pieces of a whole. There are these . . ."

"Black holes."

"Yes."

You don't say anything for a while, and then you pull a bottle of Bruce's whiskey from one of the folds of the blankets.

"Found this," you say, a sly grin sliding over your face. "Let's make some more black holes."

I laugh. "You want to make more?"

"Fuck the world!" you cry, holding up the bottle like a trophy.

"Fuck the world," I echo, laughing.

You lower the bottle. "Just you," you lean in, "and me."

"You and me."

The next thing I know

I am in the bathroom

and you are behind me

my pills are in my hand

and we are laaaaaaaughing

as I slowly

t

i

p

the pills into the toilet.

We roll around the floor

howling roaring screaming.

"Let's find our memories," you whisper. "Come back with me. To Africa."

29

Glassy, Glassy

THEN

Something has come over me. It began two long weeks ago, when Sakkie's letter didn't arrive. I checked my pigeonhole twice over, left for school, checked it when I returned. Nothing. No letter. No sign. Emptiness. I clenched my jaw and tried to forget about it, resolving to come back the following day.

The following day, nothing.

The day after, nothing.

Fourteen days, and still no word. Sakkie could have composed four letters by now, but still there is nothing.

I am flung, hourly, between deep sorrow and furious rage. I am at once a husk of insignificance and brimming over with emotions I could never categorize, let alone decipher.

Stacey and I speak less and less and are in each other's company more and more. We need no words. I have come to feel I am a hybrid of her. Perhaps I *am* her twin. Perhaps I am her clone. Perhaps she is my deity, and I am her priestess. Perhaps I am her, she is me, we are us. Perhaps I'm no more than one of the ideas that exist in the moments she has time to dream.

Two nights ago, I think Stacey sensed something was wrong. Matron has removed the padlocks from the doors now that my appointment with a doctor is looming. Stacey and I snuck out of the dorm after midnight and lay in the soft sand by the House, watching the stars twinkle above us. When a shooting star ignited the sky, I shut my eyes and made a wish, and when I turned to look at Stacey, she was doing the same. The next morning, we smiled over Bernie's head as she drew pictures in the sand and told us about how Gert spilled his milk at breakfast.

Yesterday, with one glance, I knew she wanted me to come with her, leaving Bernie struck dumb, staring after us.

Words have become superfluous.

Tonight is moonless. There have been no more trips outside, so I lie in bed, restless. I glance over at Stacey, where she lies sleeping in her ruby bedcovers. Her breathing is shallow but even. Her eyes are closed. The air is dry as sandpaper. I swallow often. I slide my hands under my pillow; they grow warm too quickly. Chena and Sal snore and nibble. I am alone in consciousness.

Drowsy with the exhaustion of insomnia, I lift the covers mechanically off me and walk out of the room into the ghostly corridor; grimacing moonbeams stain the linoleum floor. I am in a sort of daze, at the "emptiness" side of my emotional spectrum. I am the husk tonight.

I try to dig deep, to wake myself out of this zombielike trance, but the dancing moonbeams, the cold, the echoing silence, and the shadows all have me hypnotized. I feel no fear, only desire. The destructive desire to push the limit and see what happens.

In the bathroom, I stand in front of the mirror, staring at the eerie girl in the reflection, shadows behind her, demons writhing in secret spots, waiting for summoning.

I lean forward, my jaw slack. Without thinking, I stare into the dark eyes looking back at me and whisper, "Glassy, glassy, cut my arsey. Glassy, glassy, cut my arsey. Glassy . . . glassy . . . cut my . . ." I lean even closer, my mouth full of moisture, a maniacal smile on my lips. *"Arsey."*

With my final whisper, the room grows colder, more still, more empty. The shadows that linger intensify in their darkness.

I wait for Glass Man to appear behind me and slit my throat. I am sure that is how he will choose to do it. Will his fingers be made of glass, like his cold, dead eyes, the easier to slice open the artery pumping beneath the flesh? Maybe I'm not being creative enough. Maybe he will burst through the mirror and pull me back with him, into a hell full of tearing flesh and scalpel edges, where I'll cry out for eternity and no one will hear me, not even Stacey. Maybe I *will* cry tears of glass, weeping as they cut at my corneas, sobbing as the world slowly goes black.

The little hairs on the back of my neck stand on end, the way they do when someone is watching out of sight. I glance around, expectant, shivering as the cold intensifies.

I wait.

Nothing happens.

I sigh, a little disappointed. Perhaps Glass Man will use the legendary entrance we have all heard about. Maybe he will wait until my sixteenth birthday, when I am laughing and dancing, clapping and singing, blowing out the candles on my cake, opening presents, trying on pretty dresses. Maybe he will wait until then to get me, until I am beautiful and pure, halfway between the womanhood that will deform me and the childhood that cages me.

No, he'll wait until I am safe in my bed. Then, as the cool, calm night draws on, I might feel a breeze come through the window. I might feel a slow iciness trickle down my spine. I might sense something watching me in the mirror.

Then, suddenly, the room will explode, filled with a glassy tornado spinning backward, shards from every mirror and every window I've ever seen cutting into my flesh, tearing cheek from cheekbone and shredding eyes and hair. In the morning my mother might come into the room, entirely ordered, to a decapitated body lying mangled in her untouched bed.

Or maybe the only evidence of sharpness will be the slit wrists of her apparently suicidal daughter.

Maybe my blood will be missing, taken by Glass Man along with my soul, leaving nothing but a mound of bony flesh behind.

30

Persuasion

NOW

You've gone again and I'm alone. No Bruce. No Stacey. Just a whole lot of time with my own mind, and that can only be a bad thing. I have to get back to my life. Back to the real world. Back to writing Sally, and then . . . well, then I have to find another reason for living. On and on until I die.

Come back with me. To Africa.

What a stupid idea. I can barely walk most days, and I'm supposed to, what, just up and follow you back to South Africa on some hare-brained scheme to rediscover our childhood?

I scoff out loud and take another sip of my coffee. How could I even afford it? The advance for Sally's book is gone, and I put most of the royalties we get toward the mortgage. There are the savings, but Bruce and I have worked hard to amass a little nest egg in case . . . in case maybe . . . one day . . . we had a child. We haven't explicitly spoken about it, but I don't suppose it's ever been off the table either.

Suddenly I miss him. I wish he were here to hold me and tell me that everything is fine and safe and normal. I miss his smell and his big arms and his beard tickling my face when he kisses me. A secret part of me wants to shrug him away, though. To tell him to fuck off with all his love for me and pour a blue alcopop so I can have fun. To lose myself in the heavy bass of nightclub music. With you. Stacey.

I'm actually writing, for once, when I hear a tinkling sound from the bathroom. At first it doesn't register, but when it does, it's with the ice-cold, descending-into-a-yawning-darkness kind of fear.

I've heard that sound before.

I force myself to get up and grab one of my crutches. My legs feel like they might break like twigs if I work them too hard today.

Tink. Tink. Tink tink.

I swallow and hobble quietly to the en suite, *step, step-stick*, hesitating at the closed door. I don't hear anything . . . maybe I imagined it—

Tink. Tink. Tink tink.

I push open the door with agonizing slowness.

The

c

r

e

e

e

a

k

is unbearably loud.

The bathroom is empty. I sigh with relief, but the fear doesn't entirely leave, because I am staring at the mirror directly ahead of me, looking at myself (?), when it comes again.

Tink . . .

tink . . .

Like someone tapping on the glass. From the inside.

No. No, no, no.

I laugh. This isn't real. I laugh again, but in the mirror it looks more like a grimace. I hold my breath, waiting for the sound again. Waiting for something else.

Glassy, glassy, cut my—

The phone rings, shrill as a scream, and I *do* scream. Hurrying away from the mirror, feeling like something is chasing me, I close the bathroom door with a slam.

Can't get me. Can't get me.

"H-hello?"

"Bethany?"

"Bruce?"

"Yeah—what's wrong?"

I swallow a gulp of air and glance at the door. "Nothing, I just . . . I had to hurry to get to the phone."

"Are your legs okay?"

"A little sore today," I admit, diverting. "But nothing a little co-codamol won't fix."

"You sure? There's Oramorph if it's really bad. In the bathroom cabinet."

Behind the mirror.

"I'll be fine. Just need a little rest. I had lunch with Denise and I walked there."

"Why did you walk?"

"To test myself."

"How'd it go?"

"They want the book as soon as. Nothing new. I sent in the first chapter."

"You did? Bethany, that's brilliant! I knew you could do it. I knew you'd find Sally again."

Thank God he can't see my tight smile. "How's it going over there?"

"Busy. I'm hoping to be done in a week or two. I hate being away from you for this long."

"Me too. I miss you."

"You have no idea, baby. It's like I'm missing a limb. A vital one."

"Me too."

I should tell him about you. Tell him that you got in touch. I almost do, but something stops me. The memory of the look on your face when he phoned . . .

These are tranquilizers or something. He's controlling you.

"Look, Bruce, I have to go. I'm tired."

"Okay. You're taking your meds?"

"God, yes, Bruce. Yes!"

"Sorry?"

I sigh, short and sharp. "Do you have to ask me that every time you call? I'm thirty-two, not twelve."

Silence.

"I'm sorry, I'm just . . . the book is stressing me out. And you ask me every time. I'm taking them, okay?"

"I'm sorry, Bethany. Look, maybe this whole trip was a mistake. Maybe I should come home."

"No! For goodness' sake, I am capable of being alone for a few weeks."

"Are you sure?"

"Yes."

"I just love you. I worry about you. Your legs, and—"

"I'm fine. Would you trust me? Please?"

It's a while before he answers. "Yes. Yes, I trust you."

"I have to go."

"Yeah, me too. Talk later?"

"Okay."

"Love you."

"Bye."

I hang up. We both know he doesn't trust me.

He's controlling you.
Is he?

You tell me all the reasons this is a good idea. The best idea.

We can go back to the school.

We can explore the grounds.
See what it looks like now.

We can go to that memorial
for your doctor friend. It was in
Pretoria, wasn't it . . . ?

Do you remember the food?

Pap and wors? Chappies?

Guavas, monkey-gland sauce . . . ?

You have the money, from your books.
Have you traveled

anywhere

ever?

for you?

But it is what you say last, more than anything else, that convinces me:

. . . we can surprise Bruce.

31

Flying Ants

THEN

Stacey and I are alone on the green. I have tied back my hair, worried that I might become prey to an entanglement in my distraction.

I've felt distracted lately, without being able to explain why. Maybe it's because of my meeting with Dr. Morgan last week. He was a big man with dark hair and thick-framed glasses that made his eyes seem smaller than they were.

He asked me a bunch of stupid questions, like if I sleepwalk a lot and if I have nightmares. Then he asked me to make loads of fast choices: Would you rather be a sparrow or a fish? Would you rather live on the moon or underground? Black tiles or white? Do you ever talk to yourself? Do you talk to animals? Do they talk back? Do you often see things that are not there? Do you often feel afraid? Have you recently started menstruation?

He was done asking questions after that.

"It was nice to have met you, Beth," he said at the end, shaking my hand.

I froze when he used that name. "It's Bethany," I said tightly and then smiled as an afterthought.

Dr. Morgan chuckled, shook Principal Wolfe's and Mrs. Cottis's hands, too, and left. I was dismissed after that, but Sakkie's name for me rang in my ears, in both Dr. Morgan's voice and his.

It was nice to have met you, Beth.

Beth Sloane, my beautiful girl.

Ever since then, I've been lost in my mind. I was good for so many days. I didn't check the pigeonhole once. But this morning, something compelled me to (probably a tokoloshe demon), but it was empty. Nothing had been delivered. In abundance.

I can feel my controlled exterior starting to crack at every mention of the post, every time I check the pigeonhole and find it empty.

The flighty fog that is the swarm of flying ants calms me.

I had my doubts in the beginning. They were so big . . . not like any ants I had ever seen before. Their bodies were the same red of killer army ants, but their wings made them look even bigger. I remember the first time Stacey showed me what to do. I was nine. It was a warm evening; she stood in the center of the swarming insects, readying herself. Then, as quick as a bullet, she shot out her hand and grasped one wiggling ant between her fingers. Deftly, she plucked off the wings and popped the body into her mouth.

Had I been horrified? Fascinated? Both. The detail of the memory has faded, like I never did a proper backup. I plucked an ant, too, and ate it with some reservation and found, to my astonishment, that they tasted like peanut butter.

"What did Dr. Morgan smell like?" Stacey asks as we walk around the green, plucking ants and eating them.

I shrug. "Hmm . . . kind of like old cigarettes and car freshener."

"Was he old?"

I shrug. "I guess."

Stacey pulls a face I hope she never turns on me. "Truth or dare?"

"Dare."

"I dare you to smoke a cigarette."

I blink. "Huh?"

Stacey reaches into her top, where she has stored the butt of an old cigarette. The white part is about an inch in length and dirty looking.

"Where did you get that?" I whisper, wide eyed.

"On the school grounds. By the boys' side."

My head spins. "You went to the boys' side?"

It's forbidden . . . When did you go? Why didn't you tell me?

Stacey shrugs. "So? They're just boys."

The boys are as much of an enigma to us as the rarity of rain. I reach out for the cigarette, my hand shaking. Could this be . . . surely this might be . . . Sakkie's? None of the boys could get ciggys into school, surely? I try to remember if Joe smokes. No . . . I've never seen him smoke. I don't think the washerwomen smoke . . . I hope they don't. I convince myself they don't.

My hand shakes, the butt jumping up and down in my palm. Benson and Hedges Special Mild . . . his brand.

I am torn in three, between wanting to smoke it, pressing it to my lips where the phantom of *his* lips still sits; wanting to fling it as far away from me as I can; and wanting to keep it as an eternal memento.

"You need a lighter."

"Pass," I say, slipping the butt into my denim-skirt pocket.

She blinks. "What?"

"Pass. I don't like this dare. I take your default."

Stacey looks taken aback, and I feel impatient. "Baby," she says eventually, but I don't feel a barb from this. I wonder if I am becoming one of the untouchables. "Fine. Your default is to walk into the senior boys' shower room tonight and kiss the first boy you see on the lips."

I act appalled because I know it's expected and Stacey will love it. *"What?"*

Stacey smiles widely. "And I'll be watching to make sure you do it right."

"Right?"

She nods, snares an ant from the air, plucks and eats it. Then she leans forward. "Tongue," she says, grinning with delight, small pieces of the masticated ant still stuck in her teeth.

32

Marshmallow Light

NOW

The travel is a blur. You take care of everything, and I wish I had my pills. They keep me calm. *Kept* me calm. But you remind me that medication dulls my senses, keeps me trapped in a hazy half world, and you're right. Everything now is sharp and focused, and maybe I'm just not used to seeing the world like everyone else does. I've been dosed up for more than a decade.

But still. The shuddering of the plane, the talk of the passengers, the lights that flicker during turbulence . . . I close my eyes and breathe through my nose.

It's like you can read my mind, and you squeeze my hand the whole journey. Twelve and a half hours on the plane. Twelve and a half hours of constant contact. Eventually I fall asleep.

When I open my eyes, the light is different.

Orange light.

Yellow light.

White light.

I am back.

I am home.

Africa.

33

Truth or Dare

THEN

I come very close to telling Stacey that I won't go, that I *can't* take her default challenge. I am desperate to stay within the boxy confines of my bed. I cling to the edges of the mattress, my fingers straining against the sheets. Above me, where the ceiling ought to be, inky-black water pools. My mattress is an island in this inverted black sea. I can see it as clear as anything. I stare at it. It's real. If I let go, I'll fall upward into it. They'll never find my body; they'll never hear my screams.

I wonder if Glass Man has finally come for me.

"Come. Now," Stacey orders from the doorway, and I find that I have no will to disobey. After all, Stacey knows all the rules, so I should be safe. If she says come, then it must mean I can.

I slide out of bed, perspiration pooling in the dimple of my lower back, and slip on my school shoes. When I glance up at the space above my bed, the ceiling is white, empty, and firm, and I'm sure that I'm going crazy. It's surprisingly easy to admit, but I would feel better if I could write it down.

I'm going crazy. Black ink on white pages. Tangible. Instead I write it in the air.

Sal stirs in the bed beside me and then is still. How easy it is for the ~~ignorant~~ blameless to sleep. I gulp back my fear and follow Stacey along the corridor, trying to place my feet where hers have fallen first, but she has no shadow and leaves no mark so I can't be sure I won't drown.

"How do we get out?"

Stacey doesn't answer. She walks to the bathroom, to the back, where the old showers are. They are similar to the shower rooms in the boys' senior block, except the window is high up and the layout is inverted. Opposites. I have my doubts about whether we can get up high enough to reach the window, and . . . How will we get back inside?

Stacey drags the laundry bin over and then climbs on top of it. She unhooks the window and secures it as wide as it will go by placing it on the last latch. There is very little room.

"You go first," she says, climbing down. "I want to make sure you don't chicken out."

Does she think I would?

"Okay."

Once I have wriggled through the window, there is a steep drop on the other side. I land and scrape my knee on the hard earth. Was it a devil?

"Wait there," I whisper, and I run around the side of the buildings to where the wheelie bins are kept. I haul the lightest one over and put it in place so Stacey won't scrape her knee.

She follows, neatly hopping from laundry basket to window to bin to ground. I wish I could do it so gracefully.

I'm less nervous now that we are outside. The air is warm but dry, so I don't feel trapped, as I did in the dorm. I have a feeling that Stacey expects me to pass on the default. I wonder if she would be able to cut me off, call me chicken, and make my life hellish. I have no answer for this. It's almost worth doing it, just to see.

Do it, says the voice inside me. I know this voice—the truant, the rebel. I've named her Beth.

Beautiful Beth.

Beth wants me to ruin everything. She wants me to defy Stacey to see what will happen. I tell her to shut up, and follow Stacey closely.

We reach the boys' shower room, and there are still noises coming from inside, and the windows are all steamed up.

"How do I get in?" I whisper.

Stacey nods toward the sloping stairway, which goes underground like some of the houses in London. I shiver.

"Wish me luck," I say.

"Luck" is all she replies.

I take a breath and descend the steps one by one, coming closer to all those boys of powerful ages. I have a peculiar wish to knock first, but it is a stupid thought. For Stacey to be able to see, I must walk to the shower area on the left side, by the windows, and kiss a boy in there.

Do it, I tell myself. *Do it,* Beth mimics. Inside, she is at attention, ears pricked like a cat sensing its prey.

There is steam and hot, moist air everywhere; the warm particles pluck at my skin, clinging. I walk through the soggy atmosphere, my school shoes clipping on the hard tiles underfoot, and my eyes roam over everything. In the darker part of the room near the back I see a dark-haired boy watching me with a frown on his face. His closed regard hits me squarely in the chest, and I feel exposed. Why does he frown? Can Stacey see it? I tear my eyes away from him, because he's too beautiful to stare at, and I walk up to the boy closest to me, a boy with blond hair and big arms. He will have to do, since the frowning boy is far away, and if I were to choose him, Stacey would ask me why.

"What the—" someone says, noticing me.

The blond boy doesn't see me until I am right in front of him. In the corner of my eye, Stacey's head peeks in through the window, observant. It feels like I am performing for her. This idea is exciting.

I smile at the boy, lift my arms, and grab his face between my hands, and then both pull his face down and raise myself up until I have kissed his lips. He is shocked; I know it right away. Somewhere there are whistling sounds and laughter.

Remembering the challenge, I slip my tongue into his mouth and move it as I have learned to do. I press my body to him, wondering if I'm doing it right. It doesn't feel right. The front of my pale pajamas are soaked through.

"Whoa," the boy breathes when I am done.

"Goodbye," I mutter, and then I turn around and walk out, trying not to run.

An explosion of laughter behind me makes me turn back, and I can see the dark-haired boy watches me with a kind of fire in his eyes. I feel a sense of pride and a raw excitement, wondering what Stacey will think of all this.

When I get outside, she is sitting with her back to the window. Her face is white and closed off.

"Stacey?"

She doesn't respond.

"I did it. Did you see?"

I become alarmed, my excitement draining away, and with it, my strength.

I sit beside her, shivering a little in my wet pajamas.

"How?" she asks, more to herself.

"Huh?"

She whips her head in my direction. "*How* did you know how to do that? You've done it before."

I shake my head, but I don't verbally deny it.

She pinches my arm. "Tell the truth!"

I don't know what to do. If I tell the truth and say yes, will she be hurt that I never told her about it? Maybe. Would she even understand? If I lie and say no, will she suspect me of lying? Will she see the deceit behind my all-too-open eyes? Maybe.

I feel another brick fall, landing in the tiny space between us. Already I can sense the invisible wall that will divide us.

"He got a . . . a . . ." She can't say the word. Is she incapable of uttering it? No. It *can't* be. She's *Stacey*. It isn't possible that she's embarrassed. Maybe that word is a word that isn't allowed.

He got a boner, Beth sneers. *A huge fucking boner.*

"I know," I say, laughing and blushing.

Stacey glances down at my chest, and then her head snaps up and she scrambles away around the corner.

"Stac—"

"Hey!" It is the blond boy. He is wrapped in a towel, rushing over to me. "Hey, you!"

I don't want to give Stacey away, so I stand up to face him.

"Yes?"

"Who are you?"

"Bethany."

"Why did you . . . do that?"

I shrug. "Dunno," I mumble.

He looks uncomfortable. "How old are you?"

"Fourteen."

His damp hair keeps falling into his eyes, and he wipes it away with an unconsciously habitual brush of his hand.

"I'm Jared," he says with a nod. Goose pimples rise on his arms.

"You better get inside," I say, nodding to his arms. "It's getting colder."

"I can see that," he says, laughing.

I follow his gaze down to my pajamas, which are completely see-through with the water and clinging to me like a second skin. I gasp and fold my arms across my chest.

Jared laughs. "Sorry."

I shake my head; I contemplate telling him that the kiss was just a default, but I don't want to. I don't want him to ask what dare was so much harder than doing what I have just done.

"So, uh, you live on the girls' side, right?"

I nod. Duh.

"Okay," he mutters, a little awkwardly. "Well, I better get back."

"Okay."

He smiles. "See you 'round."

"Sure."

I watch him descend the stairway and reenter the bathroom. The howl of his friends and loud chatter follow his descent.

"Who was *that*?" I hear from one side.

"I like her," someone else calls, before the door swings shut and the sounds are no more than indistinct muffles.

I panic to think that I'm alone and rush around the corner. Stacey has waited for me.

"Will you see him again?" she asks.

"No."

"Why not?"

"I will if you want me to."

Stacey considers. "Maybe."

She walks around to the windows again and bends down. She is watching the boys inside, teasing, slapping wet towels against each other, laughing, punching, running.

I watch the expression on her face, which is stony as she looks at each of the boys in turn.

"HIm," she says, pointing to the boy with dark hair; he is ignoring all the fun, showering at the other end of the room. He isn't laughing. The same boy I saw first but didn't kiss.

I tense. "What about him?"

"Next time we come, bring Jared and *him* outside with you."

"Next time?"

"Tomorrow. Make sure no one else comes."

Maybe this will be something I can teach Stacey. I can sense there is a danger in us messing with older boys in this way, but something inside of me yearns for it, for the promise of a kind of destruction. Part of me hopes that there *is* danger in it.

34

Jared

"So you want me to just . . . bring them out?" I whisper.

"Yes."

I swallow, glancing at the building. "I don't know . . . How do I know that no one else will come out?"

"Just do it," Stacey insists, and her voice sounds impatient. "Get on with it. I *dare* you."

A dare, like a commandment, must not be disobeyed. Especially when it's Stacey's dare. I rub my arms, trying to get the blood flowing into them again.

With two quick deep breaths, I walk down the stairs and enter the shower room as carefully and quietly as I can. The room seems deserted, like a ghost ship. The lights are all off except for the ones in the corridor beyond the main doors.

"Hello?" I whisper. There is no response.

I am very aware of Stacey waiting for me outside, peeking at me through the window, watching my progress. Maybe she expects me to wander out into their dorm . . .

I call out again, hoping further venturing won't be necessary, and something moves at the dark end of the room. My mind fills with visions of serial killers and paranormal ghosts waiting to devour a girl like me; visions, too, of Glass Man. Do I see tendrils of shadowy smoke looming up at the back, in the rusty showers no one uses?

"Who's there?" a deep voice asks, breaking my train of paranoid thought.

"Um, Bethany . . . I'm looking for Jared."

The tall boy with dark hair steps out from the shadows with a towel around his waist. He frowns, and droplets of water fall from his damp hair onto his shoulders. My heart thumps painfully in my chest.

I feel dizzy. "Oh! It's you."

He pulls a hand towel from the rack to his left and uses it to dry his hair. "You're that girl who kissed Jared yesterday?"

I nod, throat tight, and feel myself blushing all over. "Um, yes."

"Why did you do it?"

Something about this boy makes me want to defend myself. "It was a dare. Well . . . it was a default."

"What dare did you pass on?"

"My friend wanted me to smoke a cigarette butt she found."

He pulls a face. "That's gross."

"Oh, no, she's great." *Please don't hate Stacey.* "It's just that I didn't want to smoke it . . ." I'm making such a mess of explaining that I just shut up. I put my thumb in my mouth and bite the nail; then, remembering that Stacey is watching, I pull it out and fold my arms behind my back. Stacey hates it when I bite, pick, scratch, rub, lick—or any other movement on or near—myself.

"So, you want me to call Jared for you?"

I breathe a sigh of relief. "Yes, please. But also . . . um, well, would you mind coming outside with me after you've brought Jared?"

He frowns again. "Why?"

What am I supposed to say? "Would you just come? Please?"

He looks uncomfortable, and I wonder if I should have said something different, but I don't know how to improvise. Stacey is the one with all the answers, all the moves.

"Okay," he says at length. "Sure."

He disappears out of the shower room, and I skip over to the window. Stacey is looking through, as I knew she would be. I give her the thumbs-up.

When the boy returns, he has a confused-looking Jared in tow. Both of them are dressed.

"*Bethany?*" he asks, incredulity written all over his face. He looks as if he's just been woken from a long sleep. There are pillow creases on the side of his face and crusty sand in the corners of his eyes.

"Hi," I say in a small voice, not at all sure what I am doing now that my audience is bigger.

"What's going on?" He turns to the other boy. "Rowan?"

The boy, Rowan, looks at him and shrugs, then faces me once more. I realize they're waiting for me to explain myself.

"Oh, right, um . . . Would you mind coming outside for a moment?"

Jared doesn't seem to mind, but Rowan frowns and lingers back while I lead the way out. I hold my breath, hoping he will follow. Only when I am outside and I turn to see that he is with us do I feel my stomach muscles relax and my lungs inflate again.

Stacey is standing silently a little distance off, in the darkness. I walk up to her, hoping she will now take control, but she makes no move to.

"Um, Jared and Rowan, this is Stacey. Stacey, Jared and Rowan."

Stacey ignores Jared but smiles sweetly at Rowan. "Hello, Rowan."

"Uh, hi." Rowan turns back to me. "Bethany, what's going on?"

"Well . . . my friend wanted to meet you," I say.

Something clicks in his brain. "Oh," he says slowly, eyes darting from Stacey to me and back again.

"Do you have a curfew?" I ask.

"No."

"You want to walk a bit?"

Jared perks up as Rowan is about to answer. "*Sure*," he interrupts, elbowing Rowan in the ribs. "I'd love to." He walks over to me, in front of Rowan, and takes my hand. "I know this great place . . ."

"No," Stacey cuts in sharply. "We stay together. All four of us or no deal."

Jared turns imploring eyes on Rowan, who rolls his eyes.

"Fine." Jared sighs and crosses his arms.

I glance back at Stacey to make sure she's okay. She's walking next to Rowan with her usual unreadable expression. A foot of cold air hangs between them.

We go to the Tractor Tire, climb up and sit on it, eight legs dangling into the center. Stacey's silence unnerves me, and I struggle to keep up with Jared's continuous chatter.

". . . hardly ever see a girl, so the fact that one walks right up to me and, you know, *fucking kisses me*, in front of all the guys was, well, a once-in-a-lifetime event, you know? You're the bravest girl I've ever met—who would have thought of just walking up to someone and doing that, totally at random?"

I laugh, flushing a little as Rowan smirks. "Stacey does way cooler stuff than that," I offer.

Stacey's face remains impassive. I realize with a sinking heart that she has no intention of letting me draw her out, so I decide to simply enjoy Jared's company. I can feel Rowan's eyes on my face at all times.

When Jared leans in to kiss me, I lean away.

Stacey's voice is hard enough to slap. "What's your problem?"

I glance at her. "Huh?"

"You've already kissed the guy." She glances at Jared with a smile. "Refusing him now is just plain cold."

I flush. "Oh, I . . ."

Rowan clears his throat. "So, uh, Stacey. How long have you been here?"

She smiles up at him and is drawn into a private conversation.

Jared nudges me. "So how about it? You going to be cold?"

I bite my lip. "I guess not."

He leans closer. "You wanna go somewhere?" He whispers it in my ear.

"You heard Stacey. All four or none at all. That's the deal. It's not going to change."

"You're not . . . a regular girl," he says. "Are you?"

I think, *I'm less,* but I don't say it out loud. I glance at Stacey and see that she and Rowan are completely immersed in their quiet conversation now. I think they're talking about Jared and me, but at least they're talking. He says something, and Stacey laughs, which transforms her face. A jealousy, the potency of which I've never known, erupts within me twofold, searing my throat and filling it with bile.

Rowan is warming to Stacey. But worse: Stacey is warming to Rowan. She is *laughing* at something *he* is saying. I suddenly realize that he is competition. He is a threat to my relationship with *my* Stacey, and I don't know what to do.

Jared leans in again, and I let him kiss me. It feels less wrong, knowing he is only two years older than me—so different from Sakkie—but still, I don't feel the pleasure you're supposed to feel when someone kisses you. It's actually sort of gross. I pull a face when my lips are finally released.

Both Stacey and Rowan are now looking at Jared and me. Then, at identical moments, they burst out laughing.

My face blazes hot. "What?"

They keep laughing, spurred on now by their mutual laughter.

"*What?*" I demand.

The laughter dies away into smiles, and then Rowan leans over and kisses Stacey on the lips. She looks startled for a moment, and then her eyelids drop, and she leans into him.

"Hell yes," Jared cheers, grabbing my face hard enough to bruise and kissing me hard.

He is a sloppy kisser, and there is saliva all over my chin and parts of my cheeks. I feel like I am drinking his spit, and it is gross.

I pull away from him and hold him back with the flat of my hand. "Didn't anyone ever teach you how to kiss?"

His cheeks burn a beetroot that is as patchy as I suspect his beard will be. "What?"

"Saliva control," I mutter and wipe my mouth dry. "I don't need to be digested, you know."

He blushes. I can see it even in the darkness. Rowan and Stacey have stopped kissing and are watching me. I laugh tensely and cuddle up to Jared. They go back to kissing.

What is wrong with me?

I watch Stacey move her mouth in a way that is obviously unfamiliar to her, something I reluctantly admit to myself, and seeing Rowan enjoy it angers me; I'm miserable, lonely, and utterly captivated by the sight. This just annoys me more.

I kiss Jared again, and he seems to forget my insult, though his tongue moves less enthusiastically. I stroke his thigh, shielding what I am doing from Stacey and Rowan with my body.

He groans, and I softly whisper "Ssh" in his ear. From the corner of my eye, I can see that Rowan has noticed this, and it spurs me on. I turn toward them.

"Who's brave enough to play truth or dare in the middle of the night, right here, right now?"

Stacey's eyes sparkle at the idea. This is a new challenge and no longer boring.

"I am," she says, breathless.

"Why not?" Jared adds.

"Uh, okay," says Rowan.

"You first, Bethany," Stacey says. She is curious to see what I have come up with.

I turn to Jared. "Truth or dare?"

"Truth to start," he says.

"What's the furthest you've gone with a girl?"

I think I see him blush, but in the near blackness it is hard to tell. At any rate, he looks uncomfortable.

"How do you mean?"

I roll my eyes. "You know what I mean. What base?"

"Home base," he says, a little too confidently and a little too quickly.

"Bullshit." Rowan laughs. "You can't lie."

"Shut it!" Jared hisses, shoving Rowan hard in the ribs.

Rowan laughs and coughs.

"Fine, *third*," he admits, sitting back and folding his arms.

"Tell us," I insist, "the details."

"No way, José." He laughs. "*My* turn."

I expect him to ask me the same question, but he turns to Rowan. "Truth or dare?"

I have no doubt that Rowan anticipates the same question. "Dare."

Jared looks annoyed to have been outsmarted. "*Fine*, then I *dare* you to go to third base with Stacey."

I make some kind of strangled sound and throw my hands over my mouth. I glance at Stacey, who is pale, trying to get a reading from her. Is she nervous? Angry? Intrigued? Her mask is impenetrable.

"You can't dare me to do something that another person won't allow," Rowan points out.

I glance at Stacey but don't get any sign from her.

"That's true," I add quickly. "You'll have to ask another."

Jared growls. "Fine, then I dare you to *tell* me what base *you've* been to *and* to give us the *whole* story."

Rowan laughs. "What a child you are, Jared. Fine. I've been to third base too. It was last summer when I went home. My sister brought her best friend over. Her best friend liked me, then one day we just . . . experimented."

I am captivated by the story. "Who on who?" I ask, grinning.

I catch sight of Stacey's closed face, and my smile fades.

Rowan chuckles. "I suppose details *were* part of the dare. Me on her."

I blush at the thought, warmth spreading over me like a cloak, shielding me. I blink as the warm feeling fades, leaving a surprising pool of sadness in its wake.

"Oh," I choke, smiling faintly. I wrap my arms around my chest and try to pull myself together.

"My turn." He glances at Stacey. "Truth or dare?"

"Dare," she says. I want to think she is brave, but a treacherous part of me thinks she is avoiding truth.

"I dare you to come and see me again one day."

She blinks. "Is that all?"

"Sure."

She smiles. "Okay. I accept."

He leans forward and kisses her, and Jared uses the opportunity to squeeze my butt. I'm not amused. I'm scared. There was a tenderness between Rowan and Stacey that alarmed me.

"Okay, Bethany, truth or dare?" Stacey asks me.

I don't know what to do. If I pick dare, what will my task be? Will she ask me to smoke Sakkie's cigarette? And if I pick truth . . . Will she ask the base question? Suddenly I have something of vital importance to protect: my secret.

I take a deep breath. "Dare."

I choose it because I can't face her knowing that I have been opened up and emptied out like a discarded can.

"I dare you to let Jared go to second base with you."

Jared howls, but Rowan isn't laughing. Neither am I.

"I . . . okay." I force myself to laugh like it means nothing.

I face Jared, who is warming his hands by rubbing them together.

"You have to sit there without moving, no matter what he does, for thirty seconds," Stacey adds.

Jared looks like a kid on Christmas morning, eyes wide, stupid grin plastered to his face, cheeks flushed. He is staring at me as though he doesn't know where he will start, or to ensure he gets to do everything he wants, eager little eyes flicking all over me in a similar way to how Sakkie's eyes used to.

"Okay." I glance at Rowan, whose mouth is a thin, taut line and whose eyes bore into Jared's.

Stacey positions me so I am lying flat on my back along the tire, legs slightly apart, dangling astride the tire from the knee down. Every time she moves my limbs, I imagine I am a big porcelain doll that belongs to her. She looks at her watch, presses the button on the side a few times—*beep beep beep*—then she says, "Go!" and Jared is feeling.

He runs his hands all over my breasts and stomach in a haphazard way. I can tell he has not done much of this before, even if he *has* gone to third base (which I think is also a lie). He gets more and more confident as the seconds tick away, hands turning rough.

Stop, stop, stop, I think. But the seconds just refuse to speed up. I bite down on both of my lips and scrunch up my eyes. Eventually, Jared reaches lower, caught up in the momentum, slipping his hand beneath my underwear.

"Time's up," Stacey says at last, and I breathe a sigh of relief, glad that Jared didn't get as far as he'd have liked.

Rowan's jaw is clenched, and his eyes are shadowed.

I think I'm going to be sick.

I make to sit up, but Jared suddenly jerks his fingers painfully forward, making me cry out.

"Jared!" Rowan yells, mistaking my cry of humiliating pleasure for one of pain. He leaps at Jared, knocking him backward off the tire. They hit the ground, wrestling.

"Rowan!" Stacey yells.

I'm too shocked to shout anyone's name. "Stacey," I whimper.

She wraps her arms around me. "It's okay."

Jared and Rowan are laughing by the end, though Jared has a bloody lip, swelling fast, and Rowan looks tense.

"I'm sorry, Bethany," Jared says.

Rowan shakes his head. I don't think either Stacey or Rowan know precisely what Jared did to me.

As we walk back, Stacey and Rowan far ahead of us, Jared murmurs in my ear, "You've had a home run."

I don't deny it. I don't think he's worth lying to. I can feel his fingers on me; I want more, and I hate it. I stop and face him, my back to the retreating Stacey and Rowan, and I kiss him. I run my hands all over him, lower, lower.

Yes, Beth breathes, her voice brittle as glass. *Yes.*

"Virgin," I whisper in his ear, and he blushes, heat pulsing from his cheeks and neck.

"Bethany, come on!" Stacey calls from the distance.

I remove my hands and skip to catch up, leaving Jared alone in the darkness to try to cool down. I want to step outside of myself—force myself to just *stop* this game before it gets out of hand. The two halves of me are at war, and Beth won't let me stop.

At the doorway to the shower room, Stacey and Rowan kiss, tenderly. Jared and I kiss, too, me almost drowning and my lips sore.

"It was nice meeting you," Rowan murmurs at Stacey, and my heart contracts, and tears prick my eyes.

"You too," she says.

"Later." Jared grins at me.

"Yeah, bye."

We walk without talking for a long time. Finally, Stacey murmurs, "We'll come back tomorrow."

I nod. I can sense this might be a new routine, but I wish it wasn't. I'm afraid of Jared—not because of him, but because of myself. I'm afraid of the part of me that liked what he did to me, in front of everyone. The part of me that wouldn't stop him if he grew too bold . . . the part that wants to punish me. The part that is Beth.

"Maybe I'll let Jared show you what he wanted to tonight," Stacey says thoughtfully.

"What do you mean?" I say, my chest tight with sudden anxiety.

"Well, didn't he want to go off with you? Maybe I'll let him."

"Alone?" I whisper. I feel abandoned. Surely she knows what will happen if she lets him take me off by myself?

"Sure, why not?"

I bite down on my tongue and ignore the tears threatening to leap out of my eyes. What's wrong with me? What is this ache inside my heart? In my mind, Beth taunts me with visions of Jared doing lurid things to me while she laughs and I cringe, battling both of them. But she doesn't know what is really bothering me.

I hate the idea of a new rival for Stacey's affections, but more than that—and even worse *because* it is more than that—I want Rowan's attentions for *myself.* Those dark eyes . . . and that frown between his brows when he saw Jared watching me, the way he defended me when Jared touched me . . . he captured my attention from the moment I first laid eyes on him. I think he must be the most beautiful boy I have ever seen. I swallow the lump in my throat and ignore the beat of my heart all over my body.

God forgive me.

Stacey forgive me.

35

Dangerous Waters

NOW

The hotel we check into is more of a motel. A single-story row of rooms in a long line that reminds me of classrooms. The neon light advertising vacancies hums persistently, and I can't wait until we're inside.

It takes an eternity for you to unlock the door, step inside, push me in (you were right: the wheelchair *was* a good idea), and shut it behind us. You close the curtains against the morning light, and I have an impulse to beg you to open them. I force myself to say nothing at all.

You put our luggage (one shared bag) down on the double bed on the side nearest the bathroom.

"You," you say, indicating that this side should be mine.

I get painfully to my feet and hobble to the bed, collapsing onto a springy but soft mattress. I groan. Not because the mattress is anything to write home about, but because I am bone weary in a way I can scarcely remember having ever been.

You open our luggage and begin to unpack, but my eyes are drooping, and with each blink you get fuzzier and fuzzier and fuzz . . .

◆ ◆ ◆

It's dark when I wake.

You are beside me. Facing away.

What are you thinking?

I am wearing my pajamas. You put me in my pajamas.

I reach across the small space between us and touch your curly hair.

Stacey . . .

You roll over to face me, and I feel a surge of terror. And then

your lips

are

on

mine.

36

Fortnight

THEN

We watch *Beauty and the Beast*, which has been my favorite since I was three. I lose myself in the film, even though there is something different about it tonight, something deeper. Something I have never seen before. How could Beauty love the Beast? The answer is so simple: the Beast was good. Goodness prevails over everything . . . goodness deserves love, no matter what goodness looks like. I don't know what goodness *actually* is. Mr. Mollier says all children are good, and all children are God's creation. Does that mean when I am grown, I won't matter to God? How do I know I matter now? Does he forgive the fornicators? Does he forgive those who fuck older men and lust after boys whom Stacey likes?

I cry as hard as Belle when Beast dies at the end, and the girls in the front keep turning to look at me because I'm being so loud. I don't care, though. There is a key here I have to get for myself. Some knowable truth Disney is trying to tell me, teach me. It's a clue about the nature of goodness and the nature of the Beast. Belle, in all her goodness and faith, drew the goodness and love out of Beast, who had been secluded and bitter for years. She had been a beacon of beauty because of her kindness, her innocence, her steadfast goodness. Her beast wasn't like mine—the one within. Her beast was the one who died and, from a single tear and the words "I love you," came back to her a clean and shiny man who married her and never abused her or pulled out her hair.

Inside, Beth laughs at me.

I want to tell her to shut up and leave me be, but my heart is too swollen and bruised, my mouth is too full of anguish and spit, and my mind is too cluttered with questions: "Am I . . . ?" "Is it . . . ?" "When will . . . ?"

Besides, Beth likes the hurting. She's in love with the beast.

My mother telephoned the school to say that she wanted a cabin for *two* whole weeks. This means I will be going to school like usual, but instead of sleeping in the dorm, I will go to the cabin. With her. She hasn't come to visit so soon after a previous visit since I can remember, and she has *never* stayed for two whole weeks. I wish I hadn't ignored her. If I had just apologized and spoken to her on the phone once, maybe twice, then none of this would be necessary.

Stacey helps me pack a bag for the fortnight away. Her plans for this evening have been thwarted, but I can't tell if she's upset or not. She folds and packs, she glances at me, and she folds again.

Tearfully I stick what she's folded into the bag, feeling like this parting from her might kill me. "I don't want to go," I say. "Maybe I can just hide in here."

She looks at me, blinking long and hard. "I don't think that will work."

I sigh. "Why does she want to see me *again*? And for so long!"

Stacey shrugs. "Maybe she misses you."

"I don't care. I don't miss her."

She throws down the shirt she has been folding, and the buttons slap against my case. "Bethany, just be glad you *have* a mom, okay?"

This silences me. She's right, of course. But I secretly think she's lucky that her mother is dead. If *my* mother were dead, then Stacey and I would be the same. And if both of our fathers were dead, too, then we would be like the Lost Boys in *Peter Pan*. We would be able to go to Neverland forever and never have to grow up. We would be free to have banquets of invisible food and fly with invisible fairy dust to our invisible house under the big tree.

We would always be precious to God because we'd never grow old.

"Ready?" Stacey asks when I have zipped up my bag.

I nod. "Yes."

But no. No, I'm not. I want to tell Stacey that it will be a long two weeks without her. We share no classes and don't sit at the same lunch table—besides, Mum will want me back at the cabin during lunch and after school. I want to ask Stacey to come with me. I want to tell her I hope Bernie gets a disease and is stuck inside for a fortnight. I smile at the last part, and Stacey thinks I am smiling at her.

"That's better," she says.

"Well . . . goodbye."

"Goodbye, twin."

Matron Chivon knocks on the door. She is a slim lady with not enough skin for her whole body, so her face looks especially stretched. It looks thin, too, like crispy roasted chicken, blue veins clearly visible beneath. I wonder what she would taste like.

"Come along, Bethany," she says as warmly as her icy voice will allow.

Matron escorts me right to the foot of the cabin door, as though she thinks I am a flight risk. My mother invites her in, but she gently declines.

"Thank you, but I must get back to the girls."

An impression of care. Aside from morning checks and after-school shoe-polish time, the matrons don't mind what we do.

Once Matron is gone and I am inside, my mother gathers me up into a suffocating embrace.

"Oh, darling," she says. "I missed you so much!"

I choke on the scent of sweet peach. Has she forgotten our last encounter? Well, I haven't and I'm still angry.

I glance around the room once she releases me. It's empty, and with a surge of affection I think maybe she left her crinkly husband at home and she's here *just* for me. "Is Stoffel here?"

"Of course, dear. He's in the back."

"Oh."

"You must be famished. Would you like some KFC? I brought it specially for you."

"We ate already."

"Oh. Well, never mind. We'll put it in the fridge and save it for later. Come on into the living room. We're watching TV."

I dump my bag in the little hall and follow my mother into the lounge, where Stoffel is reclining. He smells like mothballs and anesthetic.

"Stoffel, dear, Bethany is here. Say hello, Bethany."

"Hello."

Stoffel rotates his head in my direction. In my mind I can hear the creaking *tch-tch-tch-tch-tch* sounds as it swivels, the sound of a worn-out body in motion. I almost expect him to keel over right in front of me. Would anyone notice if he just died in his chair?

"Bethany," he croaks, nodding, though he says it like "*Bethhhh*-any."

We watch television for two torturous hours before I beg fatigue and escape into my room. I lock it from the inside. My mother and Stoffel rustle about for a little while, and then their bedroom door closes.

I glance out the window. It is a clear night, but there is no moon so it's too dark to see very far. I wonder if Stacey will be out, and if she will, where she'll go. Immediately I realize she would go to the senior boys' shower room to see Rowan. Maybe she expects me to be there too. Why wouldn't she assume I would come out to meet her? She'd know she could rely on me.

I slide my legs out of the bed and stuff my pillows under the duvet in a near-enough likeness of my body. Then, as quietly as I can, I slide up the window and slip out like a leaf on the wind. I grab a twig and then close the window on it to ensure I'll be able to get back inside later.

My heart soars as I run across the grounds. I am absolutely certain this is what Stacey intended. She'd have assumed I knew her plan, known I could be trusted to follow it. She is so clever.

The boys' shower room is brightly lit; it is like a beacon in the distant darkness. I skip toward it, my heart soaring.

"*Under the bumble bushes,*" I sing, "*down by the tree—boom, boom, boom—true love for you, my darling, true love for me!*"

This freedom I have managed to secure for myself is beyond perfect, and more than I expected. It is sweeter for being short.

"We're getting married, in California, with sixteen children, all in a row, row, row your boat, gently down the stream! Tip your teacher overboard and listen to her scream, ah!"

I reach the boys' block in good time. There's no one in sight. I circle the building, but Stacey is not there. I kneel by the shower-room windows and peek inside. There are five boys showering and three more wrapped in towels. In the back, where the light is very dim, I spot Rowan. Jared is nowhere to be seen. It's stupid how late they shower, how they seem to have all this freedom that we girls don't. Maybe it's because they're older in this block.

I slide down the wall until I am sitting with my back pressed against it. Where is Stacey? Surely she knew to come here? Maybe I should have gone to Joe's? But no . . . she would have come to meet me here, so she could kiss Rowan and I could kiss Jared. She was going to let Jared take me off alone, wasn't she? Wasn't that the plan?

It suddenly occurs to me that maybe Stacey never intended to come. Maybe I just *thought* she would. Maybe I was supposed to stay away too. This terrible idea makes me feel exposed on all sides, and I press myself closer to the bricks behind me, hoping they can ground me a little and push away the rising panic inside. I am suddenly afraid to walk back to my cabin alone, because surely now that I know Stacey is safe in her room, the ghosts know it, too, and they'll try to approach me. I glance up at the empty sky. No moon. No ghosts. Still, I am not ready to go.

I peek back into the window, astonished to find Rowan staring me in the eyes. He is looking through the window *at me*. He is naked—*entirely* naked. He doesn't flinch or move away, and I am warm all over, like I was the first time I saw him.

I watch him turn around and switch off the shower, then grab his towel and walk to the changing area. He faces away and dries off, then gets dressed slowly. The other boys vanish from the room one by one. Rowan is waiting for them to go. When the last one leaves, he asks Rowan something. Rowan says something short and clipped; then the other boy shrugs and leaves, switching off the light.

Maybe Rowan is going to get Jared for me, I think.

But he doesn't. He comes outside alone, hair still wet.

"Bethany?" he calls when he can't find me. I have pressed myself low against the wall, hoping I can become invisible.

Hearing his voice puts me at ease, and my heart stops hammering in my throat. I step away from the wall, wanting to clutch at him for security and warmth.

"Hello."

He laughs. "Were you hiding?"

"Sort of," I say, smiling as I scratch my arm. "I didn't mean to spy."

He glances around. "Where's Stacey?"

"Oh, she didn't come." The disappointment in my voice must be obvious.

"Why not?"

"I'm staying with my mother in the visitors' cabins for two weeks. Stacey's in the dorm . . . we didn't have any plans to come out. I just . . . needed some air. I came alone."

"Your parents suffocate you?"

"A little," I admit. "Though I feel bad about it, because my mother only got here this evening—"

Rowan bursts out laughing. "Man, you're worse than I am. I can't stand my dad's visits either. They just seem to stay a little too long, you know?"

"I know." I laugh. "I don't get it."

"Dad sends me here and then complains that I never want to see him. Is he kidding me?"

"Same," I say with a sincere chuckle. "My mother wants to talk 'girlie' to me about boys and blah blah, and all I keep thinking is—too late, Mother."

He chuckles once and then frowns. "You, er . . . you want me to get Jared?"

"No—" I say quickly, then stop myself. "No, thanks."

I rub my arms, feeling a little cold, even though the night is warm.

"You want to walk a bit? You look chilled."

"Sure," I say, and we walk in the direction of the vast open grounds. The night is dry and warm, and the empty campus feels familiar and freeing. It's good to be in Rowan's company. Good to be where I don't have to pretend.

"Why do you guys shower so late?" I blurt.

Rowan grins. "Only a few of us. Me, Jared, Mitch, Logubo—we formed a fencing team."

"Fencing? Really?"

"The school didn't have the budget for it, but Logubo's dad provided the kit and the sabers, épées, and foils. The swords," he adds, when I frown.

"Wow. But . . . why shower so late? After everyone's asleep . . ."

"We're allowed to train in the common room but only after lights-out."

"Oh."

We fall into silence for a while, the crunching of dry brush beneath our feet the only sound. Everything smells like sand and spice.

Eventually I ask, "Have you been in this school long?"

"Only a year. I hope to leave when I turn seventeen, go to college in the city for my matric year."

"What will you study?"

"Literature. It's the only thing I love. One day I'll be a writer."

"English classes are about the only class I really enjoy, only Mrs. Kilpatrick won't let us read ahead. I'd like to try my hand at harder books, like *Madame Bovary* or *Dracula* or something." I sigh and fall into silence.

"Stupid rules," Rowan mutters. "They want to keep everyone back, everyone equal, everyone exactly the same."

I nod emphatically. "Same with my maths teacher. Mr. Mollier thinks I should know about maths because *every* job on the whole planet needs it, according to him."

He snorts. "I had Mollier for maths last year too. He thinks calculus is the Holy Grail."

I blush and rub my arm uncomfortably, the memory of our encounter popping into my mind. "I know."

"He's okay," he says with a sigh, "but he doesn't realize that not *everyone* is born to be the same as him. He should focus on the students who *are* into calculus as much as he is. I'm not going anywhere near a science degree. It's not for me. I'm an artist."

"I think I am too. I mean . . . well, I don't know what I am." I glance away. "I'm just . . . nothing."

"Don't say that. You're not nothing. You're a beautiful, intelligent girl."

"How do you know I'm intelligent?"

"Well, how about '*Madame Bovary* or *Dracula* . . .'? Not many fourteen-year-olds would have a passion for the best literature in the world."

I blush at the praise, wanting it to be true so badly. "Wanting it and being able to do it are two different things."

If I were as sure as Rowan, would I be happy?

After a little silence, Rowan says, "Bethany, why did you call me out that day?"

"I . . . Stacey wanted to meet you."

He nods and looks away. "Oh."

"Are you okay?" I think I've upset him, because he doesn't say anything for a while.

"I just thought . . . I thought it was *you* who wanted to . . . you know . . . see me."

"Oh. Well . . . I did. I mean . . . Jared was sort of an accident." I suddenly feel like I should tell him everything. "You know that Jared was a default," I remind him. "The *whole* default was just to kiss the first boy I saw. He just happened to be there. I never meant to see him again, ever."

"And if you had seen me first, you would have kissed me that day?"

I swallow because I *did* see him first, but Jared was closer, and I didn't want Stacey to read into it. I nod. "Yes."

He slips his hands into his pockets. He is a lot taller than me. He's also taller and broader than Jared. I glance at his chest and imagine that if I touched him there, it would be firm.

"Would you have wanted to see me again?"

"Yes," I whisper. I gulp and look away. "I'm . . . I'm sorry that Stacey didn't come."

"You like her a lot, don't you?"

I nod. "I do."

"She's a nice kid."

"She's fifteen," I point out. She's older than I am.

He nods. "It doesn't seem like it sometimes."

"And I'm only fourteen," I add.

"You look fifteen. Anyway, age isn't that important. It's character that counts, and whether you can be yourself with someone."

I think he's right. There is a simplicity and honesty about him that makes me wonder . . . Where did he learn these truths? Maybe he got them from Disney too.

I think back to Sakkie—the man who turned me into whatever I am. And Stacey, who molded me into her image since I first arrived in this arid place. Have I ever been *myself* with them? Do I even know who that person is?

I don't want to admit it, but Rowan is the only person I've been open with. I have never spoken of my desire to study literature before, never really spoken to *anyone* about me, as a human being. Not even Sakkie. Mr. Mollier came close, I suppose, but in the end, he was just revolted by me. And why not?

"That's true," I admit, glancing away.

Rowan and I walk for hours. There seems to be no reason to end the companionable silences and invigorating dialogues, and we don't really think about where we're going. He tells me about his father, who is a trained lawyer but a practicing preacher in Cape Town. His mother died when he was young, and now he has a stepmother who is six years older than him and pregnant with his half sibling.

"It used to bother me," he says with a shrug that I only half see in the darkness. "But it's second nature now. My brother, Luke, is thirty. He lives in Pretoria with his girlfriend and has absolutely zero intention of marrying."

I laugh. "So they're living in sin, then, huh?"

Rowan chuckles, and his grin spreads wide. "You got it."

"I bet your dad wants to issue some kind of subpoena or something."

"Yeah, I think he'd change the law and *force* Luke into matrimony if he could. I just hope Luke waits until I'm there before he tells Dad that Mandy's expecting their kid."

Raucous laughter erupts from my mouth. "No!"

Rowan wipes his eyes. "I'm telling you."

I snort. "No way; your dad's going to have a kid and a grandkid the same age, and one out of wedlock too!"

We are doubled over with laughter by the time we reach the Tractor Tire. Rowan gently helps me up and then sits beside me, with his legs dangling.

"Do you have siblings?" he asks.

"No. I'm an only child."

"I feel like one. My brother was already in college by the time I came along. By the time I was three, he was at law school."

"So you sort of have the best of both worlds."

"I guess so, yes."

"I'm sorry about your mother, though," I say. "Do you remember her?"

"A little. I remember that she had dark hair, almost black, but if she stood in the sun, it was a little red. And she had beautiful eyes, sort of the color of mustard. A golden kind of green."

"Wow," I breathe. "She sounds fantastical. Like a mermaid."

"She was no mermaid," he whispers. "If she were, she wouldn't have died. She drowned in Lake Victoria."

"Shit," I whisper. "Rowan, I'm sorry. I—"

"You didn't know," he cuts in gently. He puts his hand on mine. "It's okay."

I look down at our hands and then up into his face. I'm on the edge of an abyss I can't pull back from.

Rowan leans toward me.

"I have to go," I whisper, sudden tears springing into my eyes. "I should . . . go."

"Wait, Bethany," Rowan murmurs, but I am already scrambling to get down off the tire. "Bethany!"

"I have to go," I call over my shoulder.

"Come back tomorrow," Rowan yells. "Please!"

I stop running. My heart is beating so fast. I turn to face him, and I can't breathe, though I know I am too far away for him to see it. What will I do now, with two choices placed in front of me, choices Stacey is no part of?

"Okay," I call at last. "Meet me outside the showers."

"Okay. Good night, then!"

I wave, and then I dash away, crying, laughing, heart racing, heart stalling.

I have never had a night as magical as this one. I have never felt so free.

37

Beast

My mother chatters at me for most of the day while Stoffel reads the paper, watches television, fixes his watch, and prepares the braai. We eat boerewors and steak with our hands and then potato salad and beetroot with plastic spoons. I think my mother is embarrassed by such inelegant dining, but since none of her new rich friends are here to see, or even know about, this hovel, she makes do with almost no comment, though her lips curl and her nostrils flair every time she looks at me eating in such a manner. At five o'clock Stoffel disappears for a siesta. He says the Spanish are happy all the time for two reasons: the siesta and the fiesta. I don't know what fiesta means.

The minutes seem to tick on forever. My mother talks at me for another hour, and then we all watch the news at six. After that I go for a bath, and I linger there as long as possible, watching my skin absorb water and turn prune-like. I comb out my wet hair twenty times, noticing how much it has grown since I've been here. There are no more bruises on my body, and I'm surprised to see that there is no evidence of Sakkie anywhere.

Along with the wounds outside, my insides feel a bit better, and a lot better since last night. Rowan is so . . . honest. What I see is what he is; there's no hidden agenda, no games, no power, and no tricks. When he speaks, I know I can hear what I hear and not have to dig for the hidden meaning. Even Beth seems quelled by his presence.

I plead fatigue with my mother and go to my room, where, groaning, I roll into bed and lose myself in sleep.

I wake up a long time later with my heart racing, darkness all around me. Dreams of running, falling, hiding plagued me; Beth's torture, no doubt, for keeping her so silent. Perhaps not. My mother has been into the room to cover me with the blanket. I can feel the sticky pink lipstick on my cheek where she must have kissed me good night.

I kick the covers off and tiptoe into the kitchen to check the time on the microwave. A little after midnight. I breathe a sigh of relief, realizing I'm not too late.

I repeat the previous night's activities, stuffing my bed and slipping out the window, and then I'm racing toward the boys' block.

I find Rowan sitting by the wall where he found me last night, his head back against the brick, mouth slightly open. He is sleeping.

I don't have the heart to wake him, so I stand and watch him for a while. In a position of repose, everyone looks innocent. Everyone looks at peace. Because the night is a little crisp, and because I'm drawn to his peace, I inch closer and sit beside him, trying to absorb some of the heat his body is giving off. I wish I had thought to wear some jeans instead of my thin cotton night slip. I wish I had worn shoes.

I begin to shiver, and I inch a little closer, but I nudge him, and he jolts awake with a tiny snore.

"Bethany?" he croaks, bleary eyed.

"Hi," I whisper, smiling at him. "Sorry I woke you . . . I was cold."

"No, no problem—not at all. Have I been out long?"

"Couple minutes," I say, through chattering teeth.

"Here." He slips off his jacket and wraps it around me.

"Thank you."

"If you're cold, I have an idea where we could go?"

I nod. "I am a bit cold."

He offers me his hand, and I take it. My own small palm is engulfed in his, and I shiver with the warmth and proximity.

He glances down at my feet. "You're not wearing shoes."

"I know."

He sighs and then hauls me, protesting, onto his back.

"You're not a mule," I say.

"And I'm not a barbarian either. I won't let a lady walk around with no shoes, especially here."

I blush and gently lay my head down on his shoulder, enjoying the rhythmical swaying of each of his footsteps. A lady. Is that what I am?

Beth does laugh at that.

"If you could go anywhere you want in the blink of an eye," he asks me when we've been walking awhile, "where would you go and why?"

I don't know what to say. "I . . . I don't know," I stammer. "I don't want to be anywhere else."

He smiles and looks back at me, warmth and something else behind his eyes.

I blush and look away. "You?"

"Same answer."

The blush spreads and burns. "Okay . . . If you could have any job, no matter what it was, what would you choose?"

"Novelist," he says immediately. "Rich and famous, of course."

I chuckle. "Of course. I'd be a ballerina."

"A ballerina? Why?"

"It was something I used to want to do, but the teacher I had said I was too tall."

Rowan pulls a face. "I think that's stupid. If you have the talent, then who cares how tall you are?"

I nod, even though he isn't looking at me. "I think it was more to do with my two left feet."

He laughs loudly; it bounces off the night. "Oh. Well, that makes a difference. What's your favorite car?"

I consider. "1949 Packard. In beige." I saw it in a magazine that Stoffel brought with him to the cabin once. It was love at first sight.

He whistles and raises his eyebrows. "Good answer," he breathes. "Most people would probably say a Porsche or some Lambo."

We continue the game as we walk until I realize where he's taking me. The guest cabins stand before us, dark and still and ominous.

"Rowan, where are we . . ."

"Which cabin are your parents in?" he whispers.

"This one!"

We have come to within footsteps of where my mother and Stoffel are sleeping.

"Wait here," he says, carrying me around the side of the cabin, and then he puts me down and disappears.

I step from one foot to the other in anxious impatience. Being so close to where my mother now lies sleeping feels too much like testing fate for my comfort. I count upward from one to keep my mind occupied. I reach one hundred and five by the time Rowan returns.

"This way," he says, once again taking my hand.

He leads me past three other cabins, and at the fourth he slides open the window.

"Rowan," I whisper, alarmed.

"It's empty," he says. "I checked."

The dark room beyond looks very inviting and warmer than outside.

He helps me into the room, one hand holding mine for balance and the other on the back of my thigh.

He climbs in after me and then shuts the window.

"We can't turn on the light," he warns me, "just in case."

"Okay."

I look around. The room is laid out in exactly the same way as the room I am sleeping in for the next two weeks.

"I've never done anything like this before," he says with a victorious laugh.

"Me neither." I sit on the edge of the bed.

We both chuckle and then fall silent, and Rowan sits next to me, three inches of space between us. My heart is pounding in my chest so loudly I think surely Rowan can hear it. He swallows and rubs his hands on his jeans.

"Shit," he mutters, standing up.

"Are you okay?"

He sighs. "Bethany, I—"

I already know what's coming, and it terrifies me. Beth's interest, however, is piqued.

You did it again, darling, she tells me. *You're a man-eater. A total beast.*

No . . . no. This can't happen, not to a wonderful guy like Rowan. Not to someone good and clean, like he is. I can't destroy him as well. More than that . . . *I* couldn't survive another fall.

I feel the Beast rising in me like a miasma, even as I'm trying to fight it.

"Don't tell me you like me," I plead. "Please don't."

"I can't help it." He steps close, kneels in front of me where I sit on the bed, takes my hands. "I do."

My heart hammers harder, and the Beast bares its fangs, digging its claws in. I feel the familiar stirring in my stomach, in my mouth.

"Rowan . . . What about Stacey?"

"I like her . . . I mean, she's sweet, but I don't *like* her. I talked to her and, yes, I kissed her, but only because you looked so sad when she was left out."

I gulp and panic. "I can't . . . I could never . . . Stacey is . . . important. I belong to her."

Even in the shadows, I see Rowan frown. "What?"

"She's my friend," I say quickly. "I love her." I can see he doesn't understand. "She's important. She's . . . she's . . ." I want to do this right—to convey the weight of Stacey's presence to me—but I know I'm getting it all wrong.

He sighs and buries his head in my lap. I stroke his dark hair. "What if . . . What if this was a secret? What if I still saw Stacey, to make you happy, but you and I were . . . sort of like in another dimension? In another world—*our* world."

I want it, I do. It wouldn't hurt anyone . . . and if we had our own world, I wouldn't be giving up what my whole self yearns for—including, it seems, what Beth yearns for.

"You promise you'll still see Stacey, when things are back to normal?"

He looks into my face for so long that I think he won't answer. Eventually, he says, "If it makes you happy, then I will."

"And I can see Jared," I add, thinking how perfect it all sounds.

Rowan makes a guttural sound and pushes away. He stands with his back to me, folding his arms across his chest and breathing heavily.

"Rowan?" I whisper, getting up and going to stand behind him.

I can't stop my arms. They wind their way around his torso, clasping his firm stomach. I feel it clenched, but if it is from pleasure or anger, I can't tell. Within me I feel the Beast stirring, demanding attention.

This is different, I tell it. *He's mine.*

Beth snickers but remains still.

"Will you kiss me?" I ask. My voice is smaller than I want it to be. I clear my throat and say, "Please?"

He sighs and turns toward me, face in shadows.

"Bethany . . ." He says my name so softly, like it means something to him, and he cups my cheek in the palm of his warm hand.

He bends his face low, and then his lips are on mine. I press myself into him, overcome with sweet intoxication. I have never felt *this*. This is so unique, so different, so vital. The Beast isn't in this. Something warm is wrapped around my heart, like fresh honey, filling the cracks and mending them, quenching the raging storm that the Beast tried to start.

He is awkward, his tongue new and unpracticed, but I let him lead.

He grasps at my nightdress, hands roaming under my pajamas and over my back. I sigh and grip him. He is clumsy, but keen.

He groans. "Stop," he gasps, pulling back. "Stop, Bethany."

"No, don't stop," I breathe. "Please don't stop."

I grapple with his jeans, and he is breathing so fast, and I can see he wants to stop me. So I work faster, unbuttoning and unzipping. He kisses me again, and I pull him toward the bed, but this time he does stop me.

"I've never done anything like this," he says, panting.

"You said third base."

"Yeah, I've touched a girl, but—"

I need him so badly—what is happening to me? I'm terrified by the enormity of this sudden . . . happiness, so different from the need I have felt before. So different from Sakkie.

Is this what it should have been all along?

I tug on his shirt, pulling him toward the bed. "I trust you."

He climbs awkwardly onto me, and we kiss and kiss.

More, Beth or the Beast demands.

"Bethany," he whispers, shock all over his face, and then we are one, merged together like a single being, locked in pleasure and surprise. He looks so startled that I almost laugh.

He moves awkwardly—he's never done this before—and I feel a surge of sadness commingled with affection. I guide his movements, watching every twitch of his face, listening to every breath.

There is a look in his eye, like he can't believe it is happening. I can't either. I begin to cry.

"Am I hurting you?" he asks, startled.

"No," I say, and encourage him to move again. "I'm happy."

It doesn't take long, and there is no pain. There is no pain.

Toward the end, our eyes lock, and I think, *I love you.*

"Bethany," he says, "Bethany, Bethany."

I wrap my arms around him, and I cry. Such innocence in his face—pure and without the knowledge of violence—has me crying tears I have never cried before. Open tears, not weighted down with hurt or anger. He says my name over and over, and I kiss him and kiss him, loving him all the more for making my name something profound.

"Bethany . . ."

In the bathroom, unable to take our eyes off each other, we get into the shower, slippery skin against slippery skin. Rowan washes my hair, and I wash his body. I glance at the bath and wish we had bathed together instead, submerged under scalding water. Afterward, wrapped in towels, we close the curtains and watch a late-night film on TV. At four in the morning, he walks me to my window. He never asks me if I have done this thing before. I don't know if he knows to ask.

"Will I see you tomorrow?" he says, and his face looks so different.

I kiss his lips. "Of course."

"I'll be at your window at midnight," he tells me, and then I climb into my room and watch him walk away into the night, wondering if this is a new game or if it's the only real thing in this world.

38

Little Niggles

NOW

You're gone in the morning.

I had the best sleep of my life.

A small, niggling thought but not much more.

(Bruce)

I'm not even that sore after the travel, the walking, the taxi ride . . . I feel young again.

So why do I feel so disturbed?

The door opens, and you're there, holding two coffees and a brown, oil-stained paper bag.

"Koeksisters," you say, your smile sweet and wide, but there is something sharper in your eyes.

"No," I breathe. "I haven't had a koeksister in years."

"Thought as much."

"When was the last time we ate?"

You kick the door shut with your foot. "No idea. This is it, Bee."

"What?"

"How it feels to be free. And alive."

I laugh, taking one of the paper cups. "What, hunger?"

"No. Being so busy living that sometimes you forget to refuel. It's ecstasy."

"I think you mean agony and ecstasy."

"The agony *is* ecstasy," you say, kissing me before you sit down.

Can this really be happening? Can you really have just put your lips on mine? Can we really have done what we did last night?

Don't do this.

Bruce's voice.

And I'm not so hungry anymore.

When did this turn from a girls' trip to visit our old stomping grounds and reclaim my freedom to . . . something else entirely? I glance at you, and something on your face gives me pause. It's gone in a moment.

I take a bite of my koeksister, but it's sickly sweet and the impulse to throw it away from me is nearly overwhelming.

I force myself to swallow before I speak. "Stacey . . ."

You watch me, waiting, and there is an invisible whip in your fist.

"I love my husband," I manage.

"Do you."

Prove you love me.

Your voice is so flat, so . . . dead. Just like when we were girls. I wonder if you'll punish me, like you did back then. I wonder if you'll give me a default or demand appeasement from Glass Man. The invisible whip twitches, and I squirm.

"Yes." I pause, then say it again, daring to defy you. "I love him."

The invisible walls are so high in here.

It is a long, torturous silence, and I begin to sweat. I almost look away.

But then you're smiling, and the invisible whip was never there, and there are no invisible walls, and we are not children anymore. "Bethany, relax. It was a onetime thing."

"It's just . . . I love my husband." How many times must I say it for you to believe me?

You smile, but something about it turns me cold. "I know."

"Are we . . . ?"

"Of course. We'll always be cool."

I have never felt more scared.

39

Happiness

THEN

I yawn all the way through breakfast, and Stoffel mutters about teenagers and growth spurts. Mum wants to go fishing—an eight-hour return trip—but I insist I have a mountain of maths homework and spend the whole day locked in my room. Since there's nothing else to do, I actually sit and solve equations.

In the afternoon, I go into the lounge, where my mother and Stoffel are watching *Rescue 911*, and I slouch in front of the television, desolate and hopeless.

"All finished, dear?" Mother asks.

"Yes."

"Good girl. We're so proud of you."

"Mum, I need you to send me some books when you go home," I say. "I would really like *Madame Bovary*, *Germinal*, *Dracula*, and *Huckleberry Finn*."

My mother pulls out a little pad of pink paper from her handbag and writes down all the titles, her lips moving ever so slightly as she enunciates the names.

"*Dracula*, darling? Are you sure? It's about vampires, you know."

"*Heart of Darkness* too," I add. "Thank you."

My mother adds the book to her bubble-gum-pink pad and then nods. "Okay, darling."

I feel the first little bit of affection for her. I know she is trying to make me happy after the last time I saw her, which she still hasn't mentioned. She's trying to forget I yelled for her to go and fuck Stoffel. I cringe every time I look at him and remember I actually said that. But I know my mother: she won't mention it. Silence makes the bad things disappear. We bury them, and buried they remain.

We eat again at eight o'clock (a frozen pizza), and then I disappear back into my room, my thoughts full of Rowan.

Something is . . . different with him. He makes me forget everything. He makes me forget Sakkie.

He makes me remember myself.

I clench my teeth and climb into my bed. What would Stacey do? I fall asleep still thinking about Stacey, but I wake up before my mother comes to check on me. I reach for my schoolbag and pull out the first book I find. It is my geography textbook. I pretend to have been reading it.

"Still doing homework?" my mother asks, astonished. "It's late, darling. Time for bed."

Closing the book and putting it on the bedside table, I get up, then go brush my teeth. After that I pull my brush through my hair again, staring at my reflection in the mirror. Under the hot shower I think about Rowan, and slowly I begin to feel better. I make sure to wash my body very carefully, and afterward I steal a squirt of my mother's perfume, which she keeps in the medicine cabinet whenever she comes to visit.

Stoffel and my mother move around outside my room for a while, cleaning the kitchen, putting away the blankets. Then I hear them go to their bedroom. I count to keep myself awake, and I reach two thousand. The night is dark and empty, and I have been lying still for a long time. Then, to my horror, Stoffel and my mother move on their bed. It squeaks.

I shut my eyes tightly, trying to ignore the rhythmical shriek of the bedsprings, proof that they do *it*, but the sound is high pitched and not soft enough to ignore. Eventually it speeds up.

Oh, God.

I clap my hands over my ears, swallowing down the thoughts and disgusting images, and *especially* forcing myself not to acknowledge what I feel in my own body.

Stop it, stop it, stop it!

Poor little Bethany, Beth coos.

Leave me alone.

Tentatively, I let go of one ear. The world is silent again. I breathe a sigh of relief. I don't care to look at the time. I just want to get out of here, so I stuff my blanket, buckle on my shoes, and jump out of the window. I run almost the entire way to the shower room and find I am early. Very early. Most of the guys haven't even started to shower.

I groan and settle in for a long wait.

It is Rowan lifting me off the floor and into his arms that wakes me.

"I thought I was coming to your window tonight?" he murmurs as he walks. His breath sends shivers down my spine.

"I couldn't wait," I whisper into his neck. "I had to see you."

He chuckles and keeps walking. After a while he shifts me so that he is carrying me piggyback-style again. The night is still. I rest my head on his shoulder, and the soft tread his shoes make on the cracked soil lulls me into a sort of calm semisleep.

We go to the same cabin. Rowan lays me down on the bed. I am still drowsy, so he runs his fingers up and down my arms and asks me about my favorite music, my favorite films, food, drinks, places I want to see, people I want to meet. He asks me about England as he caresses my legs, and I shiver deeply and sink, blissful, into the bed. He tells me he'll go there with me one day, to England, land of the Queen.

We create a cocoon for each other, a barrier that separates us from the rest of the world—the world of Staceys, Sakkies, Mummys, and hard, violent things. Our sex is love. Our sex is safe.

"Rowan," I whisper when we're lying naked together. "I'm happy."

"Me too," he says.

Joy that outshines my past radiates around me, healing all the little cracks and holes stagnating within me. I close my eyes and pray to God that this healing will last. That my wounds will fade. That Rowan will be mine, and Stacey's, forever. We lie wrapped around each other, gazing at everything with new eyes.

"So beautiful," he murmurs, touching his lips gently to my stomach.

He walks to the cabin's en suite and returns with a roll of toilet paper on his *thing*, doing a little dance that has me in hysterics. He climbs into the bed beside me. I've never been taken care of before.

"Don't go to sleep," he murmurs, pressing against my body and cradling my head in the crook of his arm. "I want to ask you something."

"I won't," I sigh, already feeling a land of dreams tugging at my consciousness, for surely I would have to dream to feel this happy.

40

Fateful Promise

I yawn and stretch, a satisfying burn in my muscles; light spills into the room from two directions. I frown. Was that a dream? I look up and seem to be in my room. Then Rowan sighs from under the duvet to my right.

"Rowan," I choke, "what time is it?"

His body stiffens beside me. "Oh, shit!"

"No," I gasp, throwing off the covers and running for my nightie, which is still on the floor beside the bed. I slip it over my head and buckle on my shoes.

"How did I let this happen?" he growls at himself, buttoning up his shirt and slipping into his jeans.

How gorgeous he looks, I think, and then I am back to panicking.

"My mother is going to *freak out*," I breathe, running for the window.

Rowan helps me out, and we dash across to my cabin, where there is a small group of people clustered around the front door. My mother's frantic sobs rebound off the walls and skulk out into the bright morning, where they reach my burning ears.

"Hide!" I hiss at Rowan, pushing him around the side of the cabin. "Run for it when you can."

I take a steadying breath and then walk up to the front door. Matron Monday, Principal Wolfe, Joe, and Mr. Mollier all stare at me as I pass. I avoid Mr. Mollier's eyes, reminded once again of our shameful conversation.

I'm about to open my mouth to explain when a new figure appears from behind my mother.

Sakkie.

His eyes meet mine, and I shatter.

Sakkie is here. My Sakkie. Who did this to me.

He takes in my appearance, and his lips thin as he exhales. He knows, or suspects. But his exhale reminds me to breathe, too, and I force air into my lungs.

"Bethany," my mother cries as I come closer, rushing for me.

I can't take my eyes off Sakkie, even when my mother collapses onto me, crying. No more than a beat passes before she grabs my shoulders and holds me back, her eyes furious under their moisture. Joe casts a glance between Sakkie and me, and I look quickly away.

"Bethany," she shrieks, no more than five inches from my face. "Bethany *Sloane*!"

"Hey, Mum," I say, grinning sheepishly, though my heart is struggling to beat inside me. "W-what's going on?"

"Do you have *any* idea what time it is, young lady?"

I feign confusion. "No?"

"It's after eleven! *Where* have you *been*?"

I glance at Sakkie, and all the blood in my body seems to rush to my feet. My head swims, and I briefly consider telling her I have been sleepwalking again, but I don't want the drama, especially with Matron Monday here and Sakkie watching. And especially because Joe is here, and he knows perfectly well that Stacey and I sneak out of our dorm at night.

I swallow. "Mum, I just got up early. I went for a walk."

"Your duvet was stuffed with pillows!" she accuses, her cheeks red and vein riddled.

A quick glance at Sakkie, and I see his jaw clench.

Sakkie.

Sakkie is here.

At last, Beth says.

No. No, no, no.

"That's how I sleep," I say, and I feign annoyance. "There was no need to call the whole school. I *live* here, Mum. I know my way around. Did you expect me to leave a note?"

She looks slightly more mollified, if not a little embarrassed. She glances at the principal and then back at me. "It's a school day, young lady."

"I forgot," I murmur, looking at the principal sheepishly. "Sorry, Principal Wolfe."

Wolfe clears his throat. "You've had a lot of people worried today," he says, glancing at my nightdress. "You should know better than to go wandering around dressed . . . like that. No matter if your parents are here for a visit; we still follow school regulations."

"Yes, sir."

I wonder if anyone noticed Rowan was missing, or if his friends have covered for him. Would they have even noticed my absence if Mum hadn't?

Mr. Mollier looks uncomfortable, and I wish everyone would just leave.

"All right, then." Principal Wolfe nods stiffly. "Enough of this. Bethany, I think an evening detention working in the grounds ought to teach you not to behave like this again?"

My cheeks burn, and I glance at my mother, doing my best not to look at Sakkie.

"Yes, it *will,*" she reinforces.

"You be sure to get dressed and be in your next lesson promptly." Wolfe turns to Joe. "Looks like we won't be needing you or Sakkie after all, Joe. Thanks for coming down."

Joe nods. "Not at all."

Thank God for the school's distaste for a scandal. Principal Wolfe smiles serenely at my mother, though his cheeks blush, and then he leaves after Matron Monday. Joe turns to leave and pulls Sakkie along with him, but I don't miss Sakkie's sharp stare.

When they're gone, I feel like I can breathe again.

"Now, you get *straight* into your room, little miss," my mother rants, "and into your uniform!"

"Don't nag me," I yell, too embarrassed by what's already happened and the part she's played in it to keep my composure, and I walk into my room and shut the door in her face.

Oh, God. Sakkie is back.

Sakkie . . . The Beast is purring. So is Beth.

Maybe working in the grounds for detention will mean working with Joe. Maybe that's all it will be. Joe and his snake and quiet time in the air. It doesn't mean it'll be Sakkie . . . it doesn't mean . . .

My mother has no idea what she has done.

"Bethany?" Rowan whispers from my wardrobe. The window is standing open, and his dusty boot prints are all over the floor.

I shriek with shock.

"Bethany?" my mother calls. "What is it?"

"I stubbed my toe," I call. "I'm fine."

"Hurry up now," she reminds me.

"Okay, okay!"

I shut myself in the wardrobe with Rowan, and he folds me into his arms.

"God, that was—Bethany? You're shaking! What's wrong?"

He strokes my hair, and I want to tell him that I've seen Sakkie and my whole world is ending, but all that comes out is "I want to disappear. Can you make that happen?"

He kisses my hair. "I'm sorry I fell asleep."

"I want to say 'me too,' but when I woke up . . ." I sigh, trying to hold back my embarrassed tears. "I felt so *good*."

Rowan squeezes me tighter. "Me too."

"I have to get dressed for school," I remind him, tugging on his jacket. I would give anything to be able to just spend the day with him.

I move to get up, but Rowan holds me firm. "Bethany . . . I wanted to ask you something last night. I just can't wait. I have to do it now."

"Rowan, I really—"

"Please, just let me do it quickly." He closes his eyes, takes a breath, and then stares at me. "When . . . when Jared . . ." He sighs explosively. "When Jared was going third base on you . . . Did you . . . I mean, did he . . ."

"Rowan," I whisper, "let's talk about it later, okay?"

His jaw clenches, and he speaks through his teeth. "Please, just answer me. Did he . . . What did he do . . . at the end?"

My cheeks are blazing. I don't want to talk about this with him. "Please, Rowan," I beg.

"Just . . . just tell me."

I wish I could just lie. I tell him, keeping my voice even, then add, "I'm sorry."

He will hate me now, I think.

"It's not *your* fault," he hisses through clenched jaws. "That *fucking* creep!"

"Ssh! Please, don't get me into any more trouble, *please*! She won't let me see you again if she finds out."

"I'm sorry," he grits out, shoving his fists into his eyes. "Just the thought of you and him . . . his *filthy* hands on you . . ."

My heart is pounding. "Rowan . . . you promised . . . you said that things would be the same, remember? Me and Jared, you and Stacey."

His eyes are wide, pleading. "Bethany—"

"No," I gasp. "You *promised*, you promised!"

I can't breathe. He gave me his word. If Stacey knew . . . if Stacey were left alone . . . ripples of nausea course through me, my stomach drops away, and I taste bile, bitter as gall, on my tongue. My skin tingles uncomfortably when I think of it. The possibility is too horrible to contemplate. Even Beth is alarmed.

"Rowan," I plead.

"Okay," he breathes. He takes a few long breaths and clenches his jaw. "I'm sorry, I just . . . you're mine, and . . . but . . . you're right, I did promise."

"Thank you," I whisper, kissing him firmly. "Thank you, Rowan."

"Bethany, *hurry up*!" my mother yells from outside. I scramble out of the wardrobe, throw on my school shirt, then my skirt, and rush out the front door, thinking I'm Rowan's and wondering if I was ever my own.

41

Sakkie

The grounds are dry, dusty, and empty, and the sun scorches my skin. I head over to the workers' shed, hoping Joe will keep quiet about Sakkie during my detention. Maybe he'll take pity on me and tell me I don't have to do it, that I'm free to go.

The door is open, so I head around it and step inside. The shadows are cool—a welcome break from the sun overhead. At the back of the room, a figure hammers a corrugated iron sheet to the wall, reinforcing it.

"Joe?"

The figure turns, liquid glass. "Beth . . . Beautiful Beth."

"Sakkie . . ."

I stumble back a step, the room spins, and I think I'll faint. I have no strength in me, and this is magnified by the fact that I have not seen Stacey *at all* today. I could have been breaking all sorts of rules and not even know it. The bad judges could be here, watching everything I do.

"Good afternoon," he says, smiling a toothless smile, and he puts down the hammer.

"Good afternoon . . ."

He walks to the door and closes it behind me, shutting out the light.

As he returns, he gathers me into his arms, sighing my name into my hair. "*Bethie* . . . ," he breathes. He smells of sweat and cologne, sharp as a cut. His hug is too tight, his arms crushing my bones.

I push gently away. "Sakkie, please don't—"

He laughs, taking his time to release me. "You're teasing me."

"This is stupid," I cry out, covering my face. "I'm sorry this ever happened. I'm sorry I ever knocked on your door that day! I'm sorry I didn't leave while I still had . . . whatever it was that you stole from me."

He grabs my arms, hands closing around them like vises. "Don't say that," he grits out, his eyes flashing like mirrors.

I am hysterical. "*Stay away*," I screech, scampering backward and knocking half the toolboxes and equipment over. Where is Joe?

"Beth," he warns. "What's changed?"

I gasp in lungfuls of air, and I try to blink out the endless tears that cloud my vision.

"P-please," I choke out. "D-don't ever t-touch me again!"

You know you want it, Beth tells me.

I force her away. *No. No, I don't.*

"What are you talking about?" he yells, waving his hands. "*You* wanted this, Beth; you wanted *me*!"

"I'm sorry . . . but I just *can't* see you. It's . . . wrong."

"I *love* you, god*damn* it. Doesn't that mean anything? Are you that selfish? My life's ruined because of you!"

"But, I . . ." My voice is small in my throat, clogging. "That's . . . that's nothing to do with me—"

"I'm the only one who wants you," he spits.

We stare at each other, the silence between us electric with the question of who will break whom. Who will shatter first?

"Beth," he bursts out, suddenly in tears and on his knees, his face red and puffy. "Don't do this. Let me hold you, please."

"Don't cry," I whisper, feeling so sorry for him. "Please don't cry, Sakkie."

This makes him cry harder. He sobs freely, dry and rasping, as he unbuttons my school shirt, little glass hairs pricking my skin. These cries don't reach his chest; they are not the heart-wrenching tears I have felt, the ones that seem to come from a place deeper than my body allows. These tears are shallow, but no less real. His face is so pink, and his grimacing mouth—usually so hard and thin—is pulled downward at the side, exposing his imperfect crème teeth.

"Bethie," he moans, eyes blotchy and red. "Oh, Bethie . . . Bethie . . ."

His hands are cold as glass as they run over me.

After that, there is only Beth.

By the time I get home, it is getting dark and the bobotie is sitting cold on the table. I am aching between my legs, and my wrists are still sore. At least my soul is numb, for once.

The ghosts are gone. I am alone even in this.

"How was your detention, darling?" Mummy asks without looking up.

"Fine," I mutter, and go into the bathroom.

In the mirror I don't see anyone I recognize.

Mechanically, I switch on the bath and wait for the water to get scalding hot before I climb in and scrub my skin until it is raw. Not until I am bleeding do I begin to actually *feel* something. There are new bruises on my upper thighs, two straight lines where Sakkie rammed me into his desk after the raking was done. I retch, shaking in the water. I grit my teeth and bite down on my arm, over and over, until I am causing new bruises. With every bite, the piercing inside me dulls.

That's it . . .

When I am safely in my pajamas and I'm calm enough to think, I go into the dining room, where my mother has left my cold bobotie.

She has also left a note. *Going for walk with Stoffel, dear. It's a beautiful night.*

I scrunch up the paper, beating the table with it, and then I do the same to the food. When it is little more than pulp, I throw it, along with the note, into the bin. Then I climb into bed and throw the cover over my head. I wish I could just disappear. I wish I had never been born.

42

Cane

NOW

The kombi taxi drops us outside the gate, and thankfully the driver has no questions about two women alone in the middle of nowhere.

The last time I was here, it was with my mother, and the gates were tall and proud: vivid-black iron shiny with novel possibility. Now they slump as though impaled by a truck long ago, the crimps in the iron rusting where the paint has peeled away like pencil shavings.

"Poor old guy," you say, touching one of the sharp, warped bars.

And you're right, because this gate does look like an old man, bent and broken, forgotten by the young.

"Well." You turn to me. "Ready?"

I nod, numbly, and you push my wheelchair, with some difficulty, through the wreckage of the school gate.

◆ ◆ ◆

My mother drove me down this road.

Do you want to go to a school where there are horses? she said, gripping the steering wheel. The sun was baking my skin pleasantly through the car window.

Ooh, yeah!

A school where you can ride horses, and play in big fields, and drive tractors?

Yes, please!

Okay. Good. Because we're going there now.

Yay! An adventure, I thought, tingling with excitement.

And you sleep over.

My brain stopped, and the seat didn't seem so warm anymore.

But I want to come home after.

Well, this is a special school. You sleep there.

But . . . I want to come home. Mummy, I want to come home!

I never did.

I swallow past the lump in my throat and glance at you. Your eyes have turned dully inward, and you must be thinking about the same thing. We're identical, you and me. Didn't everyone always say so? Two peas in a pod. Twins.

And I feel like that little child again. I don't want to be here. I don't particularly want to be anywhere, but I don't like this at all. You take the first step forward, but I can't, I can't—

something bad happened here

I think I always knew it. But suspecting that you had a bad school experience is very different from being back at that very same school, staring down those very same ghosts.

"I can't."

I must have said the words, because you stop pushing my wheelchair.

"We have to."

I squeeze my eyes shut. "Pandora's box . . ."

You bend over and slip your hand into mine, grounding me like an earth wire, and I let my fear go, trusting you to lead me through the thorns.

◆ ◆ ◆

The trees on either side of the long dirt drive, once so thick and tall they scared me, now stand dry and sparse, gnarled bones and splinters that reveal glimpses of the yellow fields beyond. Their grasses, so long untended, sway and dance hypnotically. I'm swimming, dizzy in that sleepy way of dreams. But this is not a dream. This is very, very real. I am here.

And so are you.

We reach a dirt roundabout of sorts, a bit of road circling a once-proud fountain, now dry and baking in the sun. Small puddles of brackish water remain, stagnant and stinking, buzzing with unfussy flies and mosquitoes. And beyond, the school building.

"I forgot about the school," I say, staring straight at the small building in front of me.

Huh. Single story. I've lived in London so long that a bungalow isn't something I can compute. A bungalow *school* even less so. One story of classes. Nothing above the heads of bored students but a ceiling and then the endless sky.

I wipe my prickling neck, and my hand comes away wet, leaving the skin behind stinging with the heat of sunburn.

"Strange," you say, cocking your head in that familiar way. "So did I. Although . . . I remember swimming competitions?"

It's a question more than a statement. An offer for me to confirm or deny.

A shadowy memory comes into slow focus. A girl, bigger than me, in a black swimming costume, her boobs wobbling like water-filled balloons as she walked. How much I wanted to poke them. I never did.

I was part of the swim team, and that commanded respect. No boob poking allowed. I was on team A. The best.

"You didn't swim." I say this with certainty, though in truth I can't remember.

"No . . . I think I watched. From stands."

I glance left, where the dirt road turns into a dirt path. "That way."

We keep going, and after a while, sure enough, a fenced-in pool area. The fence used to be a vibrant green. Now the pleated plastic is almost white with sun damage. The pool is hidden by an equally sun-bleached cover, once blue, now white. The stands look rickety, even for children, and we do not climb them.

I can hear it. The cheers of the parents and the kids watching the race. We rarely had competitions, because we were so far out. Schools from Pretoria had to drive for at least an hour to reach us, and we were even farther from Johannesburg.

A competition was a big event. It meant sweet-smelling sunscreen: pink, green, and blue, smeared on like war paint. The songs we sang were war cries. This was battle. War in water.

I can smell it. Chlorine, sunscreen, dry grass, and cloying sand, fine as flour in my nose.

V-I-C, V-I-C, V-I-C-T-O-R-Y . . . victory, victory is our cry, V-I-C-T-O-R-Y. Victory!

The voices are ghostly. But here, in my mind or out here in the baking emptiness of the pool, it doesn't matter. They are all here. Ghosts.

I look at the sky and see a pale daylight moon.

We circle the swimming area and find the old school field. The giant cement steps that lead down to it are smaller than they were, but I don't dare take them. I will tumble, down, down, like Alice, if I try. And this reality is already back to front, upside down, split in pieces. I don't want any more curiouser and curiouser.

The field is lost in gloom from the shadow of the school building and the changing building of the pool area, and I don't want to . . . I don't want to go down . . .

You point to the farthest corner. "We used to climb under the fence there. It was a secret spot where the sand looked like chocolate."

I'm going to dig.

I want to go.

Go if you want, ninny.

She's digging so deep . . . the soil is turning red.

She's going to dig us all the way to hell.

This is hell's ceiling. Are you scared?

I lean away. "I want to go . . ."

You nod. "Me too."

How long is a forever? Sometimes just one second . . .

It feels wrong here. Too many ghosts. Too many dark, dark ghosts. We turn, heading back to the dirt path that will take us to the front of the school again, and now I can see the field. This field had so many devil's thorns in it, I got them in my bottom . . . I had to pick off the pointy bits . . .

And near the end, close to the gates, where I had not noticed before, stand wooden cabins.

"Look," I say, pointing stupidly. "The visiting cabins."

You frown. "Oh yeah. I forgot. My dad and my brother would come to see me."

I nod. Something niggles   but I can't hold on.

Rowan . . .

◆ ◆ ◆

[BETHANY WHERE ARE YOU?]

"I can't believe they still grow."

We are sitting in what used to be the kitchen ladies' sugarcane patch. It is no longer a "patch"; it has spread like a forest, and we are hidden among the stalks, the crowns of leaves shading us from a brutal sun. We could be in Thailand right now, instead of here, in Settlers, Pretoria. We could be anywhere else besides this ghost school.

"Just as good as I remember them," you murmur, teeth tearing out some of the fibrous, sweet innards—the heart of the plant she hacked through.

Still destroying hearts after all.

[JESUS BETHANY I AM WORRIED SICK. TELL ME WHERE YOU ARE AND I'LL COME GET YOU.]

I grin. "We were always trying to steal this stuff. And now look at it. Like a fucking forest."

"I told you we'd have feasts of sugarcane together one day."

[BETHANY, PLEASE. I CAN SEE YOU'RE READING MY MESSAGES. BABY, TELL ME WHERE YOU ARE.]

"You did."

[DON'T DO THIS TO ME.]

"Seems pushy," you say.

"Who?"

"Whoever keeps texting you. Mummy probably died from plastic surgery overload years ago, so I presume it's the husband."

[BETHANY, I LOVE YOU. REMEMBER WHAT DOCTOR MORGAN SAID. CLOSE YOUR EYES, COUNT TO TEN, OPEN THEM. THEN TELL ME WHERE YOU ARE.]

"Bruce," I murmur, my gaze losing focus.

You grin at me. "You are hot stuff after all."

[BETHANY . . . WHO'S WITH YOU?]

I switch off my phone and put it in my jacket pocket. I grin at you, and we continue to break into the hearts of the sugarcane, ignoring the fibers sticking between our teeth. We've eaten far worse.

"Take off your shoes," you tell me.

I don't question. Wearing shoes out here is not allowed. It's against the rules. I smile, because I realize you took your shoes off somewhere along the way while my eyes were closed.

Once my shoes are gone, you whisper, "Close your eyes," in the dark.

43

ATTEMPTED END

THEN

When the silent *tck tck tck* sounds start, I know it is Rowan knocking on my window. For a moment I let myself imagine it's a blue fairy of the night, coming to see if I'm okay. Coming to take me away to their land, where children are children forever.

But then I remember that Neverland isn't real.

But ghosts are.

I don't know how long I've been sleeping, but it feels like forever. My head is heavy, my eyes are puffy, and my nose stuffy. My heart is sore, and every beat feels like an effort. The mechanism inside, the one that regulates my life, is fading away, winding down. Like an old pocket watch. *Tick, tick . . . tick . . . tick.*

It takes me a few moments to stand up, and by the time I am at the window, the ticking noises have stopped.

I slide it open. "Rowan?" I whisper, my heart raw.

His footsteps crunch on the gravel that runs around the rim of the cabin, and then he is there, reaching through the frame to touch my face.

"I thought you fell asleep," he says through kisses into my hair.

"I did," I say. I don't know how to move or what to say. I feel paralyzed and sick at heart. I feel Sakkie's prickly-glass face all over me, even now. "I'm tired tonight, Rowan. Can we just forget it?"

"Forget it—Bethany? Are you okay?"

I push him back out the window; I'm so weak the movement knocks all the air out of my lungs. "Please go away," I whisper.

"Hey, wait a second. What's going on here?"

"Leave me *alone*," I plead, my voice wobbling and cracking. "Just go."

"If . . ." He grits his teeth and takes a breath. "If you're breaking up with me, then at least do it right. Don't be a coward."

"I *am* a coward." I barely get the words out, and then my voice is gone, useless, and I'm heaving with body sobs that don't reach my face. I smother the noises in the palms of my hands—catching misery.

Rowan swallows. "Come on," he murmurs, reaching for my arms. "Let's get out of here."

I let him pull me through the window. He piggybacks me in silence, and I enjoy the familiar bounce every one of his steps makes.

"Is this about last night? Did they ride you hard about being out?"

I don't want to think about any of this. It is only an endless sequence of events in my memory, which will lead to where it *did* lead this afternoon, with me shivering on the floor, naked and humiliated. The bad judges watching with glee.

"No," I mutter. "I mean, they *did*, but that's not the reason."

"What did you say?"

"I said I left only a few hours before and that I went for a walk."

"Sounds like a reasonable excuse. I mean, you do live here, after all."

"Yeah, that's what I said."

"Well then? What's wrong? We got away with it—we're *getting* away with it."

"It's a stupid kiddie thing to be doing," I snap, punching down on his shoulder with my fist.

He drops me neatly on the ground and steps away, facing the night, back to me. Is he shaking?

"You know what? This is just *shit*, truly god-awful shit. What were you trying to do to me, Bethany? Tell me, because I really don't fucking know!"

"I'm ending this before someone gets hurt." Instinctively I slip a hand under my shirtsleeve, searching for the bite marks I gave myself. Then I pinch the skin, which is already so blue and swollen, to keep from breaking apart. The pain keeps me here, on this earth, in the now. It keeps me from floating away into myself, where there seems to be very little substance left.

Poor little Bethany.

"You're ending this to *hurt* me!"

My mouth contorts in some ugly way as a sob fights to escape my throat, where I have it trapped, and I clap my hands over my mouth. This was not what I planned at all, if I really had any plan in the first place, which I don't think I did. I just bounced from fiasco to fiasco like a lifeless Ping-Pong ball.

I'm lethal.

"I don't want to hurt anybody," I say when I can. "I just want to be myself. I want to be left alone for once."

"You want *me* to leave you alone." He isn't asking.

"Rowan, can't you see that it's *you* I want to spend time with the *most*?" Treacherous, treacherous!

What would your little Stacey say to that? I'm not in the mood for Beth's taunting.

"Can't you see that if I'm pushing you away, it's because I—" I stop myself right there. I am walking into a dangerous trap, and I must avoid it.

"Because you . . . care about me," he whispers, stepping closer.

I want to force him back, to slap his face, to yell at him and call him names—to spit if I have to—anything to get him as far away from me as possible.

Stacey once told me about the legend of the viper plant. It was a perfectly normal plant, she said, until it reached a certain age and began producing pollen. When the bees came to pollinate it, it infected itself with a deadly poison. The black gunk would seep into the pollen, tar on gold, and the bees would groggily go back to their hive and kill the entire colony. If an animal ate the leaves or petals of the plant, they would die. If the animal drank from a creek, the creek would become infected, and all the fish would die. Man would eat the fish, and man would die. All from one seemingly innocent, sadomasochistic plant.

I'm that plant. I'm poisoning everyone around me.

"Rowan . . . it's been wonderful. Sometimes I can't believe it, but now . . . you promised me you'd go back to Stacey, and I would go back to Jared."

"I promised I would go back to Stacey if I could have *you*. But you're pushing me away, so I have no promise to keep."

No! I ball up my hands and shove them into my eyes. This is horrible . . . Sakkie won't let me go; he loves me too much. Rowan won't go to Stacey unless he has me, too, and Stacey won't have me without Rowan—I know it. I can hear Stacey's voice in my head, even now, as clear as it was on the night she first saw him. *Next time we come . . . bring* him *outside with you.* The way she had said *him* told me he was hers. From the moment she spotted him, it could have been no other way.

And here I am.

"And what about Jared?" I ask. "He's your friend."

"Fuck Jared!" Rowan growls. "I don't give a flying horse's arse about him right now."

Despite myself, I laugh. It briefly occurs to me I've had the power to make two men fall in love with me. If I can do that, then I can do anything, right? But somehow I can't escape him . . . Sakkie . . . the first. Rowan is a ray of sunlight that makes Sakkie nothing more than a silhouette, but he is always there. The one who caused all this damage.

"I could sleep with Jared if you prefer," I chuckle, but Rowan doesn't laugh.

"I don't want his hands on you. I don't want *anyone*'s hands on you except for mine."

The blood leaves my face like a flushing toilet, and a hand closes on my heart. "Rowan . . ." I should tell him the truth. I should get it over with.

"I wish you'd promise me that he'll never touch you."

I step forward, unable to breathe, and he catches me before I pass out. We sit on the ground, and he asks me if I'm okay, over and over. He strokes my hair and kisses my forehead, never knowing how broken I am.

"Bethany?"

"Okay," I whisper very softly, "I won't let him touch me." And then he hugs me and kisses my shoulder.

Stupid, Beth tells me. *Stupid.* The Beast laughs.

44

Last Night

The last week of my mother's visit has passed all too quickly. In the beginning, I was dying to know how I would manage a *whole* fortnight with them. But then, I didn't expect Rowan and our secret life together. I didn't expect the wonderful feelings that were beginning to grow from under all the ashes of my heart.

Sunday night has arrived, and it is the last of the best nights of my life. My mother stands on the threshold to the cabin, looking in wistfully. The sky is growing dark very quickly; God is painting his sky.

"Well," she sighs, "two weeks." She glances down at me, and her bottom lip quivers. "It went so fast!"

I nod. "It did."

"Oh, darling, I'm going to miss you so much. I can't wait until the end of the school year, when you can come home."

"Me too," I say mechanically, though that is the time I am dreading the most. Three whole weeks at home. With my mother. With Stoffel. Without Rowan. Without Stacey.

I shudder. Even Beth hates the idea of this.

Might have to resort to desperate measures, she taunts, *like screwing Stoffel.*

I think I puke into my mouth a little bit, and Beth roars with beastly laughter, delighted she has hurt me.

"It's getting cold," my mother coos, rubbing my arms. "Better get going back to the dorm, darling. We can drive you there."

"That's okay, Mum," I say quickly. I plaster a smile to my face, and she beams at me in return. "You'd better hit the road. It's a . . . long drive. I'll walk back."

She tilts her head and rubs my arm again, chafing up and down as though she wants to warm me. "Okay, sweetie. Well, be good. Remember," she adds, holding up her index finger, "we fly back to England tomorrow, so you won't be able to reach us."

Yeah, yeah, I think. I want her to hurry up, and I know she wants to go, but there is a kind of social etiquette that she insists we play out.

"Okay," I say, waiting.

She kisses me on the top of my head, something that feels very, very redundant, and then she totters to the car, hops in, and closes the door. We have said goodbye in an acceptable manner, so her conscience is now clear. Another tick in one of her many boxes.

I wave until I see their taillights disappear when they turn onto the main road, and then I rush back inside, into my room, where Rowan has already been waiting for me for half an hour.

Because it is the last night we have, Rowan makes it special. He's stolen some candles and lit them with his lighter. We have all the hours of darkness to be together. Dawn is the hour that this dream, as it now stands, will end. We do something I have wanted to do since I first saw him in the dim side of the shower room. We bathe together. I lie in the bath with my flesh pressed against his, warm and cocooned by the water. He washes my hair for me and then rinses it down.

We pretend we're alone in the world. We pretend that there is no other life, that we are older, that we are freer. There are neither daytime school hours nor nighttime obligations to others between us. We have bridged the gap because there is no gap. Stacey is part of another world—another life.

We drink tap water out of champagne glasses, and we watch a little TV, and when he frowns at my bruises, I tell him I am a wild girl, a clumsy girl, and he kisses them better.

I cry as the dawn sun inches across the panel floors like the light form of hourglass sands, ticking down the moments that make up a life, and sometimes two lives.

"It's over," I whisper. "Two weeks have gone by . . . so fast."

Rowan holds me tighter, and he sighs into my hair. With my cheek on his chest, I hear his heart racing, counting down the last few beats of this life, which is ending.

"Bethany," he whispers through a groggy voice, "please don't sleep with Jared."

"Okay," I say. "I won't."

I clench my jaw and squeeze my eyes tightly shut to stop myself from asking . . .

"And I won't . . . with her," he says softly.

I release my breath and press my face into his shoulder, thankful and horrified about what that means to me, and what it might mean to Stacey. Knowing I have been waiting for him to say this. If Stacey ever finds out, I will flog myself for all eternity to make it right.

45

Something Bad

NOW

We walk a long time, and I see nothing. I smell everything, and my feet feel the changes in texture, from orange dirt road to dry, scratchy grass and uneven, thorny terrain.

And then you stop.

"We're here."

I inhale.

"Open your eyes, Bethany."

And . . . I do.

The cottage is small. Stained off-white walls, a messy thatched roof. A narrow, scrutinous door. Windows locked behind iron bars that didn't used to be there.

I shake my head. *No.*

"We're here." You try the door, but it's locked. "Maybe a window in the back."

I can't.

The feeling is so strong, it's a punch to my gut, and I bend over coughing.

I can't.

I can't.

Everything is spinning, and a smell—cigarettes and cocoa—hits me like a wave. Oh, God. I can't do this. I can't breathe.

I can't . . .

I can't breathe . . .

A terrible animal sound rips itself free from me, and you hear me because you come running—and where did you go?

"Beth?"

Beautiful Beth,
beautiful Beth!

You hold me, but it's a cage and I can't breathe! I'm going to die—

"Take a breath."

Your voice is far away, and dark is on the edges of the world—

"Bethany, *breathe*."

You're special, Beth. So special.

Pain. Shock. White fire.

"I'm sorry I hit you," you're saying, "but you were going blue. Jesus, Bethany."

I blink, and I breathe.

"I . . . I need . . . to go for a walk."

◆ ◆ ◆

Things start to break down around me. The sky crystallizes and cracks; the grass stills, fissuring like glass. I'm going to cut myself on the world today. I just know it. I wonder if I'll bleed.

The world doesn't cut me, though. The images in my mind do. I want to shrink away from them, or for them to shrink away from me. I make the images as small as I can, but they don't go away entirely.

Oh, no. No, no. Not this. Not this . . . I don't want to remember this.

I don't know how, but I'm lying in the dirt, curled into a tiny ball, asking the devil's thorns all around me what the fuck I've come back to.

It is much later when you find me, the heat of the afternoon sun ebbing away.

"Close your eyes," you tell me. "Good. Now get up."

I let you lead me away.

46

Stacey's Warning

THEN

My mother assumed I was safe in the dorm; Matron assumed I was safe in the cabin with my parents. I can hardly believe it worked out so well. I dump my bag on my bed and sit down with a sigh. Stacey is facing the wall. I eye her pencil-shaving bottle and wonder if I should have saved my shavings from these two weeks and given them to her. It would have been a lot to offer, a magnificent gift.

"Twin?" I whisper, hoping she is awake. Seeing her form there, so real and close after so much time has passed, has my heart pounding.

She sighs and rolls over; the movement is much more fluid than anything I can manage.

"Survived two weeks, I see," she says. Her face is impassive and closed.

My stomach jolts. Have two weeks cast me out entirely? My pulse races. "Barely," I say.

"You must have been busy," she comments, "not coming to the dorm once."

"I wasn't . . . my mother made me come straight back," I say. It sounds like I'm pleading, but for what? "Except for a detention I got and lessons and stuff."

"Still a perfect student?"

"Except maths."

Chena moans in her sleep, and her foot jiggles and pops out from under the cover.

"Should we start calling you Mrs. Mollier yet?"

My vision is all spotty. "What are you talking about?"

"I've seen how he stares at your tits all the time in the food hall and during recess. God, it's pathetic."

"He does not," I protest, but I'm dying with shame. I want to cover my chest, but I don't do it because I know it will forever be my weak spot. Until another, even weaker spot is found.

"Not surprising," she says, and her lips, but not her eyes, smile. "You're gorgeous."

I blush under the praise, but I'm confused and I don't know why. Stacey looks at me; she blinks a lot, as though with every touch of her long lashes upon her cheek, she is taking a snapshot she can look at later. I smile, hoping I look nice enough to be saved for later. She never smiles at me.

I search for a way to change the subject, but in the end, the morning bell saves me. I dump my bag in the wardrobe, strip my bed, and run to the bathroom with the others to brush my teeth. Then I return to the dorm with Stacey, make my bed, and get into my uniform.

"Ah. Back, are we, Bethany?" Matron Monday asks.

"Yes, ma'am."

She nods at me and then turns away. "Off to school with you."

She doesn't do morning inspection.

During first period, Mr. Mollier receives a note from a mousy-looking girl who leaves as soon as the paper hits his hand. He reads it, frowns, and then looks up at me. He clears his throat, then walks down the aisle and puts the note on my desk.

Bethany Sloane to attend detention with groundsman Mr. Sakkie Westerfield after school today.

I feel as though I have been punched in the gut.

Gert sees the note and sniggers. "Detention digging holes with Mr. Westerfield is torture. Sucks to be you."

"Eyes front, Mr. Van Dyck," Mr. Mollier orders.

Gert's head snaps forward, but his eyes dart back and forth to my face, to the note, to my face again. There is a furious blush spreading along his neck. I grit my teeth and shove the note under my bra strap and try to pay attention to the rest of the lesson. It's impossible. The note burns into my skin like a brand.

"Miss Sloane, remain behind, please," Mr. Mollier calls as the bell rings.

Gert hurries out of the class; I envy him.

"I have geography class now, sir."

Mr. Mollier closes the door and then takes a seat behind his desk.

"Two detentions in little more than a week."

"Yes, sir."

He sighs, lips strained. "Bethany . . . we all have to make choices in life. I hope you're making the right ones."

"Yes, sir."

"I see your maths has improved drastically. I'm very pleased."

I glance up at him through the hair falling across my face. "Thank you, sir."

He regards me for a few heartbeats. "All right." He sighs. "You may go, Miss Sloane."

"Thank you, sir."

He gets up and opens the door for me like a princess, and I hurry past his tenth graders and into the hallway. Gert is standing at his locker, eyes wide as he stares at me. I hurry past him to my own locker five spaces away and pack away my maths books.

"Bethany?"

I gasp, and the whole locker shakes with the force of my start. "*What?*" I snap. I am not in the mood for his jibes.

"I . . . just wanted to say . . . sorry, for how I acted before."

"Huh?"

"I'm sorry I was such a jerk."

I blink, my defenses starting to lower. "Oh. Thanks."

"You know, if Mr. Mollier is giving you a hard time, I can talk to my mom about him. She works on the school governing body."

I smile at his chubby, worried face. I can't believe I never noticed how childlike he looks with his red hair and freckled cheeks. I have an impulse to kiss the quivering right corner of his mouth, so I do.

"Thanks, Gert," I whisper in his ear, "but it's okay."

His breath shivers as he exhales. "C-can I walk you to geography?"

This actually brightens my day a lot. "Sure," I say, and we walk along the corridor together. We don't speak, but we don't need to. This little gesture has erased every shadow that gathered around me in Mr. Mollier's presence and since Sakkie's note.

In geography, Gert takes the seat next to mine, and when the bell goes at the end of the lesson, he walks me to my lunch table. I'm not sure what has brought this kindness on, but it has made me forget about Sakkie's note.

The lunch bell rings, and the head table girl dishes up some mash and one sausage onto everyone's plate. I slide the note out from my bra strap and unfurl it, letting my eyes roam over his letters.

I press my legs together, scrunch up the note, and try to breathe deeply, images of what will happen after school consuming my mind. Beth sighs and stretches. I can't eat. I feel like I've got live worms wriggling in my stomach, trying to eat their way out.

And what Stacey said this morning, about Mr. Mollier looking at me . . . Was that real? Is he starting to like me, infected by the inky black that seems to leak out of me wherever I go?

I try to remember how he looked in his office.

Viper, Beth taunts.

I fidget through the rest of the day, and I get let off swimming because I say I feel nauseated. Mr. Schlebler gives me written work and orders me to the library, but I just *can't* sit doing work when my insides are squirming like this. I run along the empty hallways until

I am outside Mrs. Kilpatrick's class, where I know Stacey is reading *Northanger Abbey*.

I knock gently and then enter when she calls, "Yes?"

"Sorry, Mrs. Kilpatrick, but Mr. Mollier has asked to see Stacey."

"Did he give you a note?"

I act surprised. "No, ma'am."

"Did he say why?"

"No."

She sighs and gestures at Stacey with her hand. "Very well, Miss Preston. Proceed."

Stacey rises from her seat and follows me out of the room.

"What does he want me for?"

"He doesn't," I whisper, once the door is closed. "Tell me what Mr. Mollier did."

Stacey stops walking and folds her arms across her chest. "Is that all?"

I wring my hands. "Yes."

"You're such a *moegoe*, Bethany," she says, and I feel like Bernie.

I swallow. "Just tell me—does he stare at my . . ."

"Yes, he does. And you should watch out, because old men like that have all kinds of diseases."

"Mr. Mollier doesn't have diseases."

"Not anywhere you can *see*."

"That's gross," I say, like it doesn't matter. But my heart is racing.

"Yeah, well, watch out, because if you're alone with him too much, he could infect you."

I feel exposed. I want to think that Stacey is teasing me, but what if she's right? "I'll be careful," I promise.

She astonishes me by putting her perfect palm on my cheek and sighing deeply, the softness of her breath brushing at my lips. It almost smells like flowers in spring.

"Oh, Bethany," she says, and I melt into her palm.

"I . . ." I want to say I'm sorry.

"You better be," she says, her eyes close to mine, "because he's a predator."

No, I think. He's not the predator. I'm already trapped by one of those. *He* is the predator.

So are you, Beastly Beth snickers.

I wish Stacey had warned me sooner.

"Okay," I say.

"Before supper, take a nap. We're going out tonight to celebrate your return."

I nod, and then she walks back to her class, and I stare at the empty corridor where the echo of her remains. How can things be so different after only two weeks and still look the same as they used to? I feel so torn up inside, split in so many directions that I don't know which one is *my* direction anymore. In my head I hear the song lyrics *The wheels on the bus go round and round*, and I see those wheels, ever turning, never changing, round and round in one direction, unable to stop. Fate.

The only thing that I can focus on is seeing Rowan, my little bittersweet reward at the end of a hard day. Bittersweet because I know I can look but I can't touch.

47

Games

Stacey and I sneak out of the west wing via the bathroom window when the moon is high.

"Wait," Stacey whispers, squatting on her haunches and fiddling in the pocket of her school blazer, which she has put over her nightclothes.

"What's wrong?"

She removes a razor blade with care and holds it up to her face. "We'll need this for later," she says, handing it to me.

"What? Why?"

She touches her thumbs to the tip of every finger like she does when she is calculating. "Just hold on to it."

I run with the blade pressed firmly between my fingers. My heart is thudding so hard that by the time we're standing outside the shower rooms, I'm sure Stacey will hear it.

"*Baaaa*by," Jared calls when he and Rowan exit the wing. He holds up his arms as though he expects me to run into them like some cheesy movie.

I only have eyes for Rowan.

He doesn't look at me. He reaches out for Stacey, whom he embraces and kisses on the lips chastely. My fingers shake on the thin blade; I shove it into my pocket.

"Hi," she says, grinning like she has never grinned at me.

Jared saunters over to me and wraps his long arm around my shoulders. "Don't I get a hello, beautiful?" he asks, slobbering over my ear and leaning heavily on me.

"Have you been drinking?" I whisper. His breath smells toxic and sweet, and suddenly I want a taste too.

He chuckles and reaches into his back pocket, pulling free a bottle of peach vodka. It has a sickly sweet sunset illustration on the front, all oranges and marshmallow pinks. Still, it smells good. Where did he even get this? I try to make it more interesting by imagining it's a potion that will make Stacey forget Rowan forever and love me more, but my mind can't make such a big lie true.

I glance at Rowan and Stacey having a whispered conversation, and my heart contracts.

"I want some," I say and snatch the bottle. I drink three gulps before my throat ignites and I'm coughing and gagging, trying to inhale.

"You okay?" Rowan is suddenly right next to me, hand on my arm.

"I'm," I choke out, "fine."

"Take it easy, okay?"

I look up into his eyes, glad the alcohol-induced tears are hiding the real ones underneath.

"Okay," I whisper and wipe my eyes.

Rowan's lips are tight, his eyes hard yet blazing as he stares down at me—a look so full of meaning that I panic.

Look away, I urge him . . . urge myself.

Stacey walks up to him and takes his hand, her cold dark eyes boring into my own for a split second. He steps away from me, all distance.

Jared and I walk twenty paces behind Stacey and Rowan. I wish we were in front. Then I wouldn't have to look at his arm around her waist. I wouldn't have to see her dip her head toward him or throw it back and laugh. Then their words wouldn't get carried away on the wind before I could hear what they were saying.

Jared pulls out a cigarette and lights it, taking a long drag. "Eish, it's been so fucking long, hey," he says. "All I've thought about is you."

"Hmm," I murmur, "thanks. Can I bum one of those?"

He raises his eyebrows. "Sure."

He lights it for me, and I take a drag, ignoring the immediate tightness in my chest and the insistent need to cough. After a while I am too dizzy to care if I feel nauseated. I drag and drag and drag on the cigarette. Maybe if I drag long enough, my lungs will ignite.

Rowan helps Stacey onto the tire and then reaches for me.

"Hold this, bru," Jared interrupts, handing Rowan his *skyf*, and then he lifts me up awkwardly with both hands, and I climb up across from Stacey.

"We're going to have fun tonight," she says, tapping fingers to thumb, back and forth, over and over. She nods up at the moon, which is almost full. "The ghosts will even join us."

I nod. "Sure."

Stacey watches, amused, as Jared scrambles up the tire. His pants are so loose they slide down a little as he climbs, butt crack exposed. Something long and thin makes a sloshing sound from in his long pants pocket, and Stacey frowns at it.

"What's that?" I ask.

"It's for later," he says, and gives me a wink. "None of you are ready yet."

It's obviously a bottle, but I don't press. Let him keep stupid secrets. Stacey seems uninterested and unimpressed anyway.

"I propose," she says, "that we play truth or dare—rule being that you *can't* refuse. At all."

"Whoo!" Jared punches the air. "Yeah, boy!"

"*And*," Stacey adds, "in order to dissuade any cowards from choosing truth too often, any truth-picker will also have a truth from everyone else in the circle."

Rowan looks unnerved, and I feel it too. But Jared is laughing, his tongue poking out from between his red lips.

"Let's do this," he says, slapping his thighs.

"One moment, gentlemen," Stacey insists, holding up her index finger. "There is one more contestant."

"Who?" I demand, shocked into speech.

"This way," Stacey calls. She winks at Jared and whispers, "We're going to have fun now."

"Stacey?" someone calls from the darkness.

Oh my God. It's Bernie.

48

Gathering

I sit between Jared and Bernie, biting out the insides of my mouth and feeling like I'll vomit at any moment. I want to cut off Jared's roaming hands (and wagging tongue) with the razor Stacey handed me, and make Bernie go away. Stacey sits across from me; she is so porcelainlike when her long lashes rest on her cheek as she blinks. She is serene—a goddess of the hunt with wild, untamed hair. Part goddess, part lion. All beauty, all danger. Beside her, Rowan looks like an Adonis. It hurts me how perfect a couple they are.

"Who goes first?" Rowan ventures, his voice optimistic. Is he looking forward to the game? Or is it an act to appear calm? Does he think about it all as much as I do? I send up a silent prayer—*please let tonight be okay*—but I don't know whom I am praying to. Rowan is smiling now.

I imagine we are in this together.

Stacey eyes me, and my stomach contracts. I have a niggling feeling in my chest that I want to ignore.

Stacey licks her lips. "Truth or dare—Bernie."

Bernie gasps and leans back as though physically assaulted. *"Me?"*

"Truth. Or. Dare," Stacey reiterates slowly, as though Bernie is mentally challenged. I watch as she taps, fingers to thumb—*tap, tap,*

tap. Her tongue roams the ridges of her front teeth, sliding back and forth, eagerly. *Slide, tap, slide, tap.* She is enjoying tonight. She is impatient.

"T-truth."

"How far have you ever gone with any boy?"

I notice that Jared is getting a lot of pleasure out of Bernie's discomfort, and for the first time since we began competing for Stacey's affection, I feel sorry for her. I can't help but feel bad. She's the fifth wheel. She didn't ask for this. She didn't do anything wrong, nothing to justify being an object of ridicule. I hate this, I think. I hate feeling sorry for her.

But going back to hating her is hard.

Try harder, Beth encourages.

I bite down on my tongue and say nothing, like the coward I am.

Bernie swallows. "You mean . . ."

Jared leans forward, his teeth glinting like a fox's as he smiles. "Yes, I *mean*."

"Um, I kissed a boy once at my eleventh birthday party."

"Are you a lesbian?" Stacey asks, and everyone bursts out laughing, including Rowan. His smile is open, and I know that he thinks it is all good-natured fun. I bite my lip, knowing that this is a power struggle. Shocked, I realize I didn't laugh.

Stacey noticed.

Jared takes a swig from the bottle and passes it around, then proceeds to light cigarettes from some never-ending source and distribute them as well. Rowan refuses and glances at me. I have no choice but to accept my second cigarette ever, because Stacey's eyes challenge me, and Stacey trumps Rowan, because Rowan is my secret.

I take it and put it guiltily to my lips. Rowan's eyes harden, and he looks away.

Bernie is blushing furiously. The red is marginally muted by the darkness, but the moon is high and bright, exposing her.

I glance at her, and I think, *I'm sorry*. This isn't about Bernie. It's about me. And then I'm angry—angry that I'm the subject of such scrutiny.

It must be Bernie's fault, Beth hisses. *She must have been influencing Stacey against you while you were away.*

"No," Bernie murmurs in answer to Stacey's question, holding the cigarette between her fingers.

I feel the alcohol swimming in my head. "How do you know if you've never fucked a guy?" I laugh before I can stop myself.

I see Stacey's eyes snap in my direction, and then Rowan says, "Go easy on the girl," and I love him more for telling me off.

But I would have done it again, because Stacey's eyes are bright with approval.

"I'm sorry," I say to Bernie, who frowns and leans away from me like she doesn't know who I am. As if, by being nice, I have shocked her.

"Your question," Stacey reminds me; her voice is more welcoming.

I think for a minute and then ask, "Have you ever seen your parents at it?"

Bernie's lips curl away from her teeth. "Ew! No way."

"Do you want to throw away that cigarette?" Rowan asks, and his question is so friendly I want to kiss him.

Bernie looks relieved and smiles shyly. "Kind of . . ."

He laughs and offers to take it from her. She hands it over with a grin.

"Bernie's turn," Rowan says, smiling kindly back at her.

Bernie asks him truth or dare, and he picks dare, which I think is the safer option. I won't pick truth until *he* has so that I can follow his lead. If he lies, I'll lie; if not . . . then I guess I won't either.

"I dare you to french kiss Stacey!" She giggles, and my insides squirm.

No . . . why *that*? Why *kissing*? Why *french* kissing? My heart begins to creak; the honey warmth Rowan supplies begins to drip away. I have never been this unsure or uncomfortable in my life. I have never felt such horror or pain. Fucking Bernie!

"You can only dare things with mutual consent," he says, smiling tightly.

"That's fine," Stacey says, and leans forward.

Rowan's eyes glance at me once, wistfully, and my heart does a somersault (though it feels like a trampoline is in my stomach). Then he takes Stacey's face between his hands and kisses her.

I watch their mouths move together, wet and open, and he sticks his tongue into her mouth and her tongue responds and—oh, God! I feel sick.

I turn away and try not to cry, and Jared thinks I am giving him a hug, and I let him comfort me until it's over. But I can hear the smacking noises they make as they go at it. I clench my fist and feel my nails dig little half moons into my palm.

My stomach contracts once.

Please don't be sick, Beth drawls. *What a fucking chop you are.*

"Good kisser," Stacey murmurs, and she sounds breathless. Breathless from *my* Adonis. *My* Adonis kissing *my* Stacey. The irony is that if I didn't love him as much as I do, I would be all for their relationship. I'd be yelling, "Go! Make babies! It has been written!"

I swallow a sob and wait for Rowan to speed ahead. My stomach is hollow, and the night is blacker than I have ever seen it. I can't look at him, so I just stare down at my hands.

"Bethany," he says, his voice hitching on my name's second syllable. "Truth or dare?"

I know his question will be safe if I pick truth, and anyway, I don't seem to care quite as much as I did before. I risk a glance at him. His eyes are screaming that they are sorry, but I know I asked for this, and I look away. "Truth," I say.

He nods, and his mouth quirks up a little. "Why do you—" He hesitates and then plows on: "Why do you hate your mother?"

"I . . . I . . . don't." I blink, thinking about it. "I'm just angry with her."

"Why?" Stacey intervenes, asking her question. "Why are you angry?"

"I . . . I don't know."

"You can't lie," Stacey reminds me, and her expression is so encouraging—an almost smile—that I tell her.

"Because . . . because she left me. She left me here to go and marry that gross old man, for his money, not his love. She tossed me aside like a bit of rubbish, like a slip of used paper, and then she comes here thinking she can just pick me back up again and she can't." The floodgates open. Why does Rowan know exactly the question to ask? "I hate her because she didn't help me—she didn't warn me about . . . about anything! She didn't help me, and she doesn't love me, and she doesn't deserve me!"

"What didn't she warn you about?" Bernie whispers.

The gentleness in her tone shocks me into looking at her—really looking at her for the first time in . . . well, maybe ever. I see something in her that resembles me—or used to. Innocence, curiosity, fragility . . . The thing I see in her face is the need to lock onto someone stronger than yourself because alone, you're nothing. You're lost. She has that in her eyes. Is she the me from a few years ago? Am I what she will become? This familiarity shocks and repulses me.

Please don't be like me, I plead with my eyes.

"She didn't warn me about the dangers in the world. She didn't teach me about womanly things. She didn't show me any guidance—she wasn't there when . . ." I almost lose my voice. "I needed her. She was miles away with farty old Stoffel. She chose him over me and, yes . . . I think I hate her for it sometimes, but only because I *loved* her so much. I . . . I trusted her."

Jared sucks on his cigarette, and I raise mine to my lips with shaking fingers. "What about your dad? Where's he?"

"He died when I was four. I don't remember him, not at all."

I take another drag and find that the smoke soothes my taut nerves, even as it messes up my chest.

I want to ask Rowan a question, but I know the rules. I turn to Stacey. "Truth or dare?"

I salivate with all the possibilities. *When did your mother die? Do you remember her? What was your period like? Was it like mine? What is your biggest secret, your wildest fantasy? What do you think of me? Do you prefer me to Bernie? Why don't you sleep?*

"How far have you gone with a guy?" I burst before she has chosen, knowing that it is the first, most important question that must be answered. If it's a truth, then she *has* to answer, even if it's about recounting the past.

"Dare," she says slowly, fingers tapping.

My skin flushes with humiliation, raw as salt. Shit. Shit, shit, shit. I might as well start digging a hole for myself right now. I gulp and breathe slowly; I don't think a mistake like that can ever be recovered from. Then, something occurs to me.

"I dare you to go to second base with Jared."

He laughs. "I'm game!"

If I can make her like him, I wonder if she will do a trade. Rowan for Jared, nice and simple. I glance at my Adonis, and he is chuckling.

Stacey takes her first sip of alcohol and then inches closer to Jared. "How do you want to do this?"

Rowan laughs explosively, which makes me laugh. I glance at Bernie, determinedly looking away from all of us, which brings me to a state of raucous hysterics. Jared reaches for Stacey, and for the first time I see her hesitate. I stare at her—what is she thinking? Then, steeling herself, she faces him and lifts her shirt.

I ought to look away, I know, but I can't. My heart races. This is the most intimate part of Stacey I have seen. I want to memorize it because I know when it's over, it will feel like a dream.

I can't believe she has breasts—little, like mine—and I have seen them. I feel like I'm going into shock; it is unreality.

"Yowza!" Jared breathes, staring at her breasts. He fondles them for a while until she is bored and sits back down. "Whoa, wait a minute—I didn't see—"

"Second base rules—one or the other, heaven or hell. You made your choice, *bokkie*."

I am still blinking at having seen Stacey's nakedness. I am still surprised they look just like mine, except hers aren't purple and bruised.

Stacey turns to Jared. "Truth or dare?"

"Dare," he says eagerly.

Stacey licks her lips. "You have the option of going to third base with Bernie, if she'll let you, or kissing Rowan."

"*What?* That's bullshit!"

I can hardly keep myself from laughing. Bernie is crying silently, and Rowan's lip curls downward like he's appalled.

"You've got to be fucking kidding me," Jared complains, eyeing Bernie with a grimace.

"Well, she has nice knockers," Stacey points out.

I look at them for the first time. They are, without doubt, the biggest, but I refuse to believe they are the nicest.

Jared smiles sweetly at Bernie, who shakes her head violently.

My smile fades when I see Rowan's nauseated expression.

"What if *I* refuse?" Rowan mutters in Stacey's direction.

"In that case," Stacey says, raising her eyebrows and folding her arms, "Jared has to take a default."

"Default," Jared says lazily, looking relieved.

"First, strip," she instructs, using the same tone she uses on me when she gives an order. This is her control. I can see it so clearly now that it isn't directed at me. She has control over all of us. "*Everything.* Then screw Bethany."

Rowan leans forward. "*What?*"

49

Little Girls' House

NOW

We walk and walk. I feel emptiness to my right, can hear the grass in the field, the grasshoppers, and the bees. Devil's thorns, paper thorns . . . so many enemies waiting under the yellow sea.

I remember you, they say to me now. *You humiliated us . . . plucked off all our thorns. How are we meant to defend ourselves?*

We aren't the enemy. You *are.*

Treacherous little Thorn.

We must have passed the chapel and the green.

"Bats," I mutter.

"Flying ants," you reply.

"Tasted like peanut butter," I murmur.

"Prove you love me."

I go still. "What?"

"Close your eyes."

I feel myself balk, but do it anyway, let you lead me on, blind. Don't know why I'm doing this.

You stop walking. "Open your eyes."

"My God . . . Clare House," I murmur, looking into the husk of what was once my dorm house.

Blackened and burned, the sign hangs askew.

"The little girl house," Stacey says, nodding.

"What happened?"

"You remember. *Bethie*," you breathe, "you remember."

"I'm tired."

You help me inside our old home, to our old dorm, and both of us are surprised to find our beds intact. How many children slumbered in them after us? How many jeweled rubies and blue-blocked duvet covers?

"Let's rest awhile," you offer, and I am so thankful I close my eyes without waiting to see if you will rest with me.

50

Deadly Whisper

THEN

"What?"

It's like the world loses all the power of sound after Rowan yells that one little word. Nature is dead on her feet, the wind ceases to fluster, the stars gasp and gape; all is muted to echo Stacey's silent seethe.

Jared laughs once and says, "How about it, baby?" Then he is leaning over me, sloppy wet mouth over my chin, body pressing into my stomach.

I screech as he knocks me off the tire, and we land with a thud and a flurry of dust on the cool midnight sand, among the paper thorns. The razor cuts into my thigh; I'm paralyzed and winded. Jared, drunk and high, grapples with my shirt for less than a second, ripping it ever so slightly, before Rowan throws himself full force at Jared's head to topple him. I reach into my pocket and pull free the razor, flinging it into the night.

"Rowan!" I scream as he and Jared go rolling.

Jared snarls and punches Rowan's ear, which bleeds a little all over Jared's knuckles. Then Rowan is on top, yelling indecipherable obscenities, mashing up Jared's face with punch after punch.

Terrified, I throw myself at them, grabbing Rowan under the arms and heaving.

"Rowan! Stop it! Stop, Rowan, *stop*!"

"You son of a bitch!" he is yelling at Jared, who laughs through his broken teeth even as I manage to drag Rowan away.

"*Poes*!" Jared calls, chuckling and gurgling.

I look up at Stacey, who sits atop her throne, watching the havoc she caused with an enigmatic smile. Her fingers no longer tap her thumbs. This chaos was her plan.

"I want to go home!" Bernie sniffles, whimpering into her hands.

"Rowan," I murmur in his ear, "calm down. *Please* calm down."

He shudders, and then he sighs deeply, slumping against me. "I'm sorry."

"Fucking idiots," Stacey says, but her voice is calm, an embrace. She was hard, and now she is soft. She was wrath; now she is tranquility. Her face is less rigid, more fluid; her eyes are flames, not ice. I look at her feet, where they dangle, cracked and impressive, and I am filled with gratitude, sweet gratitude, that she isn't angry with me. The nice Stacey is here, the cold one buried again.

"Shut up, Bernie," she snaps, and my heart exults. I had been cast out; I had been *frozen* out. But now I am back, I can sense it; back in her warm and protective embrace.

I step away from Rowan, and I climb the tire once more. Stacey receives me into her arms like a lost disciple returned, and I sob onto her sharp, bony shoulder.

"I'm sorry," I wail, over and over. *Please,* I think, *please don't go anywhere.*

She soothes down my hair and coos in my ear.

"Bethany?" Rowan calls, reaching for me. I know this must confuse him, but I can't explain.

"Enough excitement for one night, boys," Stacey says. She pulls a cigarette from the pack next to her, puts the long white stick between her full lips, and clicks the lighter to a flame, pressing it to the end.

I hold my breath, and she takes her first drag, expertly releasing it like she has done it a million times. And why not? Why *shouldn't* she have done it a million times?

Jared is still laughing on the ground. I can see he's lost at least two teeth, but it looks like the front ones might be okay. Surprisingly, he reaches into his long pocket and produces a remarkably unbroken bottle of green absinthe. So that's what he was hiding.

He unscrews the lid and takes a sip, smearing blood all over the mouth of the bottle.

"Ew," Stacey comments, but she looks intrigued by the bottle.

"Should we call an ambulance?" Bernie whimpers.

Rowan looks ashamed of himself as he helps his friend up, but underneath that, I can see he is hurt. *I* have hurt him, but I can't see precisely how. He glances down at his bloodied fists and frowns, jaw clenched. He's angry, and a blush spreads across his lower cheeks.

"You're not meant to drink it neat," he comments, but then he snatches the absinthe, wipes the rim, and gulps some down. "Shit," he breathes, clenching his jaw. "How did you even get this?"

Jared doesn't answer, and Stacey reaches out a hand for the bottle, taking a sip too. She doesn't react, and then hands the bottle to me. I take a small sip and cough. It's like aniseed, or licorice, but overpoweringly strong. My eyes tear, and I wonder if it was such a good idea to try some.

"Now Bernie," Stacey insists.

Bernie is delighted, thinking Stacey is trying to include her, but I know the truth. We both want to see if Bernie can hack it.

I'm not disappointed. She squishes up her face, and half of what she sipped dribbles out of her mouth. I glance at Stacey, but she seems sympathetic rather than amused.

"It's okay," Stacey tells Bernie. "Give it here."

The bottle is handed back, and then all focus is once again on Jared.

"We can't take him back like this," Rowan says. "Everyone will see."

"Will anyone be awake?" I ask.

He doesn't meet my eyes. "Yes."

"Shit."

"We'll wash him up in our bathroom," Stacey says, taking charge. "No one will be awake in our dorm. You just have to keep him quiet."

Rowan looks uneasy, but what else is there to be done? We can't exactly take Jared back to the senior dorm looking like the victim of a mugging.

We band together, all of us half dragging, half carrying Jared to Clare House, but Jared is too loud in his drunkenness. He's sure to give us away.

"This is crazy," Rowan growls. "He'll wake up half the wing."

Stacey sighs and takes the vodka bottle from Rowan, smashing it over Jared's head and shattering it into a million tiny pieces.

"Glassy," I gasp at the same time that Rowan says, "Oh my God," and Stacey's attention is suddenly burning on me.

"What?" she says.

"Glassy, glassy, cut my . . . ," I whisper, feeling faint. Glass Man is coming.

She slaps me. Hard. "Get a grip," she orders, but her face is suddenly pale.

Rowan takes half a step toward her but then stops, fists clenched at his side.

Stacey turns to him. "If you want to get expelled, then feel free to keep acting stupid. If you want to stay, then help me by watching him while Bethany and I go and get a wet cloth."

Rowan looks like he just might argue back, but I pray to the ghosts he won't.

Please don't argue, I think. *Let's just get through this.*

"Fine," Rowan says at last. "Take this, and flush it." In his tone I hear something that both terrifies and thrills me. I think the thing between him and Stacey, whatever it was, might have been irrevocably damaged.

Stacey takes the absinthe Rowan holds out. It sloshes green and hypnotic in its crystal chamber.

"Give me the cigarettes too. And the lighter. We can't be caught."

He nods and hands them over.

"Come on," Stacey tells me.

I'm honored she has picked me, but I would rather stay outside with Rowan. He'll only have Bernie for company now, which I feel bad about. Maybe he'll be kind to her . . . I realize I want that. I want someone to be nice to Bernie. I'm too much of a coward to do it myself.

Treacherous, Beth snarls. *Betrayer.*

I try not to think about the other reason I want to stay, but I picture it anyway. Rowan's eyes locked on my face, his arms wrapping around me, his voice in my ear saying "Everything is all right." I shake my head and follow Stacey instead.

We climb onto the wheelie bin and slip in through the window. It's a little awkward with the absinthe and the cigarettes and the lighter.

"Shit," Stacey mutters, when we are inside. "Trust Jared to ruin it all."

I'm glad she is blaming Jared rather than me—or, worse . . . Rowan. Stacey takes out a cigarette and lights it, drawing in a lungful of silver smoke. She closes her eyes when she blows it out, and my own eyelids droop.

"What was that?" Stacey whispers, her whole body going still as she cocks her head to the side, listening.

"I didn't hear anyth—"

"Ssh!"

Now I hear it. I think it sounds like footsteps a long way away. Matron is making her rounds. How long before she checks the bathroom? Five minutes? Less?

"Hey," Rowan calls from the window. He has climbed onto the bin. "Jared's waking up. I think I better try to get him out of here."

Stacey nods and flicks her hand. *Go,* she's saying. *Go.*

Rowan jumps down and says something to Bernie. Maybe he's said "Will you help me?" or "Give me a hand." Whatever it is, the two of them drag Jared away.

"We have to hurry," Stacey says after we have listened for a while. "Matron patrols the east wing, and then she'll come along here and finish at the bathroom."

"Okay," I say. I don't ask her how she knows this.

Stacey moves—I should have known Glass Man was watching us—and the absinthe falls, shattering on the floor like the peach vodka shattered on Jared's head. The green liquid has gone everywhere, splashing the floor, the laundry, our legs. The sound is deafening.

Stacey mutters something that sounds like *shit* or *sit*, and then her cigarette drops. Everything happens in slow motion; the cigarette spins as it falls, elegant like a gymnast, and then it happens.

The whole laundry pile, the tiles, and the hem of my nightgown erupt in sudden blue flames. First they slink over it all like sapphire liquid—a deadly whisper—then they are tall and angry, like the essence and embodiment of the absinthe's rage. They hiss and they breathe and they spread.

Stacey's eyes widen, and then I panic.

The sound is alarming—it sounds like hunger.

"Stacey!" I cry, the flames lapping at everything: the shower curtains, the towel racks—spreading across the floor where the glass and absinthe have gone. My heart chokes in the mayhem, my body paralyzed and frozen. I am beyond emotion now—beyond fear. Fear, I have left far behind.

By the time Matron reaches us, the whole bathroom is in flames, and they are spreading along the plaster ceiling and into the hall. Matron is yelling, but there is a lot of smoke, and we can't see her. The fire alarm sounds, and then the halls are filled with screaming children.

Fire, orange and blue, engulfs the entire bathroom. I have lost sight of Stacey in the blaze. I stand, calm and watchful, as the fire laps at the hem of my nightgown, dancing as it devours.

And all I can think is
I can't breathe
I'm a girl aflame

51

The Trail

NOW

You are gone when I wake.

My eyes sting in the once-familiar dryness. "Stacey?"

I'm groggy, not quite awake. But then I register the darkness in the room. The sun has set. Everything is cast in a deep-blue light, and a pulse of adrenaline flashes in my chest. *"Stacey?"*

I hear something in the distance: voices, I think. But they are faint, floating in echoes from down the corridor, which is black.

I pull my legs across the mattress and swing them down, intending to stand, but my foot hits something sharp. I hiss and draw it up.

A tiny little object is stuck to my toe.

Circular, with barbs.

A devil's thorn.

I pull it out with a grimace. A bead of blood bubbles from my toe. Your laughter echoes through the corridor into the room. I put the devil's thorn slowly onto my mattress and realize with horror what I'm staring at.

Devil's thorns. A trail of them . . . leading from my bed and out into the corridor.

Another echo of laughter, and then voices.

"Stacey?"

I follow the trail on slow, limping legs, my heart thudding *stay-back, stay-back*.

Who are you talking to?

The voices are louder in the hallway, but still some distance off. And your voice . . . it's your friendly voice. Your amused voice. Your warm voice. And now I remember there was a different one for different occasions.

"Stacey?"

The voices stop.

And

the

silence

is

horrifying.

It bends the night, it **deepens** the dark, even though I know—I *know*—that shouldn't, *couldn't* be possible.

The blood from my toe squelches on the floor. I have left a trail of my own thorns.

"Bleeding, Bethie?" you croon. "You've gotten so weak."

I swallow. "Stacey, where are you? What is this?"

"How is it," you continue, and now your voice is coming from my right side, from the doorway that leads to Gogo's old room, "that you forgot about me?"

"This isn't funny."

Your voice is farther away now. "You forgot me and our beautiful memories. Aren't writers supposed to remember everything? Draw on their experiences, their pain for that never-ending fodder in the brain files? Write what you know . . ."

Her voice is a singsong.

"Stacey, stop it."

I step forward, but the darkness is like a living thing pressing back, and I can't go farther.

"But we're playing a game! You used to love games. I remember your favorite."

"We aren't kids anymore."

Your voice is a shiver down my arms. *"Glassy . . ."*

"We're adults."

"Glassy . . ."

"Stacey—"

"Cut my . . ."

"STACEY!"

Laughter rolls off the walls, rides along the floor, undulating.

"Follow me, little Beth. Time to finish our game."

Your voice grows fainter, but you keep calling.

Come on, little Beth . . . the ghosts are out.

I'm left with the rapidly descending night and a trail of devils leading out of the charred building and out into the desert.

52

Stare

THEN

Stacey's eyes are a mucky brown. Her nose is straight and petite. She has full lips that she licks often. She has a mole on her left cheek. Her hair is curly and wild, like a goddess or a dryad. A myriad of details I try to drink in.

I glance down at her neck. Beneath the thin membrane of skin, her vein pulses with blood. Rhythmical. Predictable.

This is the only thing about Stacey that is predictable.

Her eyebrows quiver, and I think maybe she is going to frown. I stare harder, and my eyeballs dry out; I blink.

"I win," Stacey says, confirming what I haven't quite yet realized. "You lose."

I can never outstare her in our staring battles, which we started playing only a few days ago; her eyes seem moist and unaffected as she continues to look at me. Will she ever blink, or will I be looking at her until I am gray and old, realizing my whole life has been lived within the reflection in her eyes? Then she will blink and I will die. A lifetime passed in a single wink.

I smile. "You always win."

She shrugs. "You might get better," she says, though we both know I won't. She is taking pity on me.

I run my gaze over her milky skin, wishing I still looked so clean. It's been two months since the fire, and my scars still hurt me sometimes. I don't wear shorts anymore unless it's nighttime, and even then I don't wander far. I wear flowing summer dresses that reach the floor, and Stacey tells me I'm like a princess.

They are still rebuilding the west wing, so we have been moved to the north-wing spare strip. It's brand new and feels like a fresh start. The floors are white linoleum, like a hospital, and the walls gleam, nude of fingerprints or scuff marks. It is the antithesis of what the west wing has become: charred, scarred—like me. Stacey and I share a room alone, and I think maybe the fire was worth it, just for that. The beds are very close together.

"The new beds should arrive soon," Matron Monday always declares, but we are still waiting.

Everyone in the west wing missed a month of school and will have to take summer classes. I missed more than that, though, bandaged from hip to toe and strapped to a bed in Johannesburg, so I won't pass the year. The teachers don't think so anyway—except Mr. Mollier, who has been very polite to me and tried to convince me that, with enough hard work, I can do it—with only six weeks to go until the exams and cycle tests. So I'll be like Stacey—left behind. The oldest girl in my new grade.

Mother cried when she learned this—she cried even more than when she learned of the accident and my injury—but I don't see why she is so sad. I'm proud to be doing what Stacey did at my age. I'll be ahead by being behind.

"Don't worry, darling," my mother had said, holding my hands in hospital. "There's always plastic surgery. We'll ask Stoffel."

The morphine blurs my memory, but I think I tell her to go down the Tractor Tire, though she doesn't really understand what I mean, so I tell her that my scars are my new identity. They bind me to Stacey as a badge of honor. That honor is tinged with something else, too, something less palatable, but I quash it.

When Mother learns about me having to repeat the year, she says, "Don't worry, darling. We'll get you a tutor."

She knows what my eyes are telling her, but she chooses to ignore it. My failure, like my scars, is my new identity.

Stacey leans back and sighs; the bed takes her weight with a lazy eloquence.

"Are you coming out tonight?" she asks me, lying very still.

She knows the answer already. Still she asks, hoping the answer will have changed. Tomorrow makes two weeks since my return, and I've yet to leave the dorm after sundown.

"Tonight could be different," she tells me. "We could see Jared." She means it as a tempting offer, but I grimace and look away. "And Rowan," she adds a moment later.

Rowan.

I lean back and fold my arms, that familiar surge of darkness returning. The doctors said the darkness in my mind was normal. *Coping.* The truth is Rowan hasn't come to see me since I got back, and I haven't asked why. He sees Stacey, though, every night. She tells me of the wonderful things they do together now that they can be alone, and I wonder why Rowan is worth recounting the past over. Why is it okay to break her own rules, when she tells me how they dance around the Tractor Tire or kiss under the watchful gaze of the corn tower?

Glass Man doesn't seek them because he knows that they would be blind to his presence, too absorbed in one another to be scared away. And this is what forms part of the new darkness inside me. This new blackness has merged with the old, like conjoined twins. Inseparable but different.

Stacey doesn't know I want to tear off my ears rather than hear her speak about Rowan. She doesn't realize I have to bite my tongue until it bleeds to keep from asking her to stop.

How could I ever demand Stacey stop? She's in love. He seems to be as well. My brief spell away has been their honeymoon period, the same honeymoon period Rowan and I once shared, and which was torn away by my own hand. Except they had two months, when Rowan and I had a mere fortnight. Of course he fell in love with her. It's no mystery why.

Now all that is left is the deep center of the tire and Glass Man. Henry and Sarah Dertz might also be watching, keeping tabs so Glass Man knows where to find me when he decides he's ready. Sometimes I look down at my ruined legs and think the fire was an illusion. Glass Man is the one who did this to me. He cut me up with his terrible kisses as a reminder of his IOU.

"Is Bernie going?" I ask.

Stacey raises her eyebrows. "What the fuck do you think?"

"Fine. I'll come out."

I want their honeymoon to end.

I want to see the look on Rowan's face when he sees me. What will I learn from his expression in the split second before he can compose his features? Shock? Regret? Dare I even hope—affection?

Stacey leans over and kisses my cheek, and she whispers in my ear, "I love you, Bethany." There is tenderness there I have never seen before.

I tell her I love her too. I still have the scar on my arm to prove it. That day when I swiped the razor blade across my flesh seems like years ago; a laughable prelude to the magnum opus of scars I wear now. Her kiss, as it did back then, stings my skin, and somewhere inside me, Beth stirs.

I love you, too, she tells me, laughing her derision.

"Shut up," I hiss.

Stacey frowns and cocks her head to the side.

I smile apologetically, and then I notice something. "Twin . . . Where is your pencil-shaving bottle?" The bedside table is empty.

She just looks at me and smiles.

"Challenge you to a staring duel," I say weakly.

She beams at me. "You'll lose."

"I know."

53

Spy

When Stacey nudges me at close to midnight, I pretend to be asleep. I'm a coward, I know, but my brain has disconnected from my body. I don't want to go anymore. If I feign sleep, maybe she won't be offended.

It's surprisingly easy to convince her. She steps away from the bed, and then I hear her hurry out of the room. I wait ten seconds, and then I follow. Maybe just watching him will be enough for me. Maybe if I can just drink in his form one last time, it will be the end of the horrible craving inside of me. Maybe that will be enough.

She's with him, Beth tells me. Across the room a shadow looms, very real and very dark. Is it the Beast? Is it a messenger from Glass Man—a spy? *She's got her hands all over him. And he's got his hands all over her. They're a perfect match. You said it yourself.*

I stare at the shade, willing myself to be strong, but I'm shivering.

Go away, I tell her, and she does, laughing. But the shadow remains.

◆ ◆ ◆

It isn't hard to find Stacey; I am drawn to her. She and Rowan stand by the Tractor Tire, grasping one another like there has been a famine, their physical forms like the nourishment their bodies and minds require.

Seeing him smell her neck, rub her back, smile in wonder—it's enough to drive me crazy. The power of their passion is so intense I can almost feel it. They're so absorbed in one another they don't notice my presence.

"Missed you," Rowan says, in that wonderful way he used to say it to me.

Stacey sighs and leans into him. "Me too."

I think about leaving, and then I decide it is a good idea. I begin to turn, but then I notice Stacey is looking at me. She's seen me. She knows I'm here. She smiles at me, and I try to smile back, but my mouth is full of bile. Then, very deliberately, she kisses him, her lips pressed so firmly against his that it's a wonder it doesn't send both of them reeling, naked.

The bile rises again, and I throw up behind the small knobthorn tree I have been using as my shield. I sneak away, and Rowan never even knew I was there.

"I'm sorry you had to see that," Stacey tells me the next day. She is sitting in our invisible parlor, her legs crossed. The soft brown powder sand dirties her shorts, but she doesn't seem to care anymore. She doesn't brush away the filth and tell me dirtiness is a weakness, like she used to. Now she is one with the earth, like the two have a private connection. It must be, because she never gets devils in her feet and can always navigate the paper-thorn patches.

Bernie is with us. She glances up and frowns. "Huh?"

"Shut up," Stacey tells her. She turns back to me. "You should have spoken."

Bernie opens her mouth like she will speak, but Stacey throws her a dangerous look, and she falls silent.

"You were busy," I say.

Bernie frowns at me and continues to make partitions in the dirt, every so often glancing back at me like I'm an alien. I wish Stacey would tell her to leave us alone.

She laughs. "Yes. He was inspired last night."

"Inspired?" I ask.

Her eyes twinkle, and I almost faint. Stacey and Rowan had sex last night. I could have been watching. Rowan touched her like he once touched me, before I got my scars and stopped coming out to see him. The corners of my eyes sting with densely packed tears. How much humiliation and hurt can one teardrop contain?

I say, "Oh," and then fall silent. Have I been so easy to forget?

You pushed them together, Beth reminds me.

I know.

You deserve this.

I know that too.

"Want to play truth or dare?" Bernie asks suddenly. I am so distracted that her voice cuts into me, grating.

I roll my eyes and want to tell her to shut up, but Stacey has grinned and leaned in to whisper something in her ear. The way her jawbone moves reminds me of ribs and diaphragms. Organs pulsing underneath. I picture the way her tongue must twist and bend as she forms the words that will influence Bernie.

Bernie's eyes go wide. "I can't—"

"Fucking baby," Stacey says; Bernie's ears go tomato.

Bernie's face puckers. "But Bethany—"

"Leave her out of this," Stacey snaps. "Just do it."

She looks startled, but I don't know why. "O-okay."

"Later," Stacey says. "And I want the proof."

Should I ask Stacey what the dare was? Why didn't she share it with me? I can keep a secret better than Bernie can. Why hide it? And why didn't Bernie go do the dare? Why did the game end there?

◆ ◆ ◆

I'm sitting on my bed. I'm alone. The moon is high, and Stacey is outside, having sex with Rowan on a haunted tire, making sounds I used to make, touching what I used to touch. Down the hall, Bernie sleeps with her mouth hanging open, her saliva pooling in that gaping chamber until it runs down her chin like the dirty stream it is.

The silence is so loud that it hums in my head like a swarm of flies. The ghosts are out tonight. They won't let me sleep, and I won't be able to anyway, not until Stacey gets back. I wonder if Rowan will take her to our cabin, laugh with her about what we used to do there, and then drink tap water out of champagne glasses.

By the time Stacey gets back, I'm waiting in the bathroom by the window. The bathroom is identical to its charred west-wing counterpart. Stacey slides in deftly and hops to the floor on bare feet, soundless. Everything about her is silence. She's like a shadow cat. She turns around, intending to head for the door, but I am waiting just behind her, and she gasps.

She looks almost surprised—almost—but her face is cold and hard like marble, her eyes black in their anger. She raises one perfect hand and slaps me across my face.

"Spying on me again?" she hisses.

"I'm sorry," I gasp, clutching at my burning cheek. "I didn't mean to—"

Another slap, this time across the other cheek. My head whips around, and I feel a tiny crack in my neck, an air bubble popping out from between the cartilage.

"Don't *ever* do that again. Do you hear me?"

I nod. "I'm sorry."

I am too afraid to look into her eyes, so I look at her lips instead, and I see how swollen and red they are, like Rowan has been sucking on them. The blood drains from my face, and then I can't help checking for signs . . . Are her knees bloody? Does she have scratches on her neck? Bruises on her wrists? Love bites?

My stomach convulses like it is having its own little seizure. The bile I have been swallowing for nearly an hour rises up in my throat, and I vomit all over the floor. It lands loudly. I haven't eaten anything in a while, so it is just a green sludge.

"You *fucking—*" Stacey takes a breath and then opens her arms. "Come here."

I weep, stepping over the bile and folding myself into her frame. "Stacey," I whimper, my voice as small as nothing.

"Shh," she whispers, kissing my cheek so lightly it feels as if it never was. "Come to bed. Come to bed, darling."

54

A Silent Swan

"The silver swan, who living has no note,

"When death approached, unlocked her silent throat,

"Leaning her breast against the reedy shore,

"Thus sung her first and last, and sung no more:

"Farewell, all joys; Oh death, come close mine eyes;

"More geese than swans now live, more fools than wise."

Mrs. Kilpatrick looks up from the book, eyebrows raised at the class.

"Can anyone tell me what this poem is about?"

As usual, no one answers. I sit and stare at the poem, imagining the silver swan, alone and lovesick on a moonless lake, waiting for death before she will sing.

"I think," I say, "it's about awareness. I think it's about realizing that you've lost your whole life, waiting—*'Farewell, all joys'*—but I don't think she had any joys. She spent her whole life silent, waiting to sing. Probably too afraid to sing. And in the end . . . she had to die before she could free that part of herself."

"Yes," breathes Mrs. Kilpatrick. "*Yes.* You've got it, Miss Sloane. You've got it exactly. And can we not say that it is a poem of regrets? That our swan *regrets*? The geese who squawk find love, find happiness, reproduce . . . yet she, oh silent swan, dies alone, in first and last song. Like chastity spurned for the harlot."

"Beauty in death," I murmur, closing my eyes. "Beauty in death, alone."

Mrs. Kilpatrick nods. "Yes."

The class sniggers and whispers behind their hands, and I sink lower into my chair. From across the room, Gert smiles at me, his cheeks flushed.

"Now," Mrs. Kilpatrick says, clapping her hands, "I want you to turn to page sixty-six and read Thomas Hardy's 'The Darkling Thrush.' Pay close attention to what he is trying to say. Then I want you to go home and write an essay on what you think he is talking about and how he is saying it. That will be your homework for next week. Five hundred words *minimum*."

The class groans in unison, but I have already turned to page sixty-six and am reading.

"Bethany?"

I look up. The room is almost empty; students are filing out. Mrs. Kilpatrick stands behind her desk sorting through papers, and Gert stands above me.

"Yeah?"

"The bell's gone."

"Oh. Right. Yeah, thanks, Gert."

"Can I walk you to lunch?" he asks.

"Sure."

I pack away my things, head full of poetry.

"I thought what you said earlier . . . about the swan . . . I thought that was pretty clever."

"Oh. Um . . . thanks, Gert."

"Yeah, really clever and, like, *deep* and stuff."

"Thanks."

"You should write poems for a job one day maybe."

I shrug my bag onto my back. "Maybe." Those dreams I once had—and shared with Rowan—are gone now. Empty wishes.

We walk along the corridor without saying much. Gert offers to carry my bag, and I almost let him. I'm still tired. But it's probably a bad idea. If Stacey saw, she wouldn't be happy. I gently decline.

"Bethany," he says, breathing heavily, "I'm sorry I was such a . . . you know, jerk. Before."

"You already said sorry months ago," I remind him. "But it's okay. I was pretty mean too. I'm sorry I punched you—"

He blushes furiously. "Oh, yeah. It's okay. I deserved it."

He looks very uncomfortable, and his skin is a very red color.

"What's wrong?" I ask.

He releases his breath. "It's just—" He sighs. "That groundskeeper asked me to give you this." He holds out a sealed envelope. "I tried to say no, but he got all angry and said if I didn't give it to you, he would throttle me."

I stare at it blankly, feeling a kind of desperate revulsion. My vision flickers with the pulse of epinephrine that floods my body when I see the short, blocky writing on the front. *BETH.*

Beautiful Beth . . .

Has he called for me at last? After all this time?

"I didn't want to give it to you . . ."

"Thanks, Gert," I whisper.

"Bethany . . . I, um, well I . . . Is that guy giving you a hard time?"

I frown into the letter and shake my head to the left and right. "No."

"Okay. Because, you know, you can always tell me. We could get him fired and everything, you know, like I said. After all the stuff you've been through . . . first Mr. Mollier being mean and then this guy . . . well, it's not right of him."

I am too distracted to have comprehended all the words he used in that one sentence. "Huh?"

"Look, just . . . I know I was a dick to you, but I really . . . I like you, Bethany." He blushes again. "You're a cool girl. And I . . . well, I don't want—"

On impulse, I kiss his cheek like I once did, so many weeks ago. "Thanks, Gert. See you later."

"Oh, o-okay," he stammers. "See you later then, Bethany."

I am already walking away from him, away from the lunch hall. I need to find a place to read this in private. I decide the girl's bathroom is the safest bet.

It's empty at this time of the day; every student is stuffing his or her face in the ten minutes we are allotted for lunch. I lock myself in one of the stalls and sit on the toilet, lifting my legs in case anyone looks under the doors. They are wrapped in bandages under my thick tights, and as I fold them, my soft, ruined skin tugs dangerously. I'm the only girl allowed tights in the whole school. I stand out.

Dearest, has it been long enough? I am burning for you. I have to see your face. Come to me this evening. I have a surprise for you. You won't regret it, darling. Wear something white.

My heart is hammering when I'm finished. My mouth is watering, and I yearn to give in. My mind is still full of visions . . . Rowan and Stacey. Rowan in the dirt; Rowan *loving* her.

I scream once, long and loud. It is the low sound of a dying animal. The images lash at my mind like razors on the ends of whips; too much to bear. I can feel the closeness of Glass Man, and it is tipping me over the edge.

Glass Man won't wait, Beth tells me. *He won't wait until you're sixteen. He's coming for you.*

"Shut up."

Sakkie still wants me.

I rip open the stall and race through the corridors. I run into the dusty grounds, seeking, searching. I go to the sugarcane patch, the potato garden, the wheat fields. Sakkie is nowhere.

I run back to the school, wild, until I am twenty feet away from the staff room. Then I force myself to walk. I calmly push open the door and walk to the reception bar that blocks off the teachers' private room from the students outside.

Mrs. Muller is manning it today. She asks me what I want. I try to fix my hair, folding it behind my ears. I can feel how big and unkempt it is, and she is staring at it.

"Is Sakkie the groundskeeper here?" I ask in a hurried voice.

"What is it about?"

"I need to speak to him."

"Is there a problem?"

I glance up through the glass window and make contact with Sakkie's eyes. He is staring at me, worry all over his face. I feel less wild with his eyes on me, like I've already got a little bit of the destructive fix I need. I watch him get up, put down his coffee, and hurry through the door.

"Bethany?" he asks hurriedly. "What is it?"

I see Mrs. Muller raise her eyebrows and then withdraw.

"I need to see you," I whisper as soon as she is gone. "Now."

He clears his throat, straightens his top, and looks around. No one is present except the dozens of teachers behind his back.

"Okay, darling," he whispers, patting my bare arm once. His hand is hot and sticky. "What lesson do you have next?"

"Music."

"Bunk off. Come to the shed. The farthest one out, near the gates. Don't let anyone see."

I sigh, and it takes the whole of my willpower not to lean forward into his chest.

"You look bad," he says, half raising his hand and then letting it drop. "Does it still . . . hurt?"

"No," I lie. "I'm tired, though."

"Get some food. I'll see you soon."

I don't eat. My stomach is too fragile. Instead I go to the library and pull out T. S. Eliot and read "The Love Song of J. Alfred Prufrock" until I am lulled in depression.

When the bell rings, I stay in the library until it fills up. Then I check out the book of poems and head toward the shed using the long route, which avoids the music block.

I don't knock; I just walk straight in. He is waiting by the door, and I am in his arms in seconds.

55

Out

I tell Matron Monday I have a tutorial with Mr. Mollier until eight. I tell Stacey I'm not having it alone.

"Gert Van Dyck's going to be there," I tell her.

Stacey scrunches up her nose. "Gert Van *Dyck*?"

I roll my eyes in mock disgust. "Yeah, I know."

"Well, don't work too hard," she says, and I can sense that she doesn't mean this in a kind way. In fact, I sense she doesn't really believe me about Gert.

"Are you seeing Rowan tonight?" I ask, a little hesitantly. But I want to make her think about something else, and this is the surest way of doing it.

She shrugs. "No. I don't think so."

I am already flustered and panicked, and the reminder of Rowan does nothing for my nerves. Little heavy beads of sweat gather on my skin, beads that make me feel even more skittish.

"Why?"

She doesn't answer me. She doesn't blink or shrug or respond in any way. She just sits on her bed, staring at me. I'm not going to get an answer, and I think maybe she is testing him like she tests me sometimes.

I take out the white dress and put it on the bed. I have told her it's too hot for my uniform. It's a good enough explanation, but she asks about my bandages. Why am I not wearing them? It's a difficult question to answer because I can't think of a good enough lie. A lie that won't sound like a lie. I want Sakkie to see my weeping, not-yet scars. I want to see his reaction.

So I just don't answer. Eventually, she leaves me alone to finish. She lets the tights thing go.

I stand before the mirror and try to stop my stomach from flying away from me. The white dress makes me look like I have a tan. It makes me look smaller. I'm nervous being in such a delicate color without my bandages on. I'm exposed again, with nothing between the hard places of the world and me.

My legs stick out like the bleeding limbs they are. Shocking ruby against the clinical white of the cotton attempting to cast a shadow over it. They are uneven, lumpy things that don't have any place on me, and yet here they are. They are slimy in places, not fully healed.

Stacey is outside when I leave, a fact that ties my stomach in more knots than it's already in, and I'm jiggling like a druggie before I reach the shed. Maybe she is going to see Rowan after all. At a little before six, I knock on the door.

Sakkie doesn't say anything about the dress. Is it ugly? He just ushers me quickly to his car, which is parked nearby under the jackalberries.

"We're going out?" I ask. I haven't left the school since I got back from the hospital, and the thought has me sweating into his leather seats and breathing too quickly.

"Quiet," he says.

"But are we?"

"Damn it, Bethany, just let me surprise you. Let me do this right."

"What are you talking about?"

There is too much inside me, and at the same time I'm empty. I want to be filled with pain—for him to push everything else out. I don't want to remember Rowan or the bruises on my heart.

I don't want to remember Glass Man.

"Our relationship is . . . *has* been poisonous. This isn't the way I would have wanted it to start. Fuck, I never expected it at all." He takes a deep breath, and runs a hand over his prickly face. "I want to take you out and make you smile, Beth. I want to . . . do it the right way."

Is this what we have? A "relationship"? It doesn't feel like one, but maybe that's just because I've never been in one. I wonder what Rowan and I had. Was that a relationship too? It felt so different. Was that one "done right"?

He drives me into Pretoria. I immediately smell the jacarandas. I wind down the window and lean out, watching the tires of his Opel crunch the beautiful purple petals, which have scattered over the tarmac from the purple trees on either side. We park in an underground car park and take the stairs up to the street, where Sakkie leads the way toward a lit strip off to the west.

My heart thuds so hard in response to being out in the world, especially at night. I inch closer to Sakkie's tall form walking slightly ahead of me.

"We're going to eat?" I ask, astonished, when he approaches the Sheraton restaurant.

He smiles down at me. "We're going to have a proper date. A girl should have at least one date before . . . well, we didn't do things how I would have wanted. Now I can do something properly."

He has booked a table for himself and his "sister," and we are shown to a small table at the far end of the room. The table is laid out with bone china and a red, plush tablecloth.

Sick, Beth comments with a snicker.

The clinking of glasses startles me, but I don't see which of the other diners made the sound.

Sakkie drinks wine, and I have elderflower juice; then we eat mussels in white sauce, and Sakkie caresses my leg with his socked foot under the long tablecloth. It feels almost affectionate. The conversation is conservative and proper.

With full bellies, we walk the jacaranda-lined streets, and the scent later intermingles in my memory with cooked muscles, Sakkie, leather seats, white dresses, and violence of a shattering, splitting, tearing kind.

He checks us into a small motel that is all flickering neon, and which looks like no one is supposed to know about it. He ushers me inside.

"Now," he breathes, shutting the door. He steps back to look at me, and I stand shivering in the center of the room, waiting. Just like the first time.

Now is the time.

He shuts all the blinds mechanically and checks the bathroom and then comes back into the bedroom.

"Have you enjoyed the evening?" he asks.

"Yes, sir," I murmur.

He raises his hand and slaps me hard across my left cheek. My neck cranes, my teeth rattle, and I go flying across the room. I cry out once and then sniffle into my hair, huddled against the floor. Stacey slapped me only two days ago. Will I ever get used to it?

"Do you know why you deserve that?" he demands in a voice that is hard, level, and cruelly calm—like a police officer giving orders.

I shake my head.

"Before the fire . . . in the shed? I don't want to *ever* hear you say those horrible words to me again."

"W-what?" I whimper, though I do understand. I was right. He was—is—mad because I asked him to leave me alone.

"I love you, Bethie," he says very clearly, and I sob. Someone loves me. "Do you know why I did it? Why I took you out tonight?"

I shake my head as he pulls me to my feet, and I bury my face in his chest.

"When this . . . *thing* happened between us . . . I couldn't live with it."

"But—"

"*Let* me finish," he snaps, and jerks my chin up to face him. "I couldn't live with myself. With what you made me do. Because I'm a good fucking person. The more I tried to get on with my life and forget, the more I wanted you. That's why I left."

I want to ask him to change the subject, but if I open my mouth, I know I will be sick on the floor or scream until I suffocate, and he'll be angry. Besides, he is holding my chin so tightly I don't think I could speak if I wanted to.

"You messed me up," he says. "You ruined me."

How could I possibly be responsible for so much destruction? Would a child of God be capable of this much?

"But I realized something. I realized that you're *mine*."

I am so relieved he loves me that it doesn't occur to me to be afraid. Sakkie loves me. I suppose I love him back, but I don't really know how to tell. It feels like a growth inside me that still leaks sharp poison.

What about Rowan? My stomach churns violently, and I retch once.

He releases my face. "Are you all right?"

I nod. Rowan . . . sweet Rowan, who had made me feel like a whole person for a while. For those two wonderful weeks, which we stole the darkness out of, I felt like myself . . . almost like myself again. But he is Stacey's. Stacey is his. They are each other's. I am nothing. I am without.

And this is not the same. Not at all. But I shy away from the truth because Sakkie is safety, and that is what I need.

Sakkie wants me. Sakkie loves me. I am so relieved that I begin to cry again, clutching at his jacket.

"And then . . . the fire." He says *fire* like he is gasping. It is a breathy sound that has no strength. "When I heard . . . about what you lost . . . I'm sorry."

I glance down at my legs. I hadn't thought of them so much lost as ruined. My ruined legs. But I suppose I did lose them in some way. I can't go to sleep without first lathering them up and making them moist. I am forever in gauzes and bandages. Bathing is hard, and getting dressed is harder.

Yes. I have lost something.

I have lost myself.

"But it's been long enough," he says.

He touches me, and I hear the tinkle of glass again. I look around, frowning.

"So beautiful, Bethie," Sakkie says. "Tell me you think you're beautiful."

"I . . ."

There's the sound again. A tinkling crunch. A glimmering creak.

"Tell me and mean it," he insists. "'I'm beautiful, Sakkie.' Say it."

"I'm—I can't."

Sakkie walks me to the bathroom and stands me in front of the mirror, where he brushes out my hair with a cheap motel comb, but I can't look up. The comb tugs on the knots in my hair, and he pulls it roughly free, only to begin again.

"I want you to look at yourself, watch yourself, until you can tell me you're beautiful."

I don't understand this game we're playing. Still, I do what he wants. I stare into the face of the girl who is no one I recognize.

"I'm . . ."

It happens in the split second that my gaze moves from my own, to his.

It isn't Sakkie staring back at me.

It's Glass Man.

56

Feet on a Moonbeam

NOW

My legs are aching by the time I get outside, sharp pinpricks puncturing the ache like ants gnawing the bones. I won't be able to walk for much longer.

And then I realize.

My wheelchair. I left it beside the bed when we lay down, but it was gone when I woke. Did you take it? Why? What is this new game?

Or, wait. Did I? Did we bring my wheelchair at all? Did I walk into this nightmare, or did you wheel me into it?

I stagger the last few steps and exit the corpse of Clare House.

I limp into the grounds, my right leg beginning to drag, and there isn't enough oxygen, and the ghosts are out, and they are trying to talk to me with their shadowy whispers—*remember, remember, remember, little Beth*—but I don't want to remember anything else, I can't, and it is dark and I don't like the dark, I don't like the dark, I—

Crrrrrrrk.

Something behind me in the murky depths of Clare House. I pause, turning back. The dorm is still and silent, still blackened and broken, but I can hear it.

Hear what?

"*Stacey?*" I whisper.

My heart pounds. *Run. Run. Run.*

Calm down.

But it comes again.

Crrrrrrrrrk.

It rolls from the shadows. A cutting sound. Jagged, a knife ripping through the fabric of reality. Everything wobbles, bends, splinters.

What happens if the world breaks?

I turn back to the trail of thorns and focus.

Find them—my heart quakes—*before He reaches you.*

Who?

Go!

I follow a trail of thorns and moonbeams, and by the time the path ends, my feet are bleeding, my pockets are stuffed with thorns, and I am standing before the Tractor Tire.

57

Dead End

THEN

I wake up to Sakkie's furious mutterings, head thick, tongue sore. My body is not responding to anything. It takes a while for my lazy eyelids to flutter open.

"Shit!" I hear him hiss. "Goddamn it, wake up!"

Something stings my cheek, and then the other one, and I realize he has slapped me hard. Again. I groan and try to open an eye.

"Beth? Bethie?"

"Wha . . . happened?"

He helps me into a sitting position and then carries me to the bed. The softness under my back is torturous after the hard tiles of the bathroom floor.

"Are you okay? What are your symptoms?"

I lift a heavy arm and rub my forehead, which has a bump on it. "Where did I get this?" I slur.

"You hit your head on the sink as you fell," he says with a scowl. "I didn't catch you in time."

"Oh."

"Now can you tell me what the hell that was?"

I start to cry. "Don't be mean." The aching in my head magnifies.

"Goddamn it, Beth, I'm not—" He stops and takes a deep breath. "I'm sorry, okay? I'm sorry."

"Don't call me Beth," I mutter, but I don't think he's heard me, because he is pacing up and down.

"Shit."

"I don't see why you have to swear at me all the time," I sob. "I haven't done anything wrong. You say you love me . . ."

I keep talking nonsense and crying, and I have my slobbery tears everywhere, but I don't care. I feel like I'm inside a deep well looking up at a tiny speck of sunlight. I wish someone would help me out.

"Shh, sweetheart," he whispers, lying down next to me and cradling my head on his chest. "Calm down."

I focus on my breathing and slowly begin to feel better. My body is battered, but with my head on a hot, moving, breathing chest I feel more at ease.

At ten past nine, Sakkie brushes my hair with his fingers and ties it back. His cell phone rings in his jacket pocket; he curses and then goes to see who it is. His expression darkens when he looks at the number. He ignores the annoying ringing, puts the phone back in his pocket, and returns to me.

We haven't slept together tonight, and I wonder if it's a bad omen. A sign that we should have left things alone. Maybe I've lost that part of myself too. Or maybe I do have it, only it's something nobody wants.

He frowns and touches my head. "We'll have to think of a way to explain that."

I shrug. "I'll fall out of bed tonight and make it really loud."

We drive back to the school in silence.

Back at school, I sign the register at the dormitory door as 8:00 p.m. and then go to find Matron Monday. Outside her office, I adjust my hair and cover the bump on my forehead.

She's dozing in her chair with a crossword puzzle on her chest when I enter. She snores herself awake and looks around confusedly with pink eyes, and then she focuses on me.

"Sloane? What's the matter?"

"I'm sorry, Matron. I just wanted to let you know I'm back safe and sound."

"What sort of hour do you call *this*?" she asks, examining her watch.

"Actually, I got back at eight, but I forgot to come and tell you."

She blinks. "Oh. Did you sign the register?"

"Yes, ma'am."

"Very well then. Off you go to bed."

It's almost lights-out when I enter the dorm. Stacey is already in the bathroom, brushing her teeth. I get undressed quickly, hoping there are no bruises on my body, and if there are, that I'm in my pajamas before anyone notices.

I meet Stacey in the corridor.

"Matron wanted me," I say quickly, feeling both apologetic and annoyed. I'm too tired to explain anything. "I'm sorry."

She raises an eyebrow and walks past me. I don't brush my teeth. I just lean on the sink and stare into the mirror, looking for . . . what? Eventually I head back to the dorm where I climb into bed, watching Stacey.

"Are you angry?" I ask, and then can't believe I've been brave enough.

She glances at me. "You were gone a long time. For maths."

I blush. "I know. He likes to be thorough."

"And did Gert find the class useful?"

"Oh . . . yes, I think so."

Stacey smiles and is made of radiance for a fraction of a second, and then her back is to me, horizontal, and she is falling asleep.

Matron calls lights-out, and I wait for Stacey to get up and tell me to follow her into the night. I allow my eyes to close, and when I open them, it is early dawn and Stacey's bed is empty.

◆ ◆ ◆

Gert Van Dyck corners me on the way to lunch hall looking uncomfortable, like he needs to pee. He hops from one foot to the other and looks around a lot.

"Hey Gert," I say, about to walk past him.

"Um, hey, Bethany. So, um, Bernie came to see me."

I stop in my tracks as I wait for him to continue. I know what's going on. Bernie was sent to find out about me. The little spy. Why doesn't he talk faster and get it over with?

"She, uh, she asked if I was with you at Mr. Mollier's maths class last night."

"What did you say?" I whisper.

"I said I was."

I am so relieved and shocked that my eyes tear up. "You . . . did?"

"Um, yeah. So, um, what was going on last night?"

"Why did you lie for me?"

His face burns beetroot, and he brushes the floor with the toe of his shoe. "Because I . . . I feel bad for you."

"Thank you, Gert," I manage before the tide of gratitude has risen in my throat and I can't speak. "I have to go."

Nothing is what I expect it to be anymore. Gert is being nice to me despite our adversarial history, Stacey is acting . . . odd, Sakkie didn't touch me last night, Bernie is now Stacey's spy *against* me, and Rowan . . . Rowan doesn't seem to even remember me.

"What's going on with you and that groundsman?" Gert blurts out a little too loudly.

I sigh, exhausted and empty. "Thank you for protecting me, Gert. We've come a long way, haven't we?"

He blushes even more deeply and chuckles even as he shuffles his feet. I step forward with the intention to kiss him on his hot, sweat-rimmed lips, but his eyes harden, and he pulls back.

"Stop it. If this is what you and . . . I'm not like that."

"I'm sorry," I whisper, mortified at myself. "I'm so sorry, Gert. Just . . . just stay away from me."

I back away, staring at him. I don't want to have to face the reality of a rejection from a boy that I hated only a few months ago and who, I can see, likes me enough to lie for me. I turn around and I run.

"Bethany," he calls after me. "Wait!"

I don't stop to listen. I don't stop for anything. I race to the bathroom, and I stay there until the bell rings, looking into the dark, shadowy part of the room where a girl-demon is smiling at me with black and blue skin from the darkness.

I'm going crazy, I tell myself. I'm seeing things; I must be going mad. She is indistinct. It's as though she is standing in the folds of a wilting black veil, moving between her realm and mine. If she's in my mind, then I'm crazy and nothing can hurt me. But if she's the ghost of Sarah Dertz, then she must be a messenger of Glass Man, and so he must be waiting for me.

58

Window

The sun scalds my shoulders, turning my skin pink. Curse of the English, Mother used to say. She calls less often now, like she's sure everything has safely fallen back into its normal routine. She writes to ask if I'm using the medicine for my legs right. I say I am, and I leave out the part where some days I forget. Like I forget to eat, or breathe, or sleep.

I'm forgetting a lot of things. Even my dreams.

Joe potters around in the cornfields, checking the leaves for pests. The dishwasher ladies, who I've learned are also the cooks, tend to their sugarcane. I wonder if I will ever get a piece, and if it will taste like sugar. Will it taste like summertime and butterflies? It is a lazy day, full of marshmallow light.

Stacey is gone. I think she and Bernie are together, talking about me. Maybe they are playing a hushed truth or dare. Maybe they are exchanging secrets. Is this what it feels like to be cast out? Cast off? Cast away?

"Hey," someone says to my left. I have been so absorbed in my mind I didn't hear him approach.

He is wearing green today, and he looks amazing. Dark hair like midnight sun and green shirt like eternal forest. He is smiling broadly, teeth white and perfect.

"Rowan?"

"Where have you been?"

I shrug and play with a long piece of grass. I wonder if you can get a grass cut like a paper cut. "Around."

Where the fuck does he think I've been? In hospital, for one. And then here, for another. And not once did he try to see me until now. He's too absorbed in Stacey. I don't know what happened while I was away, trying to recover, experiencing the most intense pain I have ever felt. They must have been here, together, connecting. Just like I told him to. Except he's fallen for her, which wasn't the plan.

"How have you been?" I ask, because I am determined to make an effort to be nice. It isn't so hard, I find.

He frowns, and then laughs. "Good, thanks. Yourself?"

"How's Jared?"

Rowan scowls. "He's a fucking jerk, as usual. Thank God he's leaving at the end of term."

I nod. I heard something like that. Rowan did some pretty bad damage to his face. He lost the teeth to either side of his front teeth, which means he lost his cocky attitude, too, like the two were linked in some fundamental way.

Rowan's face softens. "Are you sure you're okay?"

Oh, Stacey, how lucky you are that he's chosen you. I was happy with him once upon a time, when we shared the secret hours of a stolen fortnight. And now you have him. Now he's yours. And you're his. Where is my place in all this? And when I have no place, how can I carry on, when I know that I'm your girl? I'm both of yours.

Rowan's girl.

Stacey's girl.

Sakkie's girl.

None of them want us, Bethany. Beth is right. I think she must be. None of them want me now that they have each other.

No one's girl.

"I have to go," I mutter, not answering his question.

He snatches my arm, not roughly, but firmly. "Wait. Where are you going? We've hardly spoken."

"I have to put on my medicine," I say.

He blinks and releases my arm. "Oh, I'm sorry. Will I see you later?"

I shrug. "Who knows? Later, Rowan."

I walk away, though it feels more like crawling. I go back to my dorm room, where Stacey is waiting for me. Does she sense that I've spoken to Rowan? Can she tell he grabbed my arm, or that when he did, I imagined the last night we had together?

Behind her, the window is smashed, and the broken shards of glass litter the floor, just like the absinthe bottle. The hot, sandy breeze slinks into the room, touching everything.

"What are you doing?" I say, my heart hammering inside me.

I enter with careful steps, and then I hear Matron's footsteps behind me. Stacey looks over my shoulder, then points at me.

"It was her! It was Bethany!"

"*Sloane!*" I hear Matron yell, but I'm too shocked and horrified to do anything. Stacey betrayed me. Stacey lied—Stacey tricked me. Did she do this on purpose, to get me into trouble? To punish me? Or was I just a way for her to cover her mistake?

Matron starts to haul me away, and I try to protest. "But—"

"Quiet! You're headed for Principal Wolfe's office, young lady. I've had just about enough!"

I can't believe what's happened. All I can see are Stacey's staring eyes, the tip of her finger as she points at me, like a barb reaching out to prick. A tiny part of her pink tongue sticks out between her lips, like a cat. I'm so shocked I can hardly believe it. I glance at her hand, waiting to see her characteristic finger-to-thumb tap—*tap, tap, tap*—but there is nothing but calm and her unblinking, staring eyes.

No, no, no, no!

Stacey has everything—Rowan, Bernie, me. She knows I'm her twin. She knows I would do anything for her. Why do this? Why do this to me? Why blame me?

And then I realize.

This is my test. Another test. The first since the fire. She's making sure I *am* still hers.

I am, I am, I am.

I'm radiant from the knowledge that I'm in on the plan—that I know about the task—that I won't—*can't*—fail.

I let Matron drag me down the hall, her manly hand gripping my shirt collar, and I'm laughing, cackling, screaming with glee.

◆ ◆ ◆

"Breaking school property, for the second time," Principal Wolfe mutters. He's reading a slip of yellow paper—probably Matron's "official" report. He stands behind his desk, keeping about two feet of wood between us, as though I might be catching.

"I didn't do anything wrong," I say.

"Is that so? And I suppose you didn't do anything wrong the other time either? Breaking out of the dorm at night, bringing absinthe into the west wing, lighting it on fire? Destroying school property?"

"Mr. Wolfe," his secretary, Mrs. Cottis, protests gently. She is sitting by his desk taking notes on a mechanical typewriter that ought to have been sitting in a museum somewhere. They treat me like I'm infirm because of my scars. Usually it bugs me, but now it works for me.

Principal Wolfe grunts his assent, his eyes flicker down to my legs and back. "And this time?"

"When I got there, it was already broken."

"And you have no idea how it got that way, even though Matron Monday heard a crash?"

I frown, confused. I didn't hear a crash at all. But I won't give Stacey up. "I don't know what happened."

I haven't lied, exactly.

"I'm going to give you a warning."

Principal Wolfe is soft. Had I been in his place, I would have done more to me. I would have given me detention. I would have taken away all my meager privileges. I would have caned me. But he simply writes a note on the yellow piece of paper and places it on Mrs. Cottis's desk for her to file away. She smiles at me sympathetically, and I see her take the note and slip it into her drawer. I know she won't file it. It will disappear, like the beauty my legs used to possess before I even realized it.

When I turn to leave, I'm almost laughing.

I passed.

I can't wait to tell Stacey.

59

Creepy Crawlies

NOW

Your legs dangle into the hole, and I can see you twice. You, here, now, watching me under the darkening sky, and you, then, hair wild under a cruel sun; a sickening composition.

"There could be snakes out here," you observe. "Scorpions. Army ants."

I can barely see your silhouette. We don't have torches. We don't have shoes. No jackets, no wheelchair. Nothing.

"We have to go," I say.

You hold out a hand, but I don't think I could climb up beside you.

"My legs . . . I'm too tired."

"Give them to me," you say instead, and I realize you weren't offering to help me climb. You want your devils.

I pull them from my pockets and hand them up to you, and you cocoon them in your T-shirt. I watch you pluck each thorn from your hoard, humiliate it, and throw it over your shoulder.

"You've forgotten so many of the rules."

"I—"

"Why did you do it?"

"Do it?"

"You just left me here. Left me behind."

Your head is cocked to the side, and it is getting so dark. The sun is gone.

"Stacey, we need to go . . ." But my conviction is wavering. How could I walk all the way back to the gate now, anyway? Maybe the taxi driver will come here to help. I reach for my phone—but no. It's not there. My pockets were empty when I followed the thorny path.

I look up at you slowly, my heart sinking with horror. "Stacey . . . Where's my phone?"

You continue to pluck off thorns.

"You just up and left." *Pluck.* "Went back to England." *Pluck.* "And didn't give me a second thought."

"Stacey—"

"Twins forever, remember that?"

I wipe my nose. "Yes. I remember. *Where's my phone?*"

Your smile is not a smile.

"I was a child," I say.

"I was too. I wouldn't have left you."

"We grew up. It happens. It's life." I gesture feebly. "We grew up."

You throw the last humiliated ball over your shoulder and lean forward, and your teeth and sclera are a piercing white, glitter in the shadows. "Did we?"

You watch me for a long time, but there is nothing to say because I am trying to remember what happened at the end.

Why did I leave? Why did I leave you? Why didn't I write, or call, or—anything? I wouldn't have left you. I know it.

"You were my everything," I whisper.

"Until I wasn't. And I know why."

Your voice from the past jingles in my ears.

Prove you love me.

A razor blade, glinting, evil.

Bubbles of blood on my skin.

The shock and the sting.

I am yours.

I am your twin.

Stacey's girl.

Forever.

"You forgot that, though." Your voice, here and now, is colder than the night. "You forgot *me*. You left me."

I swallow. "My mother took me back to England."

Stacey will get angry if she hears me speaking British-people words again.

"You left me before that."

I shake my head. I don't remember. I don't want to.

"Let's just go. Let's go back to the hotel."

You lean back again, and the shadows slink into the hollows of your face, erasing your eyes and your nose. "Why? We're home."

"Seriously, I don't feel well."

"Boo hoo, poor little Beth."

"Stacey, please."

And then you're holding my phone. The light is hideous, and the dark around us deepens in its glow.

"Sixteen new messages in the last thirty minutes alone. He's persistent, isn't he?"

"Bruce—"

You roar with laughter. "'Bethany, what's going on? Bethany, where are you? Bethany, who was that on the line—'"

"You spoke to my husband?"

"He just kept calling and calling."

"What did you tell him?"

"I told him you were safe with me." You smile. "And you are."

Another pang of pain sears my right leg, and I stumble to the side, gripping the tire for support. "Stacey, please. This isn't funny."

You lean forward and offer me your hand.

"Here. I'll pull you up."

My legs are shaking with pain and fatigue. I debate about sitting on the ground or letting you haul me up. Your comment about snakes and scorpions flutters past my ear, and I give you my hands. As you yank me up, my phone slips from your fingers, landing in the hole in the middle of the tire—*where Glass Man lives*—and I curse.

You know I can't get it myself, so you sit still. "Oops."

The relief of having my weight off my legs is enough to make me forget about this stupid game for a moment. But when I open my eyes and we're still on the tire and this *isn't* a fucked-up dream, a tear breaks loose and slides down my face, all the way to my chin.

Why didn't I kill Sally when I had the chance?

"Why did you take my wheelchair?"

You don't even deny it. "You won't be needing it again."

"Stop this fucking game. We're not children anymore!"

You giggle. "Aren't we?"

"What the fuck are you talking about?"

You caress my cheek. "Oh, Bethie. You're going to find out soon enough. He's almost here."

60

Assistance

THEN

It wasn't enough.

When I tell Stacey about what I did—not giving her up—she isn't impressed. She sits on her bed, legs folded beneath her, and says nothing.

"I didn't give you up," I say again.

She stares at me, never blinking, and raises an eyebrow as though waiting.

"Is there more? Was I meant to do something else?"

Matron knocks on the door. She is carrying a clipboard, doing afternoon checks.

"Everything okay in here?" she asks me, frowning slightly.

I nod. When Matron leaves, Stacey follows her—without a single word to me.

Shit.

There was something else. Something I missed. Was I meant to take the blame myself? But . . . what would that achieve? I would be sent away to Mother.

That's what she wants, Beth tells me.

"No. No, it can't be."

She wants Rowan to herself. God, you are thick.

"Shut up. Shut up!"

There has to be something more I can do.

It has been two days since I found out I failed when I thought I'd passed. Stacey is yet to talk to me. I follow her around like a puppy, and she lets me. I'm so thankful she lets me. The school grounds are very empty without her.

As empty as they were the day that changed everything. That sent me into Sakkie's world. That started this whole, stupid mess.

I just need to think, I tell Beth.

Think faster.

Is this a test too? I wish I knew the rules. If I had paid attention sooner, maybe I would have picked up on something. I would know the meaning of this riddle that I'm stuck in. Stacey will have said something in the past, something that was meant as a warning, or a clue. And because I'm so stupid, I probably missed it. Now she will be relentless. She won't let me off.

So, if I can't figure out the clue—if I can't solve the riddle . . . then I'll just do something else to impress her. Something that will get her attention and make her too happy to remember what the challenge was.

This is what you get for trying to break away, Beth tells me.

Fuck off, Beth.

I wait until the lights are out and I am snug in my bed. Stacey sneaks out at around midnight—I assume to go see Rowan—and I pretend to be asleep. It hurts a little that she didn't offer to take me with her, but I shrug it off. I have a mission. I'm like Nikita again. I have to wait until it's safe to go.

I wait.

I glance at my clock. It says 02:13. I bury my head under my pillow, and I sob into my mattress until I am too tired even for that. I look again. 02:56. It should be okay for me to go now. Stacey has been gone two hours and fifty-six minutes. She wouldn't have been spying on me for that long. I climb out of bed and sneak into Bernie's room. The shadows have left me alone tonight.

Bernie lies on her bed, which is the farthest from the door, and she is awake. I walk over to her very slowly. I've never approached her before. She looks startled and then scared, leaning as far away from me as she can.

"Can I . . . ," I whisper, indicating her bed.

She looks almost as alarmed as I feel, except I also feel revolted, but she nods.

I climb in beside her, noticing her bed smells kind of like mashed potatoes. I leave a six-inch gap between us.

"Bethany?" she asks, staring at me. She wants to know what I'm doing here. Cut to the chase.

"What did Stacey say?" I ask at last. No point beating around the bush. Either she'll tell me or she won't, stupid ninny. "That day in the Invisible House, when she whispered in your ear. What dare did she give you?"

Bernie bites her lip. "I . . ."

"Have you done it yet?"

She shakes her head, eyes wide. "No."

"So, what was it? She didn't say you couldn't tell," I remind her when she shakes her head again.

She releases the air she has been storing in her lungs and then begins to cry.

"I'm so confused," she whines.

"Just spit it out! What did she say?"

Bernie narrows her eyes and peers at me closely. "I . . . Are you messing with me?"

"What?"

She folds her arms so they rise and drop with the motion of her breaths. "Are you messing with me? You're trying to trick me."

"Oh, for Pete's sake," I mutter. She chooses *this* moment to grow a spine? "Look, you can either tell me or do it alone."

I let her take the time she needs to consider. She just stares at me, biting on her lip like this decision will change the world.

"Look, this isn't a game," I say at last. "This is serious." I swallow and try to sound sincere. "Stacey could be asking you to do something really dangerous. Now, if you tell me, maybe I'll help you."

"Why would you help me?"

"Why not? Come on, just tell me. Tell me."

"She wants me to . . . she . . ."

"Come on, Bernie. Spit it the fuck out," I hiss. I am impatient because when Stacey leaned in close to whisper her commands into Bernie's ears, I was jealous. Bernie had something I didn't. I wanted it because I knew it could be a weapon. Now I want it even more because it's my salvation.

"Sh-she . . . wants me to steal some aspirin from Matron Monday's medicine cabinet."

This is nothing like what I had expected. "Is that all?"

Bernie stares at me. "It's stealing!"

"Ssh!"

She begins to cry again, and I suppress an urge to slap her. "Shut. Up. If you stop crying for half a second, I'll help you."

"How?"

"We can go and get it right now."

This new mission has me on a high, and I can't wait to see if I can do it. The distraction is so tantalizing that it can't be ignored. The hall is still deserted and dark, drafty like someone left a window open.

No sign of Stacey.

She's with Rowan, Beth tells me.

Stop it, I tell myself. *Don't think about it.*

I swallow the bile in my throat and force back the obscene images in my head—of legs and arms and torsos twisted together in pleasure—and I creep forward, hugging the walls. Behind me I hear Bernie's heavy footfalls.

"Would you walk more quietly, please? It's like you *want* to be caught."

"I'm sorry," she whispers, sniffling.

"Just chill," I mutter, and inch forward. "Wait here. I'm going to see if it's open."

I round the corner quickly, and before I have time to think about it too much, I open the door. Not locked. *Yes* . . . I slip inside. Everything is dark. I remember from the last time I was in this room where the medicine cabinet is. It's a silver structure in the far corner, like one of those huge American fridges with double doors on it. It's like a guarded gate . . . or a secret treasure, and I didn't even need a map to find it. Are the good judges with me tonight? Or are the bad judges simply rewarding a sinner?

I try the handle, and it makes a horrible grating sound, like nails on a chalkboard, and then gives way, swinging open. I can hardly believe it's not locked. I search for the aspirin, hastily reading label after label.

Aha! I want to scream my victory when I clutch the little bottle of tablets in my hand. I check the room once before I leave, wanting to make sure everything is as it was before I came in, and then I sneak out, a grinning Bernie at my back.

We are in the main corridor when I start to laugh. "I did it!" I whisper, victory pumping in my veins.

I'm so busy being pleased with myself that I don't see Stacey at the other end of the corridor, glaring at me.

"It was so easy . . ." My voice fades away when I spot her.

"What is it?" Bernie asks, catching up to me.

Stacey walks over to me slowly, her face cold and hard like marble, her eyes black in their anger. She doesn't slap me this time. But her stare is worse: terrible and ruthless.

And empty.

"How *dare* you help Bernadette with it? Of *course* it was easy for *you*. That's why I gave it to *her*."

"I'm sorry." I can feel that I ought to cry. "I didn't mean to—"

Then she does slap me. A little muscle in my neck twinges with the force of it. I want to ask her to forgive me and take me back into her fold, but this game that she is playing will only get worse if I'm weak. Or maybe the rules have changed and I'm meant to beg. I can no longer tell.

"Always doing what you're not supposed to."

"I'm sorry. I'm sorry."

Behind me, Bernie steps forward. She puts a hand on my arm, and I can't believe how bold she is being.

"Are you okay?" she whispers.

"Get off me," I hiss, scooting backward. This is all her fault.

"Go to bed," Stacey tells Bernie quietly. Bernie keeps staring at me, and she looks so confused that I laugh, and then she looks even more terrified.

"Bethany?"

"Stacey said go to *fucking* bed," I growl at her. God, can't she take a hint? I want her away, far away from me. This is all her fault.

She shies back, clasping her hands over her mouth. She is such a marshmallow that I can't even feel bad.

"You too," Stacey says to me.

I don't delay. I turn and go to our room. When I turn back to see if she will follow, she has already left.

61

Vigil

It's dark, and everything is in a half shadow. The light is blue and black, the color of bruises, the color of Sarah Dertz's skin. I'm cold enough to shatter, but I can't seem to shiver.

"Get a move on," Stacey says from the doorway.

I'm still befuddled by sleep, but I get up and follow her, forgetting my shoes. Outside it is colder than I expect. I'm so thankful to be included.

"Are we going to the Tractor Tire?" I ask. It has been so long since we have been out together at night, and I'm surprised that she would want me to come along. Will Rowan be there? What will I do if he is? Will Jared be there, too, like before? My stomach shrinks to the size of a pea.

Stacey keeps walking without giving me any answers.

We reach the Tractor Tire just as the clouds part to reveal a perfect full moon. Stacey removes a long coil of string from behind the tire and begins to unwind it. I eye it with suspicion.

"Where did you get that?" I ask, waiting. "Stacey?"

Her eyes follow the progress of her hands, back and forth for long agonizing minutes, which we pass in silence. She winds it behind a tree and then the tire.

"Sit here," she says, indicating a spot on the ground where the two rope ends meet.

"What's going on?"

"Sit."

"I don't understand."

"This is your punishment, Bethany," she tells me. "When I give Bernie a dare, I expect *her* to carry it out."

"But I thought you forgave me."

Stacey snickers. "Why would I do that? Bad behavior must be punished. That's how it works."

I want to beg her to forgive me, because she is being so mean and cold. "But I thought . . ."

"Shut up and sit down."

I do as she says, crying, and allow her to bind my wrists very tightly so I have my back pressed to the cold hard rubber and I can't move.

"Are you going to just leave me?" I whisper.

She looks at me directly but never answers the question.

This is it, I tell myself. *Glass Man is going to claim me at last. I'm right here, waiting like a packaged gift ready to be ripped open.*

"What about Bernie?" I whimper. "Doesn't she get punished?"

"Her punishment is to leave you here."

"But . . . she's not even here."

"She's sitting in her room, awake. She knows where you are. Let's see if she can live with what I've done to you."

I already know she can. She will be ruthless, as I would have been. Such is the nature of the games we play.

Stacey lifts her leg and kicks a measure of powdery sand into my face. It goes into my mouth, down into my lungs, and I think I swallow some too.

I splutter, panicking.

When I have cried enough tears to dislodge the microscopic glass crystals from my eyeballs, Stacey is gone and I am alone with the tire.

62

Bound

At first I close my eyes and try to be patient. But as the cold intensifies and the night lengthens, shadows approach nearby. I'm paranoid about scorpions getting into my pajamas and stinging me all over, but this takes a back seat to the ice spreading over my skin as the darkness deepens.

"Stacey?" I call out nervously. She must surely be hiding somewhere, watching me from out of sight . . .

But as the silence is unbroken, the tide of panic rises. I struggle against my bonds, and they tighten on my wrists, chafing and stinging.

"*Stacey!*" I cry, overcome by the sudden terror of my isolation. Ahead of and around me, trees dance like dark shades, taunting.

I cry, I yell, I scream, but I am too far away from the school for it to be of any use. Back in the warmth of their beds, my peers lie in summertime dreams and the matron snores away her night shift in sick bay.

In the shadows I fancy I see the same inky pool of blackness I have imagined over my bed on sleepless nights. It dances a little out of sight; I am always on the edge of truly seeing and feeling it.

The skin on my wrists peels painfully away like thin wisps of tissue paper rolled up. My eyes grow weary, and I think I see a shadow in the distance, something fleeting, watching me. Now and again, I see the whisper of the girl who is Sarah Dertz, messenger of Glass Man.

"I'm not ready," I whimper at her, though it could be a tree I'm staring at. I scrunch up my eyes and will her away.

Please, Sarah, not yet, not yet. Let me have a little longer, Glass Man.

By the time Stacey comes back for me at dawn, I'm no longer shivering. I am hanging from my bonds, lying as flat as I can with my head lolling on my shoulder. She is alone and wearing her freshly pressed uniform with its perfectly knotted tie. She cuts my bonds with a razor blade, a perfect copy of the one she handed me on the night of the fire, dropping it at my feet when she is done. And then she walks away.

She never even utters a word to me.

"We'll need this for later," she had said, on that horrible, searing night. "Just hold on to it."

Is the later now? For this specific purpose? To cut me free of bonds she herself tied?

It's okay, I tell myself. *Everything is fine. You've passed through the punishment. Now everything will go back to normal.*

It takes me a long while to move. I feel as though I am once again prisoner of the Invisible House, lost in a labyrinth I can't see.

With shaking knees, sore throat, thick head, stuffy eyes, and bloodied wrists, I pick up the blade and inch my way back to the dorm, slipping the razor into the chest of drawers. I strip my bed when the bell rings, though it takes me twice as long as it used to.

I am the last to brush my teeth in the bathroom, so there's no one to see my raw wrists or the fact that I'm covered in orange dust. I stare at myself in the mirror. There are purple rings under my eyes and salt trails on my cheeks. There is dirt in my hair and on my neck. The spearmint toothpaste stings where I have bitten open the insides of my cheeks.

Behind me in the mirror, the girl watches. She stands in the shadow of the toilet stall directly behind me, behind a partly closed door, watching with dark eyes, half-clothed in gloom.

"Who are you?" I ask. "What do you want?"

She opens her mouth as if to speak, and then retreats.

"Sloane! Get on with it! We don't have all day."

I blink, disoriented. Matron Manuel is glaring at me, with her clawlike hands on her hips.

"Now!" she yells when I don't respond.

I spit out the toothpaste commingled with blood, rinse my mouth, and hurry back to my dorm. I make my bed with weak and trembling hands housing fingers that feel too fat and too stiff and turn a horrible yellow color when I bend them.

Getting into my uniform is torturous, especially doing up my shirt buttons. As punishment for tardiness, I am denied breakfast and sent straight to school, where I lock myself in a bathroom stall and wash my wrists in the toilet.

Joe finds the snake, Molly, at ten fifteen and notifies Principal Wolfe at eleven. The school is in lockdown. No one knows the exact details, only that something had happened to some pet snake found by the janitor.

I knew it was Molly. She was the only pet snake on campus. Sweet, innocent Molly. I'm sick to my stomach thinking that something serious has happened.

Gert is beside me, whispering to Thomas Smart while Mr. Mollier is looking away.

"Hey, Gert," I whisper, leaning toward him. "What happened? Do you know something?"

Gert looks a little green. "I saw it," he whispers. "I was heading that way."

"Saw what?"

"This white snake, strung up near that crappy old tractor tire." He pauses to swallow. "It . . . it was sliced open and nailed to the tire. Half the head was hanging off. It was horrible."

I cover my mouth. "The . . . Tractor Tire?"

He nods, and then sits back as Mr. Mollier begins handing out the quizzes. When we each have one, Mr. Mollier goes back to his desk to grade some other class's papers.

Gert leans forward again. "Yeah, the tractor tire. Why?"

"No reason."

But it's impossible. I was at the Tractor Tire all night. Stacey let me go just before dawn. Could Molly have been killed after that? And who would do it? How could I not have seen it? By the time I got back to the dorm, the bell had already rung. So someone must have done it during breakfast.

You know who, Beth says.

No, it's impossible. She couldn't have . . .

She could. She did. Beth laughs at me for being so blind.

Stacey wouldn't have done it, I insist, and Beth sniggers.

I glance down at my quiz and notice I've been writing *Molly* in all the answer spaces.

Gert flinches when he sees what I have done. "Yeah . . . it was pretty sick actually. I couldn't tell it was a snake at first."

"Poor Molly," I murmur, feeling tearful. "I held her once."

Gert makes as if to reach over. "I'm sorry, Bethany—"

"Van *Dyck*," Mr. Mollier growls from the front of the classroom. "You will stay after school for detention. No talking during a pop quiz."

Gert glowers at him in a surprising show of defiance and then carries on with his quiz. I just stare at the blackboard. Who could have done this to Molly? Why? Poor Joe. He must be devastated.

Glass Man's warning . . .

Near the end of the lesson, Principal Wolfe makes an announcement over the intercom.

"It is with deep regret that we have to announce that there has been some vandalism on school property. I don't want any student to worry needlessly, but there will now be a curfew for all students from eight p.m., daily. This includes weekends. Until we find out who did this, the curfew will remain in effect. Any student who knows anything may come to speak to me at any time today."

Then, with a shuffle and the characteristic beep, the line goes silent once more. The class breaks out into furious mutterings. Principal Wolfe hasn't actually said that a snake was killed, but everyone seems to know it. Word travels fast.

"Quiet down!" Mr. Mollier roars, banging his hands on the desk. The class quiets. "You have ten minutes."

I slouch into my seat and try not to cry. I have to speak to Stacey. I have to find out what's going on. Absently, I pick at my ruined wrists, itching to peel back the thin, wispy, tissue-like skin that hangs limp.

Sakkie comes to talk to me during sports class. Everyone is on the pitch playing cricket while I sit on the grass watching. He abandons his rake, not seeming to care that anyone can see us talking.

"Are you okay?" he asks, coming to sit beside me.

"Yes." Absently I pull up clumps of grass. "Poor Molly."

"Yeah. Dad's pretty upset."

I shrug. "I just don't get it. I mean . . . I was there all night. I was there at the Tractor Tire, so I don't know when she was killed. I mean . . . Wouldn't I have seen something?"

I turn my gaze up at him, pleading with him to give me some kind of answer.

He grips my shoulders. "You were *where* all night?"

"I . . ." I hadn't realized I'd said so much. What if Stacey finds out I told?

"What the hell were you doing? How did you even get out? And after what happened, can you really be *that* stupid?"

His teeth are bared and his eyes are wide.

"I'm sorry—"

"That's not good enough. Jesus Christ! Do you know what could have happened? What the hell were you thinking?"

"It wasn't me," I begin, feeling myself becoming hysterical. "It was her. She tied me to the tire. I had no choice; it was a punishment. I had no choice—"

Sakkie pulls me into his arms, squeezing me tightly. "God help me."

The knock of the ball on the bat cuts into our moment like a physical thing, and he pushes me away firmly. I glance over: No one seems to have noticed our embrace. Why would they? They don't pay attention to me.

The bell rings.

"Get to your next class."

"Okay," I say, wishing Stacey were here to explain.

I get to my feet and head toward the school building. Sakkie saunters away, and before long I notice I'm not walking alone.

"Hi, Gert."

"Hey."

I glance at him, and I catch a glimpse of the man he will one day become. Kind but strong, all because he spent his youth as a fat, awkward bully of a boy. I smile.

"What did he want?"

"Just to ask how I'm doing."

"Why do you—never mind."

"Why do I what, Gert?"

He sighs, looks briefly like he won't continue, and then says, "Why do you let him get to you? I saw the look on your face when I gave you his note, and I saw him hug you just now. I mean, are you, like"—he pauses, like he's afraid to say it—"his . . . girlfriend . . . or something? Because, I mean, that's really, really . . . it's gross."

The way his ears turn crimson is enough to make me feel sorry for him, but not enough for me to admit anything.

"Listen, Gert, I'm glad we're not at each other's throats anymore, but you don't know me. And you don't know him."

"I know he's *old*," he says, the first sign of anger showing. "And I could have told someone about this and gotten him into a lot of trouble, but you'd be in trouble too. And I don't want that."

"Well, there's nothing going on, so you can stop worrying."

He scowls at the school building, lips pursed. "You can tell someone. They can make him leave you alone."

"Thanks, but I'm really fine."

I don't have time for this. I have to find Stacey. I have to ask her what is going on. Is my punishment over? Did she hurt Molly? Is this a test too? I am so scared about what she might be thinking of me.

63

Trunkless Vine

I try to find Stacey during break because I had no time after sports. I'm burning to see her, to talk to her; she needs to love me again. I need to make it happen. I'd lay myself down in a lake of broken glass for her friendly kiss upon my cheek. I'd swim the coal seas of my shattered heart—face those dreaded demons—for her radiance once more.

I find her sitting alone by the water fountain on the sidelines of the field. She is picking the petals off a white daisy. A small cluster of denuded daisies has grown on the ground in front of her; the petals look like little white tears.

Bernie walks up and sits down beside her. I feel like I'm divided from them by some kind of barrier. At first I don't realize why. As I watch, Bernie whispers something in Stacey's ear; Stacey smiles, glances at me, eyes narrow. I feel like she is looking at me through a long tunnel, shadows on every side. All I see is Stacey and Bernie; nothing else matters.

I must be going crazy, I tell myself. What the *fuck*? What the fuck is going on? Bernie says something else, a *second* whisper; the horror that washes over me is total. Stacey smirks. The intimacy of the gesture is so overwhelmingly obvious—like a caress over naked skin—that all at once I know.

Bernie has won.

I have lost.

How could I have taken so long to see this? There is no way for me to gain ground now. I see the resolution in Stacey's eyes, and she looks at me . . . through me. My punishment wasn't a one-off—it was a casting off. No delusion could make me think otherwise, because I *am* her twin. And I would have done the same. I would have cast off the weak and chosen the loyal. I look down at my bandaged legs. Who would choose *this*?

I feel the world tilt and skew, rotating on an unstable axis. Beneath my feet, the ground begins to melt, my shoes get absorbed in the digestive juices of loamy earth. I am a lowly terricole, and I want to burrow deep—to burrow, forget, and then die.

Bernie has won and Stacey is the prize.

"Hello, Stacey," I say weakly. What else is there to do?

Even Bernie ignores me. I'm frozen out; the intensity of their cold faces has stopped my heart.

My face puckers through the frostbite, and I'm crying before I've fully turned away. I run to the girl's bathroom and lock myself in the farthest stall before I crack up completely. I hide in the tiny space, tapping the walls with my fingernails, whispering Alexander Pope, until the bell rings.

Thus let me live, unheard, unknown;
Thus unlamented let me die;
Steal from the world, and not a stone;
Tell where I lie

In sports class a few days later, Sakkie comes to see me. Once again he sits beside me, but this time there is a noticeable gap between us.

"We need to talk."

I stare at him, hearing those words over and over.

We need to talk.

He turns to look at me. In those irises I can see that something horrible is waiting. It is something that may cause irreparable damage.

But he doesn't need to say anything else. Those four words have said it all; I want to cringe away. The whole meaning, the whole conversation, has passed between us in this brief glance. The core is behind his eyes; it is in the way he bites his bottom lip.

"This has to end."

"Sakkie . . ."

"It's too late to say anything. I've decided. That night—that . . . *date*. Showed me that we can't do this. The fire, your legs, the snake thing . . ." He looks at me.

"What are you saying?"

"I'm saying goodbye, Beautiful Beth."

It's too much. I stand, and I run. I make it to the sugarcane patch before I retch. Nothing comes out. I'm too empty for that.

The bell rings but I ignore it. When I eventually go back to the field, Sakkie is gone.

◆ ◆ ◆

I try to speak to Bernie after lunch, but she walks past me with her snotty nose in the air and I am mortified. How can I possibly have come to *this*? Yet the desperation to be back in Stacey's good graces is enough to make me do anything, and I persist.

"What have I done?" I demand desperately, scampering after her, but it sounds more like begging.

She keeps walking; she's enjoying this.

"I helped you," I remind her. "I got that aspirin for you! Why are you doing this?"

Crying again is painful. I feel like my tear ducts have been soaked raw. Tears feel like shards of glass.

Bernie hesitates, opens her mouth, then frowns. She closes her mouth, her blue eyes harden; she shuts me out methodically. She knows what it means for her to be where she is. I'm a nothing now. I can be her for a while. She walks away because she knows where she is walking to and it's better than being where I am.

"No, wait! Please . . . What can I do?"

She spins to face me, eyes narrowed. The malice in her voice runs so deep I can hardly believe I've caused it. "You told me—" She breaks off, frowns and sighs. For a moment she even looks scared, but then the fear is gone, and her face turns to stone. "You're crazy. This is what you *get*. Whore."

I imagine that she is laughing; maybe she is. My stomach lurches for the second time today, and I slide down the wall beside the lunch-hall bin and breathe deeply; sweet rot fills my nostrils.

I wander the school fields, alone among the first years. It doesn't really matter what I do. I'm less than an atom now. The kids around me scream, scamper, scurry . . . all of them carefree and bondless. I dawdle in endless laps along the very farthest edges of the field.

I've screwed up my life forever. Rowan is gone. Sakkie is gone. Even Bernie is gone. Stacey won't talk to me . . . my twin won't talk to me. Can I do anything to get her to love me again? I'm too exposed without her, too naked. I feel like everyone is watching me now that she's not in the way. I don't know what to do; I don't know the rules anymore.

Do I step with my right foot first? Or was it the left? Am I allowed to pick my nose if it's for an itch and not for boogers? When am I allowed to ask about what happened at the Tractor Tire? When the sun has set or when it is newly raised? When can I ask Stacey what my dreams mean? Will she answer, or freeze me out? Is it another test?

I am approaching the most deserted corner of the field now. It is the site of the tallest trees on the property, and consequently it is entirely engulfed in thick shadow. Most of the little kids won't go here because of the time Stacey dug a hole so deep everyone was convinced she almost dug right into hell's ceiling, when the soil bled a deep, moist scarlet. I avoid the dig site by at least two meters.

I look up to make sure I am still on a straight trajectory, and I see Rowan standing right ahead, hands behind his back, watching me. I ignore him and continue my solitary march.

"Beth?" he calls as I approach.

I flinch, too fragile for painful reminders. I keep walking, one foot after the other. One, two, one, two . . . this is safest. If I break momentum, I might fall to pieces completely.

"Bethany," he says, amending my name as though he knows how painful *Beth* has become. "Please. I need to talk to you."

"Oh, hello, Rowan. How are you?"

"May I walk beside you?"

"Of course you can, Rowan. How are you? I'm fine. We're so busy this time of year. There are a lot of exams to prepare for, you know. We're always studying." I prattle on for a while longer, not really listening to what I am saying. My mouth just makes sounds and my brain disconnects. I tap my legs with every step, and this, combined with the gobbledygook I am rambling on about, makes me feel less nervous.

"Bethany," he snaps, "what the fuck are you talking about? What is going on?"

"Leave me alone."

I wish he would. It's like torture. Stacey with Bernie. Bernie with power. Rowan with Stacey. A neat little circle. Where do I fit in?

You don't, you moron.

"Shut the *fuck* up, Beth!" I growl.

I don't realize I said it out loud until I notice Rowan standing with his mouth open, staring at me. Beth disappears like condensation, laughing.

"Who're you talking to?" he whispers.

I scratch my neck. "Myself. Don't you ever do that?"

"Uh, no."

I sigh and walk past him. "See you around."

"Wait, we have to talk!"

"I don't want to. I haven't got the energy. I haven't got the h—" I don't have the heart to even say *heart.*

"What is going on with you? You're acting completely crazy. I'm trying to help you."

I look at him, and even that is painful. "If you want to help me, then leave me alone." I shake my head, exhausted. "Just . . . leave me alone."

Even now I can't say what I'm thinking. I want to tell him to choose me. Choose me over Stacey. Pick the evil twin. That will make me happy.

Instead I just turn and walk away.

In my ear canal, I hear my heart finally crack; it splits open, and the sound vibrates in every bone until I am broken all over. That would explain the strange tension I feel in my head; the last threads of my control have snapped like the support wires of an elevator fraying and breaking. I plummet down the elevator shaft.

Everything is gone. My mother is an old man's toy—a woman who killed my real mother and stuck a fake plastic replica in her place. Sakkie is an empty hole inside me that has been filling up with horrible dark things. Stacey has withdrawn her thick trunk, leaving me a weak vine without support, clinging to the air for those last final moments before I go under entirely. Bernie has broken what was left of pathetic me in half. Sakkie's goodbye sits heavily inside me, like a boulder tied to my leg, dragging me under the black waters to a quaggy grave at the bottom, and T. S. Eliot is there to meet me.

We have lingered in the chambers of the sea, by sea-girls wreathed with seaweed red and brown, till human voices wake us and we drown.

64

Nocturnal Phantasms

NOW

"What are you talking about?" I snap. "Who's almost here?"

"Not so fast. Do you remember this?" You have a razor blade between your fingers.

"No."

You laugh, because of course I do. Of course I remember, and you know it.

Prove you love me.

You put the sharp end to your wrist, and I yelp and reach for the blade. You flail, and a moment later I'm blinking at my arms in shock. At first nothing happens, but then the skin parts, seeping blood faster than should be possible.

"Rowan isn't here to save you."

I look at you, slow, stupid comprehension dawning on me. How long have you been planning this? Where have you been for the last decade or more? Have you been hiding in the shadows, devising a way to get me here, for this specific game? Everything was always a game . . . I've been so stupid.

"So, what?" I manage. "You're going to kill me?"

"You ought to die," you spit, "for what you did to me."

"Stacey, I'm *sorry*! I don't remember!"

"I know, silly chop. That's why I'm going to remind you. No shying away any longer."

You don't even flinch when you push me bodily into the center of the tire—*where Glass Man lives*—and then my phone is somehow in your hand, and you are pressing it to your ear.

I hear Bruce's voice, panicked, relieved, on the other end. "Bethany? Jesus, thank God!"

Of course. He was the last person to call me.

"I have your little friend," you say, smiling. "Just thought you should know that I'm going to kill her."

"Who is this? *Where's Bethany?*"

"Bruce!" I yell, tugging on your leg. You kick me in the face, and something crunches, and there is blood. So much blood.

"Welp, it was nice chatting, hubby boy."

"Wait—"

You hang up and smile down at me. The night is in full force, your face a skull of shadow. "I bet he's cute."

My phone pings again.

"Look at this," you say, grinning. "Your editor seems confused about your chapter."

"Stacey, *please*! Stop this!"

"Forna seems to think you've gone a bit loopy . . . let's see . . . 'Bethany, this chapter is nonsense. What are you playing at?' Oop. Looks like you're in trouble."

You turn the phone to me so I can see the screen. You click open the attachment, my chapter.

"That doesn't make sense. I sent her a chapter . . . it was good."

The phone screen is littered with words I didn't write.

Chapter 1

Sally is Stacey is Sally is Stacey is Sally is Stacey is
Sally is Stacey is Sally is Stacey is Sally is Stacey is
Sally is Stacey is Sally is Stacey is Sally is Stacey is
Sally is Stacey is Sally is Stacey is Sally is Stacey is
Sally is Stacey is Sally is Stacey is Sally is Stacey is
Sally is Stacey is Sally is Stacey is Sally is Stacey is
Sally is Stacey is Sally is Stacey is Sally is Stacey is
Sally is Stacey is a very good thorn.

I shake my head. "Stacey, I need a hospital."

My arms aren't bleeding as much as they were, but my nose is still pouring with blood, and I'm a little dizzy.

"Wrap up," you say, taking off your T-shirt and throwing it to me. The tank top beneath your tee is just like the ones we used to wear. It's like you never left this place—or maybe it just never left you.

I bind my left arm as best I can. It got the worst of the blade. I press the bandaged mess to my nose, swallowing blood and choking.

"Good. Now. Let's play another game."

There is a shuffling in the bushes, and then movement. You're not alone.

"*Why are you doing this?*" I yell.

At first I don't recognize the figure that steps up to the edge of the tire, peeking down at me where I am sprawled in spiderwebs and beetle husks.

And then her face morphs into something changed, but familiar.

"Bernie?"

65

Gravity

THEN

The staff room is full of chatty teachers who look horrifyingly human. I spot Sakkie immediately as though my eyes are magnetically drawn to him . . . as though he is the only bit of gravity I have left to keep me from floating away into the ether. He doesn't see me right away. Only when Mr. Grinyer, beside him, asks me who I'm after does he look up.

His smile falters, and his left eye blinks slower than his right.

"Ah, Bethany. Thank you for coming." He puts down his tea, and I notice how his hands shake. "Come with me, please."

I walk behind him quietly, yearning for his violent hands on my flesh. There is iron in his voice that has me shivering.

"Sakkie," I whisper, lifting my hand and meaning to touch his back, but he walks faster.

We go into an empty classroom. I don't know what to do with myself. I wait in agitation while he closes the door and draws the blind down. My actions are beyond my control now; I throw myself at him, but he grips my shoulders, holding me away. Nothing can make him relent.

"Beth, please."

"Don't," I beg, my voice high and grating. "Don't leave me . . . take all those words you said back."

"You're the one who begged me not to fall in love with you," he points out gently.

"I take it back!" I yell. "I take it all back! I *want* you to love me—I *want* you to make love to me. Please, please take me away from here. Please, Sakkie, take me away with you—I'll do anything you want—"

He pushes me down into a chair, and I'm too weak to stand up again. What is beyond exhaustion? What is beyond the beyond? What is left of the broken mirror? Useless shards with jagged edges. No shape, no recognizable form.

"I'm going back to Joburg. I'm going to fix the mess I've made of myself."

"What about the mess you've made of me?" I whisper, holding up my palms like I'm begging for money.

"You made this mess," he tells me gently, and it's like he's slit my wrists himself. It's like him *gently* stabbing me in the stomach.

"But—"

"I need to do this right," he insists.

"But . . ." My voice is small. "You said that to *me* once."

"You're bad for me." He grits his teeth.

"But . . . but you love me."

As I look at my wrists, I think—where is the blood? Where are the tears, now that I truly need them? I touch my face; it is cold and dry. "Don't you want me?"

"Oh, Bethie," he breathes. "This was poison from the start. You're old enough to see that. And after you told me that you're still sneaking out at night . . . I realized what a bad influence you are on me."

"But I was almost happy."

"Me too. But . . . you broke me in half."

Who broke me in half, I wonder?

"What happens now?" I ask, but the gravity that his proximity once provided begins to dissipate. Soon it will be all gone.

"When school's out, I'm leaving for Joburg."

"Oh."

The meeting is ending; I can feel it. He is almost closed to me now: formal, parental, dry and lustless. I've lost him; the room is growing darker.

After everything, this is it. I'm too tired to fight the storm. I'd rather drown.

"Thank you, Sakkie," I say. There is no substance to my voice now. "Thank you for everything."

He kisses me chastely on my cheek and then wipes it away with his thumb.

A kiss that never was.

An affair that never was.

A lover that never was.

I square my shoulders as best I can.

"Goodbye."

He nods and smiles that same old hard smile that doesn't touch his eyes—the one that is closed and not really there. His glass hairs glint under the lights.

That evening I huddle into the phone booth, feeling more and more like Bernie. I dial my mother's number and wait for the line to pick up. While I wait, I pick skin off my wrist and eat it.

My voice is shaking. "Hi, Mummy, it's me."

I'm in trouble, I want to say. *Just this once, please, just this once . . . can you listen?*

"Oh, darling," she says, "I can't talk right now."

Mummy, I need help. I need you. "But I really—"

"Not now, Bethany. Mummy's very busy. Stoffel's in the hospital. It's nothing serious, but I'm popping to Harrods to get him a little get-well gift. I'm thinking a Barbour."

"But, Mum, I—"

"Save your phone card, sweetie. Remember: *enunciate*. Kiss-kiss, darling. Mwah!"

"Mum—"

Click.

66

Visitor

I visit the bathroom before I go outside. I know what I am doing, who I am going to see. In my bag I carry Bernie's stolen aspirin, Stacey's old razor blade, Sakkie's old cigarette butt. I wear the lavender bra. These are my treasures; they are remnants of the people who once loved me. I stand in front of the mirror, and in the reflection, I see that lost blue girl, veiled in the darkness of the stall directly behind me. For the first time, I'm not afraid.

"I know who you are," I tell her.

She raises a hand to her mouth, and her eyes widen in a sort of vague surprise. She steps forward, raises a hand to me, and vanishes.

I turn to face the empty stall. "Beth."

I check my face in the mirror for any signs of crying. I know it's crazy, since I haven't cried in a while, but it feels like I am, so I make sure. My face feels wet, looks dry. I stare at my fingers, wondering if my tears are invisible, like the rooms in the House, which I might have been wandering through since I first stepped foot across that invisible boundary.

Sakkie left two days ago.

He lied when he said he'd stay until the end of term.

He was that desperate to leave you.

And I didn't get to ask him if he ever did get my letter. If he ever wrote back.

Getting out of the window is, as always since the accident, painful. The scars on my legs strain, begging to tear. They are still the soft scars of skin that will most likely have to fall away to reveal the shiny red skin beneath. They don't like this abuse.

I ignore their screams and keep up with my escape. Stacey is sleeping in bed. She didn't stir when I left, so I feel confident.

Once outside, I run over the cold but thirsty ground, and I don't stop until I'm standing by the tree that overlooks Sakkie's house. How long ago it feels I was here with him. How long ago since Stacey and I were inside that shack of a hut, drinking proper cocoa.

I walk up to the door, and I knock.

Joe answers, a husk of what he was the first time I saw him. He is no longer the fiery Father Christmas, with bushy eyebrows. He's just an old man. Defeated, like me.

"Hi, Joe," I whisper.

He smiles at me sadly. "Hello, *liefie*. You're out late. There's a curfew now."

"I'm sorry about Molly," I blurt out.

"How did you know?"

"A boy in my class found her. He told me."

Joe glances up, past me into the night. His eyes roam sadly over the barren bushland, and I realize how lonely he is. "Come inside, *liefie*. We'll talk."

I follow him in, taking in the familiar smells. I take the seat he offers, the one I have always taken. Only now it feels different against my bandaged thighs.

"Cocoa?" he asks.

"Extra sweet."

"*Ja, ja*," he says, and he almost smiles. "Sit tight."

I glance down at the cushion beside me, where Molly once curled herself into a knot.

Joe returns with the cocoa in tin mugs, and I take a greedy sip. I'm a little surprised when the hot sweetness doesn't revitalize me.

"What is it, *liefie*?" Joe asks. He has been looking at me while I stare into the mug.

"It's delicious, Joe. Thank you."

The concern on his face clears, and he smiles. "So. To what do I owe this pleasure?"

I lean back and close my eyes. "I don't know." It's true. I don't. I had come here looking for . . . something. Something intangible. But now that I'm here, I can't feel it. I was looking for my last bit of grounding to the earth, but I feel like I've already begun to float away.

Then I realize why I came. I couldn't ask Sakkie, but I can ask Joe.

"Did you post my letter, Joe?"

He sighs and looks into his mug. "I thought you would come asking me that one day."

"Did you?"

"Didn't you speak to him when he came back?"

I nod. "Yes. But I never asked him. And now he's gone again. For good this time, I think."

"*Liefie*, Sakkie's not a nice man. It was my stupid mistake to bring him here, but I'm his father, and he had nowhere else."

"Did you post it?"

He takes a long breath, and I think I know his answer. But then he surprises me. "Yes, I did send it. Eventually. I saw you in the grounds, so sad. You seemed to have formed an attachment to him, and I thought a letter might cheer you up."

"Didn't he . . . write back?"

"*Liefie*, Sakkie was in jail. They gave him leave to visit me for a very short time on parole. Do you understand what that means?"

"He was . . . in jail? Why?"

Joe nods carefully. "He used to work at a school up in Olivedale. While he was there, he did some pretty bad things. Things . . . that no decent man should do. I . . . I made a mistake letting him live with me.

I knew he wasn't allowed near children, but he said he was better, and he's my boy, but . . ."

My cheeks tingle as the feeling leaves them. I feel like I know the story already. It will just be a repeat of mine.

"Does the school know?" I whisper.

Joe shakes his head. "The school hired him on a cash basis on my recommendation, and he's not on any kind of official payroll or anything . . . so, no."

"What did he . . . do?"

"He . . . he got too friendly with a couple of the girls at the school. One of the girls . . . well, she said he did bad things to her against her will. She pressed charges."

"Did he do it?" I whisper.

Joe looks ill. "Yes. He did. There was . . . evidence. He hurt this little girl quite badly. It's not his fault, really. He's sick, you see. Ever since he was a boy. Sees something he wants and takes it. No concept of boundaries with him. And afterwards he feels bad . . . so bad, *liefie*. Still, it doesn't change the outcome. Doesn't change the fact that people need protecting from him."

I don't know how I feel about Joe making excuses for Sakkie. I don't know that I feel much at all.

I swallow, but my throat doesn't seem to be working, and I choke. "Oh." And "I see."

Joe leans forward in his chair. "*Liefie*, he's not a suitable friend."

"But you let him come back."

Joe's face drops. "Yes. He's my boy. He'll always be welcome here. And he'll always get into trouble and come running home, I expect."

"I thought . . ."

Thought he came back for you? You're so stupid, Bethany. So, so stupid.

"He doesn't love anyone, *skat*."

I think I'm not crying, but then a tear drips onto my knee. I have nothing left. Sakkie was a lie. I was just . . . a toy. I let him do those things to me; I let him rip open this place inside me—my soul, or my heart—and now what's left? Everything went bad after him. Stacey, then Rowan; then he came back and made it even worse, and Beastly Beth got worse . . . it all went bad because of the poison he infected me with.

And I let him.

He's not going to marry you when you're eighteen, Beth tells me. She says it gently, and I just nod.

"Thanks, Joe. I'm so sorry about Molly."

"You're a sweet girl, *liefie*. Don't let anyone get you down."

I nod. I finish off the dregs of the cocoa, and it still hasn't warmed me.

"I better go back."

Joe nods, his lips pressed together. "Before you do, *skat* . . ." He sighs, like he knows what he is about to do will be something he regrets later. "There was a letter, from Sakkie. From jail. I wasn't going to give it to you, but I suppose I had better. Doesn't make any difference now."

He walks to the sideboard near the TV and opens a drawer. He removes a letter and hands it to me.

I take it with shaking fingers.

"Just remember, *liefie*, he's a trickster. He's done this before; he can do it again." He touches my cheek. "Don't let him use you. I'm so sorry I ever let him near you, child."

I nod, and then I hug him. He squeezes me once, briefly, and then I am shown to the door, the thin envelope trembling in my fingers. Joe shuts the door behind me, and I face the black night. There is no moon out.

I walk to the tree and sit down behind it. I tear open the envelope, reading by the faint glimmer of Joe's house lights.

> Beth,
>
> You're my number one girl. My one and only.
>
> Listen carefully and do exactly what I say. I need you to get some money. Maybe ask your mom? And I need you to get a bus down to Joburg. I have some

things going on here; I can take care of you. I'm tied up at the moment, but don't worry—in about a month that won't matter.

You still love me, Beth, don't you? We can be together forever. We can run away together, but I need that money. Get as much as you can: loads and loads. Steal it if you have to. Don't worry. We'll give it all back.

Everything will be fine. Don't tell anyone what you're doing. I'll send you another letter in a few months to tell you where to go. Don't show anyone this letter, and don't go through my dad. Post the reply yourself.

Remember, I love you. I need you.

Don't forget that,

Sakkie

I wonder how stupid he thinks I am. The stationary says *Johannesburg Prison*. No wonder he didn't mention it when he came back. Maybe he thinks I ignored it, and that's why he hurt me so badly in the shed. Maybe he knows his dad would never have given it to me.

I tear up the letter and bury it in the roots of the tree.

"Goodbye, Sakkie," I whisper, staring at the dark hole in the gnarled roots. "I hate what you've done to me. To other girls. I hope they lock you away forever."

Even though I say the words and mean them, I can't help feeling like maybe I should be locked away forever too. I'm his poisonous creation, and I have poisoned others in my turn. Where does the line stop? Where does the cycle end?

And as I walk away, the last tether holding me to this earth dissolves.

67

Another Kind of Voice

NOW

"Bernie?"

"You know you're crazy, don't you?" she asks. When I don't reply, she carries on. "Since school. Pushing me aside. Making Stacey hate me. Little good it did you in the end. After everything, she chose me. Stacey chose me. She. Chose. *Me.*"

I am a thirty-two-year-old woman, I remind myself. I am married; I have a career; I am not playing those schoolyard games again.

Still.

It prickles at me. Because Stacey *did* choose her.

"You did," I mutter, glaring up at you. My lip is swelling from your kick, my nose is likely broken, but I don't care, because suddenly I hate you. I hate both of you.

"I chose her," you say, leaning forward, "because you betrayed me. With Rowan." Your eyes are cold glass. "With Sakkie." Your eyes are my black mirror.

No. No, no. Panic is a strange thing. It creeps up like vines, and once it has hold, it tightens like a boa constrictor.

There could be snakes out here . . .

You know. You always knew . . .

You laugh, turning to Bernie. "She thinks I didn't know her dirty little secrets!" You spit down at me. "Did you think I didn't know the disgusting things you did with that gross man while I was in sick bay?"

"I didn't . . . I was . . ." I shut my eyes, but the tears can't be stopped, and I need to breathe, and I need not to be here. "Please, Stacey—"

"No point trying to explain."

"You were always so . . . *off*," Bernie adds. "I guess it follows."

"I was alone, I was confused—"

Bernie sneers. "Whore."

"That wasn't my fault," I manage. "I was a child and he was the adult!"

"You sicken me," Bernie says.

"Enough," you snap, and your arm slices the air, and the blade slices more skin, but the skin isn't mine, and Bernie is staring at you, holding her throat, and this is not happening. This is not happening.

Bernie gargles, coughs, and there is blood on her lips, and then the blood is flowing between her fingers even as she tries to hold it in. She stumbles back, and I can't see her anymore, but I can hear her trying to scream and only gurgling.

"Jesus! Stacey, *fuck*!"

"I thought you were exciting," you say. "I thought you had potential. But you were just a weak, psycho, paranoid child. Obsessed with me. Even Bernie made something of herself. But you? You're still trapped here. We both are. And it's your fault." You look over at Bernie, who is making sounds I've never heard. "This is your fault, Bethie."

"Oh my God, oh my God . . ." I get to my feet somehow, and I am climbing out of the tire somehow, and you are laughing watching me, because I am slow. I know I am slow.

I fall to the ground, and the fine sand puffs up into my mouth, and I cough. But then I see Bernie staring at the sky, at the moon, a porcelain doll in blood, and I cough and cough and vomit.

Did you draw Bernie here the same way you drew me? With lies about remembering the good times?

You jump down from the tire and push me to the earth with your foot, and even now I think, *She's touching me* and *I'm going to die here*.

The old voices are back. The ones telling me I am nothing. I am no one, and I feel myself floating like I did all those years ago, hanging on by a thread. My mind wants to close in on itself and go away, somewhere deep inside, hidden where no one can find me.

And then another voice rears up. *No. You're going to fight this.*

You move over to Bernie and wipe blood from her face. "Stupid Bernie," you mutter.

You're so busy examining your work that you don't see me rise to my feet. You don't see the rock in my hand.

68

Together

THEN

I walk all the way to the Tractor Tire before I realize I have no intention of going back to the dorm. I climb up the rubber grooves and sit down, letting my legs dangle into the hole.

Stacey is almost here. I can see her coming closer, wading through the night.

"Who are you meeting?" she asks, when she has reached me. She cocks her head to the side and regards me in a way she never has before. Openly, curiously—without power.

"I'm not meeting anyone."

"You went to see Joe?"

"How did you know?"

She shrugs her shoulders to imply she doesn't know, or that it doesn't matter.

"Molly was killed," I say. "I wanted to make sure he was okay."

Stacey takes a step closer. "She was killed the day you were here. Did you see anything?"

I look away because I don't know what my eyes show. "No, I didn't. I don't understand. You came for me at dawn. There wasn't that much time for Molly to be killed and . . ."—it's almost impossible to say—"cut open and nailed up."

"How do you know she was cut?"

"Gert Van Dyck said so. He saw her first."

Stacey laughs, long and loud. "Gert Van Dyck. You like him, don't you?"

"He's sweet," I admit, my ears ringing and burning from her harsh laughter. I don't understand what is happening anymore. Are we talking at all, or are we merely thinking? Are we even moving? Have the rules lost their meaning? "Why are you turning against me?"

She ignores my question. "Maybe *you* killed Molly."

It's the calmness of her accusation—suggestion—that unnerves me. "I would never—"

"How do you know? Maybe you just don't remember."

"Stacey, why are you being so—" I break off. "Ssh! I heard something . . ."

I can still hear it. Footsteps across the sand, heading right for us.

There is an uncomfortable niggle in my head, at the back of my brain. A truth. I don't want to face this realization, but I know I'm not wrong.

Stacey killed Molly.

Stacey sliced her open and nailed her up.

Stacey is the one.

Not me.

"Bernie will be joining us shortly," Stacey says. "I told her to come."

The footsteps grow louder.

"Why?" I ask.

She sneers at me, but her eyes are empty, flat, cold. "She needs to be punished. Just like Molly. But she's very fat. It might take some work."

Discomfort becomes fear. "Maybe we should run for it." I get ready to jump off the tire, but before I can, Rowan appears out of the blackness.

"Rowan," I call before I can stop myself. I jump off the tire.

He smiles and jogs over. "Hey," he says, reaching for me. I scoot back and glance nervously at Stacey.

"What is it?" he says.

"Look who's here," Stacey sings, pointing out into the night. Before long, Bernie appears, wide eyed and shivering. Stacey is right: she is very fat. But . . . it's quite charming.

"What's going on?" she says groggily.

Stacey smiles at me, takes two steps toward Bernie, and hits her. It isn't the small slaps she's given me; it's a furious mistress of a punch, one that sends Bernie flying into the sand.

"Hey!" Rowan yells. "What the hell was *that* for?"

He runs over to Bernie and helps her sit up. She's crying loudly—like a squealing piglet—and her nose is bleeding. Stacey doesn't care about the noise. She knows as well as I that out here, we are alone. No one will find us. No one will come. No one will even hear.

Rowan whips around to look at me, his eyes hard and lips unyielding. "What the hell is the matter with you?"

"What are you talking about?" I cry, looking at Stacey. "Why is everything *my* fault?"

Bernie is sobbing, but through the snotty cries, she says three words. "She . . . killed . . . Molly!"

I gasp, gaze flickering between Stacey and Bernie. They're in this together. It wasn't enough to exclude me, punish me, abandon me. They have to ruin me as well, blame me for something I never did. Or do something just to blame me for it. I'm so sickened by the thought they could have planned this all out that I feel quite faint. All the whispering . . . Was this it? Make me a killer too? I grasp my chest, unable to process what has happened to the three of us.

Rowan looks at me like I'm a stranger. "You killed that snake? I heard that they thought it was a student, but I never thought it was . . . I feel sick."

"But I didn't, Rowan. I didn't!"

Bernie gets to her feet. "You did!" She spits bloody saliva onto the sand. "You killed that poor snake, and you loved it!"

I step toward her. "Shut up, you liar! Why are you doing this? Are you her puppet, like me? You have a brain! Can't you see what you're doing when you lie for her?"

"You fucking crazy bitch!" Bernie screeches, her eyes wide. "I'm *sick* of this, okay? I hate you!"

Rowan stands in front of Bernie, like I'm some kind of risk to her instead of the other way around. Stacey just folds her arms and watches me. I will have to pay for calling myself her puppet, even though that's what I am and have always been.

And let her do her worst.

I'm horrified by the rebellious thought, and the realization that it's a true thought.

Let. Her. Do. Her. Worst.

The invisible ropes I didn't know were binding me unwind and fall away.

I'm done.

I belong to no one anymore. Not even myself.

"It was Stacey!" I yell, my bonds finally broken. "It was Stacey. Stacey killed Molly! Not me!"

I have broken from her—oh my God—I have broken with Stacey. She will never forgive me now. She will never take me back into her fold again. Anything I do from now on will have to be on my own. What have I done?

Rowan tries not to cry, but his mouth pulls down into a horrible grimace, and I don't think he can help it. "This is fucking crazy," he says fiercely, and he is crying. "Bethany, I want you to stop it. We can get you help. Just come with us back to the dorm."

He reaches for my hand, but I yank it away. "No! I'll never go back to the dorm. You'll just tell everyone I did it, and they'll believe you! But it was her," I scream, pointing at Stacey. I've done nothing wrong, and I won't go down for it. "It was her! The window was her too. I didn't do anything! Bernie's just lying because she wants in with Stacey"—I turn to Bernie—"but she'll just do to you what she did to me—"

Rowan lunges forward and grabs my shoulders. He grips me tightly, and his face is barely two inches from mine.

"Bethany, you need help."

I take in his every detail, now that he is so close, and I have to make him understand. If Stacey is counting on one thing, it's that Rowan is hers. But he was mine first. Maybe I can show him the games she plays. Maybe I can ask him to understand me, and he will. "No, I don't—why won't you believe me, Rowan? I haven't done anything wrong. It was her; it was Stacey. It's what she does. Please, *please* believe me—"

"Bethany, Stacey is dead!"

69

The Frame

NOW

I hit you over the head as hard as I can.

You go sprawling in the dirt.

"I am not a child anymore," I growl. "I am not a lonely, confused little girl that you can manipulate." I raise the rock again. "And I am going to kill you."

You are behind me before I see you move, slashing at my back with the blade.

"You can try."

I cry out but spin to face you, and you are holding a frame in your hands. Inside it, a photo of us, arms draped around each other, grinning silly, muddy grins.

You throw it to the ground between us, and it shatters. Somehow, we both know. We always knew.

We pick up shards of glass.

It was always going to come to this.

70

Dr. Morgan

THEN

“She died in the fire, don’t you remember?”

I shake my head, over and over. “No . . . no, she’s alive. She’s right here—”

I point to where Stacey is standing—

but she’s gone.

The night is black, flat, and empty. Stacey is nowhere in sight. I look down at my hand and see Bernie’s blood seared across my knuckles.

Bernie shivers and begins to cry harder. “She’s crazy,” she tells Rowan, eyes flickering to me every few words. “She thinks she’s Stacey. She kept pretending to be her—” Her words come out at greater and greater speed until they’re merged together in a feverish muddle. “She told me to steal aspirin when she was pretending to be Stacey, and later on she came to my room asking me what Stacey had said, pretending she knew nothing about the aspirin at all! Then she stole it herself. She told me to ignore her if she ever said she was Bethany ever again, and then she acted all confused when I did what she asked. She talks to herself all night long, and she pretends Stacey is still here when everyone knows she's dead! I was so scared that I just went along with it—I thought she would kill me!"

Rowan's mouth quivers, and then he has pulled me into his chest. He kisses the top of my head over and over.

"It's okay," he says, though his chest is in spasms, fighting sobs. "It's okay. We'll fix this. Everything will be okay."

"I don't . . . I don't understand," I say into his shoulder. "Stacey's alive. She's alive. You know she is . . . you've been seeing her for months! You know she's alive."

Rowan pulls back. "What are you talking about? I've been with *you* for the last three months. Stacey is dead." He bites down on his lips, shaking his head. "I thought I'd helped you through it. I thought you were okay."

My mouth hangs open, and I must look completely stupid. "No . . . you chose Stacey over me. I . . . Stacey killed Molly . . . Stacey broke the window . . . it wasn't me."

Face it, kiddo, Beth tells me. *You're kind of crazy.*

"Shut up!" I roar at her. I have no time for her thoughts.

"Who are you talking to?" Rowan says.

"I . . ." I start to sob, but the tears are like sand. Invisible sand. "Beth."

He swallows. "Okay, Bethany, you need to come with me. Right now."

I stare at him; I try to speak. Bernie is keeping as far away from me as possible, as though I'm a deadly asp.

He steers me away. As I pass Bernie, I reach out to her. "I'm sorry . . ."

She steps back, wide eyed, and lets me pass. Rowan keeps his arm around me as we walk, and I bury my head into his chest. I can't believe what's happening to me. Can it really be true? Could I be . . . crazy? Is Stacey dead?

I can't help looking around for her. Where did she go? She was just there. I saw her . . . I've spoken to her. She was kissing Rowan; she broke the window. She can't be dead—she just can't.

"It's going to be okay," Rowan tells me. "Everything is going to be okay."

"You think I'm crazy," I whisper. "But I'm not. I'm not. But you'll abandon me anyway, just like everyone else. Mummy, Sakkie, Stacey . . . everyone will hurt me and leave."

Rowan's shoulders tense, and I realize this is the first time I have mentioned Sakkie to him. I'm so distracted and confused I can't even try to imagine what he is thinking.

He rubs my arm as we walk. "I'm not going anywhere."

Rowan knocks on the ornate door three times and then steps back to hold me again. I cling to him like I am five years old and he is my doting mother. He rubs a hot hand up and down my arm.

"It's going to be okay," he murmurs. I don't really believe him, but it's nice of him to say. I glance at him sideways. Could we really have spoken, kissed, and more . . . without my being aware of it? Is this some trick of fate? Glass Man, trying to get me to succumb to hope?

Principal Wolfe answers his own door, taking me aback. I expected a stately servant or a French maid, but no. He stands in pale slacks, staring down at us with a frown. He looks like someone who just saw a pig talk.

"What can I . . . uh . . . do for you?"

He doesn't know how to deal with kids, I realize. He's a man who, perhaps, fell into this profession, a man who deals with the paperwork and the chairpeople, but never the children.

Rowan's voice is firm when he talks, and though he is making a request, it feels like a demand. "May we come inside, sir? Something has happened."

I let out a tiny squeak of protest, but Rowan grips my shoulder more firmly, and I step obediently inside when Principal Wolfe, bewildered, nods.

"What is this about?"

"Sir, I think we had better ask one of the matrons to come and witness the meeting."

Principal Wolfe's eyes widen, and he looks at Rowan—really looks at Rowan—for the first time. Has Rowan said something he understands? Have the words *witness the meeting* had some magical effect on him?

He nods. "Very well. Take a seat through there."

He points us at a door to the left, and Rowan ushers me into the sitting room.

"What will happen?" I whisper at him.

"We'll figure out what's going on."

"But . . . Stacey?"

Rowan looks into my eyes, a frown creasing his forehead. "She'll disappear."

My heart clenches painfully in my chest. I imagine her, looking at me with her mucky-brown eyes, slowly melting into nothing, bleeding into the surrounding scenery like she never was.

I think I would disappear with her.

71

Beth

NOW

I slash at you, trying to ignore the wind that ruffles the trees like people whispering. But then there is movement again and I think, *Bernie?* But of course it isn't.

She steps out of you, pulling free ropes that glint like metal in the moonlight, and I guess I always knew I would see her again.

Beth.

Made of glass.

She stretches and groans, creaks, and fissures. Of course. You made me flush my medicine. The "anxiety pills" Bruce was so keen to make sure I took. Because they weren't anxiety pills at all. They were to keep Beth bound. To keep *you* bound.

And I remember something else I have forgotten. Long days working on Sally, ignoring the alarm on my phone. *Take Medicine.* I'll do it later . . . How long have I been forgetting to take them?

"Hello," Beth says.

"Hello," you say.

The two of you, together, two voices against my own. Two shards of glass against my one.

You laugh together and echo in harmony through the night.

But I can win this.

I will win this.

And I will kill you both.

72

Myself Again

THEN

Even today, nearly a year on, I can't remember everything that happened after the fire and after my meltdown. When Rowan told Principal Wolfe and Matron Monday my story—leaving out the parts he didn't know—they were both too shocked to speak. Matron Monday stood up and gathered me into her arms, crying into my hair. No doubt she had already begun to question my sleepwalking incident and the part she played in what followed.

Joe was sent for, and the situation was explained. I will never forget the look on his face when he was told I killed Molly. The widening of his eyes, the baggy skin pulling taut as his eyebrows rose. The laxity of his jaw as it fell open. The way he shook his head and backed away, staring at me. I still can't believe it, not really. He left pretty quickly, and I haven't spoken to him since. It's my deepest regret that I hurt him, though I think he feels the same about me—he feels a kind of responsibility, perhaps, with what his Sakkie did to me.

Dr. Morgan came to take me away. He asked me a lot of questions and had the school sign a form. Rowan wanted to stay with me, but they pried my hands from his shirt and, kicking and screaming, loaded me into a car, and that was that.

I think I finally saw a flicker of my real mother behind my fake mother's gaze on the day she arrived at the hospital. She cried a lot, but they were real tears. She told me she would be there for me, but I asked her to go home. Shocked, she complied, paying my hospital bills from Stoffel's checkbook at a distance.

I wasn't allowed to see anyone for three long months while Dr. Morgan and I tried to sort out the pieces of my broken memory. To this day I still don't remember much of my time with Stacey after the fire. At least not the parts during which I was—apparently—her. We read the witness statements, which the police released to Dr. Morgan when Joe declined to press charges. There was one from Bernie. She talks a lot about what I said to her while I was Stacey. She talks about the conversations she heard me having alone in my room. She mentions how, at times, I seemed to be having a conversation that didn't include her, even though we were the only two around. She makes me sound like a monster.

Rowan was asked to write about his encounters with me when I was Stacey. It took a long time before Dr. Morgan would let me read them.

I don't remember any of it.

Dr. Morgan says I may never remember. It is a terrifying, humbling experience to have so much taken away. To have done so much and experienced so much but to have no access to it.

We did make one breakthrough: I remembered shattering the window. It's like I have two memories of the event: one in color; the other in a faded detail, like a bad copy. In the bad copy, I was alone, smashing the window with my alarm clock. In the more colorful one, Stacey did it. Dr. Morgan says we need to explore the event more thoroughly and bring it into my conscious memory. He says that they will try EMDR—eye movement desensitization and reprocessing therapy—and hypnosis, if it's safe. He says it could take years.

I never thought of my life as moving beyond the confines of the school. I never imagined a future where Stacey wasn't in it. Some days the reality of being alone is so sharp I break down. Dr. Morgan says it's chemical. When they get my dosages right, I shouldn't have these relapses.

Gert Van Dyck's witness statement got Sakkie into a lot of trouble. But Sakkie denied ever knowing. The police came, asking me about it. I said there was nothing to tell. I am beginning to forget the details of him, and I want it that way. Sakkie was released, and he now lives in the city, far away from here.

When I underwent the physical exam, they discovered a pretty bad infection in my burns. I think that was the real reason I began to finally accept that maybe I needed help. The last time I saw my legs, they were scarred but recovering. I had changed the bandages and cared for my wounds as I was shown. But when the hospital removed my bandages, the skin was white and yellow, infected with pus. I argued with them, convinced they were trying to trick me, but I knew the truth. I had been too busy being Stacey to change my bandages, and now the wounds were festering.

They cut away a lot of the rotten flesh, but saved my legs, such as they are. I will always look a little creepy down there, like a girl with chunks bitten out of her calf—stick leg, they might call me—and purple scars where the skin has been stretched and torn. A girl with no calf muscles. I will always walk a little funny, and people will always ask me about the holes—an endless series of dents and dimples where the doctors had to dig out the pus and gangrenous flesh. The legs I knew are gone. I might need a wheelchair one day.

Another loss I never expected.

The biggest of these losses is Stacey.

Dr. Morgan finally let me see her grave after five months, after I turned fifteen. Rowan came with me. It was the first time I'd seen him since my breakdown, and though I was nervous, he hugged me to him with the same hunger I knew during our two magical weeks.

He kissed my cheek and then asked, "Do you remember anything . . . I mean, about being with me after the fire?"

I shook my head. "It's likely I never will. That's what Dr. Morgan says. It's like I was two different people. Well . . . three, including Beth."

I didn't ask him if he's okay with that. I didn't ask him if he could live with it. Instead, I told him the truth.

"I can't see you again."

He flinched. "Don't say that. We can get through this."

"I can't. Your face, your hair . . . even your name. They remind me of her."

He cried a little, then. But he didn't argue.

I looked down at Stacey's headstone. *Stacey Preston,* it read. *Beloved daughter. 1985–2000.* Here it was. Real as anything I could ever conjure in my broken mind. I knew what Dr. Morgan would ask me at that moment: *How does this make you feel?*

There was only one answer I could think of. *I don't know.*

And that was okay.

Rowan gave me a kiss, and then I was ushered back into protective custody, to the hospital that had a special mental health unit for the study of extreme trauma, and I knew I would never see him again.

I take simple classes each day, and the afternoons are devoted to my recovery. Dr. Morgan says that one day I might make a partial recovery—enough, at least, to be out in the world. But before that, we have to discover all we can about what I did when I was Stacey, why I absorbed and became her, and who Beth is. We need a diagnosis for why my mind was—*is*—broken.

But Beth has been hiding, and I don't know if she will ever come out.

One thing I do know for sure: I have a reason to be here now.

I am myself, and I am reason enough.

73

HELLO, ME

NOW

I missed the sound of the engine in the distance, but I don't miss his calls.

"Bethany!"

Bruce is here.

Of course he knew where to find me.

I turn to call out to him, but you slice my face and Beth slices my shoulder. A flap of skin hangs down my arm, and I want to run to Bruce. But if I do, you will kill me. The both of you will kill me.

So I stand and face you.

I focus on staying alive until Bruce finds me, listening to the sound of him running through the bush, calling my name. I know he will follow our voices, so I scream as loudly as I can.

We circle. We slash. We rip. There is blood and there is hair and there is skin.

Death is keeping close to us, tonight.

And all the devils are watching.

74

Rehab

THEN

Six months later, I am standing on soft, soggy grass outside the main ward, and it is a cold winter morning. I'm looking at the crispy lawn, thinking that rehab really is a deceptive word. It implies recovery when I'm not sure I really have recovered. I haven't "rehabilitated" exactly. It's more like . . . I've realized. I've stepped out of the world I was in, and I'm beginning my steps into the world that everyone else is in. I'm in transition, not wholly recovered. I may never be. I will certainly be in therapy for a good many years. Maybe forever. But at least I can do it away from hospital now, in my own home.

Dr. Morgan said I had a surprise coming, but even as the taxi pulls up and Rowan gets out, my heart leaps. I never expected this. He looks . . . different. His face is covered with an immature little beard, and his hair is short.

"Hi," he says when he reaches me. He is three paces away. Far enough that I can't fling myself into his arms.

He looks tentative.

"Hi," I manage.

"It's nice to meet you," he says hesitantly.

"What?"

He holds out an envelope. "Open it."

I do. The paper is crisp and new. It's a document, a certificate.

"My name is Bruce," he says, stepping tentatively closer.

I blink at the paper in front of me, finding the words.

"Rowan is dead," he says, stepping closer again. "Gone." Another step closer; he is right in front of me. He looks worried. "Bruce was my middle name . . . but now it's me."

I stare at him, disbelieving, barely daring to hope, reconfiguring my perception of him in this new form.

He swallows. "I'm studying nearby, so I can come see you as much, or little, as you like . . ."

My heart is racing as my mind reels. Am I hallucinating this? He did all this . . . for me? There is a moment of stunned silence, and he looks so worried I break a little.

And then I am sobbing and throwing myself into his arms. We kiss and we cry, and our noses are pink in the frosty morning, but we are warmth to each other, and he didn't go anywhere. He just gave me exactly what I needed, and I don't deserve him, but I accept him, and I will love him forever.

"I turn sixteen in a few months," I tell him when we pull apart. "Dr. Morgan is helping me to start my emancipation proceedings. He thinks that if he signs on as my power of attorney, taking me under his wing as his responsibility until I turn eighteen, I just might get it."

"Are you sure emancipation is best?"

"I don't want to be controlled anymore."

"Are you ready for it?"

I shrug. "One of the requirements will be daily meetings, and I'll have to live in the care facility for a while. And medication, of course. I'll probably be on the pills forever, but the therapy may eventually peter out. And I'll have to live in the communal flats where the other patients like me live."

I know I haven't answered his question. I'm sure he does too. But he lets it go, as I suspect Dr. Morgan is teaching him to do. He holds out a hand to me, and I take it. He gives it a squeeze, and then we walk together, slowly. I do everything slowly now.

I still see Stacey, though I don't tell Rowan this. She waves at me from across the street. She sits in my therapy sessions. She lies in bed beside me every night, watching—never blinking. Dr. Morgan was the one to point it out. How the Stacey of my mind never blinks, how she never taps her fingers, how she never does any of the little things I had told him the real Stacey did all the time. Even if she's not real, I still see her. Only now, I ignore her. I have also felt Beth stir, but the medication-induced bonds keep her tied down and silent. For now.

I suppose I will have to learn how to live like this, with parts of my memory locked away where I can't get to them, and parts of my mind tied down on purpose.

Rowan's—*Bruce's*—hand feels warm around mine. It's the only warm thing in my life.

"Thank you," I tell him. "For . . . everything. For studying nearby. For doing all this. For not hating me."

He gets this fierce look on his face, and then he hugs me again. "I'm not going anywhere."

For the last few months of my inpatient sessions, he has been in attendance. Each day we speak through our separate recollections, trying to piece together the truth. Dr. Morgan never flinches at our affair—or any of the other horrible things I reveal—and he is helping Bruce and me to understand the way I work. I'm still learning.

I think I will be learning to cope for the rest of my life.

At least now, it really is *my* life. Lived for me, and me alone.

I wonder if I'll ever see any of the people from school again. Will I see Sakkie someday, walking down the street with a bruised girl who looks up at him the way I used to? Will I see Gert, grown into a strong man? Would he even recognize me now? And Bernie . . . What of her? What will she do? What will she become? My memory of all of them is losing color and definition. Sometimes I forget their names. Trauma, says Dr. Morgan, does that to you.

Some days I wonder if I will ever be free of Stacey and Beth, and if I really want to be. Sometimes I want to be alone; other times I cry into my pillow, yearning for their return.

Lately, I've been thinking that I'm not sure I do want to be free. I think I like having their silent shadows nearby, inside and out, like accents to my mending existence, assuring me that, even if I'm crazy, I'm not alone.

75

You

NOW

The blood is everywhere, but it is done.

The glass has been dropped in the sand, and the silence is total.

Bruce pushes through the bushes. "Bethany!"

His hug is desperate, and his heart pounds beneath his shirt. He smells sweaty and delicious.

"Thank God," he says, over and over. "Thank God."

His kiss is deep, desperate. He can't see the carnage all around. He can't see the ripped skin, the hair, the bone. He can't see the blood.

"I was so scared."

"Everything's okay. She's gone."

"Are you sure?"

"Yes."

"Let's go home."

You take my husband's arm and walk away, leaving me, nothing but pieces of meat, in the dirt.

Glass Man finally came for me

in the form of you.

ACKNOWLEDGMENTS

First, a huge thank-you, as always, to my husband and my mother. I am the luckiest woman in the world to have two of the most passionate, loving, empathetic, intelligent, funny, and supportive people in my life. I love you both more than I have words to express. I also want to thank my cats for their attempts at constructive critique by sitting on my keyboard, knocking over my tea, and howling for meat at my feet with their fish breath when I just fed them half an hour ago. Couldn't have done it without you little ~~brats~~ angels. 😉

This novel, twenty years in the making, would not have been the book it is without the support of these specific people: my transplant team at King's College Hospital (and the NHS), Weronika Janczuk, Polly Nolan, Sarah Davies, Victoria Marini, Twin, Julia, Marcel, and the friends who keep me sane along the way—among them, Kat Ellis, Claire Douglas, and Ann Dávila Cardinal.

Thank you to Jessica Tribble-Wells for her enthusiasm and belief in Bethany's story, to Charlotte Herscher for her keen eye, to Jenna Justice, who copyedited like a *boss*, and to Megan Westberg, the loveliest proofreader. A massive thank-you also to Miranda Gardner, Zoe Norvell, Jarrod Taylor, and the rest of the production and art department at Thomas & Mercer. I'd also like to thank the sensitivity readers who gave this novel such a glowing endorsement. It means the world.

Thank you to the bloggers and reviewers who continue to be incredibly supportive, kind, and loving toward my work: you are deeply appreciated.

And finally, to you. Dearest reader, I'm so glad to see you on the other side. ❤

ABOUT THE AUTHOR

Dawn Kurtagich is the award-winning author of several YA horror novels, including her acclaimed debut *The Dead House*, as well as *And the Trees Crept In* (*The Creeper Man*), *Teeth in the Mist*, *Blood on the Wind*, and her first adult novel, *The Madness*.

The daughter of a British globe-trotter, Kurtagich grew up all over the world, but her formative years were spent in Africa—on a mission, in the bush, in the city, and in the desert. She leaves her North Wales crypt after midnight during blood moons. The rest of the time, she exists somewhere between mushrooms, maggots, and mold.

You can always find the author on her website at www.dawnkurtagich.com.